Baker City Brides Book 3
A Sweet Historical Western Romance
by
USA Today Bestselling Author
SHANNA HATFIELD

Corsets and Cuffs
Baker City Brides Book 3

Copyright ©2016 by Shanna Hatfield

ISBN: 978-1530970933

All rights reserved. No part of this publication may be reproduced, distributed, downloaded, decompiled, reverse engineered, transmitted, or stored in or introduced into any information storage and retrieval system, in any form or by any means, including photocopying, recording, or other electronic or mechanical methods, now known or hereafter invented, without the written permission of the author, except in the case of brief quotations embodied in reviews and certain other noncommercial uses permitted by copyright law. Please purchase only authorized editions.

For permission requests, please contact the author, with a subject line of "permission request" at the email address below or through her website.

Shanna Hatfield
shanna@shannahatfield.com

This is a work of fiction. Names, characters, businesses, places, events, and incidents either are the product of the author's imagination or are used in a fictitious manner. Any resemblance to actual persons, living or dead, business establishments, or actual events is purely coincidental.

Cover Design: Covers & Cupcakes, LLC

Published by Wholesome Hearts Publishing, LLC.
wholesomeheartspublishing@gmail.com

*To the little heroes
with the biggest hearts...*

Books by Shanna Hatfield

FICTION

CONTEMPORARY

Holiday Brides
Valentine Bride
Summer Bride
Easter Bride
Lilac Bride
Lake Bride

Rodeo Romance
The Christmas Cowboy
Wrestling Christmas
Capturing Christmas
Barreling Through Christmas
Chasing Christmas
Racing Christmas
Keeping Christmas
Roping Christmas
Remembering Christmas

Grass Valley Cowboys
The Cowboy's Christmas Plan
The Cowboy's Spring Romance
The Cowboy's Summer Love
The Cowboy's Autumn Fall
The Cowboy's New Heart
The Cowboy's Last Goodbye

Summer Creek
Catching the Cowboy
Rescuing the Rancher
Protecting the Princess

Women of Tenacity
Heart of Clay
Heart of Hope
Heart of Love

HISTORICAL

Pendleton Petticoats
Dacey   *Bertie*
Aundy   *Millie*
Caterina   *Dally*
Ilsa   *Quinn*
Marnie   *Evie*
Lacey   *Sadie*

Baker City Brides
Tad's Treasure
Crumpets and Cowpies
Thimbles and Thistles
Corsets and Cuffs
Bobbins and Boots
Lightning and Lawmen
Dumplings and Dynamite

Hearts of the War
Garden of Her Heart
Home of Her Heart
Dream of Her Heart

Hardman Holidays
The Christmas Bargain
The Christmas Token
The Christmas Calamity
The Christmas Vow
The Christmas Quandary
The Christmas Confection
The Christmas Melody
The Christmas Ring
The Christmas Wish

Holiday Express
Holiday Hope
Holiday Heart
Holiday Home
Holiday Love

Chapter One

Baker City, Oregon
June 1891

"Flames had better be shooting from the buildings in town, a dead body sprawled in the street, and a wall blown off the bank by a gang of robbers, or you're gonna have to come up with some goldurn dandy reason for dragging me away from Ian and Maggie's wedding." Sheriff Tully Barrett glared at his deputy as they walked away from the festive gathering to celebrate the marriage of two good friends.

"Now, Tully, don't go blaming poor Dugan," Thane Jordan said, slapping Tully on the back as they hurried into the heart of town. "Obviously, your presence is needed back at your office or he wouldn't have bothered you."

Deputy Dugan Durfey tossed Thane a grateful nod. "That's right, boss. I'd rather do just about anything than make you leave Maggie and Ian's reception. But there's a woman fresh off the train who um…" Dugan struggled to find the right words to say. "She's um…"

"Go on, Dugan. She's what?" Tully stopped and waited for his deputy to speak.

"She's about as worked up as I've ever seen a female and you know I've seen more than my share in this line of work. She demanded I bring you to the office. Her exact words were, 'I insist on speaking to the imbecile in charge of maintaining law and order in this horrid, reprehensible, backwater town.'" Aggrieved, Dugan shook his head. "Believe me, Tully, I tried to speak with her, but she plopped herself down at your desk and refused to move. Then that other couple came in asking after Thane, so I thought it best to fetch you both."

"It's okay, Dugan," Thane said, offering the haggard deputy an encouraging look. "Tully's pouting because he might miss out on a few dances with some of the sweet young things who constantly vie for his attentions. His absence might give the young bucks in town a chance to win their affections."

Tully glowered at his best friend as they resumed their walk to the jail. Dugan opened the door and held it as Tully and Thane preceded him inside.

Five voices combined in a discordant symphony as they stepped into the office and looked around.

A woman did indeed sit at Tully's desk, arguing with the other deputy. An older couple engaged in a lively exchange with one of the grocers, discussing the finer points of lettuce versus cabbage.

Engrossed in their conversations, the occupants of the sheriff's office failed to notice the three men staring at them from just inside the doorway.

Tully whistled loud enough to crack glass, drawing their attention. "What in thunderation is going on in here?" His rich baritone voice boomed off the walls as silence descended over the room.

Sooner than anyone could offer an explanation, Thane stepped forward and pumped the hand of the older man standing near the grocer. "Greenfield! What in the heck are you doing here?" He lifted the man's plump wife in an enthusiastic hug and kissed her cheek. "Jemma and the kids will be so happy to see you."

"Righty ho, my good man." Edwin Greenfield smiled and put an arm around his wife's shoulders. "Hattie and I missed Jemma and the youngsters so intensely that we decided to pay a visit. I realize our arrival comes as a shock, but we hope you don't mind."

"Not at all. You're just in time to enjoy some delicious cake and punch. Our friends wed this afternoon, but the celebration hasn't quite wound down. They'll be thrilled to meet you." Thane motioned toward the door. "Do you have trunks that need to be picked up from the depot?"

Edwin nodded. "We do have several trunks, but they're safe in the ticket office for the moment."

As though he suddenly remembered the others in the office, Thane turned to the sheriff. "Tully, this is Edwin and Hattie Greenfield. They were the butler and cook back at Jemma's cottage in England. In truth, they were the glue that kept everything together and they made my stay in Bolton very enjoyable."

"And here I thought it was your beautiful wife that made you reluctant to return home to America," Tully teased, tipping his hat to the couple. "I'm Sheriff Tully Barrett. It's a pleasure to meet you both. Thane and Jemma have spoken highly of you. Welcome to Baker City."

"Thank you, sir," Edwin said, politely bowing as Hattie dipped into a well-practiced curtsey.

Thane took Hattie's elbow in his hand and escorted the couple to the door. "Let's go. Jemma will be beside herself to see you. Lily will beg you to make her some decent marmalade. And wait until you hear Jack's western twang."

Tully watched as they left, pleased Jemma and the children were in for a grand surprise. He could almost hear little Lily's squeals of excitement when she saw her beloved friends from England.

Intent on ignoring the woman at his desk as she shot furious daggers at him with her unsettling blue eyes, he turned to the grocer. "Is there something I can do for you, Irwin?"

"I need to report a theft. Deputy Harter started to write a report, but we kept getting interrupted." The grocer subtly tipped his head to the irate woman. "I set a few small baskets of strawberries along with early garden peas and potatoes that came in this morning in front of my store. I placed them where I could keep my eye on them, to let people know they were available. Right before the train arrived, I glanced outside and they were all gone."

Tully thought the grocer was just tempting someone to steal his produce by leaving it outside unattended, but managed to refrain from voicing his opinions. "You didn't see anyone running off with the berries or potatoes?"

The grocer frowned. "No sir. There was nary a body in sight when I rushed outside. It was as if my produce disappeared into thin air. One minute the baskets were there. I rang up a few things for Mrs. Palmer, and when I glanced back outside, the baskets were gone."

"We'll see what we can find out, Irwin. Go on back to your store and we'll let you know if anything turns up." Tully settled a hand on the grocer's shoulder and walked him out the door.

As soon as the man left, he turned and settled the weight of his gaze on the woman. If she hadn't been scowling so fiercely, she might have been extremely pretty.

Tendrils of golden-brown hair escaped the confines of her fashionable upswept hairdo, topped with a pale gray boater bedecked with enough ribbons, silk flowers and plumes to decorate three hats. A dark blue traveling suit appeared as richly embellished as her hat, dripping with beading and expensive trims. Smooth, creamy skin and blue eyes full of fire might have drawn his interest if she hadn't been so irate and clearly unreasonable.

Her angry countenance prodded his bad humor.

For the most part, Tully was an easy-going, jovial tease. However, once someone stirred his temper, it was generally something to behold and impossible to harness until it had run its course.

"What was so all-fired important you felt the need to demand an audience with me?" he asked, moving to stand next to the chair she occupied. When she rose to her feet, he towered over her by nearly a foot.

Deliberately, he widened his stance and crossed his arms across his muscled chest. The move had intimidated hundreds of people over the years. He hoped it would send the woman running out the door in fright.

Instead, she continued to glower at him in silence.

Incensed by her attempt to control the situation, he stared back at her. "I reckon you didn't have any problem speaking your mind before I walked in here, so say your piece. What do you need?"

The woman tipped back her head and blinked at him twice, as though she gauged whether he was worthy of her time.

Out of patience, he leaned toward her. The faint hint of something soft and floral tickled his nose, further infuriating him. "Spit it out, woman! I haven't got all day."

Both deputies stared at him, taken aback by his gruff demeanor. Under normal circumstances, Tully would have used his most charming smile on the woman, teased her into a good mood, and finagled a meal with her if she was single and unattached.

Nonetheless, nothing about the afternoon's circumstances had been even remotely close to typical.

When the woman finally spoke, fury laced her tone. "I'll thank you, Sheriff, to maintain civilities, even in this barbaric town. Why, I wouldn't be surprised to see cavedwellers dragging their women through the streets, considering the impudence I've experienced since setting foot off that filthy train."

Tully sighed in frustration. "Get to the point, ma'am. I've got better things to do than stand around and listen to you slander my home."

"It's not slander when the words are true," she said, raising her nose in the air with a disdainful sniff. "While I spoke with the peevish ticket agent at the train station, some despicable purloiner stole my bag. It is of the utmost importance that you find it."

A snort burst out of Tully before he could stop it. "Sorry, your highness, but the probability of your bag turning up is slim to none. I'd have to assume you brought several trunks along, so I'm sure you won't miss whatever was in it."

The woman's anger rolled over him in a palpable wave that nearly threw him off balance. Indignant, she huffed, setting the plumes on her hat to bobbing. Tully lifted his chin to keep one of the pink feathers from batting him in the face.

"I assure you, I have only one trunk and my bag. The trunk is with the ticket agent, but the bag is essential to my future livelihood. I must insist you do everything in your power to retrieve it."

"Fine. File a report and we'll investigate the theft." Tully started to turn away but a small, gloved hand on his arm tugged his gaze back to the woman. Brief as the contact was, her touch left him ill at ease and even more on edge.

"Please, Sheriff? Would you see to the recovery of my belongings yourself? Not that I don't trust your deputies." She glanced at the two men as they leaned against a desk across the room and offered them a coquettish smile. "Nevertheless, this matter requires your expertise and supreme discretion."

Tully cocked an eyebrow and rocked back on one hip. "What's in that bag of yours? What, exactly, requires the utmost discretion, as you put it?"

"It's a delicate topic that should be handled with prudence and care."

Another sigh rolled out of his broad chest and he sank onto the chair at his desk. He opened a drawer and pulled out a form, slapping it on top of the scarred wooden surface of the desk. The tip of his tongue moistened the end of the pencil he picked up then held poised above the paper, prepared to write.

"What's your name, darlin'?"

She stiffened. "It most certainly isn't darlin' or darling. Must you address me with such familiarity and improper speech?"

Summoning the last bit of patience he possessed, Tully tamped down the urge to snatch the woman's hat off her self-righteous head and stomp it beneath his boots. "Your name, please. I need your name for my report, Mrs....?"

"It's miss. Miss Dumont."

Tully wrote her last name on the report then glanced at her again. "First name?"

"Surely that is unnecessary for your report. You certainly won't be referring to me by my first name. Miss Dumont will suffice."

"Have it your way." Tully scribbled something on the paper. "What does your bag look like?" He refused to acknowledge the woman as she settled herself into the straight-back chair on the other side of his desk.

"Brown leather. It's fairly new. It's about this size." Miss Dumont held her hands out in front of her, indicating a large bag. "The clasp and buckles are brass and it has the initials G. A. D. on the front."

"Gad? What's that stand for?" Tully looked up at her and caught a glimmer of tears in those intriguing blue eyes before she chased the emotion away.

"My father's initials."

Tully nodded, writing the information on the form. "Is there anything attached to the bag or inside it with your name or address?"

"Yes. There are a few letters from my father's mine partner."

"Mine partner?" Tully pinned her with a glare. "Your father has a mine partner in the area?"

"Yes. That's why I'm here. I came to check on his holdings. Once I've concluded the business affairs are in order, I will eagerly leave this town." Warily avoiding his gaze, she fussed with her gloves.

The woman was withholding information, of that he was certain. Tully didn't trust her any further than he could throw an angry bull. "What's the partner's name? I know most of the miners around these parts."

"Mr. Clive Fisher. He and my father have been business associates for three years."

Chuckles he hadn't meant to release escaped, incurring the woman's wrathful glower.

"What, precisely, is so amusing to you, Sheriff?"

"Oh, nothing at all, ma'am." Tully wished he could be there to see the look on prissy Miss Dumont's face the moment she encountered the grizzled old miner. The only thing Clive Fisher hated more than taking a bath was women. "Let's get back to your report. I need a detailed list of the contents of the bag."

Much to his astonishment, Miss Dumont's cheeks turned pink and she dropped her gaze to her lap again. "You see, um… that's to say, the contents are of a nature that one does not…"

"Either you tell me what's in that bag, or I wad this paper up and stuff it in the stove." Tully pointed to a pot-bellied stove in a corner of the room. Although the heat of the day prohibited a fire burning in it, the threat sounded good.

She nodded, causing the plumes on her hat to attempt an escape by flapping away. "In addition to the letters I mentioned from Mr. Fisher, you'll find a family Bible, and a copy of *Rose in Bloom* by Louisa May Alcott. The bag also contained a hair brush and hand mirror, my toothbrush and a tin of tooth powder, a bottle of French perfume, and a nightdress."

Miss Dumont folded her hands on her lap and sat so straight, Tully wondered how she could maintain such a formal posture. He leaned back in the chair and tapped the pencil on his desk. "So, your future livelihood depends on keeping your teeth clean, or is it finishing that book you were reading?"

Bristling, the woman looked as though she'd dearly love to reach across the desk and slap him.

He'd like to see her try. "What else is in the bag, Miss Dumont?"

A long moment passed before she nodded once in resignation. When she opened her mouth to speak, Tully leaned forward with a threatening glare.

"No more of your nonsense about tooth powder and books. Either you tell me the truth, or I'll toss you out the door."

She held his gaze, her own cool and affronted. "You, sir, are no gentleman."

Snickers from the deputies made Tully grin. "I never once claimed to be. Now what is in the confounded bag?"

Miss Dumont cast the deputies a guarded glance before turning back to Tully. "I'd prefer that information remain confidential."

"If you want our help in finding your bag, we all need to know what we're looking for." Agitated, Tully tapped the pencil again.

He didn't know what it was about the woman that rubbed him the wrong direction, but he'd taken a healthy dislike to her the moment he set foot inside his office. Generally, he liked most everyone.

A good judge of character, he could easily sift the liars and thieves from folks who were good-hearted.

Within a few seconds of meeting her, he'd pegged the woman as someone who had secrets and planned to keep them. "What'd you do? Rob a bank? Steal priceless jewels? Hide a murder weapon in your spare bloomers?"

Miss Dumont sucked in such a large gulp of air that she choked and coughed into a scented handkerchief. Dugan hurried to pour her a cup of water while Seth stepped beside her, waiting to see if he needed to whack her on the back.

She took the cup from Dugan and sipped the tepid drink then wiped moisture from her eyes.

Tully didn't show the slightest hint of sympathy or remorse. "Come on, princess. What else is in that bag?"

"Corsets," she whispered.

"What'd you say?" Tully leaned closer to her again, looking at his two deputies. They'd resumed their post at the desk on the far side of the room, removing the possibility of hearing her whisper.

Red suffused not only her cheeks, but also her entire face as she forced her gaze to meet Tully's. "Corsets."

For the length of several heartbeats, he stared at her then smiled, revealing the dimples in his cheeks. "If corsets are the thing essential to your livelihood, then I'll point you in the direction of the Gilded Spur. It's the nicest brothel in town. Zed's fair to his girls and he'll take good care of you. Why didn't you…"

"My word!" The woman jumped to her feet and shook a finger in Tully's face. "How dare you utter such... such... I've never been so insulted in my entire life. Do I look like a woman who would... the kind of person that..."

Tully stood, mostly to keep her from poking his eye with her flailing finger. "Now, ma'am, just settle down. I didn't mean to imply anything, but you came in here ranting about needing some secretive item from your stolen bag and finally fess up that the item in question is your corset. What other conclusion am I supposed to come to?"

Slightly mollified by his explanation, she returned to her seat. "The corsets aren't of exceeding value, but you said you needed a complete list of the contents of the bag. It isn't proper to speak of such things and that is the reason I hesitated to mention their inclusion in the list of stolen property. There are three corsets in my bag and, um... other personal items such as one might need for a change of clothes."

"Bloomers and petticoats I understand, but three corsets? What in tarnation do you need with three corsets?" Tully's hazel eyes traveled over her with an intense, penetrating perusal. "Appears to me you've got one on right now."

"Indeed, Sheriff." Crimson highlights continued to stain her cheeks under his scrutiny. "However, the last item for your list is the five hundred dollars I had hidden in the false bottom of the bag."

Softly, Tully whistled then looked at her as if she had rocks rolling around in her head instead of brains. "Don't you know you shouldn't carry that kind of cash around with you? Especially in a bag anyone might steal."

"Yes, well, I realize now it would have been fortuitous to have carried it on my person, but that is neither here nor there. The money is gone and I'd very much like for it to be retrieved. At the very least, I'd appreciate the return of my belongings. A few items, such as my family Bible, are priceless to me and can't be replaced."

Taken aback by the tears in her eyes and the sincerity in her tone, Tully stood and walked around his desk. "We'll try to find your bag, Miss Dumont, but I can't make any promises. If you've no objections, Deputy Harter will escort you back to the depot to retrieve your trunk then accompany you to a hotel. I assume you need a place to stay while you're in town?"

Barely perceptible, she tipped her head upward in acknowledgement he had assumed correctly.

"I believe the Hotel Warshauer would be to your liking." Tully looked to Seth. The deputy nodded in agreement.

Miss Dumont rose to her feet. "Thank you, Sheriff. I do apologize for taking you away from the nuptial celebration of your friends. Best wishes to the happy couple."

Tully's face appeared impassive. He remained silent as Seth left the office with the maddening, fascinating woman.

If she wasn't such a haughty little thing, puffed up with self-importance and a generous helping of exasperation, he might give her a second glance. It was hard to overlook her lovely eyes, golden brown hair, smooth skin, and kissable lips.

Disturbed by the direction of his thoughts, Tully strode out the door back toward Maggie and Ian's reception.

The lingering sting he experienced from the sharpness of Miss Dumont's tongue strengthened his resolve to avoid her as much as possible until the snippy female left town.

Chapter Two

Brianna Dumont sank onto the bed in her hotel room and released a weary sigh.

Exhausted beyond words, she couldn't believe someone stole her bag out from under her nose.

No matter how badly she wanted and needed her bag returned, she didn't possess a great deal of hope the sheriff would locate it.

That infuriating man had been less than helpful and incredibly rude. In fact, she'd call him arrogant, irritating, and far too handsome for his own good.

Why did exceptionally attractive men often come with such a conceited, belligerent attitude?

She supposed he could say something similar about her. Short-tempered and demanding, she hadn't made a very good impression on him, the two deputies, or the nitwit ticket agent at the train depot.

Raised to be a lady, and trained in the finest finishing schools, Brianna knew she'd been difficult. But her entire future rested on finding that bag.

She removed her hat and tossed it on the bed then unpinned her hair, shaking out her long tresses.

The first thing she wanted to do was to take a bath and wash off the nearly two thousand miles of dust and soot from her journey across the country.

After that, she might think about food unless sleep claimed her first. The train ride from Rhode Island had offered little opportunity for her to rest. She'd kept a vigilant watch over her bag lest anyone try to make off with it.

Under the pretense of being recently widowed, no one questioned the propriety of her traveling alone. Although she didn't wear black, she was in mourning and didn't think anything would ever ease the ache in her heart.

A determined mental shake scattered her maudlin thoughts as she hastily pinned up her hair and fastened her hat into place.

After picking up her reticule and locking the door to her room, she hurried down to the front desk.

A thin young man with pale skin and a bookish demeanor looked up from the paperwork in front of him as she approached. "May I help you, Miss Dumont?"

She offered him an engaging smile. "Why, yes, Mr. Isaac. Might I inquire if there is a mercantile in town?"

The young man nodded. "There are three mercantiles, seven grocers, and quite an assortment of other stores, but if you want the best, go to Miller's Mercantile. He keeps his store stocked with a little of everything and it is good quality. If you go outside and take a right, walk down two blocks, cross the street to your left, and go down one more block to First Street, you can't miss it."

"Thank you, kind sir." Brianna slid a coin across the marble top of the hotel desk then rushed outside into the sunshine. She wished she'd had some idea of how horrifically warm it would be in Eastern Oregon. Accustomed to the cooling breezes blowing in from the Atlantic Ocean across Narragansett Bay, the sagebrush-covered hills surrounding Baker City's valley did nothing to dispel the summer heat.

Quickly making her way to the mercantile, she opened the door and stepped inside, inhaling the scents of coffee, dill, furniture oil, and something floral that made her smile.

The store teemed with customers and excited chatter. Many shoppers appeared to be dressed in their best finery. Brianna assumed they were probably guests at the wedding the sheriff seemed so irritable to miss by returning to his office to speak with her.

She wandered past a display of garden tools and canning jars then made her way through the store to where the items she needed were located.

Several people smiled and offered her a sociable hello as she made her way down the aisle of the mercantile. Although she did not intend to stay in Baker City, she didn't wish to offend anyone. The manners instilled in her from an early age enabled her to smile politely and offer appropriate comments when necessary.

For the most part, the other shoppers left her alone as she studied the selections available in the well-stocked store.

The clerk at the hotel had been correct in that the mercantile offered a vast array of items. The quality was also acceptable to Brianna's high standards.

She picked up a woven basket from a nearby stack and began adding items she needed before she could take a bath.

When she'd gathered replacements for all the personal items lost with the theft of her bag, she made her way to the front counter where a friendly man rang up purchases and spoke kindly to the customers.

As she waited in line, Brianna noticed a display of perfume. Much to her delight, she saw a bottle of her favorite French perfume and added it to her basket along with a bar of scented soap, a jar of face cream, and a bottle of hand lotion.

Mindful of her limited funds, she refused to return the luxury items to the shelf. The perfume and scented soap would remind her of happier times and people she loved while the lotion and cream would be essential in the harsh heat of the area.

Before she talked herself out of the indulgent purchases, she stepped back in line. Only one more person was ahead of her when she spied a puckish little fellow watching her from around the edge of the long front counter. Blue eyes twinkled from beneath shaggy blond bangs and a dusty flat cap. A sprinkling of freckles marched across a pert nose and a scabbed-over cut decorated a stubborn chin.

Aware of the child's stare, Brianna pretended not to notice the boy as she stepped up to the counter.

"Are you new to the area, miss?" the clerk asked. "My name's Frank Miller and this is my store."

A smile rose to her lips as she greeted the man. "It's a pleasure to meet you, Mr. Miller. I'm Miss Dumont and I arrived in town today."

"Welcome to Baker City." Frank gave her a questioning glance. "Have you moved to the area or are you visiting?"

"I'm only here for a short time on a business matter," Brianna explained. "An unfortunate loss of my traveling bag left me in need of several items. The front desk clerk at Hotel Warshauer suggested I shop here."

"I'll have to thank Mr. Isaac for the referral. If there is something you need I don't have in stock, Miss Dumont, please let me know. I'm happy to order anything at all. Most often, it can be here in just a few days. With the train running through daily, we try to offer as many conveniences as some of the bigger cities."

Brianna smiled again. "That's wonderful, Mr. Miller. I do so appreciate your kind offer. If I find myself in need of something unavailable in your fine establishment, I will most certainly inquire about the possibilities of placing an order."

Frank Miller grinned. "Do you wish to purchase the basket, Miss Dumont?"

"I do. I'm also in need of a…" She glanced at the jars of candy on the counter then winked at the child who continued to watch her. A little finger pointed to a glass jar of sassafras drops. "A dozen pieces of those sassafras drops."

"Certainly," Frank said. He scooped the candy into a small paper sack and added it to Brianna's basket. Abruptly noticing the child hiding at the end of the counter, the storeowner made a shooing motion toward the door. "Sammy, you go on and quit bothering my customers."

The child raced out the door, but Brianna caught a glimpse of the boy as he peeked back in the window.

Frank shook his head. "Don't mind the little scamp. He doesn't talk, but he's a good boy, at least from what I've seen."

Brianna paid for her purchases and picked up the basket. "Did he suffer from some malady that took his voice?"

The storeowner shrugged. "Don't rightly know. He's been like that since he started coming into my store a few months ago. Only reason I know his name is because he wrote it out for me. Thank you for shopping here, Miss Dumont. I hope you'll come again."

"I'm sure I will, Mr. Miller. Thank you for the excellent service." Brianna strolled out the door and looked to where she'd last seen Sammy peering inside the store. The boy sat on a wooden bench, observing her.

With unhurried movements, Brianna took a seat on the end of the bench and set the basket down beside her. Slowly, the child slid closer to her.

Studying the small face, Brianna guessed the boy to be around six or so. His features were almost delicate enough to be feminine, but the rough and tumble air about him definitely belonged to a rambunctious lad.

"It seems I purchased far more candy than I can use. Do you think you might be able to take it off my hands?" Brianna held back a laugh as the child's head bobbed up and down in excitement. She took the small sack of candy from her basket, removed one piece and popped it into her mouth then held out the sack to the boy.

A grubby little hand reached out for it, but stopped before it connected with the paper. Blue eyes lifted to her in question and she nodded her head reassuringly. "You may take them, just don't eat them all at once and spoil your dinner."

The child smiled broadly and took the sack, stuffing a piece of candy in his mouth. He tucked the sack of candy into the pocket of his short pants then gingerly reached out and patted Brianna's gloved hand.

She covered the small fingers with her other hand and smiled. "You're most welcome, Sammy. Go on, now, and stay out of trouble."

Sammy touched the brim of his dusty cap then jumped off the steps and raced down the street, disappearing around the corner.

Amused by the child, Brianna sucked on the candy and quickly made her way back to the hotel.

After setting down her basket and reticule, she removed her hat and gloves then went to the private bath in her room and turned on the water to fill the tub. When the deputy carried her trunk to the hotel, she had little expectation of finding somewhere to stay that provided even the most basic comforts. However, the Hotel Warshauer offered luxurious touches that made her appreciate the sheriff recommending she stay there, in spite of his surly behavior.

Stripping out of her filthy clothes, Brianna took a moment to remove the money she'd stashed in secret pockets inside her petticoats and hid the funds in the pockets of a clean petticoat she pulled from her trunk. There wasn't more than ten dollars in the bag she lost at the depot. However, she was smart enough to know the sheriff wouldn't have bothered to look for it at all if she hadn't stretched the truth to say there was cash inside.

The bag didn't have a false bottom, but the hidden contents of the bag were worth thousands of dollars. That was why she hoped and prayed the local members of Baker City's law enforcement would find the thief and return her bag posthaste.

Too tired to dwell on the possibilities of what might happen if the bag was never recovered, she sank into the tub with a relieved sigh. After washing her hair and scrubbing every inch of her skin, she leaned back and closed her eyes, letting the cooling water refresh her.

When she opened her eyes again, her fingers were as wrinkled as the dried prunes her grandfather used to eat. She stepped out of the tub and dried herself then combed through her hair. In the mirror above the bathroom sink, she rubbed her recently purchased face cream into her cheeks and forehead.

Unable to think of anything but sleep, she donned a nightgown from her trunk, drew her drapes closed and climbed into the welcoming softness of the bed.

Bright sunlight danced around the edges of the drapes when she awoke. The air in the room felt stifling and heavy from the heat. Although she'd left the windows open, the heavy fabric of the drapes had blocked much of the breeze.

Hastily climbing out of bed, Brianna pulled back the drapes. She glanced at the clock on the dresser, shocked to see it was nearly two the following afternoon. Her stomach felt empty and hollow. The realization she'd not only missed lunch and dinner yesterday, but also breakfast and lunch today made her stomach growl.

Focused on finding sustenance, Brianna hurried into the bathroom and splashed cool water on her face then brushed her teeth with her new toothbrush and powder.

She grimaced at the snarled state of her hair and spent several minutes combing out the tangles before pinning up the weight of the tresses. Without it holding her body heat against her neck and back, she felt cooler almost instantly.

Impatient to eat, she opened her trunk and dug through the gowns she'd brought along, selecting a lightweight cotton lawn ensemble in a shade of blue that matched her eyes. She slipped on her shoes, pinned on her hat, and tugged on her gloves. Quickly snatching up her reticule and room key, she rushed out the door.

Mr. Isaac greeted her with a friendly nod as she approached the front desk.

"Is the dining room still open?" she asked, hoping it was.

"They just closed, but they'll reopen at five for dinner service." The young man gave her a knowing look. "If you're looking for a place to find a little something to eat, we have two bakeries. My personal favorite is across the street and down two blocks on the right. They're open until four."

Brianna thanked him and did her best to maintain a dignified pace to the bakery instead of picking up her skirts and running as her empty stomach compelled her to do.

The yeasty aroma of bread blended with the hint of sweets as she opened the door and stepped inside the bakery. After selecting a sweet roll, she took it to a nearby park and sat on a bench, eating every bite. She watched a few children playing and mothers keeping watchful eyes as they sat on wooden benches. A young couple strolled hand-in-hand, so enamored with each other, she wasn't sure they realized there was anyone else in the vicinity.

A beautiful flowering bush drew her gaze and she meandered over to where butterflies flocked to the bright pink blossoms. She bent over to sniff the fragrant flowers when a deep, resonant voice spoke behind her, making her suck in a startled gasp.

The branch in her hand broke off with a loud snap. Butterflies took flight around her and wild flutters filled her stomach.

The sheriff's scowl greeted her when she turned around to face him.

"I don't know how you're used to doing things, but around here, leaving your trash for others to pick up isn't acceptable. I could haul you in for littering if I was of a mind to." Tully shook the paper wrapper from her sweet roll in her face. "I could also fine you for defacing public property." He pointed to the branch in her hand.

Brianna snatched the discarded paper away from him and wadded it into her hand. "I wasn't littering. I walked over here to look at this bush and left the paper on the bench. If you hadn't jumped to erroneous conclusions and nearly accosted me, I would have picked it up in a minute."

In hopes of getting away from the exasperating man, she marched across the park. Unfortunately, he matched his long strides to her shorter steps.

Disconcerted by the breadth of his shoulders and the noticeable strength of his tall form, she stopped and glared at him. "Must you follow me?"

"I want to make sure you don't destroy anything else," he said, staring down at her.

"Do you harass every newcomer to town or am I the only one to receive such special treatment, Sheriff?" Brianna fought down the urge to slap the smart-alecky look off his face.

"Oh, you are special. No doubt about that, Miss Dumont." Sarcasm fairly dripped from his tone. "In fact, I'm sure you think you're more special than anyone else in town, maybe even the entire West, or possibly the country."

Indignant, insulted, and infuriated, she smacked him across the chest with the branch in her hand, sending a shower of pink blossoms dancing through the air.

Tully's eyes widened in shock and Brianna realized she'd just struck an officer of the law.

"I… I… I'm sorry, sir, I don't…" At the menacing look in his eye and the growl that worked free from his throat, she took a hurried step backward into a muddy puddle. The heels of her shoes sank in and she would have fallen on her backside if the sheriff's arm hadn't caught her around the waist and pulled her forward.

Immediately, he released her, but bent down until his nose nearly touched hers. Fiery amber lights flickered in his eyes and his breath smelled pleasantly like mint as it blew across her face. "Unless you'd like to discover how fun it is to spend the night in a jail cell, you'd dang sure better not do that again. Run along, Miss Dumont."

"But I…"

"Get your bloomers in gear and go!" Tully ordered, pointing his finger in the direction of the street. His voice boomed like thunder around her, causing other patrons of the park to turn curious gazes their direction.

With as much decorum as she could muster, she lifted her skirt hem ever so slightly and hastened out of the park.

After seeing Ian and Maggie off at the train depot for their honeymoon trip to the Oregon coast,

Tully had walked through town, checking to make sure all was peaceful and quiet.

He'd turned a corner and noticed Miss Dumont leave the bakery with a paper-wrapped treat held in her hands like it was a cherished treasure.

Out of curiosity, he followed her to the park and observed her from a distance as she ate the sweet roll. Convinced the woman was hiding something, he wondered what brought her to Baker City. If she really came to town to check on Clive Fisher's mine, that meeting alone would send her scurrying back east to wherever it was she belonged.

For reasons beyond his ability to fathom, Tully felt a need to keep an eye on the annoying woman. He'd never met a female who irritated him so thoroughly with nothing more than her presence.

The moment she'd smiled as she watched children play, her entire face lit up. Some crazy, stupid part of him felt drawn to her beauty and feminine softness. He wondered if her kiss would taste as sweet as the pastry she'd just eaten or more like the honey her golden-brown hair brought to mind.

Infuriated by his thoughts, he grabbed the paper she left on the park bench and purposely startled her when she rose to admire the nearby bush. He'd never arrested anyone for littering in the park, but he felt the need to goad her, to leave her as unsettled and unsure as she made him.

Unable to put his finger on the exact cause, something about the woman left him cranky and nervous, two things completely out of character for him.

When she'd stepped back in the mud and almost fallen, Tully grabbed her waist out of instinct. Further discombobulated by how good it felt to wrap his arm around her, he almost lost the ability to think rationally when he bent down and watched bright flames dance in her blue eyes. The scent of her perfume, something that held a hint of a soft floral fragrance, filled his nose and pushed him toward the edge of reason.

His lips itched to taste hers so badly that he had to do something to distance himself. The quickest thing that came to mind was to make her mad and send her on her way.

However, it didn't help that he surveyed every inviting sway of her skirts as she rushed out of the park toward the hotel.

If he wanted to survive the uppity woman's visit to town unscathed, he needed to do a better job of ignoring her.

Chapter Three

Livid beyond anything she'd ever experienced in her lifetime, Brianna stormed back to the hotel room. In a huff, she changed out of the mud-speckled dress then asked Mr. Isaac to send out her clothes to be cleaned. He assured her Wang Ping's laundry was the best in town and would have her clothes ready the following day.

She ate an early dinner, borrowed a book from the hotel's expansive library, and retired to her room.

As she tried to focus on the book in her hand, her thoughts drifted to the pompous sheriff. If she wasn't mistaken, she thought she'd heard his friend introduce him as Tully Barrett. The name seemed inordinately fitting for such a cocky, vexatious man.

Exactly what she'd done to get on his bad side she didn't know, but she'd definitely gotten off on the wrong foot with him.

Perhaps she could conclude her business in town and be on her way without enduring another encounter with the sheriff. Something about him, something rugged and raw and a little wild, made her heart beat rapidly and her breath catch in her throat when she thought of him. The effect he had on her was enough to leave her ill at ease, but then there was the brutish, boorish way he behaved.

If he treated everyone with such a heavy hand, it was a wonder he had any friends at all.

Determined to shove thoughts of him from her mind, she readied for bed. The mud covering her shoes stirred her anger once again. She ought to make him clean her shoes since it was his fault she'd stepped into the mud at the park.

Hastily pulling on a wrapper, she opened her door and set the shoes in the hall. Often, when she and her father had traveled, they left their shoes in the hall at night for the hotel staff to clean and polish. The next morning, a pair of shiny shoes would wait outside her door.

Only when Brianna opened the door the next morning to retrieve her shoes, they weren't there.

Miffed that her shoes hadn't yet been returned, she went to her trunk and dug inside until she located her spare shoes.

"No, no, no!" The black ankle boots in her hands would never do. Instead of a matching pair, she held two left shoes. Since all her footwear was custom-made, there was no way she could wear a left shoe on her right foot.

Disgusted with herself, she stamped her foot and tossed the shoes back into the trunk, slamming the lid. In her haste to pack, she hadn't even thought to add a pair of slippers.

Quickly glancing down, she hoped her skirt hid the fact she didn't wear any shoes. She could have left off a layer of petticoats to lengthen her gown, but she wouldn't dare leave one lying around with money hidden inside it.

In an attempt to focus on positive thoughts, she pinned on her hat, picked up her reticule and rushed downstairs to the front desk.

Mr. Isaac smiled in greeting. "Good morning, Miss Dumont. How does this day find you?"

"Quite well, except for one small matter. I'm in desperate need of my shoes, Mr. Isaac. Have the staff returned the others?"

"The others?" The young clerk appeared completely confused. "I'm not sure I understand what you're asking, Miss Dumont."

"Last night, I set my shoes in the hall to be polished. This morning, they should have been left outside my door, but weren't returned. Would you please have someone bring them to my room?" Fast losing patience, Brianna glared at Mr. Isaac. "You do have my shoes, don't you?"

"I'm sorry, but that is not a service we offer here at the hotel. If you set your shoes in the hall last night, my only guess is that someone took them." Subtly, Mr. Isaac backed away from the counter. The furious woman leaning against it looked like she wanted to hit something — or someone.

"You're saying someone stole my shoes?"

"Yes, Miss Dumont." Mr. Isaac slid a little further out of reach. "You could report the theft to the sheriff's office. I'm sure he'll…"

Before he could finish speaking, Brianna spun around, marched out the hotel and down the street in the direction of the jail.

She'd just crossed an intersection on the main street of town when she stepped on something sharp and pain sliced through her foot.

With no dignified way to examine the wound, she took a deep breath, trying to determine if it bled without raising her skirt to look.

"You look like you had persimmons with a side of lemons for breakfast this morning."

The deep voice, becoming all too familiar to her, caused her to spin around and spear the sheriff with an enraged grimace.

"Don't you have anything better to do than continually harass me?"

Tully shrugged and offered her a false smile, one that only served to make her angrier. "As a matter of fact, I do." He started to walk off, but Brianna reached out and placed her hand on his arm.

He stopped and stared down at her, raising an eyebrow in question. "Do you need something?"

"Indeed, I do. If it wasn't for an unfortunate circumstance that mandated I speak with you in person, you may rest assured I would do my best to avoid speaking to you at all." Despite her intention to remain calm, she glared at him. "At any rate, I've been the victim of a theft once again and require your assistance. Perhaps if you spent more time chasing down the thieves swarming around this town, you'd have less time to grieve upstanding citizens."

Tully rocked back on one hip and hung his thumbs from the pockets of his denim trousers.

"You really know how to sweet talk someone, don't you?"

Brianna released a beleaguered sigh. "I need to report a theft, Sheriff. Will you or will you not provide assistance?"

"What'd you lose now? A petticoat? Was it your stockings? Maybe your bloomers? Should I check to be sure you still have a pair of 'em on?" The teasing grin he shot her dissipated when her hand connected with his cheek in a resounding slap.

"You, sir, are a despicable cad!" Brianna would never have guessed someone as big and brawny as the sheriff capable of moving with such lightning-fast speed. However, before she could turn away, he'd fastened heavy iron cuffs around her wrists. He grabbed her upper arm in his hand and propelled her toward the jail.

"What in the world do you think you're doing?" She struggled against his iron grip around her arm.

His fingers tightened while the cold stare he fixed on her made a chill slide through her body. "I'm taking you to jail, Miss Dumont. You might get away with assaulting officers of the law where you live, but I don't tolerate it. Not at all."

Her jaw dropped open as she gaped at him. "This is ridiculous. Remove these cuffs and release me, this instant."

"Not happening, your highness." He swung open the door to the jail and escorted her through the office back to the cells. No one else was in the building, something for which Brianna was grateful. Mortified to be manhandled in such a manner on the way to the jail, she certainly didn't need any spectators to her unexpected imprisonment.

Tully marched her into a cell then removed the cuffs. A smile played around the corners of his mouth as he slammed the door and turned a key in the lock. "You're under arrest."

Furious, she spluttered in protest. "For what? I have done nothing more than demand you carry out the responsibilities of the job the good citizens of this town entrusted into your care. You have no right…"

Tully took a step back as she grabbed hold of the cell bars and rattled them. He smirked. "You are under arrest for assaulting an officer of the law."

Defiant and insulted, she lifted her chin. "You deserved the slap after that impudent comment."

Tully ignored her and continued. "You're under arrest for assaulting an officer of the law, being a public nuisance, harassment, and disorderly conduct."

Incensed, she rattled the bars again. "I did no such thing, and you know it. This is an outrage. You, sir, are a bully and a beast! I demand an immediate release. Wait until your superiors hear about this. I'll have you removed from your position. In fact, I won't stop until the governor of this state has you tossed in prison!"

"Good luck with that, sweetheart." Tully stalked over to the door, leading to the jail's office, his gaze hard and penetrating. "Your time might be better spent reflecting on how you ended up in here, Miss Smarty Britches."

Tully would have shut the door that separated the cells from the office, but there weren't any windows in the back. As much as he'd like to throttle the lone occupant of the jail, he didn't want her to suffocate from the heat.

Instead, he went to his desk drawer and pulled out two pieces of cotton batting, stuffing them into his ears as Miss Dumont continued to rant and rave about the injustice of his behavior.

Ignoring her pleas and protests, he sat down at the desk and spent the next few hours catching up on paperwork.

His stomach told him it was close to noon when the door to the jail opened and Thane Jordan strode in with his daughter, Lily.

"Uncle Tully!" Lily squealed, launching herself at him. Tully lifted her in his arms and kissed her on her little button nose.

The child patted his cheeks then leaned back, noticing the cotton sticking out of his ears. "What's that for? Are you sick?" she asked.

Tully yanked the cotton from his ears and dropped it into a desk drawer. "No, honey. I just got tired of listening to a wild cat hiss and spit."

Lily's eyes widened and she looked around uncertainly, expecting to see a cat prowling through the office.

"There's nothing to worry about, sweetheart, I think the cat went to sleep and all is fine now." Tully settled Lily on his knee. "What brought you and your dad into town? Don't tell me... you've decided to join the circus and your daddy brought you in to catch the train."

"Don't give her any ideas," Thane warned as he gave Tully a pointed look.

Tully chuckled and bounced his knee, making Lily giggle. "You're gonna take a job working at Wang Ping's laundry?"

Lily wrinkled her nose. "No, silly."

Tully rubbed a hand over his chin, pretending to be deep in thought. He snapped his fingers and grinned at the precocious child. "You've decided to take over management of the lumberyard while Maggie and Ian are gone."

Lily shook her head, causing her curls to dance into a complete state of disarray. "No. Ian's daddy is taking care of the lumbers. Don't you 'member?"

Tully nodded. "I must have forgotten. Thank you for the reminder. So, if you aren't here to join the circus or take over the laundry or run the lumberyard, what are you and your daddy doing in town?"

"We came to take you to lunch with us and then me and Daddy are going to shop and then Ian's mommy and daddy are gonna go home with us for supper. Are you coming for supper, Uncle Tully?"

"Of course, I am, sweetheart, but only if I get to sit by you."

"Yep! You can sit by me!" Lily scrambled upward until she stood on Tully's leg and wrapped her arms around his neck. "Did you know my birthday is soon?"

"I think I did know that, but tell me again how old you're gonna be? Will you be as old as Mr. Bentley who drives the sprinkler wagon?"

Lily giggled and shook her head again. "No! I'll be this many." She held up four fingers. "You'll come to my party and have cake, won't you, Uncle Tully?"

He hugged the child then set her down, kissing her on the cheek. "Wild horses, bank robbers, cranky cats, and exploding mines wouldn't keep me away."

"Oh, goodie!" Lily clapped her hands in excitement then ran back over to Thane, wrapping her arms around his leg.

"Would you like to join us for lunch, Tully?" Thane asked, resting a hand on his daughter's profusion of soft curls.

"I'd be happy to. Dugan should be here in a minute and then we can go. I've got a prisoner in back I don't want to leave unattended."

"We aren't in a rush." Thane settled into a chair across from Tully.

"Where are Jemma and Jack?" Tully expected Jack to be with Thane if anyone accompanied him to the jail.

"Jemma is busy getting ready for Mr. and Mrs. MacGregor's visit for supper. Jack decided he'd rather ride fences with Ben this afternoon than come into town."

"You better be careful or you're gonna turn that boy into a real cowboy."

Thane leaned back in his chair. "I certainly hope so. The best thing for that boy is a summer spent out in the sunshine learning about the workings of a ranch. However, his mother is adamant he continue with his lessons during the summer months."

"She's not making him play the piano, is she?"

"No. I put my foot down on that account," Thane said. "The poor boy pleaded his case well and suggested fencing as a strong alternative to piano. But Jemma declared he'd either poke his eye out or cause Lily's demise if we let him pursue that. I'm teaching him how to shoot instead."

Tully laughed. "I'm sure Jemma approved of that."

"Not exactly, but she's coming around. Jack killed a rattler yesterday out behind the barn."

"How many buttons on the tail?" Tully asked.

While the men continued their discussion, Lily quietly wandered over to the doorway leading to the cells.

Brianna had listened to the dialogue between the sheriff and the youngster. If she hadn't despised the man so much, the way he interacted with the child might have softened her heart toward him.

As it was, she'd been amused by the conversation between him and the little girl named Lily.

A head full of strawberry blond curls peeked around the doorway. Brianna smiled and waved at the little girl. The child disappeared then peeked back around again. Brianna winked and waggled her fingers. The third time, Lily walked inside and over to the cell where Brianna stood.

She watched the child approach, trying to think when she'd ever seen such an adorable little girl. The head full of curls, springing every which direction, had most likely been combed into some sort of order earlier in the day since a pink satin bow nestled in them. A pink frock, trimmed with a lavish amount of lace, spoke of wealth and elegance.

The lively spark in the little one's copper-colored eyes and the appealing grin on her rosebud lips endeared her to Brianna.

"Who are you?" Lily asked, standing in front of the cell and staring at Brianna with wide eyes.

"My name is Miss Dumont. Are you Lily?"

"Yes, ma'am." Lily dipped into a curtsey.

Impressed by her manners, Brianna smiled. "It's a pleasure to meet you, Lily. Is your father speaking with the sheriff?"

"Yes. My daddy and Uncle Tully are bestest friends." Lily gazed at Brianna. "Do you have a bestest friend?"

"Sadly, I don't believe I do."

"Oh, I'm sorry." Lily appeared lost in thought a moment, then her face brightened. "I know! You can be my friend."

"I'd like that very much," Brianna said, squatting down to Lily's level.

The little girl giggled and latched onto the cell bars, hopping off one foot to the other. "Uncle Tully said there was a wild cat in here. Did you see it?"

"I guess I must have missed it." If Tully Barrett ever let her out of the cell, she'd show him a wild cat.

"We're going to lunch with Uncle Tully. Do you want to come?"

Brianna reached through the bars and stroked her hand over the child's head. "As lovely as that sounds, Lily, I'm afraid I'm stuck here for a while."

"Why? Only bad mens are supposed to be in here and you're a bee-you-tee-full princess." Lily rubbed a finger over the ornate beading on the sleeve of Brianna's pale-yellow gown. "And you smell very nice. My mama and Aunt Maggie always smell like flowers, too."

Brianna smiled. "I greatly look forward to making the acquaintance of your mother and aunt."

"You should come to supper tonight. Mama is making all kinds of good things to eat and so is Sam."

"Who is Sam?" Brianna watched as Lily swung back and forth from the bars of the cell. The child seemed incapable of standing still.

"Sam is the bunkhouse cook and he keeps everyone in line when my daddy isn't home. He makes the best biscuits. Oh, I mean cookies. We called them biscuits at home, before we moved here."

"I see. So, you lived in England?" Brianna had noticed the child's accent as soon as she spoke.

"Yep! Then Uncle Thane came and brought us to 'Merica on a big boat and then he was my daddy."

"Oh, that must have been wonderful." Brianna struggled to make sense of the child's words. Apparently, the little girl was adopted, which meant she most likely was not related to the reprehensible sheriff. In Brianna's mind, it was impossible to think a child so loveable could be a blood relation of such a horrid man.

"Lillian Jane Jordan! What are you doing?" Thane called to her and the little girl scampered toward the doorway. She stopped and waved at Brianna before disappearing from sight.

Brianna heard Lily talk about the beautiful woman in the cell and then heard the low rumble of men's voices.

Footsteps thudded across the wood of the plank floor. A man she recognized from the first day she'd arrived in Baker City stuck his head around the door and looked at her. He reached up and tipped his hat. "Ma'am. I hope Lily wasn't bothering you."

Brianna smiled. "Not at all, sir. She was a welcome diversion."

The sound of the outer door opening and another male voice speaking to the sheriff let her know a deputy had arrived.

Lily raced past Thane and back to Brianna's cell. "I hope you'll come visit us, Miss Dumont. My mama would be pleased to meet you."

"Thank you for the invitation, Lily. I shall…"

"Daddy, Miss Dumont has an owie," Lily interrupted, pointing to spots of blood visible on the cell floor when Brianna moved.

Thane walked over to the cell and took in the blood then stared at the woman. "Miss Dumont, is it?"

"Yes, sir."

"Are you injured?" Thane asked, picking up Lily and settling her on one strong arm.

"I believe I am, sir. I stepped on something, but that occurred moments before the sheriff took it in mind to arrest me this morning."

Thane turned toward the doorway and yelled, "Tully! Get your worthless hide in here and let this poor woman go."

Tully sauntered into the room, glaring from Thane to Brianna. "Since when do you get to tell me what to do with my prisoners?"

"Since you locked this one up with an injury. She needs medical attention for her foot." Thane pointed to the blood on the floor. "I've never known you to be cruel, Tully, but this might be pushing it."

"I didn't know the dad-blasted woman was hurt." Tully jammed the key into the lock and swung open the door. "Why didn't you tell me you were injured?"

"You didn't offer an opportunity. Besides, I was preoccupied by the fact you slapped those dreadfully heavy iron cuffs on my wrists and dragged me here for no reason."

"Oh, I've got plenty of reason, your highness, but that will wait until later. Let me see your foot." Tully stepped into the cell, filling the space with his presence and masculine scent. Brianna backed away from him until the wall behind her brought her to a halt.

"Let me see your foot," Tully demanded.

"No." Brianna wanted to cower as Tully towered over her, but she straightened her spine and lifted her chin, daring him to force her to comply.

"Have it your way." Tully bent down and set his shoulder against her midsection, lifting her up like a sack of feed. Her head dangled down his back and her hands thumped against his solid thighs as he lifted her petticoats and grabbed her flailing foot.

Shocked by his crude handling of her, Brianna was further aggravated when she noticed how well Tully's trousers fit him and the unyielding strength of his body as he held her on his shoulder.

"Where in blazes are your shoes, woman?" Tully thundered, tramping out of the cell and depositing Brianna on top of his desk while Thane, Lily, and Dugan observed.

"That's what I've been trying to tell you all morning, Sheriff Barrett. Someone stole my shoes last night." Brianna attempted to push down the skirts Tully continued to lift as he examined her foot.

"How in heck did someone steal your shoes? You aren't dumb enough to sleep with your door unlocked are you?"

Brianna glared at him. The knowledge that he'd return her to the cell straight away was all that kept her from slapping him again.

"No, sir. I left my shoes in the hall at the hotel for the staff to clean. After someone practically shoved me into a mud puddle yesterday, my shoes were in dire need of a thorough scrubbing and polish. When I opened the door this morning, they were gone."

Tully rolled his eyes. "What did you expect? This isn't New York City or whatever fancy place you're used to staying. If you set things out, most folks assume that means the item is free for the taking. First, you lost your corsets, now your shoes." The sheriff gave her a look full of reproach. "Use your head, Miss Dumont, or pretty soon I'll have to throw you in jail for public nudity. As much as I might like to see that, not everyone would be excited if you marched through town like the next Lady Godiva."

Thane coughed, trying to hide a bark of laughter, while Dugan excused himself outside. When the deputy stepped back into the jail, his chest shook as he worked to contain his chuckles.

"While I haul her to Doc's office, can you arrange to get her a pair of shoes, Dugan?" Tully turned to the young deputy. "If you run over to see James at his shop, I'm sure he can help."

"Sure, boss. Do I need to lock her up when Doc finishes with her?"

"Nah. She served enough time today."

Wisely, Brianna held her tongue. At least until Tully swept her into his arms and headed out the door with Thane and Lily following close behind.

"Put me down this instant, Sheriff! I insist!"

"You can insist all you want, darlin', but the only place I'm setting you down is at Doc's office. From there, you can do whatever you please."

Brianna glared at him. "Never, in my entire life, have I met a man so pretentious, conceited, and altogether overbearing."

Thane chuckled and looked away.

Tully and Brianna both stared at him. "What's so funny?" Tully asked.

"Miss Dumont sounds a lot like Jemma did when we first met. She called me so many names that I finally gave up keeping track of them."

"Did you deserve to be called any of those names?" Brianna asked.

Thane nodded. "I sure did. That woman infuriated me to the point I couldn't see straight let alone think with a lick of sense."

Brianna cast Tully a smug look. "So, it's a trait indigenous to the men of Baker City?"

"Oh, I don't know about that, but Tully and I are quite a bit alike." Thane smirked at Brianna. "Jemma is the love of my life now, but she didn't much like me the first month or two we were married."

Brianna's head snapped up. "She married you, even when she didn't like you?"

"Yes, ma'am." Thane glanced down at Lily as the little girl rode in his arms. "Her sister married my brother and gave us two beautiful children to care for. The only problem was that Jemma and the kids were in England. I didn't know they existed until my brother passed away and I traveled over there to settle his estate. I needed to bring Jack and Lily back to America and Jemma couldn't bear to be apart from the children, so we wed for their sakes. Neither one of us planned on falling in love."

"What a wonderful, romantic story." Thane's tale distracted her from the tribulation of being carried through town to the doctor's office in the sheriff's arms.

"And it had a happy ending," Tully said, shifting Brianna in his arms as Thane opened the door to the doctor's office.

Doc happened to be speaking to his assistant in the waiting room when they walked inside. The man motioned for Tully to follow him back to an examination room, where the sheriff gently deposited her on an exam table.

After he set her down, Tully leaned forward until his face was just inches from hers. "Don't you dare set foot outside until Dugan comes for you. Understood?"

"Perfectly, Sheriff." Brianna wanted to scream and shout at the awful way the sheriff had treated her, but she feigned indifference as he gave her one last warning glance then disappeared from the room.

His enticing scent lingered behind and she rubbed her finger beneath her nose, hoping to dislodge it.

The doctor cleaned the cut and wrapped it in a bandage. After helping Brianna back to the waiting room, he was in the midst of warning her to stay off her foot a day or two when Dugan appeared with a man carrying a box full of women's shoes and ankle boots.

"Miss Dumont, this is James Caldwell. He owns a shoe shop here in town. He can custom make anything, but he had a few ready-made pairs. One of them ought to fit you," Dugan said, leaning against the wall while James set down the box in his hands.

"Let's give this one a try," Mr. Caldwell said, holding up a pair of sturdy ankle boots with a short heel. While still fashionable with buttons up the side, they would also provide more stability than the dressy shoes Brianna had been wearing.

The boots were slightly big, so Mr. Caldwell helped her try on a smaller pair.

She stood and took a few steps around the room, pleased at how comfortable the boots felt on her feet.

"These are perfect. Should I return with you to your store to settle the bill?" she asked, glancing at the shoemaker.

"That's not necessary, miss. The sheriff took care of the bill." Mr. Caldwell tipped his hat to her and left with his box of shoes.

Brianna turned to pay for her bill to the doctor, only to discover Tully had taken care of it as well.

Shocked speechless, she stared at the deputy, trying to gather her wits. Why would a man who had been so rude and horrible to her pay her doctor bill and purchase her new shoes? It made no sense. None whatsoever.

"Are you ready to go, Miss Dumont?" Dugan asked, opening the door and waiting for her to precede him.

"Yes, Deputy Durfey. I believe I am," she said, limping outside. The sun bore down on her and her stomach growled, offering a reminder she'd missed breakfast and it was nearly past time for lunch.

"If you get tired of eating at the hotel, there's a nice little restaurant just down the street there." Dugan pointed down the block.

"I value the information." Grateful, Brianna tipped her head his direction. "It is always helpful to have options at your disposal."

"Yes, ma'am."

Dugan remained silent as he walked her back to the hotel, holding the door for her as she made her way inside. "Have a pleasant afternoon, Miss Dumont." Politely, he tipped his hat to her.

"Thank you, Deputy Durfey. Your assistance is greatly appreciated." Brianna smiled at him then continued inside the lobby.

Rather than go to her room, she made a beeline for the restaurant and indulged in a filling lunch. All the while she ate, her mind played over the events of the morning, starting with the theft of her shoes and ending with the maddening sheriff.

It seemed imperative she conclude her business and leave town before that infuriating man wormed his way any deeper into her thoughts.

Chapter Four

Brianna sat in the hotel's restaurant, sipping a cup of tea even though most of the other patrons had left. She spent the previous day in her room, allowing her foot to rest, but she couldn't bear the thought of being cooped up staring at the same four walls another day.

After dressing with care, she made her way to the restaurant in the hotel and enjoyed a delicious breakfast. A discarded newspaper caught her eye at the empty table next to hers, so she picked it up and read the news on the front page.

Several articles garnered her interest as she worked her way through the paper. The sip of tea she'd just taken spewed out her mouth and she choked as she read the headline over the sheriff's report of arrests and incidents.

Woman Named Fred Claims Theft, Arrested For Assault!

Based on her continued refusal to share her first name with the high-handed sheriff, he'd informed the paper her name was Fred. From the way the story was written, it made it sound as though she'd invented the incident of her missing bag and shoes then viciously attacked the town's beloved lawman.

"That man has positively gone too far!" Brianna stood and slapped money on the table to pay for her meal. In her haste to defend her honor, she forgot all about her sore foot as she rushed to the front desk.

"Mr. Isaac, I am in dire need of directions to the newspaper office."

At the look on her face, the poor desk clerk didn't even bother to smile or offer good-natured remarks. He pointed toward the door. "Cross the street and go down three blocks, turn right and go another block, you can't miss it. It's not far from Mr. Miller's mercantile. There's a sign hanging up outside."

"Thank you." Brianna gave him a curt nod then marched off in the direction he indicated.

At the newspaper office, an elderly woman sat at a desk facing the door. "May I help you?" she asked with a pleasant smile.

"Yes. I'd like to speak to the editor."

"I'm terribly sorry, but he's out of the office. You're welcome to leave him a note or try back tomorrow."

"I'll leave him a note." Brianna took the paper and pencil the woman slid across the desk to her. When she finished writing the missive, the woman handed her an envelope. She tucked the letter inside then handed it back. "You will see he receives this?"

"I promise I'll give it to him as soon as he returns to the office."

"Thank you," Brianna said, mustering a half-hearted smile just for the sake of attempting to be polite before she stormed out the door.

Intent on finding the sheriff, she stomped down the street. She rounded a corner and spied the insufferable man speaking to Mr. Miller of the mercantile.

Tully Barrett laughed at something Frank Miller said. Dimples filled his cheeks and Brianna couldn't help but notice his engaging smile. It appeared he wasn't rude to everyone, or more pointedly, was rude only to her. She'd seen him laughing and joking with several people around town in the few days she'd been there. He seemed to reserve all this surly behavior just for her.

Regardless of his demeanor, she intended to take him to task for publicly humiliating her in the misleading report.

"Sheriff Barrett!" she called as she approached him.

As though someone had poured a bucket of ice water down his back, Tully's entire countenance changed. He snapped his mouth shut and glared at her.

"Good morning, Miss Dumont," Frank Miller said, escaping inside his store at the enraged look on her face.

"To what do I owe the displeasure of this visit, Miss Dumont?" Tully spied the newspaper in her hand and smirked. "Or should I refer to you as Fred?"

"You intolerable, presumptuous, supercilious cretin! How dare you!" Brianna shook the newspaper in Tully's face. "Not only is the information in this article incorrect, it is slanderous."

"I believe you're the one who said it isn't slander if it's true." Tully's contemptuous grin nudged her past the boiling point and completely beyond the grasp of reason.

"My name is not Fred. That's not even close. Had you asked nicely instead of demanding, I would have given it to you in the first place. To clarify, someone stole my bag even though you doubt the truth of it. It is a matter of great importance it be returned. Furthermore, one of the many crooks who reside in this… this… depraved community stole my only pair of shoes!"

"Well…" Tully took a step back and studied her from the tip of the blue plume on her hat to the toes of her new boots barely visible beneath the hem of her exquisite gown. "You must have made it through a whole day without losing any more clothes because it looks like you've got your corset, petticoats, and bloomers on today. Maybe I better investigate, just to confirm the fact." He bent down and started to lift the hem of her skirt.

Outraged, she smacked him across the back with the newspaper. "You are despicable and disgusting."

When she raised the newspaper to smack him again, Tully grabbed her wrist and fastened an iron cuff around it. Before she could pull away, he latched a cuff onto the other one and turned her around.

"You're under arrest. Again."

Brianna attempted to set her feet and refuse to move, but he merely pushed her forward. "You can't arrest me again when I haven't done anything wrong."

Tully took her arm in his hand and marched her into the jail. Seth Harter glanced up from the desk where he sat filling out a report. Taken aback by the sight of a woman in cuffs, he remained silent as Tully directed Brianna back to the cells. A drunk snored in the one farthest from the door and she wrinkled her nose at the smells emanating from him.

Quickly opening the cell nearest the door, Tully pushed her inside then removed the cuffs. After he locked the cell, he glared at her. "You're under arrest for assaulting an officer of the law, disturbing the peace, and…"

Brianna crossed her arms and sneered at him. "You can't even think of a third reason to arrest me, can you?"

"Unlawful annoyance." Tully leaned toward her and pointed a finger toward the drunk. "If you make as much racket as you did the last time, I'll move you next to his cell and shut the door."

"Humph!" Brianna turned her back to Tully, but remained silent.

Tully dropped the cell keys on his desk and removed his hat, forking his fingers through his thick brown hair. He lifted his gaze to Seth, mindful of the deputy's shocked expression.

Not in the mood to discuss what he'd done, he settled his hat back on his head. "Can you keep an eye on things for a while?"

"Sure, boss. Are you really gonna leave Miss Dumont in there?" Seth tipped his head toward the jail cells.

Tully stepped close to the deputy's desk and dropped his voice. "Let her go as soon as ol' Boyd wakes up."

Seth nodded and Tully ambled out the door into the fresh morning sunshine. He hurried through town and out to his property. As he neared the pasture where his horses grazed, he emitted three sharp whistles.

A buckskin horse trotted his direction. Tully easily looped a rope around his neck and led him over to a rail just outside the barn. He saddled Cotton, in need of a ride to clear his head.

A few minutes later, he headed off toward the tree line, anticipating the cooler air and shade provided at the higher elevation.

As he rode, he contemplated where his day had gone so terribly wrong.

He'd started off the morning with his favorite breakfast at the restaurant in town, eating two orders of bacon, three eggs fried the way he liked them, and two fluffy biscuits smothered in fresh strawberry jam. After his second cup of coffee, he made a round through town, visiting with folks he'd known for years and others who were relatively new to the area.

He made a point of stopping by the lumberyard to see if Angus MacGregor needed any help as he watched over operations in Ian's absence. The affable man told him he had everything under control, but thanked him for his concern. They discussed the fine meal Jemma had served the other evening and laughed over the antics of Lily and Jack as the children showed everyone around the newly finished house after supper.

Tully bid him good day then remembered he had a special order he needed to place with Frank Miller at the mercantile.

If only he hadn't stood outside talking to Frank a few moments, maybe the troublesome Miss Dumont wouldn't have found him. Despite her proper appearance, he had the idea she was like a dog with a bone once she set her mind to something.

For whatever reason, she'd set her mind on disliking him. Thoroughly and completely.

The feeling was mutual.

If he hadn't loathed her so entirely, he would have admired the sunlight streaming through the light brown curls around her face. And the way her blue jacket and skirt, edged in dark blue stitching and beads, made him think of periwinkle flowers. A blouse of thick creamy lace called his attention to her graceful neck before it dipped behind a waistcoat constructed of the same blue fabric as her dress.

The bright blue gloves on her hands stood out in stark contrast to the cuffs he'd wrapped around her delicate wrists.

The slightest possibility existed that he'd overreacted to her slapping him with the newspaper.

In all fairness, he deserved it for telling Bowen Packwood at the newspaper office her name was Fred. Bowen was aware it was all in fun, but printed the article anyway.

Tully knew if Miss Dumont caught wind of the article, she'd be fit to be tied, but something in him wanted to rile her.

Disturbed by his continual need to provoke her, Tully couldn't understand the reasoning behind it. He kept the peace, not stirred up trouble. Over the years, he'd played plenty of jokes on his friends, but it was harmless and taken in the vein it was intended.

Miss Dumont brought out the worst in him and Tully didn't like it. Not one bit.

Thane had taken him to task for locking her up the other day, especially in light of her injured foot. Guilt pricked at him for not noticing her wound. He hadn't given her the opportunity to say anything, plugging his ears and ignoring her the entire time she'd been in the jail until Thane and Lily arrived. If it wasn't for the little girl pointing out Miss Dumont's blood on the floor, Tully might have left her suffering in the cell the rest of the day.

The crazy woman hadn't sat down the entire time she'd been in there, refusing to dirty her dress in his filthy prison, as she called it. His cells were among the cleanest anywhere because Tully wasn't keen on the idea of any vermin creeping over to his desk and taking up residence on him. He hired someone to clean the cells every week.

Nevertheless, his conscience nagged him about treating a woman so disrespectfully. It wasn't like him to do such a thing.

To make amends, he'd paid her doctor bill and had the cobbler send him the bill for her new shoes. Yet, he'd turned right around and told Bowen to call her Fred.

Although he wouldn't admit it to her, he'd discovered her name was Brianna shortly after her arrival in town.

Once the wedding reception ended, Tully went to the depot and questioned the ticket agent at length, learning Brianna Dumont arrived from Warwick, Rhode Island. She didn't purchase a return ticket and had queried the ticket agent about the most prosperous mines in the area and lodging options. She'd set down her bag to dig a coin out of her reticule to pay him for keeping an eye on her trunk. It was in that moment that someone made off with her bag.

Tully grinned, recalling how incensed she'd been when he'd teased her about her corsets.

Truthfully, thoughts of her corsets made him wonder what she'd look like under all the prim and proper attire she wore.

The moment he'd laid eyes on her, he knew she wasn't the type of woman to set foot in the Gilded Spur. He'd made that offhanded comment about her working there just to watch the sparks ignite in her summer-sky eyes.

The more she reacted to his teasing, the stronger he felt the need to prod her. The way her eyes flamed with anger and she rebelliously raised that proud chin only egged him on.

Since she'd set foot in town, his world had shifted out of balance.

No matter what story she tried to sell him, he knew she wasn't telling the whole truth about what was in her bag or her reasons for being in Baker City.

If he could keep his head on straight around her for more than five minutes, he planned to find out what really brought her to town.

Chapter Five

Determined to ride out to Clive Fisher's mine, Brianna donned her fullest skirt and retrieved a pair of thick leather gloves from her trunk. If the mine was as successful as she imagined, there might even be a grand house located at such a prosperous enterprise. No doubt, Mrs. Fisher would invite her to stay with them for the duration of her visit in the area.

With no idea how long it would take to reach the mine, she concluded she might need something to eat before she returned to Baker City. A biscuit she'd saved from breakfast and wrapped in a clean napkin tucked easily into the pocket of her skirt.

Before she changed her mind or let her fears hold her back, she marched to the livery Mr. Isaac said had the best horses in town. Thus far, his information had proved most helpful.

After paying to rent a horse for the day, Brianna asked if they had a sidesaddle she could borrow.

Milt Owens, owner of the livery, stared at her so long, Brianna thought perhaps something was grievously wrong. Finally he spoke, jabbing his thumb over his shoulder toward the tack room. "I'd feel better about putting a western saddle on the horse for you."

"I assure you, sir, I've been riding sidesaddle for nearly as long as I have walked. In fact, I earned the women's championship title for horsemanship at my father's club three years running."

"But, Miss Dumont, the terrain around here isn't what you might be accustomed to. There are rocks and sagebrush and rattlesnakes not to mention badger holes and…"

"I'll be fine, Mr. Owens."

He disappeared inside a room and returned with a sidesaddle. Although it was far from new, it looked to be of good quality.

Without saying a word, he saddled the horse then led it outside into the bright June sunshine. "Are you certain you wouldn't rather have a regular western saddle, Miss Dumont? It would just take me a minute to switch saddles."

"No. I prefer to ride this way. I do thank you for accommodating my request," she said, giving the man what she hoped was a sweet smile.

He cracked a grin and held out his linked hands for her to use as a step in mounting the horse. Once she settled her skirts around her, she smiled at him again. "Do you know how to find Clive Fisher's mine?"

Milt raised both eyebrows so high they nearly meshed with his hairline. "What does a nice lady like you want with a crotchety ol' coot like him?"

"He and my father are partners in a mine. I came to Baker City to check on our investments."

The man blew out a long breath then walked around the horse and pointed toward the distant mountains. "See that little ribbon of trail that leads up into the trees?"

"Yes," Brianna said, straining to see that far into the distance with the sun shining in her face.

"Once you hit the timberline, take the second trail to your left. Ride about two miles and you'll see a burnt stump. Turn there and you'll be at Clive's mine." Milt looked at her one more time. "Are you sure…"

Brianna held up a hand to stop him. "I'll be perfectly fine, Mr. Owens, but I do thank you for your concern. Have a pleasant day."

"I'm sure mine will be better than yours," he said cryptically, then hurried back inside the livery.

Brianna rode over a few blocks then followed the road that led out of town. At the sedate pace she set, the sun was high overhead when she reached the area where coniferous trees grew on the sloping hillside heading up to the top of the mountain.

Despite Mr. Owens' fears she might have problems, the road she'd taken was established and she'd ridden without incident.

She'd waved to a few wagons carrying families toward Baker City. Lest any of the men riding into town arrive at any false conclusions about her, she kept her eyes averted as she encountered them in passing.

The temperature dropped as she rode through the trees, although the path became harder to navigate. Holes, tree roots, and dust a foot-thick in some places made her advance at a cautious pace.

Focused on maneuvering around a rather large rut in the road, the hair on the back of her neck suddenly stood on end. Nervous, she glanced around and sucked in a gulp when a pair of yellow eyes glared at her from beneath a nearby tree.

The animal looked rather like a dog with gray fur on its back, a white belly, and a bushy black-tipped tail. However, the pointed ears and narrow pointed face did not seem doglike or in the least bit friendly, especially when it growled at her.

Brianna screamed, startling the horse. It bolted forward and she had to work to retain her seat on the saddle.

The horse lunged onto a side trail and continued galloping even though Brianna tugged on the reins and pleaded for it to stop.

Unable to control the animal, Brianna held on as it veered off the trail. Tree branches slapped at her face and yanked the hat right off her head.

Panic beat strong in her breast and she swallowed down the fear in her throat threatening to choke her.

With no warning, the horse came to an abrupt halt and Brianna flew off, landing in a creek. The water was so cold it made her sit up and gasp in shock. Before she could scramble to her feet and grab the reins, the horse turned and trotted back the way they'd come.

Alone, frightened, soaked to the skin, and fighting the urge to cry, Brianna ran after the horse in her soggy clothes. Without a way to ride off the mountain, she really would be in trouble.

A few hundred yards later, a catch in her side made her stop and press a hand to her ribs. Whoever invented corsets never tried to chase down a runaway horse wearing one. The combination of the higher elevation, getting tossed off the horse, and an engulfing sense of fear left her lightheaded.

Fainting was not an option, so she closed her eyes a moment to gather her composure.

She made it back to the trail and sighed in relief as a man rode toward her with the livery horse trailing along behind him.

"Miss Dumont?" the man asked as he stopped beside her.

Brianna recognized Thane Jordan and released a relieved sigh. "Oh, thank goodness you found the horse," she said, accepting the reins he held out to her.

He stared at her for a long moment. The corner of his mouth quirked upward, as though he held back a laugh. "Have a little trouble, Miss Dumont?" Thane stepped out of his saddle and helped Brianna mount her horse.

"There was some furry beast with yellow eyes that startled me and I screamed. The horse bolted and dumped me in the creek," she said, pushing wet hair out of her eyes.

"Probably just a coyote. They're harmless, for the most part." Thane mounted and looked over at her. "I don't know where you found that sidesaddle, but I'm surprised Milt Owens let you put it on one of his horses."

"Mr. Owens strongly debated the wisdom of me riding astride, but it simply wasn't a topic I wished to discuss." Brianna settled her wet skirts around her.

Thane shook his head. "My wife refused to ride astride, but I didn't leave her any options. Now, she enjoys her western saddle. When Maggie gets back from her honeymoon, go by her shop. She can set you up with some riding skirts that make it much easier for you women to ride."

Brianna wouldn't argue with the man who came to her rescue. "I'll take that information under advisement."

Thane tipped back his hat and looked at Brianna again. "What are you doing this far up in the hills?"

"My intent was to locate Clive Fisher's mine. My father invested as a partner in his holdings and I'm here to evaluate the success of that endeavor." Although the summer heat warmed her, Brianna felt chilled to the bone. She urged the horse forward until it stood in a patch of sunshine. "You wouldn't happen to know how to find it, would you?"

"I sure would. It's not too far from one of my mines," Thane said, turning his horse back in the direction he'd come. "I heard Tully tossed you in the calaboose again."

"If you mean manhandled me into one of the jail cells without cause, you would be correct. I don't understand how you can be friends with such a loathsome man as the sheriff."

Thane worked to hide a grin, but not before Brianna caught sight of it. "Oh, I wouldn't say Tully is loathsome. Once you get to know him, he's not such a bad guy and a handy fellow to have around if you run into trouble. Tully's saved my neck more times than I want to count."

Brianna rode in silence for a few minutes before she looked at Thane. "How long have you known Sheriff Barrett?"

"Since I was sixteen. Tully and I were both orphans. We met on the way to Texas but ended up traveling with a wagon train here to Oregon. Maggie MacGregor and her first husband were our traveling partners. When Daniel died in a mining accident, Tully and I did our best to help Maggie. We're both happy for her to find love again with Ian."

"Has she been a widow long?"

"More than ten years," Thane said, guiding his horse past a burnt stump and down a little-used trail.

"Ten years is a long time to mourn a spouse." Brianna thought of all the years her father had mourned her mother's death. She'd only been five when her mother passed away from some wretched illness that ate away at her until there was nothing left of the vibrant woman. Twenty-one years later, her father had still missed her mother every single day.

"It is, but I think I'd mourn beyond a lifetime if something happened to my Jemma." Thane turned in the saddle and glanced back to make sure Brianna made it down the steep trail without any problem.

She offered him a reassuring nod. "I greatly look forward to meeting your wife, and Mrs. MacGregor. I've heard nothing but good comments about them both."

Thane smiled. "They both are fine, fine women. I'm sure Jemma will look forward to meeting you, too. Perhaps you'd like to join us for lunch after church on Sunday. We often eat at the dining room at Hotel Warshauer after the church service."

"Oh, that would be lovely. I'm staying at the hotel, although if I'm going to spend too much more time in town, I may need to seek out a less expensive alternative."

"If you're planning to stay more than a week or two, talk to Maggie and Ian when they return. There's a recently vacated apartment above her dress shop."

Thrilled by this tidbit of news, Brianna would make a point to seek out Mrs. MacGregor as soon as the woman returned from her honeymoon trip.

Brianna was about to offer a comment when a shot kicked up dirt a few feet in front of them. Although his horse reared, Thane kept the big stallion under control. Whether Thane's presence or that of the other horse calmed her mount, Brianna was glad the horse didn't bolt again. It merely shied to the left a few steps.

"Clive, it's Thane Jordan! Put that gun down and come out here." Thane cupped his hands around his mouth so his voice carried farther.

Brianna watched as a grizzled old man who looked half-demented shuffled out of a ramshackle building into the open, holding a rifle in one hand and a pickaxe in the other. Her dreams of having a luxurious home to stay in while she was in the area crashed around her.

"Thane! What in the…" The old man glared at Brianna. "What sort of disease have you dragged up the mountain?"

"No disease, Clive. Miss Dumont is the daughter of your business partner. She came all the way to Baker City to check on her father's holdings."

"You're George's girl?" The old man dropped the pickaxe and shaded his eyes as he scowled at Brianna.

"Yes, sir." Brianna rode up beside Thane, hoping he'd stay long enough to make sure the old man didn't shoot her.

When the miner turned and shuffled toward the shack, Thane motioned for her to follow him. "You'll be fine, Miss Dumont. Clive's bark is worse than his bite. Can you find your way back to town?"

"Yes, Mr. Jordan. I made note of the trail and will be able to return without further assistance. Thank you so much for your help." Brianna smiled at the man then urged the horse forward, following Clive.

"Take care, Clive, and stay out of trouble," Thane called then turned and rode up the trail.

Brianna slid off the horse and followed the miner to his shack. She tied the reins around a sturdy post.

Clive frowned at her as he stood in the doorway. "I ain't got no use for women, even if your father seems like a good man. Why didn't he come instead of sendin' you?"

"My father was recently murdered. I didn't even know about your mine until I was going through his papers. From the letters the two of you exchanged, it seemed he held great hope for your claim being prosperous. I understand Father maintained a forty percent share of ownership in the mine."

"He did, and I reckon with his death, the ownership passes to you, much as it galls me to think of a sharin' my mine with a woman." Clive spit a stream of tobacco that landed only a few inches away from Brianna. She did her best not to wrinkle her nose.

Suddenly, the breeze changed direction. A stench, a revolting cross between a rotting corpse and something left to ferment far too long, blew in her face. Disgusted, she realized the smell came from Clive.

His clothes were so filthy the fabric hinted that it might stand upright, even if he wasn't wearing them. Although his hair wasn't long, it looked as though he'd whacked it off with a dull knife as it stuck up this way and that around his head.

Convinced she could see bugs crawling in his hair, she took a step back, hoping none of them tried to jump onto her.

"I'm right sorry to hear about your father, Miss Dumont, but you traipsed all the way out here for nothin'." Clive stomped inside the house and slammed the door.

Brianna hid her surprise the entire building didn't collapse around him, so ramshackle was its state.

"Mr. Fisher? Mr. Fisher! I insist we discuss matters. If you have no desire to collaborate with a woman, I'm more than happy to sell my father's shares back to you. Would that be a satisfactory arrangement?"

The sound of muttering and banging around followed by a string of cursing made her turn her back to the cabin and cover her ears.

Unless a bear or a wolf jumped out at her, prepared to eat her alive, nothing else would have driven her to set foot inside Clive Fisher's humble abode. Just when she was ready to give up and try talking to him another day, he opened the door and strode outside.

He handed her a cup of steaming coffee and motioned to two stumps set by a circle of rocks ringing a pile of ashes. While Brianna settled her skirts on one of the stumps and took a small sip of the coffee, he built up the fire, pausing in his work to look at her and grumble every so often.

When a warm fire blazed with cheery welcome, Clive took a sip of his coffee and settled onto the other stump.

"I don't like women, missy, and I don't like anyone pokin' and proddin' in my business, but your father was an honest and fair man. Out of respect to him, I'll shoot straight with you."

Brianna tried not to squirm when Clive fixed his narrowed gaze on her. His pale blue eyes looked like murky water had frozen in a lake devoid of color. Gray stubble sprouted on his face, although he didn't have a beard.

Stooped as he was, the old man was barely taller than she was. As he sat beside her, sipping coffee and casting furtive glances her direction, she concluded Thane Jordan was correct. Clive Fisher was harmless.

"Thank you for building a fire. It's cooler up here in the mountains than I expected." Brianna smiled at him and took another tiny sip from her cup, trying not to think about dirt or bugs, or the stout flavor of the drink.

"Looks like you took a dunkin' on your way here. Horse get away from you?" Clive didn't look at her as he talked, but he grinned into his cup.

"As a matter a fact, an animal scared me and spooked the horse. He managed to unseat me in a creek that was as cold as any water I've ever felt. If it hadn't been for Mr. Jordan's fortuitous arrival, I'd still be on foot, trying to find the horse."

"That's what you get for ridin' one of those death contraptions." Clive pointed to the sidesaddle. "Right there is a perfect example of why women are nothin' but troublesome nuisances. They don't use their noggins when it comes to just about every single decision that rolls down the road. I got no use for the stupid rules of society and propriety." Clive crooked his pinky finger in the air as he took a loud slurp of his coffee. "It's all a bunch of nonsense. Most females ain't got nothin' between their pretty little ears besides a bunch of air and ridiculous expectations."

"Well, I'm glad we got all that out of the way," Brianna said, setting down the cup and holding her hands out to the fire. "Now that you've established I'm too dumb to understand anything about this business, I'd like to know how much the mine is producing and examine the facility."

"Now, just hold on to your skirts, missy. Nobody goes in the mine but me, and I ain't of a mind to tell you a thing. How do I know you're really George's girl?"

Brianna pulled a locket from beneath the neck of her blouse and opened it. She laid it on her palm and held it out toward the old man. "That's a photo of my father and mother on their wedding day."

Clive whistled, but with a missing front tooth, the sound came out more like the mating call of a deranged bird. "Girlie, you look just like your mama. She was a very beautiful woman."

"Thank you." Brianna stared at the photo, proud that she bore a strong resemblance to her mother.

Clive pointed to the locket. "Your father sent me a photo of himself so I'd know what he looked like if he ever ventured out to visit the mine. That's him in the picture, even though he was younger there."

"We've established that I am Brianna Dumont, daughter of George Dumont. Now may I see the mine?"

"No." Clive took another sip of his coffee. "The thing is, missy, the mine hasn't done very well the last few years. Your father knew that and told me in his last letter to keep workin' at it."

"If you were to pay me for Father's share of the profits today, what would it total?" Brianna watched as Clive disappeared inside his shack. More banging ensued before he eventually reappeared with a little glass jar and handed it to Brianna.

"There's about forty dollars worth of gold in that jar and that's your father's share."

"Forty dollars? Oh, surely you jest, Mr. Fisher. Why, from the letters you and Father exchanged, it sounded as if you both expected this to be a profitable mine. If that is true..." Brianna rattled off figures and facts from research she'd done about the gold mining business.

The old man's jaw dropped open and he gawked at her. "Well, I take that back. There might be one woman alive whose head isn't completely full of ridiculous nonsense." He stood and motioned for Brianna to follow him.

Much to her surprise, he gave her a tour of the mine and answered her numerous questions. To Brianna's relief, they returned to the stumps near the fire and Clive threw another chunk of wood on the coals. Her clothes had almost dried and she'd almost warmed up from her dunking in the creek, but not completely.

"Why are you really here, missy?" Clive asked, drinking from his cup of cold coffee.

"Father owed a great deal of money to a very powerful man upon his death. By coming here, I hoped I could sell his portion of the mine, pay his debts, and restore his good name." The starch went out of Brianna's spine. "I suppose I'll have to figure out another means of acquiring the funds."

"Well, girlie, don't go losin' all hope in the Felicity. Not yet."

Brianna stared at Clive as a slow grin spread across her face. "A man who hates women named his mine Felicity? How is that possible?"

"That's a story for another day." Clive stood and pointed to the sky. "There's a storm brewin' and if you want to beat it back to town, you better get. If you stick around for a few weeks, I'll see what I can do to come up with some money to buy back your father's shares."

"I appreciate your help and concern, Mr. Fisher, but don't go to any bother on my account. I'm sure I'll see you again before I leave Baker City."

"Most likely, girlie. Be careful ridin' back to town. Do you need me to come with you?" Clive took a few steps toward a corral that looked like it might disintegrate if anyone touched it. A mule brayed and stuck its head over a rotting pole.

"Thank you for that kind offer, but I can find my way back to town." Brianna led the horse over to a stump and climbed into the saddle. She settled her skirts and gave Clive Fisher a parting glance. "I extend my gratitude to you, Mr. Fisher, for your hospitality and tour of the mine."

"Just be careful and don't get lost. The last place you want to be is out here on the mountain in the dark, especially a woman as pretty as you." Clive waved as she headed up the trail.

Brianna kept watch for any animals as she rode toward the main trail. When she reached it without incident, she released a sigh and headed back down the mountain.

With a rare day off to do as he pleased, Tully spent it repairing a section of fence on his twenty acres at the edge of town. After lunch, he removed the barn door that had been busted for a few weeks. He was in the process of hanging a replacement when Thane Jordan rode up.

"What are you doing in town today, you contrary cuss?" Tully asked as Thane dismounted and sauntered over to him.

Thane held the door while Tully tightened the screws in the hinges. "I rode out to one of my mines today. You won't believe who I found on foot up in the mountains."

Tully lifted his gaze and shot Thane a questioning glance. "Please tell me it's the horse rustler I've been trying to track down. If you found him, I hope you dragged him behind Shadow the whole way to town."

Thane shook his head and grinned. "I did not find him, although I'm sure you will. He's bound to make a mistake sooner or later."

"Most likely," Tully agreed, turning his attention back to tightening the screws holding up the door. "If it wasn't the rustler, who was it you saw?"

"Miss Dumont."

The screwdriver in Tully's hand slipped and jabbed into his finger, drawing blood. He muttered a few choice words and sucked the blood off his finger before turning to glare at his friend.

The urge to punch Thane hard enough to knock the smirk off his face nearly made him draw back his fist. "What in tarnation was that thick-headed, wearisome woman doing up in the hills?"

"She was trying to find Clive Fisher's mine. From what she said, a coyote spooked her and the horse took her for a wild ride before dumping her in the creek. The horse ran off and she was trying to catch up to it when I happened upon her. She's darn lucky I came across her mount before someone else did. That fool woman was up there on a sidesaddle." Thane lifted the door a little higher as Tully tightened the last of the screws. "I suggested she purchase a riding skirt from Maggie before she makes another attempt riding somewhere."

"Did you take her to Clive's place?" Tully gave the screwdriver one final turn then stepped back.

"I did. Clive only shot at us once on our way in. He must be going soft in his old age." Thane pulled the door shut then pushed it open. "Good work on the door."

"Thanks." Tully gathered his tools and set them inside the barn in a toolbox he kept on a high bench near his tack. "You left her up there with Clive?"

"Yeah. I stopped by his place to ride back with her, but she and Clive were nowhere to be seen, so I assumed she'd already left."

"What if he killed her and tossed her body down a shaft?" Tully lifted his saddle from a rack and carried it outside. He whistled for Cotton and the horse trotted over to the fence.

Chuckles rolled out of Thane. "Clive wouldn't kill her, or anyone else for that matter. He just likes to put on a good show."

"Still, I doubt that woman could find her way out of a cracker box let alone off that mountain." Tully settled the saddle on the back of his horse and tightened the cinch while Thane slipped on Cotton's bridle. "I finally get a day off and I'm gonna have to spend an hour or two of it chasing down some nincompoop female who isn't smart enough to ride like a normal person or stay in town where she belongs." Wound up, Tully huffed in frustration. "For that matter, she needs to go back to wherever she came from. I've endured more irritation and frustration since she arrived than I've had in the last dozen years."

Thane hid a grin and listened to his tirade. He ran a gentle hand along Cotton's neck and patted the horse as Tully swung into the saddle. "It's too bad she's so pretty and smart, too. That probably just makes it even worse, doesn't it, you cranky ol' buffoon."

Tully scowled at Thane as his friend mounted his horse and rode alongside him to the road. "You coming with me?"

"Nope. I'll leave you to handle Miss Dumont. I told Jemma I'd pick up a few things she needed at the mercantile on my way home. You know you're welcome to join us for supper if you're of a mind to ride out to the ranch."

"If it doesn't take me the rest of the day to find that mule-headed woman and the storm we're about to get doesn't settle in, I'll be there." Tully thumped Thane on the back. "Thanks for helping with the door."

"Anytime," Thane said, turning toward town.

"Tell Jemma and everyone hello for me." Tully called over his shoulder as he headed west and rode toward the hills.

He'd only gone about a mile when a lone rider drew his gaze.

Backlit by the sun, a golden haze surrounded Brianna Dumont as she rode his direction. Her hair fell in a tumble of waves around her shoulders and down her back. Sunlight streaked through it, making it look like warm honey shot with gold. Tully's fingers itched to bury themselves in those wild, thick tresses.

A smudge marred her creamy cheek, her skirt had a tear near the knee, and she looked as though she might have wrestled with a pig from the dirt covering her dress, but Tully thought she'd never appeared more appealing.

Lively blue sparks danced in her eyes and her lips turned up in a smile. The wind and sunshine had given her skin a pleasant, rosy hue.

He didn't think he'd ever seen a woman so full of life and vibrancy. Drawn to her youthfulness, he wondered how old she was. At that moment, as she rode so carefree and unhampered by the constraints of society, she seemed more like a girl than the full-grown woman he knew her to be.

When she caught sight of him waiting on the trail, she slowed the horse as a frown replaced her smile.

"Good afternoon, Sheriff Barrett." She offered a polite nod as she rode past him.

He turned Cotton around and quickly caught up with her. "It looks like you've been on quite an adventure. Did you enjoy your visit with Clive?"

Brianna turned and glared at him, as though she tried to discern how he could possibly know where she'd been. Finally, she nodded her head. "We got off to a bumpy start, but I do believe Mr. Fisher is not nearly as curmudgeonly as he prefers everyone believe. He even gave me a tour of the mine."

"You're joshin' me." Tully leaned back in the saddle and stared at her. "Clive doesn't let anyone see The Felicity and he sure doesn't like women around his place."

"Why is his mine named The Felicity?" Brianna glanced over at Tully. "I assume it doesn't have anything to do with a state of bliss."

Tully chuckled. "No. I don't think there is a single felicitous thing about Clive Fisher." He studied her a long moment. "I reckon if I don't tell you the story, you'll ask around until you find out anyway. Once upon a time, Clive was married. Even had a little girl named Felicity. One winter, his daughter took sick and died. His wife ran off, claiming she couldn't take living in the wilds of Oregon another day. That's why Clive despises women and why the mine is called The Felicity."

"Oh, that's so sad. The poor man must be utterly heartbroken." Brianna's heart ached for the old man. No wonder he hid himself away from the world by working the mine.

"It happened a long, long time ago."

Brianna glared at Tully and reined in her mount. "Does that mean he should just forget about what happened and pretend his daughter never existed?"

A sigh rolled out of Tully as he stopped so close to her, their legs almost touched. "I never said or even implied that, Fred. What kind of burr is riding in your britches that makes you turn everything I say into an argument?"

As he expected, Brianna straightened her spine and lifted her chin before turning her cool glare to him. "You are a boorish, fractious man, Sheriff. Now if you'll excuse me, I must return this horse to the livery."

"By all means, Fred, take the horse back. Next time, be smart enough to leave the sidesaddle there. You could have gotten your neck broken or yourself killed."

Brianna narrowed her gaze and lifted an index finger to shake his direction. "You'd like that, wouldn't you, Sheriff? There is nothing that would please you more than my demise."

"I can think of a few things that would please me more, Fred." Tully's voice sounded unusually low and husky as he spoke while heat emanated from his hazel eyes. The thoughts filling his mind sure weren't any he ought to be having.

"And don't call me Fred!" she said, tossing her hair off her shoulder.

The fire flaming in her eyes and the color in her cheeks had scattered most of Tully's sense, but the moment she shook that tempting mane of hair, he was a goner.

Before he could think about what he was doing, what repercussions it might bring, he grabbed the finger she shook at him and pulled her toward him. His hands sank into her hair and his mouth lowered to hers.

A few seconds passed as she resisted him. The moment she surrendered to the passion sparking between them and fully engaged in the romantic interlude, he deepened the kiss. His hands trailed down her arms and settled at her waist, prepared to lift her onto his lap.

Suddenly, she came to her senses and jerked her head back.

"Oh! You… you…" Unable to find the words she wanted to say, she slapped the reins across the rump of the horse and charged into town, leaving Tully alone on the road.

He watched her go, wondering what possessed him to do something as dimwitted as kissing prickly Miss Brianna Dumont. Not only would she be even more difficult to handle, he didn't know how he'd ever get that kiss out of his mind or the sweet, honeyed taste of her off his lips.

Chapter Six

Upon her return to the hotel, Mr. Isaac greeted Brianna with a fretful glance.

"Are you well, Miss Dumont?"

Brianna realized she must look a fright, but there was no help for it until she could take a bath and change her clothes. "I'm perfectly well, Mr. Isaac. However, your concern is appreciated."

Politely, he tipped his head then reached beneath the desk. "A letter arrived for you today while you were out." The young man handed her an envelope.

The name of the local newspaper office covered one corner of the parchment rectangle she held in her hands.

Curious, Brianna thanked Mr. Isaac then hurried up to her room. She tore open the envelope, withdrawing a single sheet of paper.

Miss Dumont,

I received your missive about the article naming you as Fred. Please accept my sincerest apologies for the misunderstanding.

If you have a moment to spare, I'd like to discuss the matter with you. Please come by my office before five o'clock today or by noon tomorrow.
Sincerely,
Mr. Bowen Packwood, Editor

Gratified the editor wanted to discuss Tully's ridiculous report, Brianna hurried to take a bath, wash her hair and dress in one of her finest walking suits. With the summer heat permeating every corner of her room, it didn't take long for her hair to dry. She twisted it up on her head, leaving a few tendrils to wisp around her face then fastened her hat at a sprightly angle.

Quickly tugging on her gloves, she picked up her reticule and room key, grabbed her parasol, and hurried out the door.

At the newspaper office, she asked to speak with Mr. Packwood. She waited only a moment before the friendly receptionist escorted her into his office.

"Miss Dumont, what a pleasure to meet you." A jolly-faced man with a rotund girth and a soothing voice greeted her as he stood from his desk and walked around it. "Thank you for meeting with me today."

"It's my pleasure, Mr. Packwood." With grace and decorum, Brianna tipped her head and sat in the chair he held out for her.

The editor walked back around his desk and lifted her letter from a pile of papers on the large, cluttered surface. "That was quite a letter you wrote.

In fact, I was very impressed that you worked so many four and five syllable words into such a short missive."

"Thank you, sir. I do hope you took my request into consideration." She offered Mr. Packwood a satisfied smile, gratified someone in town finally saw the sheriff's true colors.

Bowen leaned back in his chair. "To be clear, Miss Dumont, I've no intention of running a retraction or refuting anything Sheriff Barrett stated." At her dismayed gasp, he hurried to continue. "The reason I asked you here was because I want to offer you a job. Obviously, you have a stronger grasp of the English language than about ninety percent of the people in this town and I'm quite certain you are capable of writing articles. After seeing you in person, though, I think you have the potential to become a star reporter for our paper."

Miffed the man did not intend to call out Tully Barrett as a deluder of truth, she tamped down her irritation. With no hope of garnering any funds from her father's share of The Felicity, the idea of a job at the newspaper held a great deal of appeal.

Not only would it be something that stirred her interest, it meant she could begin accumulating the funds she needed to pay her father's debts. Even if she never planned to return to her former home in Rhode Island, she was determined to restore her father's good name and clear any debts he owed.

"I would be interested in a position," Brianna said, sitting a little straighter as she eyed the newspaper editor. "What did you have in mind?"

"You'd be perfect to acquire the intricate details for some of our more probing articles." Bowen steepled his fingers over his round belly. "Men will spill their guts to a pretty girl like you and not think twice about it."

Offended, Brianna started to rise to her feet, but before she did, Bowen waved his hand at her.

"Now, don't march out of here affronted and mad. I'm just laying the facts out on the table." Bowen scribbled something on a scrap of paper and held it out to Brianna. "That's what I'm willing to pay you if you work for me full-time."

"What would working for you entail?" Brianna asked, shocked by the amount of money Mr. Packwood was willing to pay. Women typically made far less than men did for doing the same work.

"I'd expect you to produce a few stories each week, since we publish daily. I might ask you to help edit some of the news that's submitted for publication."

Slowly, Brianna nodded her head. "And what type of articles would be of interest to you and your readers?"

"I want you to work on hard-hitting news. Things my other reporters can't seem to track down. Scandals in town, things no one wants to talk about. You can dig up all kinds of dirt because no one would expect you to be the one reporting on those types of stories. They'd expect you to be writing about the Eastern Star Lodge's upcoming tea and that sort of thing." Bowen stood when Brianna rose to her feet. "What do you say, Miss Dumont? Will you give it a whirl?"

"I believe I shall, Mr. Packwood. When would you like to see my first article on your desk?" Brianna walked toward the door.

"Why don't you come Monday morning, ready to get to work? If you don't have any story ideas by then, I'll assign you something to get you started. I'll let Mrs. Warden know to expect you."

"Very well, Mr. Packwood. Thank you for this opportunity." Brianna held her hand out to him and he shook it. "I'll see you Monday."

Although it bothered her that the editor was clearly in the sheriff's pocket, she found the idea of becoming a newspaper reporter intriguing.

Mulling over possibilities for her first story, she stepped outside and cringed as thunder boomed so loudly, the windows of the newspaper office rattled behind her. A bolt of lightning streaked across the sky and she watched it, mesmerized by the bright light.

Hastily snapping open her parasol, she took a few steps down the sidewalk. A firm hand pulled her to a halt and yanked the parasol out of her hands.

"I know you're crazy, Fred, but are you trying to get yourself killed? You look like a lightning rod with that silly thing over your head." Tully closed the parasol and handed it back to her.

"I'm not speaking to you." Brianna turned her back to him and marched down the block.

Unfortunately, Tully walked beside her. "That's fine. It'll make it easier for me to apologize for my behavior earlier. I didn't mean to um... That is, I wasn't planning to..."

Abruptly, Brianna stopped. Tully bumped into her and would have knocked her down if his arm hadn't wrapped around her waist, holding her upright. Immediately, he released her and took a step back.

She glowered at him. "Sheriff Barrett, is there some reason you insist on tormenting me?"

"No, Fred, other than the pure delight of it." His cocky grin wasn't entirely lost on her as dimples popped out in his cheeks through the rakish stubble he continually sported. There wasn't enough growth to call it a beard, but too much to assume he had merely forgotten to shave.

It gave him a rugged, almost dangerous appearance that seemed at odds to those all-too-attractive dimples and the warm light in his eyes. If Tully Barrett's name didn't linger at the top of her list of men she greatly disliked, it would have been easy to fall for him. Especially after his kiss left her so rattled, she could barely remember her own name.

Instead, she mustered up a scowl. "I do believe I asked you to cease referring to me as Fred."

"Where's the fun in that?" He fell into step beside her when she resumed her walk toward the hotel. Fat drops of rain began plopping around them as they turned the corner.

"Come on." Tully took her elbow and guided her inside a restaurant she had not yet visited. A waitress soon seated them and poured two cups of hot coffee. Although the air had been stifling earlier, the rain brought a cooling breeze.

"What are you doing?" Brianna asked as Tully removed his hat and sipped the coffee.

He gave her a chagrined look. "Buying you dinner, to make up for earlier."

She started to rise from her chair, but Tully's hand shot out and grasped her wrist. "Please stay, Miss Dumont. I'm sorry about what happened. I didn't intend to get so carried away and I won't let it happen again."

"Fine, I'll stay, but just this once." She sat down and removed her gloves, uncertain if she appreciated his vow not to kiss her again. It had been the single most wonderful kiss she'd ever experienced, even if it should never have transpired.

Determined to push it from her mind, she looked around the restaurant. In the excitement of the day, she'd missed lunch. The biscuit she'd taken with her had turned to mush in the creek and she certainly wouldn't have eaten anything Mr. Fisher offered, had he been that polite.

The rich, delicious smells of food made hunger gnaw at her and her stomach growled.

Tully grinned at her. "Sounds like you're hungry."

Embarrassed, Brianna fussed with her napkin, draping it over her lap. "It's terribly impolite to notice my stomach has defied the rules of society."

His grin broke into a wide smile. "I never did set much store in those rules."

Brianna looked up at him and her mouth quirked at the corners. "I am indubitably aware of that fact, Sheriff."

Tully leaned back in his chair and took another sip of coffee. "Why are you really here, Miss Dumont?"

She started to speak, but he held up a hand. "Don't start that nonsense about checking your father's holdings at Clive's mine. That crazy ol' goat barely scratches up enough gold dust to keep himself clothed and fed."

"I discovered that today. From the letters he and my father exchanged, I fully expected the mine to be quite prosperous. I'd vainly hoped there might even be accommodations available there, but that was not the case."

With great effort, Tully held back a snort. "That shack he lives in ought to be condemned. You didn't go in it, did you?"

"Absolutely not. Goodness only knows what sorts of pests inhabit that derelict abode." Brianna took a sip of her coffee then smiled at the waitress when she came to take their orders.

When she left, Tully studied Brianna for several minutes. "Are you here because you broke up with a beau and wanted to drive him mad trying to find you?"

Brianna glared at Tully. "Certainly not. If I had a beau, I wouldn't play games with him and I certainly would never run away from the man I loved."

"You robbed a bank and are on the lam, trying to stay one step ahead of the law," Tully teased.

The look she shot him held smug satisfaction. "If that were the case, you had a wanted fugitive in your jail twice and let me go both times. That can't be good for your reputation, Sheriff Barrett. What if word gets out that you are incapable of keeping criminals incarcerated?"

"I can haul you back there right now if you enjoy your cell so much." Tully touched his chin with his fingers, pretending to be deep in thought. "Maybe we should hang a sign that says, 'Fred's Place,' on your cell door."

"Be my guest, but you and I both know you won't arrest me again." Brianna took another sip of her coffee, watching Tully over the rim of the cup.

"Don't be so sure about that. You have a tendency to cross the line, Fred."

Resolved to keeping her temper at bay, she ignored his continued insistence on calling her Fred. "Regardless, I don't plan on making a third visit to the jail."

"Good for you. I'm glad to see you planning ahead." Tully grinned again. "Now, let's get back to your reason for being here in town. If you didn't break some fool's heart or rob a bank, and you're still desperately searching for a bag full of unmentionables, maybe you really did come to town to work at the Gilded Spur. Why, I…"

Brianna clapped her hand over his mouth, eyes wide as she frantically looked around to see if anyone heard them. No one appeared to pay the least bit of attention to their conversation. She released the breath she'd been holding. "Would you please refrain from speaking so... uninhibitedly, about matters that are confidential?"

Tully took her hand in his, kissing the back of it before she jerked it away and placed it on her lap.

"Must you always be such a tease?" she asked, unsettled by the tingles racing up her arm from the touch of his lips to her skin.

"I must, Fred, otherwise, life is just too dad-gummed serious for my liking." Tully looked up as the waitress brought their meals. After offering grace, he picked up his fork and knife, cutting off a bite of rare steak.

Brianna tried not to look at the pool of pink juice on his plate as she forked a bite of steaming beef casserole to her mouth.

As they ate, Tully told her a little of the town's history and how he came to be there, reiterating the story she'd already heard from Thane.

From the way he spoke about Thane and his family as well as Maggie and Ian MacGregor, she could tell he loved and respected each of them.

"What made you decide to leave your home and venture west?" Brianna asked as she sipped a cup of tea and Tully enjoyed a glass of lemonade after they finished their meal.

"Let's just say I needed to find a place to call home. I knew as soon as we arrived, Baker City was where I wanted to sink my roots." Tully appeared lost in thought for several moments while silence settled around them. Finally, he looked over at her. "You still haven't told me the truth, Miss Dumont. Why did you come to Baker City?"

"I truly did come to check on my father's holdings with Mr. Fisher's mine. Honestly, I had a much different vision of what his share of the business would be." If it wasn't for the newspaper job, Brianna didn't know what she would have done. Her funds were quickly dwindling and she wouldn't return to Rhode Island if at all possible.

"Why didn't your father come with you?"

Brianna avoided his probing gaze. Her fingers nervously traced a pattern on the cloth covering the table. "That would have been impossible."

"Why?"

"Because my father is dead." Tears burned her eyes and she swallowed hard to keep the emotion from overwhelming her. Everything had happened so quickly, including her unplanned trip to Baker City, there had been no time to mourn her father. As long as she kept busy, kept from thinking about his death, she could almost convince herself he was still alive and waiting for her at home.

"I'm sorry." Tully reached across the table and placed his warm hand over hers, giving it a gentle squeeze.

The comforting touch unsettled her, but she didn't pull her hand away. It had been too long since she'd enjoyed another human's touch offered for no reason but to make her feel better.

With a sigh, she raised a watery gaze to Tully. "My father died a few weeks ago." Her voice broke.

"I'm sorry, darlin'. That's a hard thing for anyone to handle. What about your mother?"

Brianna shook her head. "She died when I was a little girl. It's just been Father and me for the last twenty-one years." She took a handkerchief from inside her sleeve and dabbed at her eyes. "A large sum of money is required to keep his business enterprises afloat. I found the letters from Mr. Fisher in some of Father's papers and thought if I could convince the miner to buy back Father's shares, I could keep our cotton mill operating."

"You plan to run the business yourself?" Tully asked, not surprised that Brianna would attempt it.

"There is a plant manager, but yes, I would have taken over the business decisions. I often worked with Father, albeit from home."

"What are you going to do now?" Some primitive part of Tully wanted to protect and shelter Brianna. The fact he felt anything for the woman, beyond annoyance, left him ill at ease.

"I don't know. Mr. Fisher encouraged me to stay in town a few weeks and I'm in no hurry to return to Rhode Island."

Tully released her hand and sat back again. "I could make a few inquiries, find out…"

"No!" Brianna's eyes held fear and pleading when she looked at him. "Please don't, Sheriff. I'd prefer to just leave things as they are."

Convinced there was much more to the story than she shared, Tully decided to go along with her request, for now. "Whatever you say. It looks like the rain let up. May I walk you back to the hotel?" Fascinated, Tully watched as Brianna pulled on her gloves, smoothing down each finger of the creamy yellow covering.

The pale green walking suit she wore fit her perfectly and brought out rosy blossoms in her cheeks. A buttery yellow lace blouse provided a hint of contrast that highlighted the streaks of gold in her brown hair.

Hair that Tully hadn't been able to stop thinking about since he'd run his fingers through it earlier. It had been a colossal mistake to kiss her, but danged if he didn't want to do it again and again.

Mindful of the disastrous road his thoughts tried to travel, he tugged them back under control. He took Brianna's elbow in his hand, guiding her outside.

"How could it be so sweltering this afternoon and so nippy this evening?" she asked, concerned her teeth might start to chatter in the cool evening air.

For once, she was grateful for the presence of the sheriff at her side. The warmth of his big body permeated the air around her and blocked most of the chilly breeze. With effort, she forced herself to ignore how handsome he looked in the stormy evening light. She wondered what it would be like to be held in those strong arms against his solid chest.

When he'd buried his hands in her hair that afternoon, she'd never known such knee-weakening sensations existed. The feel of his hands sliding down her arms and resting on her waist made her so languid she could have slid off the horse to the ground in a boneless heap.

Then she'd come to her senses.

No matter how charming and good-looking the sheriff might be, he'd been little more than a thorn in her side since she arrived in town. Although he'd been moderately well behaved throughout their shared meal, she knew it wouldn't last.

Tully proved her right when she stopped outside the hotel.

"Thank you for dinner and seeing me back safely." Brianna backed toward the door, baffled by the odd light shining in Tully's hazel eyes that appeared almost golden in color.

"Anytime, Fred. Have a pleasant evening." He turned and sauntered off in the direction of the jail. Before he'd taken more than half a dozen steps, he looked back at her. "As soon as I find that bag of corsets you lost, I hope you'll plan on modeling them for me."

The wink he sent her confirmed he was nothing more than a roguish reprobate.

Mortified, heat seared Brianna's cheeks as she looked around, hoping no one heard Tully's comment. An older couple peered at her in shock while a young cowboy surveyed her with interest.

Brianna turned and rushed inside the hotel, plotting revenge on the sheriff.

Chapter Seven

"Miss Dumont, we're so pleased you could join us this morning." The pastor and his wife greeted Brianna with genuine warmth as she made her way out the door of the church after the Sunday morning service.

"It was a lovely service, Pastor Eagan. I thought your…"

"The sinner has come to repent, is that it?" Tully's baritone interrupted her words and train of thought as he spoke behind her.

The pastor and his wife smiled at the sheriff as he grinned at Brianna.

Incensed, she ignored him and walked down the church steps. He followed close behind her. "I was surprised to see you here this morning."

She continued to pretend she couldn't hear him. Thane waved and motioned her over to their buckboard. "Miss Dumont, will you still be able to join us for lunch today?"

"I'd love to," Brianna said, smiling at a beautiful auburn-haired woman standing at his side. "This must be your lovely wife I've heard so much about."

"Please, call me Jemma, Miss Dumont." The woman held out a gloved hand that Brianna took in hers. "I absolutely love your gown. Is it a Worth?"

Brianna glanced down at the raspberry pink fabric, highlighted with accents of black lace. "Yes, it is, but your gown is splendid. That's not a Madame Beauchene, is it? They're impossible to acquire."

Jemma rubbed a hand along the front of her coral-toned skirt. "It is. If you ever want to order one from her, I can send a letter of recommendation. However, we have an incredibly talented dressmaker right here in town. Maggie's designs could rival any house of fashion."

"Speaking of Maggie, she and Ian will be back this afternoon," Thane said, looking at Tully. "Will you still be able to meet them at the train?"

Tully nodded. "I planned on it, although Ian's dad said he'd take the wagon and meet them. Most likely, Mags will have filled at least one new trunk with purchases on their trip."

"You two leave Maggie alone," Jemma chided. "A woman should not be limited on the number of trunks she needs when she travels."

Thane chuckled. "So declares the woman who packed thirty-two trunks to bring to America."

"Thirty-two? I only hauled fourteen out to the ranch," Tully said, surprised.

"That's because Mr. Jordan ordered half of them to stay at the cottage." Jemma grinned, recalling how she'd tricked Thane by only packing fourteen trunks but allowing him to think she wanted to take all thirty-two. She turned to Brianna.

"Forgive us for going on and on. Shall we venture to the hotel?"

"Certainly." Brianna looked around. "Where are your youngsters today? I haven't had the pleasure of meeting your son, but I did make the acquaintance of Miss Lily."

Jemma smiled and looped her arm around Brianna's as they strolled toward the hotel. Thane and Tully fell into step behind them. "Jack and Lily took Mr. and Mrs. Greenfield to the hotel to save us a table."

Brianna vaguely remembered Thane introducing a British couple to Tully the day she'd first arrived in town. She thought their name was Greenfield.

"Are they settled in at your place?" Tully asked as they waited to cross the street.

"They are, for the most part. We've tried to talk them into coming to work for us, but they are adamant they're just here for a visit." Thane glanced at his wife and then at Tully. "I wish we could convince them to stay. Lily will be heartbroken if they leave."

"She won't be the only one," Jemma said, looking back at Thane. "I can't bear the thought of them leaving, even if they have agreed to stay for the summer."

"Well, that gives you a few months to figure out a way to keep them here." Tully waved to a deputy as he walked on the opposite side of the street. "What do they plan to do when they return to England?"

"That's just it... they haven't any plans," Jemma said with a sigh. "Perhaps some miracle will occur between now and the end of August and they'll change their minds."

"If I hear of anything, I'll be sure to let you know," Brianna said. Her work at the newspaper should provide access to information that might be helpful.

Tully snorted. "And what information will you be privy to, Fred?"

Jemma glared at him while Brianna feigned indifference to his comment. Thane jabbed him in the side with his elbow as they walked up the hotel steps, shooting a look of warning his direction.

As they entered the hotel's dining room, Lily ran to them with her wild curls bouncing every direction. "Mama! We saved you a seat. Oh, hello, Miss Dumont. Will you sit by me?"

"I'd love to Lily. Thank you for asking." Brianna took the child's hand, following her to a table where an older couple sat with a handsome boy who greatly resembled Thane, except for his copper-colored eyes and straight brown hair.

"Miss Dumont, it is our pleasure to introduce you to Edwin and Hattie Greenfield." Jemma smiled at the couple.

Once they exchanged words of greeting, Jemma placed her hands on the boy's shoulders. "And this is our son, Jack. Lovey, this is Miss Dumont."

Jack bowed then held out a chair for her as she took a seat.

Impressed with his manners, Brianna beamed at him. "What a fine gentleman you are, Jack."

"Thank you. Mama tries hard, although Dad and the fellas at the ranch don't think it's that important." A western twang intertwined with Jack's British accent, causing Brianna to hide a grin.

Lily climbed onto the chair next to Brianna. As she watched the little girl wiggle and squirm on the seat, the familiar scent of the sheriff enveloped her. She glared at him as he settled onto the seat on her other side.

With a disdainful sniff, she shifted slightly so her back was nearly to him and focused all her attention on Lily.

The child chattered about an enchanted bird that belonged to a fairy princess living in the juniper tree behind the barn.

Jack leaned forward from his seat across the table and tipped his head toward his sister. "She likes to make up stories."

Tully chuckled. "So does Miss Dumont. Lily and Fred ought to get along like two peas in a pod."

Jack's eyes widened and he gaped at Brianna. "Is your name really Fred?"

Brianna narrowed her gaze and scowled at Tully. "It most certainly is not. My name is Brianna. For reasons beyond my ability to comprehend, Sheriff Barrett has decided to call me Fred."

"Fred, Fred, with a pretty hat on her head," Lily chanted in a singsong voice, grinning at Brianna. "Beautiful lady, that's Miss Fred."

"On that note, let's order our lunch," Thane said, motioning the waiter over to their table.

Despite Brianna's trepidation about sitting next to Tully, he kept up an interesting and engaging conversation. He managed not to tease her once during the meal.

Brianna learned Mr. and Mrs. Greenfield had served Jemma's family as butler and cook for more than thirty years. No wonder the woman was so determined to keep them close. They seemed more like a beloved set of grandparents than former hired help.

For a moment, Brianna considered the servants her father had employed over the years. Most had been loyal to the family. She would greatly miss their cook and head housekeeper. The two women had done their best to mother her and she'd turned to them with girlish tears more times than she could count.

Lost in her maudlin thoughts, a touch on her arm made her glance down as Lily leaned against her. "Do you like to sing, Miss Dumont?"

"I'm afraid singing is not among my particular talents." Brianna smoothed a hand over Lily's curls, amused by the impish child. "However, I would warrant a guess that you like to sing."

"Oh, I do! I love to sing and dance." Lily started to jump out of her chair to demonstrate, but Thane grabbed her and swung her onto his lap. Distracted by the tickles he delivered to her sides, she leaned against her father and sighed contentedly.

Brianna admired the way the tough cowboy appeared to melt around his wife and children. His face visibly softened as he looked at them with undeniable, unconditional love. Brianna wondered if she'd ever experience similar devotion from anyone in her lifetime.

Involuntarily, her gaze drifted to Tully as he sat beside her, finishing the last few bites of a piece of berry pie. Why the infuriating lawman would come to mind when she was contemplating true love, she had no idea. The very notion of him being anything beyond a tease who took great pleasure in her discomfiture left her agitated.

"I reckon we better head back to the ranch. That rain we had sure settled the dust, but it looks like another storm is brewing and I don't want to get caught in it." Thane shifted Lily in his arms and pulled cash out of his pocket to pay for their meals.

Lily stretched a hand out to Brianna. "Will you come to my birthday party? Please? We'll have cake and ice cream and all sorts of wonderful things to eat. Mrs. Greenfield promised to make marmalade and crumpets."

Brianna smiled. "Oh, that sounds lovely, Miss Lily, but perhaps…"

"You can ride out with me." Tully wondered when his mouth had completely detached from his brain, because the last thing he wanted to do was spend time around Miss Dumont. If she went with him, that meant he'd have to take a buggy and the trip would last twice as long. He'd be stuck with her for two hours of travel time, not to mention the hour or two they'd spend at the party.

Thoughts of her jostling beside him on a buggy seat, with her floral perfume assaulting his senses and her enticing appearance tempting him, made the collar of his shirt uncomfortably tight.

All eyes looked to him as he swallowed hard. "I could drive you out since I'm going anyway. Ian and Maggie would welcome you if you wanted to ride out with them."

"They'll be bringing his parents, so I'm sure there won't be room in Ian's buggy," Jemma said, smiling at the sheriff. "It's so kind of you to offer to bring Miss Dumont, Tully. We'll plan to see you both at the party."

Brianna glanced at Tully, wondering how she'd endure his presence for the duration of the trip to the Jordan Ranch. For the sake of her new friends, she would make a concentrated effort to remain civil to the sheriff.

Chapter Eight

Monday morning, Brianna rose early and dressed in a summer-weight walking suit. After eating breakfast at the hotel's dining room, she hurried to the newspaper office.

Bowen Packwood happened to see her walk inside and motioned for her to follow him to his office.

"It's nice to see you're punctual, Miss Dumont," he remarked as they walked down the short hallway.

"Yes, sir." Brianna took a seat in front of his desk as he settled into his chair amidst creaks and groans from both him and the piece of furniture. She ducked her head to hide her smile and opened a new notebook, taking a pencil from her reticule.

"Have you come up with any story ideas?" Bowen leaned forward until his arms rested on the desk in front of him.

"What do you think about an article detailing the hazards of mining?"

Bowen shook his head. "That's been done and done again. Unless someone is stealing gold, trying to stake a claim that isn't theirs or something along those lines, I'm not interested. What else have you considered?"

"Perhaps an article about the soap factory, it could have a humorous spin about cleaning up the county with their manufacturing facility."

The editor stared at her for a full minute before slowly nodding his head. "You may write that article, but I don't promise to publish it. Don't put it at the top of your list, but plan to get to it in the next week or two."

"I could write an article about the meteorological station, something about the changes they've seen in the weather since the office opened here in town." Brianna found it fascinating a report on the weather conditions was sent to the chief office twice a day, every single day, at five in the morning and again at five in the evening.

"That wouldn't be a bad story to have on hand to run on a slow news day. Add it to your list, but put it right below the soap factory." Bowen narrowed his gaze. "I want some hard-hitting news from you Miss Dumont. Something that will sell papers. Something that will get people talking."

Brianna held back a sigh. She hadn't been in town long enough to know what issues concerned the citizenry and Mr. Packwood hadn't been terribly helpful in providing her with any direction. "I did hear some gentlemen discussing a horse rustler after church yesterday. Apparently, he's stolen more than a dozen horses so far."

The loud smack of Bowen's palm hitting his desk made Brianna jump and drop the pencil she held in her hand. She retrieved it then stared at her employer with wide eyes.

He waggled a finger her direction. "Now that's the kind of news I'm talking about. Find out who lost horses, where the robberies are taking place, what the sheriff is doing to track down the thief, that sort of thing." Pleased, Bowen leaned back in his chair. "While you're at it, add a story to your list about the Chinese. There's always something newsworthy going on with them."

"The Chinese, sir?" Brianna asked. She'd noticed a few Chinese men with long queues and strange hats walking around town. The hotel had assured her Wang Ping's laundry was the best in town for cleaning her clothes. However, that was the extent of her knowledge of the local Chinese community.

"Chinatown is located just west of the Powder River, down on Auburn Avenue. There are a handful of Chinese stores, a gambling house, and a joss house. It seems like someone's always down there stirring up trouble. Just be careful if you venture that direction. It's mostly men." Bowen gave her a long look. "On second thought, you best stay away from Chinatown, but see what you can turn up on that horse rustler. As soon as you have a story together, come back and see me."

"Do you have any other work you'd like me to see to, sir?" Brianna asked as she stood and tucked the pencil back in her reticule.

"Nope. I want you out there," Bowen jabbed his thumb toward the window behind him, "drumming up facts. Stay out of trouble, Miss

Dumont. If you're in jail it will be hard for you to track down any real news."

Brianna nodded her head then took her leave. A visit to the sheriff's office was essential to gain any information for the story about the horse rustler.

Anxious to put off seeing Tully Barrett as long as possible, she made her way to Maggie Dalton MacGregor's dress shop. She wasn't sure if Mrs. MacGregor would be there, since she and her husband had just returned from their honeymoon trip the previous afternoon, but an open sign assured her the woman was in the store.

A bell jangled above the door when she opened it and stepped inside.

"Good morning!" a cheery voice called from the back. "I'll be right there."

Brianna watched as a dark-haired beauty rushed out from the back room and offered her a welcoming smile. "Welcome to my store. How may I assist you today?"

"Are you Mrs. MacGregor?" Brianna asked, admiring the woman's exceptionally crafted gown, done in a shade that made her think of sun-ripened peaches.

"That's me."

Brianna smiled. "My name is Brianna Dumont. Yesterday, I dined with Mr. and Mrs. Thane Jordan following the church service. Mrs. Jordan said your work could rival any dressmaker and she is absolutely correct in that assessment."

"It's a pleasure to meet you, Miss Dumont. Jemma's not the least biased, either." Maggie winked then waved a hand around her store. "I'm usually closed on Mondays, but since we've been gone for a week, I wanted to come in and take care of a few details this morning. How may I help you?"

"First, I heard you have an apartment above your store you might be interested in renting. I'm searching for a place to stay for a month. I've been at the hotel this past week, but I'm seeking a more affordable option. Although I checked at the boarding house, it appears the property is up for sale and in quite a stage of transition. The sheriff and Mr. Jordan happened to mention your apartment."

Maggie looped her arm around Brianna's, escorting her through the store to the workroom. Brianna took in the neatly stacked bolts of fabrics as well as tidy baskets of trims. A large worktable and two sewing machines took up a good portion of the space. A staircase led to the second floor near a back door.

"Come on and I'll show it to you." Maggie led the way up the stairs and opened a door at the top. "There are two bedrooms, the sitting room and a kitchen. I'm planning to leave most of the furniture, but I do have a few things I still need to pack and take to Ian's..." Maggie blushed. "I mean to our home."

Brianna smiled and squeezed Maggie's hand. "Congratulations on your recent nuptials. I've heard nothing but good things about you and your husband. I had the pleasure of meeting Mr. MacGregor's parents at church services yesterday. They are quite an unusual, but lovely couple."

Maggie gave her a conspiratorial look. "I met them myself a few days before the wedding. Ian certainly takes after his father, although I dearly love his mother."

Satisfied the apartment would meet her immediate needs, Brianna turned to Maggie. "How much do you think you'd like to receive in rent?"

In the past, Maggie would have rattled off a number, but she wanted to discuss it with Ian before she made any decisions.

"To be quite honest, I hadn't thought about renting it. If you wouldn't mind giving me time to consult with my husband on the price, I can get back to you later today." Maggie studied her a moment then grinned. "Better yet, why don't you join us for lunch and we can discuss the matter then?"

"Oh, I wouldn't want to impose, especially since you and Mr. MacGregor are just returned from your honeymoon trip." Brianna was convinced she'd feel awkward and out of place with the newly married couple.

"Nonsense. You may as well join us. Ian's mother will have something ready to eat." Maggie offered her an encouraging look. "I insist. It will give us the opportunity to get to know you a little better."

Brianna nodded. "Very well. I accept your kind offer."

Maggie showed her all the rooms then led her back downstairs. "Is there anything, other than the apartment, you wanted to discuss?"

"Actually, I'd like to purchase a riding skirt from you. The other day I rode a horse with a sidesaddle and it has been made abundantly clear I should refrain from doing so in the future."

Maggie laughed. "With the men in this town, I'm sure you probably heard more than you cared to. Strong opinions and a tendency to share them are hallmarks of several men around here."

"That would certainly be true for your sheriff." Brianna stared at a beautiful ice-blue gown Maggie had on display. Ecru lace dripped off the cuffs and hem while soutache trim highlighted the front of the jacket and skirt. The simplicity of the gown's design gave it an elegant appearance.

Aware of her interest, Maggie pointed to the gown. "Would you like to try it on? It would be perfect with your coloring, especially your eyes."

"Although it's beautiful, Mrs. MacGregor, I must keep my focus on riding skirts. What would you recommend?"

"That you call me Maggie," the woman said with a sassy grin.

An hour later, Brianna had purchased a riding skirt, two simple cotton blouses, and a brocade vest.

"I'm so glad I had some things in stock that fit you," Maggie said as she totaled the purchases.

While Brianna took money out of her reticule, Maggie wrapped the clothes in a piece of plain brown paper and tied the package with a length of blue ribbon.

"You're welcome to wait here until noon and then I can show you where we live," Maggie said as

Brianna picked up the package and moved toward the door.

"I have a few errands to run." Brianna glanced down at the watch pinned to the front of her jacket. "I shall return a few minutes before the noon hour."

"I'll see you then, Miss Dumont. Thank you for your purchases this morning."

Brianna smiled at Maggie as she opened the door. "Please call me Brianna. I have a feeling we'll be friends and I can use as many as I can find these days."

"Enjoy your morning, Brianna." Maggie waved as she hurried down the street in the direction of the hotel.

Brianna deposited her new clothes in her room then ran by the mercantile to select a small gift for Ian and Maggie and asked Mr. Miller to have it delivered to their home that afternoon.

With a fortifying breath, she walked to the sheriff's office and opened the door. It was the first time she'd entered without being angry or in handcuffs.

She stepped inside and smiled at Deputy Harter as he sat at his desk with a stack of paperwork. The sheriff was noticeably absent.

The deputy stood and tipped his head toward her. "Miss Dumont. It's a beautiful day, isn't it?"

"Yes, it is, Deputy. I had a few questions for the sheriff. Is he available this morning?" Brianna offered the young man a bright smile.

His chest puffed out slightly and his mouth kicked up at the corners. "He had some business to take care of, but he hoped to be back this afternoon. May I give him a message?"

"No, thank you. I'll speak with him another time." Brianna moved toward the door as the deputy followed her. "Enjoy your day, Deputy."

"Yes, ma'am."

As she stepped outside and hurried down the street, she felt him watching her and wondered if all the men in town could use a lesson in good manners.

She strolled over to the soap factory and made an appointment to speak with the manager the following week, then rushed back to Maggie's place.

Eager to see the MacGregor home, she opened the door to the dress shop and stepped inside. Maggie leaned against a tall, blond-haired man as he stood with his arms wrapped around her, kissing her thoroughly and passionately.

At the sound of the bell jangling, the two of them broke apart, turning her direction. Maggie's face was red with embarrassment but her husband wore a mischievous grin as he looked at Brianna.

"Miss Dumont, is it? Ian MacGregor at your service." He bowed to her with a flourish of his hand before he straightened and wrapped his arm around Maggie. "My bonny lass said ye plan to join us for lunch. It'll be a pleasure to have ye eat with us."

"It's a pleasure to meet you, Mr. MacGregor. Your wife was most helpful this morning. Baker City is quite fortunate to have such a talented dressmaker." Brianna smiled at the man so clearly besotted with his bride.

"Indeed, we are. Maggie mentioned yer interest in rentin' the apartment." Ian glanced at the ceiling then back at her. "Do ye have any references?"

Maggie scowled at Ian but held her tongue.

Brianna's smile faded and she refrained from sighing. "I've only been in town a little more than a week. My father owned forty percent of a mine in the area. Perhaps you know Clive Fisher?"

Ian held back a snort while a lively light danced in his blue eyes. "Ach, lassie, ol' Clive isn't exactly a glowin' reference. Why are you here in town?"

"I came to check on my father's holdings at the mine." At his look, she shrugged. "I had no idea it wasn't a large mining operation. I discovered the truth the other day when I rode out there. At any rate, I've taken a job working at the newspaper and decided to stay, at least for another month. Although the hotel is wonderful, I need to find accommodations aligned to my current financial situation."

"So ye've gainful employment and aren't up to nefarious deeds, is that right?" Ian's teasing grin made both women smile.

"That's correct, Mr. MacGregor."

"Verra well, then. If my Maggie wants to rent ye the space, I have no objections." Ian nudged Maggie forward and pointed to the door. "Let's go see what Mother has rustled up for lunch. We can discuss the details on our way there."

Taken aback that Ian turned over the decision about renting the apartment to Maggie, Brianna decided perhaps most men in Baker City weren't pompous, overbearing dolts like the sheriff.

Maggie named a price for the rent Brianna thought was more than fair. They agreed Brianna would give Maggie a few days to clean out what she wanted and plan to move in on Thursday.

After arriving at the house and greeting Ian's parents, Brianna followed Maggie to a table outside beneath the shade of the trees. A gentle breeze blew up from the creek, carrying both cooler air and the sound of the gurgling water.

"What a lovely setting," Brianna said, impressed with the MacGregor's home and the lavish landscaping. "It's so peaceful here."

"At least it used to be, until you found your way to Ian and Maggie's table."

Brianna's shoulders tensed at the baritone sound of the sheriff's voice as he strode across the yard to join them.

"Tully! What a thing to say," Maggie scolded as she hugged him then motioned for him to take the seat next to Brianna.

"Oh, Fred's used to it," Tully said, winking at Brianna then removing his hat and hanging it on the back of his chair.

"Fred?" Ian asked, looking from Tully to their guest.

"Miss Dumont refused to tell me her name the first two times I arrested her, so I decided to call her Fred."

"Arrested?" Maggie's eyebrows shot upward and her voice rose in volume. "Why did you arrest her?"

"Twice?" Ian stared at Tully.

The sheriff leaned back in his chair and ran a hand through his hair, fluffing the ring his hat left behind. For an insane moment, Brianna wished she could have followed the trail his fingers made. His short brown hair, thick and wavy, had drawn her interest from the first moment she saw him without his hat. The black Stetson he wore hid most of it from her view, but it didn't keep her from admiring it when she could.

"Why did you arrest Miss Dumont?" Maggie asked, glaring at her friend.

"Assaulting an officer of the law, public nuisance, harassment, and…" Tully glanced at Brianna with a teasing grin. "What was the last one, Fred?"

She huffed and draped the napkin across her lap before lifting her gaze to the sheriff's. "Disorderly conduct."

Ian's mother appeared stunned into silence while both Ian and Maggie stared at Tully, baffled.

Tully took a long drink from a glass of cold lemonade, ignoring their questioning looks.

Finally, Maggie spoke. "What, exactly, did she do, Tully?" The graceful, elegant woman was the epitome of refinement. Maggie couldn't imagine her doing anything that might result in one arrest, let alone two.

"She slapped me across the face, yelled at me in the middle of the street, and refused to go peacefully to the jail." Tully smirked at Brianna. "I should add resisting arrest to your charges."

Brianna ignored his comment and looked at Maggie when the woman reached out and clasped her hand. "What did he say to you, Brianna?"

Pink blossomed in her cheeks and Brianna shook her head, refusing to repeat what Tully had said in front of Ian and his parents. When Maggie gave her an imploring look, Brianna leaned over and whispered in her ear.

Maggie rocked back in her chair, anger sparking in her deep brown eyes. She glowered at Tully. "Tully William Barrett! I ought to slap you silly for saying such a thing. How could you?"

"Now, Mags, don't go gettin' all in a fit. Fred's forgiven me." Tully smiled at Brianna. "Haven't you?"

Brianna held his gaze. "At least until the next time you feel inspired to insult or offend me."

Mindful of the tension crackling around the table, Ian's mother smiled and nodded to her son. "Ian, ask the blessing so we may eat our meal while the food remains palatable."

"Yes, Mother."

After lunch, Maggie gave Brianna a tour of the large stone home while Tully caught Ian up on the news around town.

As they stepped outside and meandered down the front walk, inhaling the sweet scent from the profusion of flowers growing in pots and flowerbeds, Brianna smiled at Maggie. "Thank you for inviting me to lunch and for allowing me to rent your apartment. I assure you, I'm not nearly the degenerate Sheriff Barrett makes me out to be."

Maggie laughed and wrapped an arm around Brianna's shoulders. "I never thought you were. Don't take anything Tully says to heart. He's an overgrown child who loves to tease, but he's been a wonderful friend to me. Just give him time to get to know you. He'll come around."

"I've surmised as much," Brianna said as they meandered out the gate bearing Ian's brand. Ian and Tully walked around the corner of the house and waved at them. "The sheriff hasn't been completely awful, although he works quite diligently at it."

The two women giggled as the men approached, ignoring their questioning glances.

"Might I escort you back to town, Fred?" Tully held out his arm to Brianna.

Hesitant, she finally nodded her head and placed her hand on his forearm. "Thank you, Mr. MacGregor, for your hospitality."

"Ach, lassie. Please call me Ian." He smiled at her as he settled his arm around Maggie's waist and pulled her close to his side. "It was a pleasure to have ye join us."

"Thank you, Ian, and Maggie, for the lovely meal and the opportunity to visit your beautiful home. If you need more time to move your things, just let me know. I'm not in a rush." Brianna politely inclined her head toward the couple.

"Thanks for lunch, you two. I'll talk to you later." Tully tipped his hat at Maggie then began the walk into town. Ian and Maggie's home was located across a lush meadow behind Ian's lumberyard on the edge of Baker City.

"They have an incredible home," Brianna commented as they walked past the lumberyard office. Tully lifted a hand in greeting to several of the men working there but didn't stop to speak to any of them.

"It is a beautiful home. I'm very pleased for them. They deserve to be happy, especially Maggie." Tully appeared to survey everything around them as they strolled down the street. He cast Brianna an inquisitive look. "What did you mean when you said you weren't in a rush and could give Maggie time to move her things?"

"Maggie was kind enough to allow me the opportunity to rent her apartment. The hotel is wonderful, but I look forward to staying somewhere more affordable."

Tully appeared puzzled. "Why don't you stay at the boarding house? It's clean and safe, and the price is reasonable."

"The owners are trying to sell it. The situation there appeared to be in a very discordant state when I stopped by this morning to inquire about a room."

"Is that so? I suppose I should go see what's going on over there." Tully turned his head toward the boarding house as they stood at an intersection, waiting for a wagon to pass.

Brianna worked up her courage and smiled at the man who intimidated and fascinated her. "If you've no objection, Sheriff, I would like to ask you a few questions about the horse rustler I heard you discussing with Mr. Jordan yesterday."

"Why in the heck are you interested in a horse rustler, Fred? That's no information a lady needs to know." Tully glared at her then slipped into a cocky grin. "Unless you're in cahoots with him. I bet that's it. You're supposed to be the pretty distraction that turns all attention away from him while he makes off with our horses."

With the option of taking his words as a compliment or insult, she weighed the possibilities before responding. "I'm not in cahoots, as you put it, but I am working on an article for the newspaper. Mr. Packwood asked me to unearth all the details I could in regard to the subject. The most knowledgeable person about the matter is you."

"Bowen told you to talk to me?" Surprised, he stopped in the middle of the boardwalk. "You're working for Bowen? When did that happen?"

"I officially began work this morning. My first assignment is writing an article about the horse rustler. Now, will you allow me to glean what information I can from you or shall I search for an alternative source?" Brianna smiled sweetly, wondering how Tully could be so maddening yet undeniably attractive at the same time. The twinkle in his hazel eyes and the dimples in his cheeks made her wonder what he'd looked like as a boy. She pictured him being every bit as ornery and full of life as he was now.

Tully took her elbow in his hand and guided her to the nearby park. After settling on a bench, he leaned back and crossed one booted ankle over the opposite knee.

"Ask away, Fred, and I'll tell you what I know."

Grateful she'd tucked a small notebook and pencil into her reticule, Brianna pulled them out. "When did the first robbery take place?"

Tully spent the next twenty minutes answering her questions. Taken aback by her intelligence and thoroughness, he treated her as he would any reporter from the paper — with respectful professionalism.

"Now that I answered all your questions, how about you answer a few of mine?" Tully leaned forward with both elbows resting on his knees.

"What could you possibly want to ask me?" Brianna appeared dubious as she tucked the notebook back into her reticule.

"You haven't told me the whole story of why you're here or what your intentions are. There's still a secret you're hesitant to share."

Caught off guard by his astute observation, her mind scrambled to conjure a flippant reply. To her relief, Deputy Durfey ran up to them, rescuing her from answering.

"Son of a gun, Tully! I ran all over town trying to find you. A few miners came into town and started a fight over at the assayer's office. Right now, they're bustin' up Howard's saloon."

"Let's go." Tully jumped to his feet and took a few running paces before he stopped and turned around. "Can you get yourself back to the hotel, Fred?"

"Of course, but I'd like to accompany you." Brianna hurried toward him, despite the horrified look on both men's faces. "It sounds like a story for the newspaper."

"Absolutely not. And don't get it in your head to follow me, either. I'll toss you back in jail if I have to." Tully took a step toward her with a menacing scowl.

Brianna backed away and shook her head. "I'll stay, but you have to promise to tell me what happened."

"Fine. Later." Tully ran off with Dugan beside him.

Annoyed the man threatened another trip to the jail to keep her from tagging along, she returned to the park bench and sat down, watching the other occupants of the park. From the corner of her eye, she noticed a puckish little face peering at her from behind a tree.

Brianna smiled and waved a hand in the child's direction. "I'd be happy to have you sit with me, Sammy."

The child ducked back around the tree, hiding from view. Brianna pretended not to notice and continued sitting on the bench with an open expression on her face.

Only a few minutes passed until Sammy edged around the tree and scampered her way. The child plopped down on the opposite end of the bench from Brianna.

"It's certainly a lovely day, isn't it, Sammy?"

The child nodded, keeping his gaze focused on his dusty, bare feet. Brianna had noticed many children running around without shoes or stockings, enjoying the feel of cool grass between their toes. For a moment, she wished she could be as carefree as the youngsters and shed her shoes and stockings.

"Are you engaged in any activities this afternoon?" Brianna slid a little closer to the charming imp.

Sammy shrugged, staring at Brianna. The little one pointed at her then in the direction of the sheriff's office.

"Why was I talking to the sheriff? Is that what you want to know?" Brianna asked.

Sammy nodded his head.

"I was merely trying to gather information for a story for the newspaper. Mr. Packwood hired me to write a few articles for him." Brianna rose to her feet and held out her hand to the boy. "It's much too hot out this afternoon. What do you say we go get an ice cream or a soda?"

The child smiled and took Brianna's hand, pulling her toward the drugstore located a few blocks from the park.

The boy looked at her with adoration as they entered the store and Brianna held back a sigh. If only it were as easy to win over Tully Barrett with a dish of ice cream.

Chapter Nine

"How's the story on that horse rustler coming, Miss Dumont?" Bowen Packwood asked when Brianna tapped on his office door.

"The sheriff is following a few leads, but still hasn't made any arrests." Brianna sat in the chair Bowen indicated and pulled out an article she'd written the previous evening. "In the meantime, I did discover there is talk of organizing a Women's Christian Temperance Union here in town."

Bowen groaned and settled back in his chair. "Heaven help us all if that's the case."

Brianna shot him a cool glare but slid the article she'd written across the desk.

The editor lifted the papers and read the story. He picked up a pen and made a few notations then looked over at her. "Despite the fact I'm not thrilled with the topic, you stuck to the facts and wrote an informative piece." He pushed the article back toward her. "Read those changes I made and you'll see how it makes the story stronger."

Quickly, Brianna scanned through his notations and nodded in agreement. "Thank you, sir. Does this mean you'll publish the story?"

"It does, but stay on that horse rustler story and anything else of interest you might find."

Brianna grinned and took a folded sheet of paper from the bag she'd carried with her. "Do you know the sheriff well, Mr. Packwood?"

He raised an eyebrow and gave her a curious look. "I do."

"Then you are aware of his tendency to tease and joke with others?"

"I certainly am." Intrigued, Bowen leaned forward. "What do you have in mind?"

"I wrote an article about the sheriff. If you find it to your liking, what do you think of printing a special copy of the newspaper just for Sheriff Barrett?"

Bowen snatched the story from her hand. First, a chuckle burst out of him, followed by a snort then a deep belly laugh rang through the room. "It would be my pleasure to print this just for Tully. I'll make sure one of my boys delivers it to his office the moment the ink dries."

"Of course, you'll leave my name off the article, won't you?"

"Of course." Bowen grinned and stood, holding out his hand to Brianna.

Pleased he'd accepted her first two articles, she shook it then rushed out of the office. Inspired, she headed off to see what other news she could unearth in town.

On her way back to the hotel that afternoon, she stopped when Maggie MacGregor darted out of her shop and called to her.

Brianna crossed the street and hurried toward the woman. "Hello, Maggie. It's lovely to see you."

"And you, Brianna. I wanted to let you know Ian and his folks helped me clean out the apartment yesterday, so anytime you'd like to move in, it's ready for you."

Brianna clasped her hands beneath her chin, excited at the prospect of moving into her own place. "If you've no objection, I'll take occupancy tomorrow morning."

"That would be just fine." Maggie motioned Brianna inside the shop. "I've got a key for you and I'll show you how everything works."

The following morning, Brianna smiled as a young man carried her trunk from the hotel to Maggie's shop. After breakfast, she'd given Mr. Isaac a generous tip for his help during her stay at the hotel. He offered to send one of the bellboys up to carry her trunk for her and she readily accepted. Although Maggie had volunteered Ian's assistance, Brianna didn't want to bother her friends.

With the young man following her, Brianna walked down an alley and along the back of Maggie's shop to the rear door. She unlocked it and held it open as the bellboy stepped inside then hefted the trunk up the stairs. At her direction, he set it in the larger of the two bedrooms. He accepted the tip she handed to him then disappeared down the stairs with a, "thank you, Miss Dumont," tossed over his shoulder.

Brianna wandered through the apartment, surprised Maggie had left so much furniture behind.

Then again, Ian's house was fully furnished and she couldn't imagine where they'd put Maggie's things.

In the kitchen, Brianna would have built a fire in the stove and made herself a cup of tea, but she didn't want to heat up the apartment. With limited culinary skills, she planned to eat very simply or take her meals at the restaurant down the street.

She pushed open the window to catch the morning breeze. The table beneath it would provide the perfect place to write articles.

Leisurely, she unpacked her trunk then carried a framed photo of her father and one of her parents on their wedding day into the sitting room and placed them on the mantel. Although Maggie had left a comfortable sofa and chair behind, the room seemed rather bare without paintings on the walls or other bric-a-brac to give it a homey feel.

If Brianna planned to stay longer than a month, she might add a few touches, but she didn't see the point in spending the money on unnecessary frippery. Before her father died, she wouldn't have thought twice about purchasing whatever she pleased the moment the whim struck, but she had limited funds and felt a determination to learn to live within her current means. The missing contents of her bag might have helped her situation, but until it was found, she had no other options.

The last time she'd asked Tully about her stolen bag, he warned her it might never turn up. He told her it was likely someone grabbed it and jumped on the departing train. Aggravated and dismayed by the loss, she needed to forget about it and move on.

"Brianna?" Maggie called up the stairs, pulling her from her thoughts.

Hastening to the top of the stairs, Brianna smiled at her friend. "Good morning! I hope you don't mind that I'm here early."

"Not at all." Maggie smiled as Brianna joined her at the bottom of the steps. "You're welcome to come and go as you please. I noticed the door to the apartment was open and wanted to make sure it was you up there. Do I need to send Ian to collect any of your things?"

Brianna shook her head and followed Maggie into her workroom. "I appreciate the offer, but one of the bellboys carried over my trunk. I'm settled in and so appreciate all the things you left in the apartment."

"With Ian's house fully furnished and decorated, there isn't anywhere for most of my furniture. I took over a few pieces that have sentimental meaning, but the rest of them can stay here." Maggie removed her hat and gloves then turned back to Brianna. "Have you had breakfast? We could run down to the bakery if you haven't."

"I ate at the hotel, but if you decide you need a break this morning, I'd be happy to go with you then."

Maggie nodded in agreement. "I like the way you think. Perhaps we could plan to go about ten. Will you do most of your writing for the newspaper here or there?"

"Here," Brianna said, fingering a bolt of airy fabric that looked like spun sugar. She wished she could figure out a way to have the rest of her things shipped from home. She'd dearly missed her expansive wardrobe, but she wouldn't dare contact anyone for fear of the wrong people finding out her location. "Mr. Packwood has been generous in allowing me to work wherever I choose, as long as I write a few stories for him each week. I've turned in two and am almost finished with a third."

"That's wonderful, Brianna. I look forward to reading your articles." Maggie set a bolt of dark blue twill on her worktable and unwound several yards. From a drawer, she took out pattern pieces and began placing them on the cloth. "When does the first one come out?"

"Today. I asked Mr. Packwood not to use my full name, so they are written by B. E. Dumont."

Maggie smiled and picked up a pincushion, pinning the pattern pieces where she'd positioned them. "I'll look in the paper when we go home this evening. What does the E. in your name stand for?"

"Evangeline. It was my grandmother's name," Brianna turned toward the stairs. "Enjoy your morning, Maggie. I'll pop down around ten and we can make that trip to the bakery."

"Thanks, Brianna. If you find you need anything for the apartment, please let me know."

"I will, and thank you for renting it to me, despite the fact I've been arrested twice since I arrived in Baker City."

Maggie laughed. "I wouldn't worry about that."

Brianna returned upstairs and settled herself at the kitchen table with a sheaf of papers, an inkwell and pen. Instead of writing, she looked out the window and watched Tully Barrett make his way down the street, tipping his hat to women and shaking hands with men.

The way he charmed everyone he met, he could have been a politician stumping for support.

Although she wanted to dislike him, it was difficult when he stopped and greeted a woman with a baby. The silly faces he made caused the little one to giggle and wave chubby arms in the air.

Except where she was concerned, he certainly seemed to be a friendly, easy-going man.

Tully whistled as he made his rounds around Baker City. He loved talking to friends and neighbors as he walked through town, ensuring all was peaceful. If someone had told him as a boy he'd grow up to be the sheriff of one of the largest cities in Oregon, he would have thought they were crazy.

He stopped and helped the Morrow family load the last of their trunks on a wagon headed for the depot. After only a few months in town, they'd decided to move to Portland.

Although he liked the couple and their younger children, the older daughter had been a thorn in Ian's side the entire time he'd courted Maggie. When his friend made it clear he had no interest in Eunice, she hadn't taken the news well. It didn't surprise him the family was leaving. Eunice had barely left the house since she humiliated herself at a dance the previous month and he had an idea nothing in town was quite like the couple expected.

Once he bid them well, he continued on his way. The chubby cheeks of a healthy baby drew Tully like a magnet. The baby smiled and cooed as he made a funny face and waggled his fingers at her. Politely tipping his hat to her mother, he ambled to his office, content and happy with life.

Other than the horse rustler he had yet to catch and the annoying presence of Brianna Dumont, Tully decided life couldn't get any sweeter.

Rather than examine why Miss Dumont bothered him so, he shoved thoughts of the exciting, exhilarating emotions she stirred in him to the back of his mind and opened the door to his office. He checked on their lone prisoner, a man who'd tried to forge a title for a piece of land east of town, then sent home the deputy who had kept watch during the night shift.

The heat of the day kept him from stoking the fire in the stove and making a fresh pot of coffee. Instead, he took off his hat and settled into his office chair, reviewing a pile of wanted posters that had arrived in the previous day's mail.

A name jumped out at him and he reread the poster. Dale Darcey had taken several hundred dollars from Thane back in November during a collapse at one of the Jordan mines. Thane had given Dale the cash and asked him to go into town for help and supplies, but the thief took the money and disappeared.

From the wanted poster in his hand, Dale Darcey had added a bank robbery in Wasco County, attempted murder, and assault to his transgressions.

Tully set aside the poster, planning to show it to Thane. His friend would want to see that his former employee had turned to a life of crime.

He glanced up from his desk when a freckle-nosed boy ran inside the office and handed Tully that day's newspaper. The boy grinned and touched the brim of his flat cap when Tully took a coin from his pocket and tossed it to him.

"Thanks for bringing my paper, Sammy. You stay out of trouble and have a good day."

The boy nodded and scampered out the door.

Tully leaned back in his chair, trying to recall anything he'd heard about the boy. He'd noticed him around town in late spring, but no one seemed to know anything about him. It was challenging to get information from the child due to his inability to speak.

Although he'd made it clear Sammy could come to him if he ever needed anything, the child seemed oddly self-sufficient. Tully wondered if Bowen Packwood knew anything about him, since Sammy sometimes delivered papers. He'd have to remember to ask the man.

With a snap of his wrist, Tully opened the paper and read the front page. At the bottom, a headline made him tightly clench his jaw. Quickly scanning the article, he stood so fast, his chair tipped on its side.

Enraged, he slapped his hat on his head and strode out the door. He nearly plowed over Dugan as he arrived to start his shift.

"What's wrong, boss?" Dugan asked, stepping to the side and making note of the fury on Tully's face. It took a lot to make the sheriff angry and Dugan wasn't sure he'd ever seen the man so outraged.

"I'm gonna throttle a meddlin', busybody woman, that's what's wrong," Tully shouted, waving the newspaper at Dugan before marching down the street in the direction of Maggie's shop.

He strode around to the back and opened the door with such force it swung inward and bounced off the wall.

From her spot at a sewing machine where she worked on a basting stitch, Maggie yelped in surprise.

Not saying a word, Tully charged up the stairs of the apartment, taking them three at a time, and knocked the door at the top open.

"Miss Dumont!" he bellowed as he stalked inside.

A clatter from the kitchen accompanied by a startled shriek drew him into the room. Brianna frantically mopped a puddle of ink before it soaked into a sheaf of papers.

The glare she sent him held enough venom he should have dropped to the floor in the throes of death, but it didn't faze him.

"What in the…" Tully snapped his mouth shut in an attempt to gather his thoughts and composure. He took a deep breath and tossed the newspaper on the table. His index finger pointedly tapped on the article that sent him into such a fit. "What gave you the right to write such nonsense? I ought to haul you to jail for slander."

The smug look she gave him as she gracefully rose to her feet did nothing to cool his temper. "It isn't slander if it's…"

"True." Tully stepped forward, moving so close Brianna could see gold and green flecks dancing in the fiery fury of his eyes. "You and I both know that article isn't true. Why would you do something like that? Write something that could destroy my credibility in town?"

"Brianna?" Maggie's voice carried into the kitchen. "Is everything okay up there?"

Mindful that the article would upset the sheriff, Brianna never guessed he'd hunt her down, looking for all the world like he might strangle her with his bare hands.

Anxious to escape his anger, she tried to step around Tully, but he blocked her in at the table. When Maggie walked into the kitchen, Tully thrust the newspaper at her. "Read what she wrote about me."

Maggie took the newspaper. Her eyes widened as she read the headline aloud.

Baker City's Sheriff Manhandles Women
Makes Unjust Arrests and Harasses Citizenry

"Oh, my," Maggie whispered, glancing from Brianna to Tully before returning her attention to the article.

Sheriff Tully Barrett may seem like a friendly, amicable fellow to those who don't know better, but he preys upon innocent women when no one is looking. The modern-day wolf in sheep's clothing hides his true nature behind a dimpled grin and handsome smile.

Recently, he has tormented an innocent with such relentless determination that the person in question is terrified to set foot outdoors.

In the last week, he has made two false arrests, based on nothing more than a foul temper and thwarted attempts at improper overtures. A good deal of soap may be required to scrub away the bold, scandalous comments he made to a lady of high regard. Reportedly, he...

Stunned by the article, Maggie sank onto a kitchen chair. "Brianna, did you write this?"

"Yes." Brianna did her best to look chagrined although it was hard to hold back her smile. "Don't you think it is a well-crafted story?"

"Well-crafted!" Tully hollered, taking off his Stetson and slapping it against his leg. Puffs of dust shimmered in the morning light.

Brianna watched the particles dance in the sunbeam streaming in the window, considering how long she should let Tully suffer.

Maggie placed a calming hand on his arm when he returned the hat to his head and balled his hands into fists. "Tully, take a deep breath. You and Thane have never cared what people had to say about you, so why are you so upset by this? Anyone who knows you will know this isn't true."

Tully paced the length of the small kitchen then glowered at Brianna. "It's that she felt the need to write such a spiteful article and submit it to the paper, portraying her lies as facts. If I'm not tarred and feathered before the day is over, it'll be a miracle. You know how people are around here."

Disappointed in her new renter, Maggie looked to Brianna. The woman and Tully had clashed since the moment they met. She'd heard enough from Thane and a few of their other friends to know Tully was fighting his attraction to the lovely Miss Dumont tooth and nail.

From what Maggie had observed, Brianna was equally attracted to Tully and every bit as determined to ignore the spark that sizzled between the two of them.

However, none of that explained why Brianna felt the need to defame Tully in such a public way. The article could stir up no end of trouble for him.

"Why did you write this article, Brianna?" Maggie asked, placing the newspaper on the table. "It does seem rather…"

"Spiteful. Cruel. Mean. Without a grain of truth." Tully's clipped tone belied his hurt at what the woman had done.

Brianna returned to her seat at the table and picked up the newspaper, fanning it in front of her face. "Are you sure about that, Sheriff Barrett? Correct me if I'm wrong, but you did arrest me twice without any true reason. You've made numerous comments about my um… about inappropriate topics of conversation. Furthermore, you've gone out of your way to bully me since I arrived in town."

"Well, shoot!" Tully plunked down in a chair and nervously jiggled his leg. "It was all in fun,

Fred. I didn't know you took it all so seriously. I certainly never thought you'd retaliate by writing something like that." He pointed to the newspaper she continued to fan in front of her face. If he hadn't been so mad at her, he might have been entranced by the breeze she created as it temptingly stirred wispy tendrils of hair around her face.

"I have come to realize it was in fun, Sheriff. From my observations, you take great pleasure in teasing people, playing jokes on your friends."

"That's true, Tully," Maggie said, then glanced back at Brianna. "But that still doesn't explain the article."

Unable to help herself, Brianna giggled. "I know, but I decided to see if Tully could take a dose of his own medicine. Apparently, that bitter pill is one he can't swallow."

He stilled and stared at her. "What does that mean?"

"It means, Sheriff, you might want to hang onto this particular copy of the newspaper because it is the only one in which the article was printed. Mr. Packwood agreed it would be quite amusing to let you think the story went out in all the newspapers. He printed one special copy and made sure it was delivered straight to you."

Relief didn't quite override the justifiable resentment Tully felt toward Brianna and Bowen Packwood. He'd be sure to get back at the newspaper editor later.

At the moment, he struggled between wanting to hug the infuriating woman who wrote the article and telling her he was proud of her for getting the best of him, or turning her over his knee and paddling her backside for upsetting him like that.

A sound drew his attention to Maggie as she tried to stifle her laughter. She coughed and rose to her feet. "I think I hear the bell in the store. I'll talk to you both later." The sound of her giggles carried up the stairs after she disappeared to her workroom.

Tully narrowed his gaze and studied Brianna. "Are you working to get on my bad side, Fred?"

She shrugged and went to the sink, trying to wash away the ink she'd spilled when Tully had frightened her half to death with his arrival. "I thought I already had a permanent place there."

"I was just starting to think you might not be an infernal pest, and you had to go and prove me wrong." Tully moved behind her, angry she'd scared five years off his lifespan, but so attracted to her he couldn't have kept his hands to himself if someone had cuffed them behind his back.

He reached out a finger and trailed it along the exposed expanse of her neck. Goose bumps popped out on her flesh and he grinned, satisfied by the result of his touch.

Brianna spun around, slinging water as she shook off her hands and glared at him. "What are you doing?"

"Nothing, Fred. If I was gonna do something, you wouldn't have to ask. My intentions would be clearly evident." The urge to kiss Brianna's lips was so strong, the pull toward her almost set him off balance.

Refusing to surrender to the desire, he backed away and picked up the newspaper. "I believe I need to go see Bowen and give him my regards for assisting you in your underhanded deeds." He grinned as he stepped into the hallway. "Maybe I'll let him think he's under arrest and haul him down to the jail."

"Don't be too hard on him, Sheriff. The story was my idea. He just agreed to print it." Brianna hated to be the cause of more trouble, although from what she'd seen, both Tully and Bowen enjoyed a good joke.

"Rest assured, Bowen deserves whatever I toss at him. I still haven't gotten him back for something he did last fall. This should settle the debt and then some." Now that Tully had a moment to absorb the fact that he wasn't about to lose his job or be run out of town by angry citizens, his good humor was restored. One of his favorite things was playing a joke on someone, and he quickly formulated a dandy for the editor of the newspaper.

"Thank you for not arresting me," Brianna said as Tully started down the stairs.

He stopped and glanced back at her. "You're off the hook, at least for today. If you see the patrol wagon roll by with your boss in the back of it, don't be too concerned."

Brianna smiled and watched Tully rush down the stairs and out the back door. For a moment, she'd been sure he wanted to kiss her. Had he tried, she would have let him.

Chapter Ten

Brianna strolled to the mercantile, intent on finding a gift for Lily. As she walked up the steps to go inside, she noticed a familiar little face peeking around the corner of the building.

"Come inside with me, Sammy. You will provide great assistance with my shopping." She held a hand out to the child.

Sammy ran over and clasped Brianna's gloved hand with fingers that weren't entirely grubby. The little boy lifted a questioning gaze to her.

"I need to find a gift for Lily Jordan. Do you know her?"

The boy shook his head.

Brianna walked inside the store, still holding the small hand in hers. "What do you think a little girl would like for her birthday?"

Immediately, Sammy went to a display in the women's department and pointed to a child-sized parasol made of pink lace with a smooth cherry wood handle.

"My gracious, Sammy. Lily will adore that." Brianna picked up the parasol and smiled at the child. Taken aback by the little boy's selection, the gift suited Lily perfectly. "I think you need a gift, too."

Sammy snapped his head around and stared at Brianna then pointed to his chest, questioning if she spoke to him.

Brianna laughed softly and placed an arm around his thin shoulders. "Yes, you, Sammy. Why don't you pick out something you'd like to have, just for fun?" Fully expecting the child to choose something like a harmonica or a surplus of candy, the boy hurried over to a display of books and selected a storybook.

Surprised Sammy wanted a beautifully illustrated copy of Hans Christian Anderson's fairy tales, Brianna bent down close to the child. "Are you sure that's what you want, Sammy?"

Vigorously, the boy nodded his head. The hopeful glimmer in his blue eyes pinched Brianna's heart. Again, she wondered what kind of life the child led. He ran wild about town half the time, when he wasn't delivering papers for Mr. Packwood or following her around.

Without the ability to speak, it was hard to question Sammy about his life, but Brianna planned to inquire into his well-being with Tully. Even though Sammy appeared fed and clean, the fact he seemed so alone bothered her.

"Do you know how to read?" Brianna asked as they made their way to the front counter.

Sammy nodded and clutched the book tighter against his chest, as though fearful Brianna might take it away.

Soothingly, she rubbed her hand across the boy's back when they reached the cash register. While Mr. Miller wrapped Lily's parasol in a piece of shiny paper, Brianna asked Sammy to pick out some candy while she purchased more ink and another writing tablet.

When they left the store, they walked to the park. Sammy sucked on a peppermint drop while Brianna read a fairy tale from the book. At the end of the story, Brianna closed the book and felt an odd contentment as Sammy leaned against her, asleep. Gently moving the child so he rested with his head on her lap, Brianna relaxed in the shade of a tree, happier than she could recall being for a very long time.

There was something so oddly satisfying about the unbridled affection of a child. The sweet innocence on the little boy's face stirred maternal feelings she'd never experienced.

While the boy slept, Brianna watched people in the park and began gathering her thoughts for a new article she planned to write. If Mr. Packwood didn't want it, perhaps she'd send it to a magazine. Several national publications might be interested in her writings.

She grew up pampered and spoiled, but she was determined to forge a successful future based solely on her own skills and talents.

When he awoke, Sammy seemed embarrassed to have fallen asleep. Brianna gave him a hug and sent him on his way with his book held like a prized treasure and a handful of candy pieces in his pocket.

The next day, Brianna impatiently awaited the time to leave for Lily's party. Tully had asked if she wanted to take a buckboard or ride a horse out to the Jordan Ranch for the little girl's celebration.

She decided to try riding astride a western saddle and told Tully she'd prefer to travel on horseback. He asked her to meet him at his house at half past four that afternoon.

Although she would have argued the fact had anyone pointed it out, she'd checked the clock so often, the hands seemed to cease moving forward. The reason had to be her excitement to see the ranch and the Jordan family.

It most certainly couldn't have a thing to do with the good-looking sheriff and the idea she'd be alone with him both going to and returning from the ranch.

Finally, it was time to leave. She checked her image in the mirror one last time, grabbed Lily's gift, and hurried out the door. As she strode through town in her split skirt, enjoying the freedom it offered, she waved to Pastor Eagan and his wife. A glance behind her as she headed toward the edge of town confirmed Sammy followed, attempting to remain unnoticed.

Brianna turned a corner and stopped, waiting for the little boy to sneak around it. When he did, she wrapped her arms around him and said, "Boo!"

The boy turned on her with such a glower of indignation and fury, Brianna couldn't help but laugh.

Sammy pushed away her hands, but Brianna gently squeezed his shoulder. "I'm sorry, Sammy, but I'm riding out to the Jordan Ranch. You can't follow me clear out there. Do you need anything before I leave town?"

The boy shook his head then raced off without another glance back at her.

Brianna resumed her walk to Tully's place, pondering over many things, including the little boy. One of these days, she might just follow him to see where he lived and have a conversation with his parents about letting the child roam freely about Baker City.

At the edge of town, Brianna walked a few hundred yards when she noticed a lane and saw a farmhouse and barn behind some trees. Convinced it had to be Tully's place, she turned and followed the pasture fence as it led to the house.

Shirtless, Tully stood in front of a hand pump near the barn, splashing water over his face and chest.

Brianna watched every movement he made with rapt interest. The sheriff had to be one of the finest male specimens she'd ever seen, not that she'd witnessed any men half-dressed as he was.

Sun glistened through the droplets of water clinging to the hair covering his muscled chest and stomach. As he straightened and wiped a towel over his face, his shoulders seemed wide enough to carry the worries of the world.

Completely intrigued by the splendid sight of him, humiliation burned over her face and down her neck when he looked up and caught her ogling him.

"Hey, Fred, I was just wondering if I needed to come get you or if you'd find your way out here."

Tully grinned and draped the towel over the pump handle. "Glad to see you made it."

A proper gentleman would have covered his form and offered an apology for his unclad state. However, Brianna had already learned there was nothing proper about Sheriff Tully Barrett.

The arrogant man plucked a leaf off a plant and stuck it in his mouth then sauntered toward her in a rolling gait that only served to highlight his impressive form. Her gaze traveled over the tousled waves of his hair to his dimpled cheeks and charming smile to that spectacular chest and down the length of his long, solid legs, encased in the denim trousers he and Thane Jordan seemed to favor.

The cocky grin on his face broadened when she lifted her gaze to his. Mischief and merriment twinkled in his eyes as he stepped so close to her, the tips of his dusty boots brushed the hem of her riding skirt. The pleasant aroma of mint mixed with his alluring masculine scent.

"If I didn't know better, I'd think you're staring at something you like seeing an awful lot, Miss Dumont," Tully teased. He widened his stance and, much to her combined elation and dismay, flexed his many muscles.

Helpless to look away, she remained in mesmerized fascination, pondering why Tully Barrett had been blessed with good looks, charm, strength, wit, and a rugged appeal so hard to resist.

The man was full of himself, annoying, frustrating, and… entirely alluring.

Brianna's fingers itched to reach up and trace across Tully's chest, to see if the muscles felt as firm as they appeared.

Ignoring the intense longing, she stepped back and forced her gaze to a pasture where several horses grazed. Two saddled horses waited in front of the barn, their reins tied to a hitching rail. She recognized the buckskin the sheriff usually rode, although she hadn't previously seen the other horse.

"Do you need anything before we leave, Fred?" Tully asked. "I can get you a glass of water or the outhouse is right over there." He pointed behind the barn.

"No, thank you." Brianna tried to keep from staring at Tully as he walked with her toward the horses. Enthralled with the raw power and masculinity of the man, her eyes continued darting his direction. In dire need of a distraction, she took a deep breath and inhaled the minty aroma again. "Why do you often smell of mint?"

"I like to chew on it," he shrugged. "Reckon it's a habit. Why? Do you not like mint?"

"No, I do. The aroma is pleasing."

"Well, I'm happy to hear you don't think I stink." Tully lifted his hat from a fence post and settled it on his head.

Dumbfounded, she frowned at him. "Surely you don't mean to ride out to the Jordan Ranch like that."

He glanced down and rubbed a hand over his chest, her eyes following where her hands couldn't go. Pure devilment shone from his face when he met her gaze. "I thought maybe you'd prefer I leave my shirt off. From the way you slobbered all over yours, I might have to let you borrow my kerchief to use as a bib."

The furious blush that seared her cheeks left them feeling singed. "Sheriff Barrett! The things you say are not only rude and uncivilized, they're just…"

Tully chuckled. "Downright true. The things I say are true and you know it, Fred." He picked up a shirt wadded into a ball by the pump and motioned toward the house. "I'm just funnin' ya. I planned to change before you got here, but I'm running a little late. You can sit in the shade over there while I find a clean shirt. I'll be right back."

Before she could say another word, Tully dashed across the yard, up the porch steps, and went inside the house.

Brianna had envisioned him living in a primitive cabin, not a large farmhouse with a porch that wrapped around the front and sides, and an inviting swing near the front door. No flowers grew in pots or flowerbeds, but he did have a yard. Nibbled down to nearly nothing, she assumed he allowed animals to graze on the grass.

Although his place lacked the obvious care and attention of the MacGregor property, Tully's home appeared snug and the barn sturdy. His fences stood straight and tall and no weeds grew around the house or barn.

While she waited for Tully, Brianna touched her shirtwaist to see if she really had drooled. With Tully's teasing nature in mind, she realized he probably watched out a window to see if she'd check.

A smile quirked the corners of her mouth upward and she relaxed, considering his playful nature. Tully might push the boundaries of propriety but he wouldn't completely cross them, no matter how much he teased and pretended otherwise.

The sound of a door closing drew her attention to the house as he took the steps in one long stride and hurried her direction.

He wore a dark green shirt with a green and gold paisley silk kerchief around his neck. He'd changed out of his denims into a pair of tan canvas pants and switched out his dusty Stetson for one that looked new. As he approached her, he carried a small box beneath his arm while he tugged on a pair of leather gloves.

"Ready to go?" he asked, tucking the box into a saddlebag draped across the back of his saddle.

"I believe I am," Brianna said, moving out of the shade where she'd waited on a stump beneath a big cottonwood tree. Tully took the package from her hands and stowed it in his saddlebag then walked around Cotton to the other horse.

The gentle palomino glanced at Brianna then closed his eyes, as though her presence meant nothing to him.

"This is Hoss. He'll take good care of you," Tully said, patting the horse on the neck and freeing his reins from the hitching rail. He led him around in front of Brianna.

She rubbed her hand along the horse's neck to his withers then let him sniff her before she moved to the side, wondering how she'd get her foot into the stirrup.

Tully wrapped his hands around her waist and lifted her up before she could further contemplate the best way to mount. Startled, she sucked in a gasp of air, refusing to acknowledge how much she enjoyed his touch, even for the briefest moment.

"Does the saddle feel okay?" Tully asked as he shortened the stirrup for her.

"I've never ridden astride before, so I'm not sure what to expect." She wiggled on the seat, settling into it.

"If you have any problems, speak up. I don't want you to get any sores from something rubbing."

Brianna arched an eyebrow at him. Tully grinned, flashing his dimples as he walked around Hoss and adjusted the length of the other stirrup. When he finished, he handed her the reins and placed a hand on her leg.

Out of habit, she stiffened and glowered at him for his inappropriate touch on her thigh. "Sheriff, it is unseemly for you to be so familiar with my person."

"Shoot, darlin', this ain't nothing. If you weren't so all-fired prim and proper, I'd do more than just touch your leg." The wicked wink he cast her direction only made her work harder to appear affronted.

"You should be taken out and whipped for being so free with your speech and manner. What would Pastor Eagan think if he heard you say such things?" Brianna refused to admit just how much she enjoyed and even looked forward to the outlandish things Tully uttered.

"Pastor Eagan wouldn't care one way or the other. He's too busy trying to redeem lawless felons such as you." Tully swung onto the back of Cotton and turned the horse toward the lane.

"Humph!" Far too amused with Tully and entirely too thrilled about the party with their friends to be upset, Brianna remained silent as they rode through town and headed south.

About half a mile into the sagebrush-covered hills on a trail thick with dust, Tully glanced at Brianna. "Are you doing okay, Fred?"

"I'm well. Thank you for inquiring," Brianna said, exhilarated by the experience of riding astride. Rather than feel as though she might topple to the ground like she often did with a sidesaddle, the western saddle made it easy to maintain her balance. "How far is it to the ranch?"

"It's about four more miles." Tully pushed his hat back and studied Brianna for a long moment then glanced away, as though he wanted to say something then changed his mind.

Unsettled by the intensity of his perusal, she turned to observe the passing scenery. She watched a snake slither beneath the cool shadows of a rock and a shiver slid down her spine.

Tully noticed and pointed to the reptile. "Those bite and they're poisonous. If you hear something rattling, back away without riling it."

"Good heavens!" Brianna stared at him then glanced back at the snake as it coiled beneath the rock and flicked its tongue at them. Another shiver passed over her.

Tully settled a hand on her shoulder, giving it a gentle squeeze. "Generally, they're more afraid of you than you are of them, but try to avoid rattlesnakes just the same."

She nodded her head, wondering why she ever thought it would be a grand adventure to ride out into the hills. They didn't have things like rattlesnakes and coyotes and cougars where she grew up. The two-legged beasts who roamed the city pretending to be upstanding citizens were the most dangerous animals she'd ever encountered.

They'd traveled another mile when he looked to her again. "Are you sure you're doing okay on Hoss?"

Brianna nodded. "He's a very well-mannered horse, which seems improbable considering his owner." The frown he shot her made her giggle. "It does seem unlikely for one such as yourself to have an animal that behaves far better than you."

Tully slapped a hand to his chest in feigned insult. "You wound me, Miss Dumont. How could you make such unfounded claims against an officer of the law who is so dedicated to this town?" He grinned at her. "Then again, you wrote that article about me, telling the world how appalling and reprehensible you find me."

Once he got over the shock and anger of reading the article in the paper, Tully made quite a show of going to the newspaper office to arrest Bowen Packwood. Both men knew he did not intend to do such a thing. For fun, Bowen climbed inside the patrol wagon Tully had parked in front of the newspaper office and rode in it to the jail. After Tully marched Bowen inside the sheriff's office, the two men sat at Tully's desk enjoying a few laughs. Humored by the story, Tully had framed the article and hung it on the wall behind his desk at the office.

Without warning, a sage grouse flew out of the brush, startling both horses and drawing him from his musings. Hoss took off at a run, and Tully dug his heels into Cotton, terrified Brianna might fall off and get hurt.

When he caught up to her, she wore a big smile while her eyes glowed with life and excitement. The horse was under control, even if she continued to let him gallop down the road.

"Want to race to the ranch?" he asked, tugging down his hat.

"That's not fair, I don't know where we're heading." Brianna reached for her hat as it blew off.

Tully snatched it midair and held onto it, offering an encouraging grin. "Come on, you can't miss it."

Together, they rode down the dusty road and soon topped a rise where Tully reined in Cotton and Brianna pulled Hoss to a walk beside him.

"That's the ranch," he said, pointing to a series of buildings in the distance. Brianna admired the green pastures of fat cattle and corrals with horses. A large two-story house beckoned them in welcome as they rode into the ranch yard. A cowboy ambled out of the barn as they rode up.

"Howdy, Tully. Glad you could make it." The friendly young man named Ben offered Brianna a charming smile. "Nice to see you again, Miss Dumont."

Brianna nodded to the handsome cowboy she'd met at church. "It's nice to see you, Mr. Amick."

Tully swung out of the saddle and draped her hat over his saddle horn. He started around Cotton to help Brianna, but Ben beat him there, lifting her to the ground before taking the reins to both horses.

"Thane and Jemma are up at the house. Lily's been flittin' around like a bee plumb full of fermented honey all afternoon." Ben tipped his head toward the house. "Go on over and I'll see to the horses."

Tully slapped the cowboy on the shoulder then grasped Brianna's elbow in his hand. "Thanks, Ben. Appreciate it."

Brianna glanced around at the barn, a large log structure Tully told her was the bunkhouse, and a small cabin where Thane and Jemma had lived until they finished building the house.

There were several other outbuildings, like a smokehouse and springhouse, equipment shed, and chicken coop.

As they neared the house, Lily caught sight of her guests and raced toward them.

Brianna couldn't help but grin as the child's curls danced in disarray around her head.

"Uncle Tully! You're here!" Lily launched herself at him.

The sheriff swung the little girl into his arms and spun her around before kissing both her cheeks and her nose. "Happy Birthday, Lily."

"Thank you," she said, hugging him around his neck before lifting her head and smiling at Brianna. "Hello, Miss Dumont."

"Hello, Lily. Happy Birthday to you."

"Thank you." The little girl bounced in Tully's arms and pointed to the yard where Jemma and Mrs. Greenfield finished setting a table in the shade provided from the house.

"Hello!" Jemma called, waving to them as they approached.

Tully set Lily on her feet and kissed Jemma's cheek then tipped his hat to Mrs. Greenfield.

Brianna took the hand Jemma held out to her and gave it a gentle squeeze. "Thank you for inviting me. Is there anything I can do to provide assistance?"

"If you wouldn't mind, we still need to place the napkins and cutlery." Jemma pointed to a basket on the porch.

"I'd love to help." Brianna watched as Jack Jordan walked with Tully in the direction of the barn. He soon returned with the presents they'd brought for Lily and set them on a table where a few other packages waited for the little girl to open them. She caught Tully's eye and gave him an appreciative nod before returning her attention to the table.

The expensive linens and lace covering the table seemed completely at odds with the rough surroundings of sagebrush and cattle in the background, but the contrast made it particularly appealing.

Brianna liked the idea of Jemma bringing such refinement to the rugged setting.

Once they finished with the table, the women returned inside the house to complete meal preparations.

Lily and Jack followed them inside and the children volunteered to give Brianna a tour of the house.

She stared in amazed surprise at the bathrooms the Jordan family had in their home. The one thing she dearly missed at the apartment above Maggie's shop was a bathroom. The outhouse she shared with two other businesses made her cringe every time she used it. Not only that, but taking a bath involved heating water and filling a small tub then having to dump out all the water when she was clean.

A streak of envy sped through her as she took in Jemma's large claw foot tub.

Lily pulled her into a bedroom that would thrill any little girl, decorated in shades of pink, white and green. While she showed off her room, the child chattered about the fairies that lived in her dresser and the magical pony hidden beneath her bed.

Jack rolled his eyes and sighed. As Lily flit around the room, he leaned closer to Brianna and dropped his voice. "She makes up stories and songs all the time. Mama says she'll outgrow it. I sure hope it happens soon."

Brianna hid her smile and gave Jack a commiserating look. "I'm sure she will, Jack." In truth, she enjoyed hearing Lily's made-up stories.

The wild tales illustrated the child's active imagination and quick mind.

"What about you, Jack? What are your favorite things here at the ranch?" Brianna asked as Lily began singing a song about a calf and a raccoon.

He stepped over to the window and pushed aside the lacy curtain then pointed to a pasture where horses grazed. "My horse, Nick. Dad gave him to me when we moved here. I love to ride."

"Nick is a beautiful horse," Brianna said, moving behind him and gazing out the window. "What else do you enjoy?"

"I made most of the shingles for our house and helped with the design. Mama says I might be an architect when I grow up, but only if I get to be a cowboy, too."

Brianna laughed as they walked out of the room and down the hall. "I'm sure you can find a way to do both."

When she and the children returned downstairs and went outside they discovered, Ian, Maggie and his parents had arrived, along with Pastor and Mrs. Eagan.

Lily squealed and ran to Maggie, then hugged everyone, becoming more energized by the minute.

"She might burst from excitement before we make it through dinner," Tully whispered in Brianna's ear.

Brianna didn't know if the proximity of his big body, the minty warmth of his breath, or the fact he'd silently moved beside her left her most unsettled.

She turned and discovered his face so close to hers, she could see the gold and green flecks floating in his inviting gaze.

Swiftly tugging the ends of her unraveling composure together, she took a step away from him and nodded her head. "I concur with your assessment. She might just flit away."

Tully chuckled. "Most likely, she'll get so worked up she'll have one of her temper fits. They aren't for the faint-hearted. Lily doesn't do anything by half measures."

"That is an undisputable fact." Brianna smiled as Lily greeted each of the cowboys who worked on the ranch with hugs and kisses.

The meal went smoothly with Tully taking a seat beside Brianna while Ben somehow settled into the chair on her other side. The breeze outside felt refreshing until clouds rolled in and the air suddenly dropped in temperature.

Fearful of a storm, Jemma and Thane urged Lily to blow out the candles on the cake Mrs. Greenfield had made. While the birthday girl opened her gifts, the guests ate their cake with scoops of creamy ice cream. Thane had somehow managed to haul home enough ice for Jemma to make the treat.

Sitting between her parents, they told Lily whom each gift was from as she opened it. Brianna was impressed when the little girl examined each present and thanked the giver before moving on to the next one.

When she opened the parasol, Lily jumped off the chair and twirled it over her head. She raced over to Brianna and gave her an exuberant hug. "Now I can look like Mama when we go to town. I'll be a fine lady, too."

Jack mumbled something about that never happening.

Brianna worked to swallow back her smile while Tully hid a snort behind a cough.

Lily opened the box from Tully and squealed so loudly, the family dog howled and leaped off the porch.

Everyone watched as the child pulled a pair of miniature boots from the box, fashioned just like the boots worn by the cowboys around her.

"Tully, these are incredible," Thane said, examining one of the boots.

Jemma didn't appear as thrilled by the gift as Thane and Lily. "Now she'll be into even more mischief with the men." Jemma frowned at Tully then offered him a smile. "She'll love these boots so much, Tully. Thank you."

He grinned. "You are welcome. A good cowhand like Lil needs to dress the part."

The little girl kicked off her shoes and squirmed on Thane's lap as he pushed the boots onto her feet. Proudly twirling her parasol over her head, she clomped across the porch and back again then dove into Tully's arms.

He gave her a hug and kissed her rosy cheek before she raced off to open the remaining presents.

After she opened the last gift, the Eagans and MacGregors headed back to town. Brianna and Tully stayed to help clean up, but when the temperature dropped even further, Tully hurried to the barn to saddle the horses.

"Take this, Brianna. You might need it before you get back to town." Jemma handed her a fine woolen wrap.

"Oh, I'm sure I'll be fine." Brianna hesitated to take the shawl.

Jemma placed it in her hands and walked with her outside where the chilled air blew around them. "Perhaps I should fetch you a coat." She started back inside the house, but Brianna grabbed her hand.

"The shawl will be fine, Jemma, and much appreciated. It probably just feels colder than it really is because it's been so hot."

Skeptical, Jemma gazed at the darkening sky. "That's a possibility, but it certainly looks like a nasty storm is brewing. It might be best if you and Tully stay the night. I hate the thought of sending you off into a downpour with darkness approaching."

"Please don't worry on our account. I'm sure we'll be back in Baker City before it has a chance to rain." Brianna hugged Jemma and lifted Lily in her arms when the child bounded up to her with her parasol.

"I love my present, Miss Dumont. Thank you for coming to my party." Lily gave her a tight squeeze before Brianna set her down.

"Thank you for the invitation, Lily. It was my pleasure to share in your special day." Brianna bent down and lightly tapped her index finger on the end of Lily's button nose. "I'm so pleased you like your parasol."

"It's bee-you-tee-full!" Lily swung it around, almost accidentally hitting Brianna with it before she raced back into the house.

Jemma released an exasperated sigh. "We so appreciate you coming for Lily's party. The parasol is adorable and she'll greatly enjoy it."

"It's particularly fetching with those boots." Brianna wondered how Tully had found such a tiny pair then realized he most likely had them custom-made for the child. The fact that he'd go to such bother for the little girl made her heart soften toward him even more than it already had.

"I imagine we'll have to wrestle those boots off her when it's time to tuck her into bed tonight." Jemma smiled as Tully led the horses to the end of the walk. "Thank you for everything, Tully. As you may have surmised, Lily adores her boots."

"I'm glad she likes them. Thanks for a fine supper, Jemma. Tell Thane I'll be out on my next day off to help him with the hay." Tully would have told Thane himself, but his friend had hurried off with his hired men to secure the outbuildings and run his thoroughbreds into the barn before the storm hit. He waved a hand at Brianna, motioning her to join him. "Let's get moving, Fred. I don't want to ride home in the rain."

"Why do you insist on calling her Fred?" Jemma asked as Brianna hurried down the walk and stepped next to Hoss.

Tully boosted her up to the saddle and handed her the reins before he swung onto Cotton. "As far as I'm concerned, that's her name until she gives me a reason to call her something else."

Brianna grinned at Jemma. "I suppose I should feel fortunate he didn't decide to call me stupid or ugly, or Aloysius."

Jemma laughed and waved as the two of them rode out of the ranch yard. Before they made it to the top of the hill, big drops of rain started to fall. Tully settled Brianna's hat on her head and untied a rain slicker from behind his saddle.

"Put this on." He held it out to her.

She shook her head and pushed his hand away. "The shawl Jemma loaned is sufficient. You wear it."

Tully tried to drape it around her, but she grabbed it from his hand and threw it at him. "I won't wear it, so unless you want it trampled by the horses, you put it on." She glowered at him.

Finally, he shrugged into the slicker and pulled his hat lower on his head. "Are you sure you want to ride home. I could leave you with Jemma and come back for you tomorrow."

"No. I prefer to go home. I'm sure the rain won't get any worse."

The temperature continued to drop and soon the rain turned to snow. Incredulous, Brianna glared at Tully through the flurry of snowflakes. "It's nearly July! How can it snow this time of year? The temperature has been almost unbearably hot. This abrupt change in the weather makes no sense."

Tully sighed. "It can snow any time, although it's rare to get any storms between May and

September. We can still turn back if you want to stay at Thane and Jemma's place."

Brianna shook her head, concerned she would freeze to death before they reached either the ranch or town. "I'd prefer to return to Baker City."

"Then that's what we'll do." The snow fell so hard, Tully struggled to see more than a few feet in front of him, but he knew the road well and it wasn't yet dark, so he wasn't overly concerned about making it back to town.

However, Brianna frantically glanced around, trying to get her bearings. The lost, frightened look on her face combined with the chattering of her teeth finally forced him to rein both horses to a stop.

"Confound it, woman! You're gonna break every tooth in your thick head if you don't stop them from clacking together like that. It would be a shame to damage such pretty, pearly teeth." Tully scowled at her as she pulled the shawl tightly around her shoulders.

She wished she had accepted the coat Jemma offered. In fact, she wished she had stayed at the ranch instead of deciding to ride back to town. "I… I'm… trying," she said between chatters.

"Dad-blasted summer storms and contrary women…" Tully mumbled under his breath. Frustrated, he reached over and grabbed Brianna, settling her across his lap. He wrapped the ends of the slicker around her, sharing his body heat with her.

"What… are… you… doing?" Brianna asked through frozen lips.

"Warming you up and getting you home. Now hush up and hold on." He grabbed Hoss' reins in his hand then urged Cotton forward.

The heat radiating from Tully instantly penetrated Brianna's cold body. She snuggled against his chest, grateful for his warmth and his brawny form that blocked the frigid wind.

As the snow swirled around them, she lost all track of time and place. They might have ridden for hours or minutes — she couldn't tell.

All she knew was nothing in her life had ever felt as good as being in the sheltering circle of Tully's arms. Content and drowsy, she closed her eyes, ready to fall into a peaceful slumber.

"Fred! Don't you dare fall asleep. I need you to stay awake until we get back to town." Tully glared at her, but she refused to open her eyes. Gently, he jostled her. "Fred! I mean it. You open those beautiful eyes and look at me right now or else…"

Unable to obey his orders, her mind wondered what sort of threat he'd carry out. No matter how much she wanted to, her eyelids weighed too heavy to force open.

"Brianna? Please, darlin', open your eyes." Worry etched vertical lines between Tully's eyes as he gazed at the woman in his arms. Concerned if she fell asleep, she might succumb to hypothermia, his mind scrambled for an idea to keep her awake.

Later, that was the reason he gave for pressing his lips to hers until he teased a response out of her. When she slid her hands up his chest and wrapped them around his neck, he shifted in the saddle so he could hold her closer.

Overcome with a need to hold her, to love her, Tully deepened the kiss and masterfully shared the ardor that made his blood zing in his veins and heat churn in his gut.

In the length of a few heartbeats, they both went from nearly frozen to feverish.

Despite her innocent response to him, passion drove her to return his kisses. The sparks that had flickered between the two of them from the moment they met caught fire and combusted.

While he continued to work a spell over Brianna with his kisses, Tully glanced up and realized they'd reached town. The streets were empty and not a soul was in sight, so he kissed Brianna all the way to Maggie's shop. When he stopped the horses out front, he slid from the saddle with her still in his arms and carried her down the alley to the back of the shop.

At the door, he kissed her neck and nuzzled her ear. "I need the key, Fred, if you don't want to stand out here all night."

As though she'd awakened from some enchantment, Brianna opened her eyes. Shocked, she realized they'd not only reached Baker City, but stood at the back door to Maggie's shop.

Suddenly aware that Tully held her against his chest, she glanced at him and took in the yearning on his face as his eyes glowed with desire.

All the way into town, she thought she'd been dreaming of Tully's touch and kisses, but it hadn't been a dream. It was real. He was real, and so very tempting as he held her in his arms.

Before she fully regained her senses, Brianna pulled his mouth to hers again and engaged in a kiss that should have melted snow from where he stood all the way back to the Jordan Ranch.

Tully moaned and held her even closer against him. "Give me the key, Brianna." As he said her name, his voice was so husky and deep, the sound of it sent a delighted shiver trailing through her.

Mistaking her response to his affections for a reaction to the cold, Tully set her on her feet. He reached up to a support beam in the overhang above the back entrance and retrieved a key. Quickly unlocking the door, he picked her up again, carrying her up the stairs and into the sitting room.

Tenderly depositing her on the sofa, he built a fire in the stove, then one in the kitchen. While he worked, Brianna curled up, tugging a crocheted afghan off the back of the sofa over herself. She felt as though she might never be warm again.

The chill came not from the snow, but from Tully setting her down. The world seemed like a cold, bereft place without his arms around her.

Nothing in her past had prepared her for the remarkable experience of falling in love with the handsome, teasing sheriff. He evoked emotions in her she hadn't even known existed.

She heard Tully moving around in the kitchen. Eventually, he reappeared with a cup of hot tea and placed it in her chilled hands.

"Do you need me to stay with you, darlin'?" he asked, placing a hand to her forehead. Her skin was cool but not overly so.

However, his hands felt like they were on fire. Every part of him longed to take Brianna in his arms and love her all night long.

"I'm fine," she whispered, sipping the tea. "Thank you for taking such good care of me."

Fearful that he might surrender to the voice in his head screaming at him to steal more honey-sweet kisses from the gorgeous woman, Tully took a hasty step toward the stairs.

"Are you sure you'll be fine?"

"Yes, Tully. Will you be able to make it home in the storm?"

He grinned. "This little skiff isn't anything compared to some of the blizzards Cotton and I have been through. You get those wet clothes off and get warmed up." Suggestively, he waggled an eyebrow at her. "Unless you'd like me to stay and help you with that."

"No, thank you, sir." She feigned an indignant huff. "I do believe it's time for you to go home, Sheriff."

Tully nodded. "I'll check on you in the morning. Good night, Fred."

"Good night."

Tully hurried back out into the storm, hoping the snow would cool the inferno Brianna had set ablaze in him.

The fire burning in her blue eyes did nothing to temper his longing. Sheer force of will was all that kept him from racing back up the steps and claiming her as the love he'd waited his whole life to find.

Chapter Eleven

Although the snow melted not long after the sun rose, the amorous tension crackling between Brianna and Tully didn't ebb.

When he stopped by early that morning to check on her, Brianna could feel something pulse between them that left her frightened yet fascinated.

Nervously twirling his hat in his hands and shifting his weight from one foot to the other, Tully must have felt it, too.

Neither of them spoke of the ardent, driven kisses they'd shared the previous evening among the swirls of snow.

"Are you sure you feel well, Fred?" Tully asked, studying her face. "I could take you to see Doc."

She shook her head. "I'm perfectly healthy, Sheriff, but I do thank you for your concern and for seeing me safely home."

He nodded and moved to the landing. "If you need anything, be sure to let me know." Before she could speak, he clattered down the stairs and said a few words to Maggie then left.

Brianna sank onto her sofa, convinced Tully's handsome appeal increased every time she saw him.

Recollections of how good it felt to be in his arms, to know the delicious, rich taste of his kisses, to see sparks burst to life in his expressive hazel eyes, made her lean back with a careworn sigh.

A relationship with Tully was not only out of the question, it bordered on ridiculous. They were both too determined to have their own way, opinionated, and strong-willed to get along. Tully had an obvious lack of interest in proper behavior. Fine manners were something she not only valued, but also insisted upon for maintaining an orderly lifestyle.

A hundred reasons why they were ill suited popped into her head, but it did nothing to change the whispers from her heart telling her Tully was the one man she could love for a lifetime.

Annoyed with herself and her infatuation with the good-looking sheriff, Brianna pinned on her hat, picked up her notebook and pencil, grabbed her reticule, and rushed out the door.

She interviewed a dozen people about the snowstorm and the damages it caused. She spoke with the person who managed the meteorological station and recorded his input about the freak summer storm.

To finish the article, she needed a quote from Tully and walked to his office. When she stepped inside, he was alone at his desk, writing what appeared to be a report.

He glanced up at her and smiled. "Hey, Fred. What can I do for you?" Politely, he stood and held out a chair at his desk for her.

Once she was seated, he sat in his chair and leaned back.

Brianna took out her notebook and pencil. "I'm nearly finished with an article about the snowstorm and wanted the sheriff's thoughts on any adverse effects it caused."

Tully supposed she probably wouldn't appreciate him making a flippant comment about the effects she'd had on him last night. After he made it home and settled the horses in the barn, he stood out in the snow for a long time, trying to cool the fever he couldn't shake.

Every time he thought of her, of how good she felt in his arms, he'd heat up all over again.

Even now, as she sat across the desk from him all prim and proper in a dress the same shade as whipped butter, his mouth watered at the thought of tasting her sweet kisses again. All he'd have to do is take two steps around his desk and she'd be in his arms, with those delectable lips pressed to his.

"Sheriff?" Brianna asked in a tone that made it clear she was there only on business.

"Problems with the storm, huh?" Tully yanked his thoughts together and gave her a generic comment about any damages he'd witnessed. He cautioned people to be prepared for inclement weather any time of year, and to be mindful of the dangers of hypothermia and frostbite.

Rapidly taking notes, they both glanced at the door when Dugan Durfey ran inside. "Boss, Luden

Scott just sent word in that the horse rustler struck his place and took Loco."

Tully lunged to his feet. "That's it. I'm hunting him down and I don't care how long it takes." He started out the door then looked back at Brianna. "Can you get yourself home, Fred?"

"Yes, of course." She watched as he ran out the door, heading toward his place.

Brianna left the sheriff's office and hurried to the newspaper office where she left the snowstorm article for Bowen. He happened to walk by as she was about to leave.

"Any progress on the horse rustler story?" he asked.

"Tully just received word he struck again last night. I shall request he allow me to accompany him to the location where the horses were stolen."

Bowen laughed and shook his head. "You can try, but Tully won't let you tag along. Just talk to him when he gets back."

Brianna gave her employer a look that expressed her determination to do as she pleased then rushed out the door.

Sammy fell into step beside her and she glanced down at the boy. "Did you see the sheriff run out of town?"

The child nodded then lifted his hands, as though asking a question.

"A rustler took some horses, including one named Loco. Is that the sheriff's horse?"

Sammy's eyes sparkled with amusement and he grinned. He pointed to the side of his head then made an outlandish face that caused Brianna to laugh.

"The horse is crazy, is that it?"

Sammy nodded.

"So, he lives up to his name?"

Another nod.

They'd reached the back door of Maggie's shop. Brianna pulled a coin from her reticule and hastily scribbled a note, handing both to Sammy.

"Sammy, would you please run down to Mr. Owens' livery and give him that note? I need him to saddle a horse for me. And make sure he uses a western saddle." Brianna opened the door and ran up the stairs to her apartment.

Faster than she'd ever changed in her life, she yanked off her dress and pulled on a riding skirt, blouse and vest. She grabbed a jacket, then unpinned her hair and braided it, tying the end with a ribbon.

She dropped her reticule in the bag she used to carry her notebook and tossed in a few extra pencils.

After snatching a pair of leather gloves from the dresser, she raced down the stairs and to the livery. Sammy waited there, rubbing a hand over the muzzle of a saddled horse.

"I got your note, Miss Dumont," Milt Owens said as she approached.

"Thank you, sir." Brianna pulled money from her bag to pay for the rental of the horse and handed it to Milt. He gave her back the coin she'd given to Sammy.

"The boy gave me the coin. Thought maybe you were making a deposit." Milt grinned when Brianna put the coin into Sammy's hand and kissed his forehead.

"Thank you for your help, sweetheart." She cupped Sammy's chin in her hand. "You stay out of trouble until I get back."

Sammy nodded then ran off with the coin tightly clasped in his hand.

Milt helped Brianna mount. She turned to him with a grateful nod as she draped her bag over the saddle horn and accepted the reins he held out to her. "I don't know what time I'll return."

"Don't worry about that, Miss Dumont. I trust you won't skedaddle with my horse."

She tipped her head to him then guided the horse down the street. At the edge of town, she wondered how she'd convince Tully to let her go with him. She was almost to his lane when the sound of running hoofbeats reached her ears and she watched Cotton take the turn onto the road at a fast lope before Tully urged him into a full gallop, heading north of town.

Brianna squeezed with her knees and made a kissing noise that sent her horse racing forward.

Since Tully didn't give her the chance to ask, she would just follow him wherever he was going. She stayed far enough back she hoped he wouldn't notice her. Several miles later, he reined the horse off the road onto a lane.

Slowing her mount to a walk, she made her way up the lane. Trees surrounded a big corral where Tully had stopped and spoke to another man.

Impatient to hear what they were saying, she tied her horse to a branch out of sight and crept closer to the corral.

Bent down as she edged along the fence, she studied the variety of horses in the enclosure. If the horse rustler took the sheriff's horse, she wondered why the thief didn't steal them all.

Before she could further contemplate the reasoning of a thief's mind, Tully mounted and rode back to the road.

Desperate not to lose sight of him, Brianna made her way back to her horse and managed to climb into the saddle. She rode him down the lane in time to catch a glimpse of Tully continuing north on the road.

Another mile later, he and Cotton turned onto a little used path that led into the hills. Brianna followed behind him and stopped her horse when Tully dismounted, studying an area of churned mud. He mounted and continued deeper into the hills, riding to the north and west.

The air was cool and Brianna was glad she'd thought to bring her warmest jacket. She stopped long enough to slip it on before trailing after Tully.

When she topped a rise, she saw him walking around what could have been a makeshift corral, constructed of tree limbs and fallen timber.

She dismounted and left her horse tied where she was sure Tully wouldn't see it then made her way toward the enclosure.

Intent on watching her footsteps, she sucked in a gulp as a twig snapped behind her.

"You better have a dang good reason for being here, Fred."

Brianna turned around with her hands held in the air, relieved it was Tully and not some hardened criminal who'd come upon her. "I can explain, Sheriff."

Tully holstered the gun he'd held pointed at her then rocked back on one hip. "I'm waiting."

"The first-hand knowledge I could glean from accompanying you would prove invaluable to the story. I planned to ask your permission, but you were already galloping down the road when I arrived at your place."

"You decided to come along." Tully's gaze raked over her, taking in her golden-brown braid, jacket and riding skirt. "If you think you were being sneaky, I knew you were back there before Cotton ever hit full stride. I don't have time to take you back to town, darlin', so you either do exactly what I tell you or you turn that horse around and get your sweet little backside home."

"Sheriff! You mustn't speak in such an uncouth manner." Secretly, Brianna thrilled that he'd called her backside sweet, but she certainly didn't want him to know that. "Your choice of words is highly unacceptable."

Tully's hands were on her arms so fast, she didn't know when he'd moved. Roughly, he pulled her against him and lowered his head until his lips hovered above hers. "From now until I get you home, you'll put up with whatever I say and do. Is that clear?"

When she started to protest, he pressed a hard, unyielding kiss to her mouth then raised his head. "Is it clear, Miss Dumont? You listening to what I say could mean the difference between life and death for us both."

Rattled by his kiss as well as his proximity, Brianna nodded her head. "I'll do what you say," she whispered, wishing he'd kiss her again.

"Good." Tully picked her up and carried her back to her horse, setting her on the saddle. His hand brushed down her leg and he patted her knee. "Ride over to where I left Cotton. I'll be right there."

Befuddled by his kiss and touch, she nudged her mount forward until they waited next to Tully's faithful horse.

The sheriff appeared from behind a large rock, carrying a piece of frayed rope covered in blood.

Eyes wide, she looked at him in question.

"The rustler isn't as smart as he thinks," Tully said as he swung onto Cotton's back and rode along a faint trail. "Thanks to the storm and warm temperatures this morning, he's leaving tracks even a toddler could follow."

Brianna didn't know about a toddler, but she could see tracks in the mud, although she had no idea what they meant.

Tully pointed out four different sets of prints. "I think there's one rider with three horses. Luden said the rustler took three horses sometime between when he checked on the horses last night and when he went out to feed them this morning."

"And one of the horses is yours?"

"Yep." Tully stopped and studied the tracks then turned Cotton into the trees to his left. They rode up a steep hill before cresting the top. In the distance, a man rode at a leisurely place, leading three horses.

Tully motioned for Brianna to ride closer to him. The moment her leg brushed his, he leaned toward her and spoke in a hushed tone. "We're gonna ride down this hill as quiet as we can and get closer to our rustler. When I give the signal, you grab tight to your reins and keep control of your horse."

Before Brianna could ask any questions, Tully straightened and clucked to Cotton. Curious what the sheriff had planned, she would do as he commanded.

Smug with the success of his thievery, the rustler remained oblivious to their presence as they closed the gap between them. They were only a hundred yards behind him when Tully pointed to Brianna. She took a tighter grip on the reins and stopped her horse as Tully tugged off his glove and set two fingers in his mouth.

The shrill whistle emanating from him made Brianna cringe and wish he'd told her to plug her ears.

One of the three horses the rustler led reared and struck at him, knocking him from the saddle. He landed in an unconscious heap.

Tully raced forward and had the thief in handcuffs before Brianna had moved more than a few feet.

Quickly grabbing the reins of the rustler's mount and the lead ropes of two of the horses, Tully gave them to Brianna to hold.

The horse that had knocked the rustler to the ground continued to rear and snort.

Tully grabbed his lead rope. Softly talking to him, he didn't make any move to touch him until the horse kept all four hooves on the ground. Unhurried, Tully sidled closer to the horse and ran a gentle hand along his neck.

The horse visibly calmed as Tully brushed a hand across his muzzle. He pulled something from his pocket and let the horse nuzzle it from his hand.

With a relieved sigh, he turned to Brianna. "Fred, I'd like you to meet Loco."

"Well, he certainly appears to live up to his name." She studied the handsome gelding, admiring his straight lines and unique coloring. "What is he?"

"Besides a little crazy?" Tully grinned at her and continued to rub a calming hand over the horse. "His father was a mustang and his mama was a quarter horse. He gets that pretty chestnut color and long legs from his mother, but the rest of him is all mustang."

"Is that why his mane and tail are both dark and light?" Brianna thought the flaxen color mixed with black quite striking.

"The proper term, since you're so insistent on them, is bi-color. He also has a dorsal stripe down his back. Loco isn't so much loony as he's just opinionated about how he wants to do things." He handed Brianna Loco's lead rope then grabbed the rustler by the back of his coat collar and hauled him to his feet as the man came to.

"Dale Darcey, you've got some kind of gall showing up around here. To add insult to injury, you rustled horses while you're at it. I have a few friends who'll be most anxious to see you."

The man blinked to clear his vision and stared at Tully, realizing he'd been caught. "Sheriff. I'd like to say it's a pleasure, but it ain't."

"Where are the rest of the horses, Dale?" Tully gave the rustler a shake hoping it would loosen his tongue.

The young thief just sneered at him. "You think you're so clever, figure it out."

"If I had to guess, I'd say you run the horses up to the mining road then into Haines and board them on the train to The Dalles. You have a partner there waiting for their delivery." Tully shoved the young man onto his horse and took the reins from Brianna.

Dale gaped at him. "How could... How did..."

Tully winked at Brianna then turned back to Dale. "After the horses arrive in The Dalles, you haul them to the stockyard and then..."

"That ain't true. We line up buyers and sell them one at a time." Dale winced when Tully tightened a rope around his ankle and tied it to the stirrup so he wouldn't fall or jump off the horse.

Tully looked over at Brianna. "You're the witness to his confession, Fred."

"Yes, sir," she said, amazed at how easily Tully had overcome the thief and tricked a confession out of him.

She watched as Tully tied Dale's cuffed hands to the saddle horn. Before he did, he looked at the young man's bleeding palms. "One of the horses almost got away from you back there a ways, didn't he?"

"Sure did." Dale scowled in the direction of Loco. "That beast is plumb berserk. If I'd known he was your lunkheaded cayuse, I woulda left him alone."

"I'm kind of glad you stole him, Dale. I was tired of trying to track you down." Tully took the lead ropes from Brianna then boosted her up to the saddle. When she was settled, he gave her a questioning glance. "Can you handle these two lead ropes, Fred? I don't want to lead Loco, my prisoner's horse and the other two, but if you'd rather not try, I'll manage."

"I can take them," Brianna said with more confidence than she felt. Although she was comfortable around horses and a good rider, she'd never had to lead a horse for any distance. They were miles from Baker City and it would be dark in a few hours.

Tully nodded at her and mounted Cotton. Rather than go back the way they'd come, he rode east before heading south.

Dale Darcey bragged about all the people he'd robbed since he'd taken Thane Jordan's money and left him to die at the mine along with his men last November.

Shocked and repulsed, Brianna almost cheered when Tully stopped long enough to pull Dale's boot off his foot and remove his sock.

"Good gosh, almighty!" Tully turned his face away and wrinkled his nose, quickly shoving Dale's boot back on his smelly foot. "You had a bath in the last year?"

"There's no call to be insulting, Sheriff." Dale frowned at him. "I ought to…"

After stuffing the malodorous sock in the idiot's mouth, Tully yanked the kerchief off the thief's neck and tied it around Dale's face to keep him from spitting out the dirty sock.

"That should make for a much more peaceful trip," he said as he mounted Cotton again and continued toward Baker City.

For the next hour, Tully acted as if he and Brianna were out for a scenic ride. He pointed out plants native to the region, and mentioned the delicious berries that grew wild in the area.

The discussion about berries made her stomach growl. She'd missed lunch and the dinner hour had come and gone. Hunger gnawed at her, leaving her uncomfortable and wishing she'd taken time to pack food and a blanket.

Brianna was cold, tired and considering what Tully would do if she begged to stop for a rest when he pointed to a clearing ahead near a creek.

"We'll stop there for the night," he said, over his shoulder.

"Are you insane?" Brianna asked, riding closer to him. Loco kicked at one of the horses she led so she dropped back and raised her voice. "We can't stay there."

"Why not?" Tully stopped and swung off Cotton's saddle.

"Because… it's… we shouldn't…" Brianna didn't want to tell Tully her reputation would be in tatters if she spent the night alone in the hills with two men, even if one of them was in handcuffs and the other was the sheriff.

"I promise everything will be fine, Fred. Don't worry your pretty little head. It'll be too dark soon to see the trail and I don't want this ignoramus trying to get away." Tully tied Loco's lead rope to a sturdy tree then lifted Brianna from her mount.

He handed her the reins for Cotton and Dale's horse before he untied the ropes holding the young man to the saddle. With a jerk, he pulled the thief to the ground and dragged him over to a tree where he tied him up so he couldn't escape.

"Are you planning to leave him like that?" Brianna asked, somewhat relieved the rustler couldn't go anywhere. From watching Tully with the young man, she surmised that he held little mercy for those who broke the law and flaunted their lawlessness in his face.

Although the first time she'd met him, she assumed Tully Barrett was a thickheaded, conceited bully, she realized there were many facets to his character. Around women, he was as charming as he could be. His male friends and peers were given respect along with a generous helping of teasing and jokes. Children were entertained, protected, and loved.

"He's lucky I didn't string up a rope and leave him dangling from a tree." Tully grinned at Dale when the thief's eyes bugged and he looked panicked. "After all, he not only stole more than a dozen horses, including mine, he's wanted for robbery and assault, attempted murder, not to mention what he did to Thane."

Brianna watched as Tully let the horses drink from the creek before tying their lead ropes and reins to thick branches. With practiced ease, he removed the saddles and saddle blankets. He looked over each horse before leaving them to nibble on the rich carpet of grass.

"What did Mr. Darcey do to Thane?" Brianna asked, observing Tully's movements as he kicked a spot clear of grass with the heel of his boot then hauled up rocks from the creek to line a circle around the bare patch.

He motioned for Brianna to follow him as he walked into the pine trees. "Last year, right around Thanksgiving, Thane rode out to check on his mines. He owns several, spread all over the area. Anyway, he was almost to the last one when there was a loud explosion. By the time he got there, the tunnel in the mine had collapsed and his men were trapped inside. Two men were at the mouth of the mine when the explosion happened. One of them was injured badly but the other one barely had a scratch.

"And the one who barely had a scratch was Mr. Darcey?"

"Yep. Thane had an injured man in need of nursing and a bunch of men stuck in the mine in need of supplies from town to free them. Rather than leave Mr. Darcey at the mine, Thane chose to stay and sent Dale into Baker City with instructions to find me. Thane gave him more than enough money to cover the costs of necessary supplies and waited for his return."

Much to her surprise, Tully removed his hat and gathered a few handfuls of pine needles and dried moss, tossing them inside his upturned head covering. After handing the hat to her, he selected several twigs then picked up some smaller pieces of wood. Together, they walked back to the campsite.

"What happened?" Brianna asked as Tully piled the pine needles and moss in the middle of the spot where he planned to build a fire.

"Mr. Darcey, over there, took the money from Thane and disappeared. Those poor men were left in the caved-in mine tunnel for five days and the injured man almost died before some of Thane's ranch crew located him." He arranged twigs around the top of the pile so that it almost looked like a teepee. From his pocket, he pulled a small piece of flint and a knife.

"Oh, that's horrid!" Brianna scowled at Dale Darcey over her shoulder then jumped when a spark Tully produced from striking the knife blade against the flint caught in the moss and a flame flickered.

Tully bent down and blew on it until the moss and pine needles began to burn. The twigs soon caught fire and he gradually added bigger pieces until a warm, cheerful fire burned.

Amazed at Tully's skills, Brianna held her hands out to the blaze and smiled at the sheriff. "You are a man of many talents."

He cocked an eyebrow at her and grinned. "Don't forget it, Fred." The gleam in his eye, a mixture of longing and something that sure seemed a lot like love, made her shiver.

Tully started to remove his coat to hand to her, but she shook her head. "I'm fine, Sheriff. Really."

He carried the saddle blankets over to the fire and made a place for her to sit off the rapidly cooling ground then retrieved a pouch of jerky and hardtack from his saddlebags.

When he handed her a piece of the dried meat, she sniffed it, deciding it had a beefy aroma mixed with a few spices. "What is it?"

"Jerky. It's the best you'll get for supper tonight, so dig in." Tully took a small coffee pot from his bedroll to the creek and filled it with water then set it on a smooth rock by the fire.

He removed the kerchief and sock from Dale's mouth and shoved in a piece of jerky. The young man had no choice but to chew it or go without any food.

Brianna held back a giggle, but Tully caught the amusement on her face when he returned to the fire.

Eventually Dale demanded something to drink. Tully held a tin cup full of creek water for him, gave him a piece of hardtack to eat then disappeared into the darkness.

Brianna stared into the flames until he came back with an armload of wood. He added a piece to the fire and settled down, leaning his back against a log he'd rolled over to make them more comfortable.

"Sheriff, it's kind of cold and dark over here," Dale whined. "And I could sure use a trip into the woods to do my business unless you want me to do it right here."

Appalled, Brianna shot the rustler a scathing glare before she turned back to Tully. "He's disgusting."

"Yep, he is." Tully got to his feet and untied Dale, escorting him away from their camp. While they were gone, Brianna removed the ribbon from the end of her braid and unwound the strands then braided it again. During the course of the day, so many wisps had come out of the braid, more of it hung free than remained restrained. She took another piece of jerky from the pouch Tully had left beside her and leaned back against the log.

Inspired by her surroundings, she retrieved her notebook and pencil. She jotted down notes in the light from the fire, recalling everything she could about Tully tracking down Dale, the rustler's capture, and building the fire.

By the time Tully returned with Dale, Brianna had filled four pages in her notebook. At the thief's continued whining that he would freeze to death if Tully didn't let him stay by the fire, Tully tied him to a tree that was marginally closer.

"Sheriff, this ain't gonna work. I can't get no sleep trussed up like a turkey. I promise I won't vamoose if you just let me sleep on one of those saddle blankets by the fire."

Tully snorted and stared down at his prisoner. "What makes you think I care if you freeze or die? You're a wanted criminal, Dale, and this isn't a luxury hotel. Shut up and go to sleep."

Dale huffed and whined, so Tully returned the dirty sock to his mouth and tied the kerchief over the top. "Sweet dreams, Mr. Darcey."

Brianna swallowed back a giggle at the disparaging look on Dale's face.

When Tully sank onto a saddle blanket beside her and released a weary sigh, he held out a blanket he'd taken from a bedroll behind his saddle. "Take it, Fred. It'll be a long, cold night if you don't, even with the fire."

She accepted the blanket but gave him a questioning glance. "What about you? Won't you get chilled?"

"No, darlin', I'll be fine." Tully poured a cup of coffee and held it out to Brianna. After she took a sip, she handed it back to him and he took a long drink, watching her over the brim of the cup.

The intense light in his eyes and the look on his face left her unsettled and nervous. In need of a distraction, she asked Tully about the various mines, and the town's distinctive title of Queen City of the Mines.

"Did you know the hotel where you stayed houses the third elevator to be constructed west of the Mississippi River?" Tully's deep baritone voice sounded soothing as he spoke.

Brianna shook her head. "I did not know that. What else is unique about Baker City?"

"Other than having the most handsome sheriff west of the Rocky Mountains?" Tully teased.

She laughed. "That is not a fact, but an opinion, held almost exclusively by you and a few of the twitterpated young girls in town."

He leaned close to her and nudged her arm with his. "I don't care what those little ninnies think. However, I do care about the opinion of one incredibly beautiful woman named Fred."

At that moment, with Tully pressed close to her side, Brianna could have easily fallen into his arms and remained there throughout the night. In the firelight, he looked like a bronzed statue she'd once seen on display in New York City.

No matter how much she refused to tell him she found him unbelievably appealing, Tully Barrett was one of the most attractive men she'd ever seen.

"If I ever meet a woman with the horrid name of Fred, I'll inquire as to her thoughts of a puffed up, arrogant officer of the law."

Tully chuckled and tossed another piece of wood on the fire. They both watched the sparks dance upward.

Silence settled around them and Brianna contemplated how she'd ever get to sleep, especially when she needed to, as Dale Darcey stated earlier, do some business.

She refused the coffee he held out to her and seemed unable to settle down. Tully figured out the reason for her restlessness and stood then pulled Brianna to her feet.

"Come on, Fred. Why didn't you say you needed to make a trip into the bushes?" He lifted a burning branch from the fire, took her hand in his, and led her away from the camp.

"Of all the inappropriate topics you've broached, that may be at the top of the list." Brianna allowed him to lead her into the darkness with only the glow of their improvised torch lighting the way. Propriety dictated she should release his hand and demand he leave her to her own defenses, but common sense prevailed.

"Surely, not. My inquiries about your corsets and drawers should rank higher, don't you think? If I haven't discussed them enough to be number one on your list, I could launch into a conversation about them right now. Perhaps I better do an inspection to see what you're wearing." Playful, he reached down toward the hem of her split skirt.

For his benefit, she slapped his arm and pretended to be affronted. His teasing made her feel safe and cared for, even if she wouldn't admit it.

"There's a bunch of bushes right over there where you can take care of your needs. I'll wait here for you." Tully gave her a slight push in the direction he indicated.

Brianna hurried over to the bushes then caught him watching her. "Turn your back, Sheriff! Have you no decency?" She walked around the bushes until she was out of sight on the other side.

"None whatsoever."

When Brianna rejoined him, he handed her the branch then filled his arms with firewood on the way back to their camp.

After dumping the wood he'd gathered onto a pile he'd started earlier, he walked over to where Dale slept against the tree. Carefully, he removed the kerchief and sock from the thief's mouth then draped a saddle blanket over him.

"Why did you do that?"

Tully shrugged. "I don't want him to choke on that thing while he sleeps. As long as he stays quiet, I'll leave it out."

Surprised by Tully's kindness to the rustler, she kept her thoughts to herself. Tully rolled back the log they'd leaned against and spread out the two remaining saddle blankets end to end, making her a bed.

"Go on and get comfortable, Fred. I'll cover you up with the blanket when you get yourself settled."

She stretched out on her back, longing for a pillow. Tully flicked the blanket and it settled over her, wrapping her in its warmth. It smelled of wood smoke, leather and horse with a hint of Tully. Wishing she could write down the smell before she forgot it, she breathed deeply, attempting to memorize the masculine scent.

A startled squeak burst out of her when Tully stretched out beside her on the outside of her blanket.

"What are you doing?" she whispered, turning to look at him.

He set his hat on the log and folded his arms behind his head. "Looking at the stars."

Brianna lifted her gaze and stared at the velvety sky above her, twinkling with thousands of stars.

"Oh," she whispered, enchanted by the sight. "It's beautiful."

"Yes, it is," Tully studied her, not the sky.

Afraid he might kiss her again, and worried he wouldn't, Brianna pointed out a few constellations her father had taught her.

"I'm sorry about your dad, Brianna. It sounds like you were close," Tully said, glancing over at her again.

Tears stung the backs of her eyes and she nodded her head. "We were close and I miss him every day." Determined not to cry, she looked inquisitively at Tully. "What about you? Do you have parents who worry about you? A brother or sister?"

Tully remained silent so long, Brianna wondered if he'd gone to sleep with his eyes open, but he finally released a weary sigh. "No, I don't have anyone, just Thane and his family, Maggie, and now Ian. Thane and Mags have been all the family I've had since I was seventeen."

"I'm, sorry, Tully." Brianna worked a hand free from her blanket cocoon and managed to grasp his hand in hers. His skin was cool to the touch and she worried that he was going to freeze, lying on the cold ground. She yanked on the blanket beneath him until he rolled to the side.

When he stared at her, she held up the edge of the blanket. "If you can behave yourself, slide under here so we both stay warm."

Tully thought it was the single worst idea he'd ever heard, but he couldn't tell her no. He didn't plan to stay there long anyway. As soon as Brianna fell asleep, he'd sit up and keep an eye on both her and Dale.

Slowly, he rolled beneath the blanket then slid an arm under her back, pulling her close to him. Her head rested in the curve of his shoulder while his hand settled at her waist. Content and strangely happy, he could have stayed in that position the rest of his life.

The faint fragrance of flowers tickled his nose while the amber glow from the fire turned Brianna's creamy skin into a temptation he found hard to resist.

As though she read his thoughts, she grasped at the thread of their maudlin conversation to take their minds off the attraction sizzling between them. "What happened to your family? Where were you before you met Thane and Maggie?"

The last thing Tully wanted to do was tell her about his past, but something about being with her, about staring up at the stars together, loosened his tongue and weakened his resolve.

"I was seven when both my folks died one winter of small pox. My sister, Becky, and I went to stay with a distant relative. I don't know if he was an uncle or cousin. We'd never seen him before, but he made us call him Uncle Blye. We only lived with him a few weeks before he started beating on us, and then he tried to… um… Becky was twelve, you see, and looked mature for her age. He um... he tried to…"

Brianna squeezed his hand and he cleared his throat. "I brained him with the bottle of whiskey he'd spent the evening drinking and the two of us ran into the nearest town. The pastor let us spend the night then took us to an orphanage the next day. We stayed there until Becky was eighteen. They forced her to choose between living on the streets, working in a brothel, or marrying a man who would pay the director of the orphanage a tidy sum for furnishing him with a young bride. She opted to marry. The beast who took her strangled my sister two days after they wed."

"Oh, Tully." Brianna's heart ached for the pain Tully had endured.

He swallowed hard before he continued. "When I found out she'd died, I wanted to kill that man with my bare hands. I might have done it, too. I ran away from the orphanage and headed over to the jail. Blinded by my grief and fury, I wasn't thinking straight. On my way there, a rancher stopped me and asked if I'd help him load his wagon with a shipment of lumber that had arrived on the train. I tried to refuse, but he insisted on me going with him. As I helped him load the lumber, I told him what had happened. When we finished, he paid me for my help and offered me a job. I worked on his ranch until I was fifteen."

"Why'd you leave? Did he treat you poorly?"

Tully glanced down at her, shifting slightly so she rested more comfortably against his shoulder. "No. He was good to me. From him, I learned about grace and forgiveness, and reacquainted myself with the Lord. That rancher treated me like a son, but then he died. His only child, a spoiled rotten girl who'd moved to the city, returned with her husband and took over the place. The new owners and I didn't see eye to eye on anything, so I left."

"Where did you go?" Brianna could picture a young Tully, putting up a brave, defiant front to hide the depths of his emotional wounds. To some degree, he still did the same thing.

"I wandered from town to town, working odd jobs. Then I ran into Thane and we became fast friends. Shortly after we met, we took up with Maggie and her husband, Daniel. We came to Oregon and that was that."

"But, Tully, you endured so much as a child and went through your adolescent years largely alone. How on earth did you become such a fine man?"

Pleased Brianna thought he was a good person, Tully tried to be, even if he sometimes fell short of the mark. "Maggie, Daniel, Thane and I were good for each other. We helped each other grow up and we knew with unwavering certainty we could count on each other. Thane's brother mostly raised him, and he was a wonderful person, or at least from what I've heard. Maggie and Daniel both had good parents. My parents were the best, they just passed away far too soon. I think all of us had a good foundation, even if life tossed us around a bit."

Brianna reached down and squeezed his hand where it rested at her waist. "They'd be so proud of you, Tully Barrett. Now tell me how you became the sheriff."

"Well, after Daniel was killed in a mining accident, I wasn't too interested in mining anymore. Thane begged me to continue for a little while longer. It wasn't long after Daniel died that we hit a rich vein of gold. Maggie and I sold our shares of the mine to Thane. She started her dress shop. I bought my place on the edge of town and went to work for the sheriff as a deputy. Thane kept mining. He bought the ground where the ranch house is and started purchasing more property and mines. He owns one of the largest spreads in the area, as well as gold mines and one silver mine. As for me, when the sheriff retired, I got his job."

"And you love every minute of it."

Tully's chuckle vibrated through her, making a sweet tremor pass over her. He assumed she was cold and cuddled her closer, tucking the blanket around her shoulders.

"Now that you know everything about me, I think it's your turn to divulge all your deep, dark secrets."

Brianna did not intend for Tully or anyone else to know the real reason she'd fled to Baker City, but she loved listening to his deep voice rumble in the stillness of the night and wanted to keep him talking.

"I told you my father passed away, didn't I?" she asked.

"Yep. You mentioned he died recently. You also said you needed to come up with some money to keep his cotton mill operating."

"That's correct. Father was robbed and brutally stabbed on his way to the bank." Brianna sniffled and willed her tears away.

"Oh, sweetheart, I'm sorry." Tully kissed the top of her head. "What happened?"

"The cotton mill has been in my family for four generations. It's been a very lucrative business, but Father ran into some financial hardships a few years ago. He borrowed heavily from the bank, worked hard to get things back on track, and began paying on the loan. The last year, he'd done so well, he'd saved enough to repay all the debt early and was on his way to make that final payment to the bank when someone robbed him and stabbed him to death."

"Brianna, that's terrible. Is there anything I can do to help? Did they catch his killer? Find the money?"

She shook her head. "Unfortunately, no. The man who killed him escaped and the payment wasn't made to the bank. I have until the first of August to make the payment or the bank will take the factory, my home, and all of Father's holdings."

"And that's why you were so dead-set on selling your father's partnership in Clive's mine."

"Yes, but you know how that turned out. The money I make at the paper would be only a tiny drop in the bucket of what is owed." She sighed. "I do so wish my bag would turn up."

Tully laughed softly. "Are you still thinking if you had those corsets you could get a job at the Gilded Spur?"

"No!" She jabbed an elbow into his side and he grunted. "You're positively detestable!"

"As long as we're both clear on that," he teased, trying to tickle her side. She didn't so much as move let alone giggle. "Don't tell me you're one of those people who aren't ticklish."

"I might be ticklish, but I won't tell you where."

Tully's breath blew across her cheek in tantalizing tendrils as he bent his head down close to her face. "I'll look forward to discovering that very spot one of these days."

She turned her head and attempted to glare, but his face was enticingly close to hers. "I don't know what sort of woman you think I am, Tully Barrett, but I'll have you know I don't…"

He silenced her with a tender kiss that effectively scattered her thoughts. Unable to recall what she meant to say, nothing else mattered except how wonderful she felt resting in Tully's strong arms against the solid warmth of him.

Twice more he tantalized her lips with his kisses before he lifted his head and smiled. "Close your eyes, Brianna. Close your eyes and relax. I'll keep you safe," he whispered and started to hum a lullaby she hadn't heard since before her mother died.

Content and at ease with Tully, she stared up at the stars, wishing on the brightest lights overhead. Wishing for a future with the man she loved with all her heart.

Sparks danced like fireflies in the midnight sky when Tully added a log on the fire. He poured a cup of coffee and nursed it as he watched Brianna sleep.

The glow of the fire highlighted her face as she rested on her side, snuggled beneath the blanket he'd tucked around her.

Once she closed her eyes, she'd fallen right to sleep. The sound of her soft, even breathing assured him she slept, so he carefully moved his arm and rolled away from her.

The temptation to hold her all night was almost more than he could bear. Nippy night air did little to cool his feverish longing for her, but it wasn't the time or place to make any declarations.

As she spoke about her father and his brutal death, Tully knew she still hadn't told him the whole story. Miss Brianna Dumont was hiding something. He wouldn't rest until he found out what, exactly, had driven her from her home, chasing the hope of a prosperous mine clear across the country.

Something about her father's death seemed strange and he planned to find out what.

For now, though, he studied the sweet way Brianna's lips turned up at the corners and her eyelashes fanned her smooth cheeks.

Never, in all his life, had Tully wanted a woman like he wanted her. He'd never even imagined wanting someone so much it made his heart ache with every beat. The yearning for her wasn't just a physical longing.

Something about her spoke to his heart, whispered to his soul, and connected them in ways he couldn't begin to fathom. A part of him felt like he'd known her forever. In other ways, he felt a brand-new excitement bubbling in him every time he saw her.

Earlier, when she cuddled close to him as they stared at the stars, Tully experienced the sensation of finally coming home. Brianna was the place he'd been searching to find. Although he'd set down roots in Baker City, his heart had been waiting for her to come along to claim its home.

Not that he'd spent a lot of time dreaming of a wife, but Brianna was nothing like the vision he'd pictured for a spouse. He always assumed he'd remain free and unfettered, but after Thane married Jemma, Tully realized he wanted a love like the two of them shared.

Doubtful he'd ever find true love, he'd offered to marry Maggie when she seemed so lost and heartbroken in the spring. Wisely, she turned him down and gave her heart to Ian.

Tully grinned as he thought of how hard he'd worked to make Ian jealous and convince him he had plans to wed Maggie. Thane teased him about getting a job with a traveling theatrical company based on his performance. Proud of how well he'd played the part of an enamored suitor, he realized he really was one when it came to the woman sleeping a few feet away from him.

Brianna arrived in town a spoiled, demanding, snobbish thorn in his side. Now, he'd do anything for her, to keep her safe and protected. He'd been amazed how quickly she'd dropped her pretentious demeanor, at least with everyone but him, and adapted to life in Baker City.

A chuckle almost worked its way free of his chest as he recalled catching her muttering about how thoroughly she despised the privy behind Maggie's shop. There wasn't any doubt in his mind that Brianna was accustomed to a life of lavishness.

Tully shook his head. What did he have to offer a woman like Brianna Dumont, other than his heart? It seemed precious little compared to the wealth and luxury to which she was accustomed.

As dawn approached, Tully made a fresh pot of coffee then checked on his prisoner. Dale spent most of the night snoring like a bear in a beehive.

To shake off his melancholy thoughts and awaken himself, Tully splashed cold creek water on his face and neck, and breathed in the fresh morning air. Alone, he spent a few quiet moments sending up prayers, grateful to greet another new day. When he returned to the fire, Brianna sat on her knees, rubbing the sleep from her eyes.

"Mornin', Fred," he said, walking up behind her.

The look she tossed over her shoulder made him want to kiss her in the worst way, but he tamped down the urge. Instead, he handed her a piece of jerky and took one for himself.

"How far are we from town?" she asked, getting to her feet, although she kept the blanket wrapped around her shoulders for warmth.

"It'll probably take us about an hour and a half, maybe two to get back to town. As soon as sleeping beauty wakes up, we'll head out." Tully tipped his head toward the tree where he'd tied Dale.

Brianna grinned and took a sip of the coffee from the cup Tully handed to her. "I thought perhaps some wild animal had wandered into our camp for all the noise he produces in his slumber."

Tully grinned and took the cup back when she held it out to him. "At first I thought the racket came from a moose in mating season, but it's just him." He handed Brianna a few more pieces of jerky with a grin.

While she ate her meager breakfast, Brianna folded the blanket then walked away from the camp.

"Be careful and don't get lost," Tully called after her.

"I'm perfectly capable of finding my way back," she said, insulted he thought she might lose her way in broad daylight.

On her way back from taking care of her personal needs, Brianna stopped to wash her hands and face at the creek. The frigid temperature of the water made her draw in a sharp breath. At the same time, the crisp air and cold water left her invigorated.

She rocked back on her heels and stared at her likeness in the clear water of the creek. At the mussed reflection, she finger-combed her hair and braided it again. The wrinkles in her clothes, though, were beyond her ability to repair without a hot iron.

Determined not to give her disheveled appearance another thought, she looked around, admiring the lush grass surrounding her and the scent of pine in the air.

Her gaze drifted across the creek. The pair of beady little eyes watching her forced a scream out of her throat, breaching the morning stillness.

With another shrill scream, she scrambled to her feet and ran toward camp. Turning to glance over her shoulder, she collided with a solid form.

Tully wrapped his hands around her arms as he caught her, worry etching lines between his eyebrows. "What is it, darlin'? What happened?"

"There's some horrid creature over there." Brianna pointed to the creek.

Much to her dismay, he led her back to the bank.

He looked around then pointed to a spot several feet up the creek. "That's just a muskrat, Fred. No need to carry on like he's the harbinger of death and destruction. You probably scared the little critter more than he did you."

Brianna shuddered at the sight of the rodent's furless, scaly tail. "I highly doubt that." Covered in thick brown fur, the muskrat pushed webbed feet in the water as it swam away from them.

"What's all the ruction, Sheriff?" Dale called from his spot at the tree.

Tully laced his fingers with Brianna's as they walked back to the camp. "Dale ought to thank you for screaming. If it hadn't brought him awake, I was ready to fill the coffeepot with creek water and pour it over his head."

"Maybe you should do that anyway," Brianna whispered as they stepped into the clearing.

Dale looked their way and she giggled while Tully chuckled. "Maybe I will."

Brianna poured the last of the coffee into the tin cup then rinsed the pot while Tully untied Dale and took him into the bushes.

When they returned, Tully gave his prisoner a piece of jerky and the cup of coffee. While Dale complained about the empty hole in his belly that the coffee and jerky didn't fill, Tully watered the horses then saddled the ones they planned to ride.

Loco snorted and stomped when Dale moved too close to him. The rustler frantically scrambled away from the horse, tripping in the process.

Tully lifted him by the back of his collar and unceremoniously plopped him on his mount. After he tied his hands and feet, he helped Brianna mount her horse then handed her the lead ropes for the two horses she'd led the previous day.

"Let's go," he said as he mounted Cotton and led their little procession in the direction of town.

An hour later, he detoured through the trees and rode into the back of a property Brianna thought she recognized from the previous day.

A man waved and hurried their direction when they neared the barn.

"Well, I'll be, Tully. You said you wouldn't come home without the rustler, and there you are. Which one of you has the beautiful accomplice?"

Tully stepped out of the saddle and grinned. "Luden Scott, this is Brianna Dumont. She's a nosy newspaper reporter who wanted first dibs on the horse rustler story." Tully winked at Brianna. "Miss Dumont, meet Luden Scott. He's one of the finest horse trainers I've ever met and he's been trying to work some of the crazy out of ol' Loco."

"You obviously have your work cut out for you, Mr. Scott. I wish you all the best in your endeavors," she said, smiling at the cowboy.

"I'll need all the help I can get with Loco. He is one thick-headed ol' son of a gun." Luden took the lead ropes from Brianna while Tully led Loco to the corral. "I appreciate you finding my horses while you were rescuing Loco."

"It's the least I can do," Tully said, turning his horse loose with the others. Loco bucked a few times before running around the enclosure and stopping on the far side. "Hopefully, we won't have any more problems with horses disappearing around here."

"Except for that one." Luden pointed to Dale as he tried to ride off unseen. He'd only gone a few yards when Brianna grabbed his reins, putting a swift end to his attempt to flee.

"That boy seems to have more rocks rolling around in his head than brains." Tully shook Luden's hand then swung back onto Cotton. He took the reins to Dale's horse from Brianna and grinned at his friend. "Thanks again, Luden. I'll stop by soon to see how Loco's progressing."

"Be sure you do." Luden tipped his hat to Brianna. "It was a pleasure to meet you, ma'am."

"You as well, Mr. Scott. Have a pleasant day."

Luden smiled. "I plan to, Miss Dumont. Safe travels back to town."

With only Dale's horse to lead, Tully set a faster pace as they rode to Baker City. It was nearly nine when he stopped in front of the jail. Deputy Harter ran out to greet them, taking over the duty of shoving Dale into a jail cell.

Sore from riding and weary from her adventures, Brianna wanted to take a bath, eat a hot meal then sleep for several hours.

First, she had to muster enough energy to swing her leg over the back of the horse. Tully came to her rescue, grasping her waist in his hands and lifting her out of the saddle before setting her on her feet.

"You go on home, Fred. I'll take care of returning your horse to Milt and explain why you didn't bring him back yesterday." Aware of many sets of eyes watching them, Tully handed Brianna the bag that contained her notebook and raised his voice just enough those intently listening could hear. "It was a surprise to run into you on the trail this morning. Next time you decide to go for a sunrise ride, be sure you let someone know where you're heading. You might not be so lucky next time to encounter a handsome man of the law."

Befuddled by his words, Brianna gave him a confused look then noticed the crowd gathering around them. Mindful of Tully's attempt to salvage her reputation, she glared at him. "If I happen to encounter such a man, I'll be sure to let you know." The clipped tone of her voice and curt nod of her head led those around them to believe she still loathed the sheriff.

A few of the men chuckled while some of the women smiled as she stalked away from him, heading in the direction of Maggie's shop and her apartment.

With no time to watch her walk away, Tully focused on the business of contacting a U.S. Marshal to take Dale Darcey off his hands.

Chapter Twelve

Throughout town, people talked about the newspaper article Brianna wrote detailing Dale Darcey's arrest. She'd even managed to get a quote from Thane and his mine manager, Mr. Gaffney, about Dale's role in leaving them stranded at the mine in November.

She'd wanted to make Tully sound like the champion she believed him to be, but stuck to reporting the facts. If others called him a hero, it wasn't because she'd created any bias in his favor. Although she maintained her pretense that she and Tully were still at odds, she was pleased so many of the townspeople respected and admired the sheriff.

He worked hard to keep the town safe and peaceable, and deserved whatever praise they cast his way.

Bowen Packwood had danced an excited little jig in his office when Brianna turned in the story. He'd been so happy with her article, he generously told her she could write an article about any topic of her choosing and he'd publish it.

While she considered penning something about summer fashions or the Eastern Star Lodge's pie social, she mulled over her options. Whatever she wrote, she wanted it to impact their readers.

Unbeknownst to Tully, Brianna also wrote an article about her experience with an old West lawman in tracking down a wanted criminal. She painted pictures with her words of the beautiful scenery and described the scent of the trees and the brisk fresh air. In detail, she observed the western lifestyle of which many people only dreamed remained alive and well in Eastern Oregon. With her heart wide open, she allowed herself to write about Tully through the eyes of love.

When she finished, she signed it B.E. Dumont and mailed it off to a newspaper in New York, hoping they would be interested in publishing the article.

A week later, she received a telegram from the paper. The editor was thrilled with her submission and wired her a bank draft for an amount that made her read it twice to make sure she wasn't mistaken.

The paper promised to mail her copies of the article and encouraged her to send more submissions in the future.

An idea for a series of stories, based on Tully and his adventures, niggled the back of her mind until she'd considered asking if he'd be willing to join forces with her.

Consumed with her ponderings of how best to broach the subject with him, Brianna wandered down the main street of town, glancing in store windows and wishing for a breeze to dispel the relentless summer heat. After the snowstorm, the weather turned blistering hot, making for miserable afternoons and stuffy evenings.

Without paying any mind to where she walked, Brianna stepped into the street as Mr. Bentley drove by on the sprinkler wagon. The old man drove the wagon shaped like a barrel up and down the streets of town in the summer, sprinkling water to keep down the dust.

Heedless to anything around her, Brianna just happened to be in the line of fire as water sprayed across the street. Dust stirred up by the wheels of the wagon and the horses coated the pale-yellow fabric of her gown, clinging to every drop of water soaking into her skirt.

"Oh, gracious!" she said, stepping onto the boardwalk and glancing at the old man who cackled from his seat high on top of the barrel.

"Stay out of the way, missy, or you'll turn into a mud pie."

Incensed, she glowered at his back as he continued on his way. "What a contemptible…"

A familiar baritone behind her made her jump. "Now, Fred, you be nice to Mr. Bentley. If it wasn't for him, the dust on the streets would be a foot deep." Tully grinned at her as he glanced down at her soggy, soiled skirt. "Maybe next time you should pay attention to where you're headed."

Since he was right, she refrained from saying anything. Instead, she turned and walked toward her apartment so she could change. Tully fell into step beside her.

"If you'd stop racing off in a huff, I have a question for you," Tully said in a hushed tone as they walked past a group of women in front of the Crystal Palace, a shop specializing in items for the home. Lamps, clocks, and gleaming china glistened in the window.

"What is it?" Brianna asked, slowing her step although she didn't turn to look at Tully. If she did, she might surrender to the need to be back in his arms. Since the night he'd held her beneath the stars, she'd wished a thousand times he'd hold her like that again.

"The Fourth of July festivities are tomorrow and I wanted to invite you to share lunch with me."

He appeared to struggle to get the words out. The self-assured sheriff couldn't be nervous about inviting her to accompany him to the festivities — could he?

Fires, floods, rabid beasts, and bloodthirsty raiders would have to descend on the town all at once to keep her from going with him, but she didn't want to agree too quickly. "What transpires during the festivities?"

"There are contests and speeches, and a community picnic. Some people set up booths to sell trinkets and such. At dusk, there's a big fireworks show that's quite something to see." Tully looked both ways along the street and noticed a few people watching them. He tugged Brianna around the corner into an alley. The shadows of the buildings hid them from prying eyes. "Please, Brianna, say you'll go with me."

As though he needed to give her a reason to say yes, he brushed his thumb over the curve of her cheek and along her jaw, turning her knees and resistance to mush.

Unable to speak as his fingers trailed along the exposed skin of her throat, she mutely nodded her head.

"I'll stop by Maggie's shop for you at ten. Would that be agreeable to you?" Tully's eyes burned into hers, but he took a step back.

Finally finding her voice, she nodded again. "That would be fine, Sheriff."

"Good." He disappeared around the back corner of the building, leaving her alone.

Brianna leaned against the side of the furniture store, willing her heart to settle back into a regular beat and her legs to return to normal. It took a few moments before she was convinced she could walk without looking like a stumbling drunk and continue the rest of the way back to her apartment.

After changing her gown, she decided to go to the park and sit in the shade of the trees where she hoped to find relief from the heat. As she relaxed on a bench and watched children play, a wiggling presence slid close to her. She smiled down at Sammy.

"Hello, Sammy. I haven't seen you for a few days. Are you well?"

The boy nodded, but looked sad.

"Is everything okay at home? Is there something I can do to help you?"

Sammy shook his head then leaned against Brianna, as though in need of a comforting touch. Without hesitation, she wrapped an arm around the child's thin shoulders and pulled him against her.

"If you decide you need my help with anything, Sammy, please come find me anytime."

He sniffled once and closed his eyes. Only a few moments passed until little puffs of air coming from his mouth indicated he slept. Brianna removed his dusty cap and settled him on the bench so his head rested on her lap.

Tenderly, she brushed the hair from his face. She studied the freckles on his stubby little nose and a smudge of dirt on the stubborn chin.

She must remember to ask Tully what he knew of Sammy and his family. Although she meant to inquire many times, she always got distracted around the sheriff.

Quietly, Brianna opened the notebook she'd brought along and worked on a story for Mr. Packwood about the creamery in town opening a new cheese division. She'd sampled some of the cheese and it was delicious.

Thoughts of food made her question what she could contribute to the community potluck the following day. Any attempts on her part to make something would result in her unintentionally poisoning someone if she didn't burn down Maggie's shop in the process.

No, the best plan was to purchase something someone else had made, but she had no idea what it would be. She finally decided to visit the bakery just down the street from her apartment and see what they might have available.

Sammy stirred and sat up, rubbing his eyes and yawning. Suddenly, he realized he'd used Brianna for a pillow.

He started to run off, but she grabbed his hand before he made an escape. "Sammy, I need to go to the bakery. Would you like to accompany me?"

Eagerly nodding his head, the boy snatched his flat cap from where Brianna had set it on the bench and tugged it on, then grasped her hand in his, pulling on it.

She laughed and tucked her notebook and pencil back into her bag. Quickly rising to her feet, she held Sammy's hand as they made their way through the park to the bakery.

Delicious, yeasty scents greeted them at the door, mingling with the mouth-watering aromas of cinnamon and chocolate.

Sammy glanced up at Brianna and grinned, pointing to display cases full of pastries, miniature pies, cakes, sweet breads, and cookies. A shelf behind the front counter held jar after jar of colorful candy. It looked as if a sugary rainbow had burst and been captured in the shiny glass containers.

"What would you like, Sammy?" Brianna asked as they walked around the displays. The boy wavered between a display case full of cookies and one holding slices of cake. Finally, he pointed to a piece of chocolate cake with a thick layer of frosting.

"We'd like two pieces of chocolate cake, a glass of milk, and a cup of tea," Brianna said, smiling at the woman behind the counter. Brianna also paid for six dozen assorted cookies, asking to have them boxed up to take with her.

Sammy plopped down at a small table by the front window and dug into his cake. The child appeared to relish every bite, and Brianna wondered again about his home life. Although he wasn't starving, Sammy always seemed hungry and there was a fearful, lonely light that lingered in his blue eyes.

After he finished his cake and guzzled his milk, Brianna took one last bite of hers then slid the cake across the table. "Would you like to finish mine, Sammy? I'm still rather full from lunch."

Immediately picking up his fork, Sammy made short work of the cake then finished his milk. Brianna sipped her tea then smiled as the clerk carried over the box of cookies and took their dirty dishes from the table.

"Thank you for joining me, Sammy. It's no fun to eat alone, so your company is much appreciated." Sammy grinned and stood as Brianna rose and pulled her gloves back on her hands.

The little boy started to lift the heavy box of cookies for her, but Brianna took it. Sammy rushed to open the bakery door and hold it for her as she stepped outside.

Brianna smiled. "Those are lovely manners you have, Sammy. Be a good boy and enjoy the rest of your day. I'll plan to see you at the park tomorrow."

The boy nodded and waved before racing down the street and disappearing around the corner of the saddle shop.

The next morning, Brianna ate a leisurely breakfast of sugar sprinkled on slices of buttered bread and a glass of cold tea. She took her time dressing in a white gown made of light lawn fabric. Carefully styling her hair, she settled a smart straw hat adorned with blues roses and ribbons on her head. Tipping it at a saucy angle, she fastened it with a hatpin, gathered her reticule, parasol, and the box of cookies before she made her way down the stairs.

Her foot reached the bottom step at the same moment Tully knocked. She set the cookies on a small table, turned the lock and opened the door.

"Hello, Sheriff. You're right on time." Brianna smiled, taking in Tully from the spotless hat on his head to the toes of his recently polished boots. He'd trimmed the stubble on his face so it looked almost newly sprouted. The crisp white shirt he wore with a dark blue vest accented the tan of his skin and the breadth of his shoulders.

Admiration for the man filled Brianna as she forced her gaze to move from his chest back up to his face. For the briefest moment, she indulged in the luxury of studying his sculpted lips, recalling how much she'd enjoyed his kisses.

The light flickering in his eyes drew her in, but she tamped down her interest and moved to pick up the box of cookies.

"Let me get that," Tully said, taking the box from her then holding out his arm.

Gingerly, she placed her hand on it, anticipating the tingle that would trail up her arm at the contact.

Ignoring it, she closed the door and opened her parasol. "Lead the way, Sheriff."

Tully grinned and sauntered down the alley in the direction of the park. "What's it gonna take for you to start calling me Tully? You didn't seem to have any problem calling me by my given name the night you spent in my arms."

Terrified someone might overhear the conversation, Brianna glanced around.

Tully chuckled. "Oh, stop fussing, Fred. No one's listening. Besides, you're too fine a lady for anyone to believe you discuss your unmentionables with me on a fairly regular basis."

Her face bloomed with color and her gaze held an icy frost when she glared at him. "You're impossible and…"

"Save your breath, darlin'. I already know what you think of me," Tully said, offering her a roguish wink as they neared the park. "What would you like to do first?"

Brianna tipped her head toward the tables set up to hold the food. "We should leave the cookies on the dessert table then perhaps we could stroll among the booths."

"Did you make the cookies?" Tully took her elbow in his hand as he guided her through the crowd to the food tables.

She glanced at him over her shoulder and grinned. "You didn't see smoke rolling out of Maggie's place, did you? If I'd done the baking, something would have caught fire."

Tully's smile faded as he set down the box and they strolled toward the booths. "You can't cook? Not at all?"

"I can make toast and tea." As she studied a booth with a display of small flags, she missed the disappointed look on his face.

"This won't work, Fred, not at all." Tully stepped away from her.

"What won't work?" Baffled, she had no idea to what he referred.

"Us. This. I can't be seen around a woman who doesn't know one end of a frying pan from the other." He took another step back. "A woman of your beauty and brains is a great temptation, but all deals are off if you can't cook."

For a moment, she almost believed his teasing then she noted the mischief in his eyes and the way his mouth twitched at the corners as he fought down a smile.

Amused, she turned her back to him and strolled to the next booth. His long strides quickly placed him at her side as she looked over an assortment of embroidered handkerchiefs.

"I thought you'd decided to find someone who knew how to cook, Sheriff." She lifted a beautiful linen square decorated with a bouquet of forget-me-nots in one corner.

"I reckon I might as well stick with you, at least for today."

Brianna offered him a wry smile and quirked an eyebrow upward. "That's quite generous of you. If you see a girl more to your liking, by all means, chase after her with my blessing." She set down the handkerchief and turned to scan the people filling the park.

"How about her?" Discreetly, Brianna pointed to a young woman who stood out in a canary yellow gown and hat. "She seems rather flamboyant. Is that more to your liking?"

"No, she certainly is not. I'll have you know she works at Zed's... Never mind where she works, but no, she is not more to my liking." Tully offered her his arm again and they continued meandering through the booths.

"What about her?" Brianna tipped her head to a booth selling boxes of chocolates. A portly girl purchased a box and ripped off the lid, stuffing her mouth full of the candy in a most undignified manner.

Tully scoffed. "Now who's being mean?" he asked.

"Point taken." Brianna glanced around. "That one, over there."

He followed the direction of her gaze, watching old Mrs. Jepson teeter across the park, leaning heavily on her cane.

Brianna giggled. "I'm sure she knows how to cook."

His only response was a noise that sounded like a growl.

With a broad smile, she pointed to a head full of strawberry-blond curls. "There is the perfect girl for you, Sheriff. She's always game for an adventure and has told me she might marry you when she grows up, if she doesn't join the circus. I know for a fact she can make a lovely mud pie."

Lily Jordan squealed and ran their direction, launching herself into Tully's arms. He swung her around and kissed her rosy cheek before the little girl grinned at Brianna.

"Hi, Miss Dumont."

"Happy Fourth of July to you, Lily. Did you just arrive?" Brianna asked then turned to smile at Lily's parents and brother.

"Jack and Lily barely waited for the buckboard to stop moving before they jumped down. They've been excited for days to come to town for this," Jemma said, giving Brianna's hand a squeeze. "Did we miss anything exciting?"

"Not yet," Tully said, motioning for their group to claim a few empty chairs in front of a podium where the mayor and other dignitaries were about to offer speeches.

As soon as the last speaker finished, Pastor Eagan asked a blessing on the community meal and the picnic began.

Jemma brought along blankets for everyone to sit on. Thane and Tully spread them in the shade of a tree then took the children to fill their plates. Jemma and Brianna greeted Maggie and Ian when they arrived.

"You missed the speeches," Jemma said, hugging Maggie.

"And for that, I'm most grateful," Ian teased. "The mayor and his cronies blow more wind than a broken set of bagpipes."

Edwin Greenfield chuckled and the women rolled their eyes as they made their way to the food line.

Brianna glanced down when someone bumped into her and smiled into Sammy's face. The little boy seemed particularly excited as he waited for his turn to fill the tin plate he held in his hand. At the curious glances of Jemma and the others, Brianna introduced the child to them. When Sammy looked around for a place to eat, Brianna put a hand to his shoulder. "Please sit with us, Sammy."

He nodded and followed her over to the quilts where Thane and Tully sat with Jack and Lily.

The two children grinned as Sammy sat down close to them. "Sammy, this is Jack and Lily." Brianna patted Sammy's back and smiled at the other two children. "Sammy doesn't talk, but he manages quite well to express himself."

The little boy gave her a warm smile then bit into a piece of crispy fried chicken.

The variety of tasty food made Brianna want to eat with as little restraint as the girl with the box of chocolates. Instead, she maintained a perfect posture and took small bites, as she'd been taught from the time she was younger than Lily.

The women sat together, discussing flowers, fashions, and the fact the Greenfields had decided to stay in town and run the boarding house. They'd signed the paperwork making the purchase and their ownership official the previous day.

Jemma and Maggie offered to help Hattie clean it, so Brianna volunteered her services, too. She knew only marginally more about cleaning than she did cooking, but it sounded like a fun day she could spend with her friends.

"Congratulations on your new venture," Brianna said, offering Hattie a warm smile. "If you and Mr. Greenfield are in agreement, I'd be happy to write an article about the boarding house now being under your capable ownership and management."

"That would be wonderful and very much appreciated, Miss Dumont." Hattie returned her smile.

"Please, it's Brianna. Just tell me when you're ready, and I'll come for an interview."

Hattie nodded in agreement. "Perhaps sometime soon, after we've had an opportunity to clean and spruce the place up a bit. Edwin already hired painters to give the outside a fresh coat and I wanted you girls to share your thoughts on the wallpaper in the hallway and parlor. I think it needs to be replaced, but Edwin thought it might be repaired."

"It sounds like you have many plans for it." Brianna smiled at the older woman.

"Plans for what?" Tully asked as he turned his attention from the men's discussion to Brianna.

"The boardinghouse. You know Mr. and Mrs. Greenfield purchased it, didn't you?"

"I did know that, Fred. Are you gonna write a story about it?" he asked as he snitched half a buttered biscuit off her plate. She glared at him and moved her food out of his reach.

Neither of them noticed the pleased, knowing glance that passed between Jemma and Maggie.

"That is my intention, Sheriff." Brianna lifted her chin in the direction of the food tables. "I suggest, sir, if you are still hungry you refill your plate instead of stealing my food."

"Well, shoot!" Tully winked at the children and grabbed the chicken leg Brianna had yet to taste. "It's so much more fun to torment you than go stand in line."

Lily and Jack laughed while Sammy's little shoulders shook with mirth.

Brianna released a beleaguered sigh, but smacked Tully's hand when he tried to pilfer a strawberry off her plate.

"You are a miserly, mean woman, Brianna Dumont." Tully's dimpled smile softened his words as he rose to his feet and sauntered over to the food table. The children hopped up and accompanied him.

Brianna watched him walk away, taking in every nuance of his gait, the way his trousers fit his long, muscled legs, and how bereft she felt with him gone.

"August or September?" Maggie asked Jemma.

"August," Jemma said.

Hattie smiled and all three women looked to Brianna. She dragged her gaze away from Tully and noticed them studying her. "August? What's happening in August?"

"Your wedding to Tully, of course."

It was a good thing Brianna hadn't taken a bite of something because she would have spewed it out in a most unladylike manner.

Her mouth hung open as she gaped at her friends. "Has the heat baked your brains? I'm not marrying Tully Barrett. The man is an insufferable, uncouth, deplorable beast."

Maggie grinned and turned back to Jemma. "Definitely August."

Brianna was still spluttering indignantly when Tully and the children returned. He placed a piece of chicken on her plate, along with a slice of cake before focusing his attention on the youngsters. The silly questions he asked them had them all laughing.

After everyone had eaten their fill, contests began throughout the park. There were games for the children and competitions for the men.

A roped off area at the back of the park drew many spectators. In the center of the square area was a pile of rocks, several sledgehammers, and a large gathering of men. The few women in the crowd stood out with parasols held over their heads, keeping the hot sun from beating down on them.

Jemma and Hattie stayed to watch the children play games, but Maggie and Brianna accompanied the men.

"What is this?" Brianna asked, watching as one man knelt by a large rock with a tool in his hand that a second man hit with a heavy hammer. Every time he struck, the man holding the tool would turn it slightly, as though they bore into the rock.

"It's a rock drilling contest," Tully explained. "You've read about sinking shafts and driving tunnels, I assume?"

Brianna nodded. "It requires explosives."

"That's right. A series of holes are drilled into the rock. The holes are then loaded with explosives and detonated. The debris is cleared out, the opening trimmed to size, and support timbers installed. Then the drillers start all over again."

"I read about the process, but I didn't realize drilling the holes was such laborious work."

"It is, and it can be dangerous, too." Thane added. "The drill is basically a steel rod that has a flared chisel-shaped tip so the hole is slightly larger in diameter than the rod, allowing the bit to be withdrawn."

"How does this two-man operation work?" Brianna asked, fascinated by the method.

"Cornish miners brought the process to our country," Thane explained. "One man holds and turns the drill, changing it out when the bit gets dull, while the other wields a sledgehammer. That's what they're doing here. The team that makes the hole the fastest without cracking their rock wins."

They watched two teams compete then Tully grinned at his long-time friend. "What do you say, Thane? We used to be pretty good at this"

"I might be a little out of practice." Thane smirked at Tully. "But that never stopped me before."

Thane removed his vest, tie, and hat, handing them to Maggie, while Tully handed his things to Brianna. The urge to bury her hands in the thick waves of his hair made her fingers itch, but she resisted.

"Are you sure you want to do this?" Maggie asked, glancing from Tully to Thane. While both were in prime physical condition, neither of them swung the heavy sledgehammer on a daily basis.

"Ach, lassie, let 'em have at it," Ian said, reverting to his brogue as he watched the proceedings with excited interest. "If the two eejits want to pretend they're still young, fit, and handsome like me, don't stand in their way."

Thane and Tully both scowled at Ian while Brianna and Maggie laughed.

"Do you want to hammer or hold?" Thane asked when it was their turn.

"I always had better aim than you," Tully said, picking up the sledgehammer.

Thane lifted a drill from the pile and set the bit against a rock. "Fine, but you better not smash my hand. My wife would be quite put out with you."

Tully looked over at the three judges who sat in chairs nearby then glanced down at Thane. When his friend nodded, Tully hefted the hammer and swung, hitting the drill dead center. Quickly, Thane rotated the drill and Tully hit it with consistency.

As the two men worked in harmony, Brianna couldn't move her gaze from Tully. The fabric of his shirt stretched taut across his chest and shoulders. With each swing of the heavy hammer, the muscles of his arms flexed.

Entranced as she imagined what it would be like to watch him without his shirt on, her cheeks seared with heat.

She waved Tully's hat in front of her face to create a breeze and ignored the nudge Maggie gave her as he swung the hammer again and again.

"I'd forgotten how much fun it is to watch them," Maggie said, wrapping her hand around Ian's arm.

"They are a well-matched pair, for certain," Ian observed, cheering loudly when Tully's last strike finished the hole they drilled into the rock.

"You're slowing down, old man," Thane taunted Tully as they wiped sweat from their faces and retrieved their vests, ties, and hats from the women.

"Me? You were barely keeping up. Jemma might need to put you out to pasture." Tully grunted when Thane's elbow connected with his side in a playful jab.

"I think ye both did verra well, considering ye don't do that sort of work every day." Ian shook both their hands then they all watched as another team competed in the contest.

The competition ended with Thane and Tully taking second place to a pair of young men who'd recently moved to the area.

"I knew you're getting too old to do this sort of thing," Tully goaded Thane after they accepted their award.

"Me? I'm not the one with all the gray hair." Thane gave Tully's head a pointed look.

Tully's eyes narrowed and he yanked the hat off Thane's head full of thick hair. "At least I'm not going bald." He tapped his friend on the top of his head then snickered when Thane reached up a hand and slapped his hat back down.

"That's enough, you two. You're worse than a bunch of bickering dunderheads," Maggie said. She led the way back to where Jemma and the Greenfields watched the children play from the shade of the quilts beneath the tree.

"What did you two do?" Jemma asked, startled by Thane and Tully's overheated appearances.

"We joined in a friendly little competition," Thane said, plopping down beside his wife.

"And we would have won if this decrepit old fogy could have hustled a little faster." Tully stretched out on the blanket.

Thane laughed. "It wouldn't have mattered how fast I went when our winning depended on this lazy ol' cuss moving with more speed and agility than a half-blind, rheumatic granny."

"Rather than listen to these two toss insults back and forth, I'm going to get some ice cream," Maggie said, tugging on Ian's hand. "And you're buying."

"Yes, my bossy lass." Ian grinned and followed Maggie over to a booth.

The remainder of the afternoon and early evening passed pleasantly among the friends. At one point, Brianna thought she recognized someone in the crowd from her life in Rhode Island, but decided that was preposterous. No one knew where to find her and the one person who cared enough to search for her was dead.

Chasing away her sad thoughts, she rejoined the lively conversation taking place among her friends. As soon as dusk settled, they watched the brilliant sparks of fireworks fill the sky.

Lily shrieked and covered her ears at the first explosion. Once Thane convinced her the world wasn't about to end, she sat between Jack and Sammy, watching the colorful bursts overheard.

Surprised Sammy stayed with them most of the day, Brianna wondered if the boy would be missed by his family.

Once the fireworks ended, the crowd dispersed, prepared to go home. Brianna looked around for Sammy, but the child had already disappeared.

"May I walk you home, Miss Dumont?" Tully asked, bending down so his breath blew warm and soft across her ear.

The hint of mint made her smile. "You may, Sheriff."

Brianna wasn't in a hurry for the evening to end, so she slowly meandered through the park with Tully at her side. He kept his hands in his pockets as they walked and seemed lost in his thoughts.

"Do you know anything about Sammy?" Brianna asked as they turned onto the street where Maggie's shop was located.

"Not much. I first noticed him around town in late spring. Other than the fact that Sammy seems to spend a lot of time wandering around town and occasionally works for Bowen, that's the extent of my knowledge." Tully studied her. "Why? You're not planning on writing an article about him, too, are you?"

"No, don't be ridiculous," Brianna said, turning down the alley that would take them to the back door of the shop. "I'm merely curious. Sammy seems so forlorn sometimes, and hungry. He's most always hungry."

"I've yet to meet a boy who didn't have at least one hollow leg." Tully guided her around a drunk who'd fallen asleep at the back of the alley. He frowned at the man, planning to roust him on his way back to the park. Celebrations like Independence Day meant he had a long night of work ahead of him.

"Apparently, you never grew out of that stage," Brianna observed dryly as she took a key from her reticule and unlocked the back door. "Is that why you prefer a woman who cooks to any other type?"

Tully followed her inside and closed the door, drawing a startled glance from her. "I prefer a woman with a sharp mind who isn't afraid to speak her opinions, stand up for what she believes in, and mothers sad little boys."

He looked at her with such a soft, tender expression on his face, Brianna wondered how her heart could continue to function when it felt entirely melted.

One step brought him close enough that she could see embers burning in his eyes. A second step put him so near, the heat of his presence encircled her as he stared at her.

"You're the type of woman I prefer, Brianna. And I don't give a flying fritter if you can cook or not."

The sound of his deep voice saying her name made it difficult for her to remain upright as her legs quaked.

Unsettled, she would have moved away from him, but he wrapped a brawny arm around her waist and drew her flush against him.

"In case I wasn't clear earlier, I like you. You're beautiful, intelligent, kind to everyone but me, and full of sass and pluck."

Brianna watched his enticing lips move as he spoke, more interested in them pressing against hers than anything he said. "Pluck," she muttered as she mentally braced herself for the impact of his kiss.

He lifted her up until their lips met in a fiery, heated clash that sent her senses reeling.

"Tully," she whispered, knocking off his hat and trailing her hands through his hair.

What might have happened next would remain a mystery. Shots sounded from down the street and Tully lifted his head with a sigh.

"There are moments I purely hate my job." He touched his forehead to hers then kissed her cheek. "Right now is one of them."

He set her down and picked his hat up off the floor, settling it on his head. With one last quick peck to her lips, he opened the back door then glanced at her. "I enjoyed spending the day with you, Fred. Be a good girl and don't open this door tonight for any reason."

"I won't, Tully. Thank you for today." Brianna reached out and squeezed his hand as more shots rang out. "Please be careful."

"Always," Tully said with a cocky grin then ran down the alley. Brianna watched until he disappeared around the corner before shutting the door and locking it.

Her heart floated on air as she made her way upstairs to her apartment, convinced Tully cared for her, at least a fraction of how much she cared for him.

Tully raced down the street toward one of the busy saloons. As soon as he found the muttonhead who started shooting up the town, the idiot would wish he'd stayed sober or remained at home.

Accustomed to being called to duty at all hours of the day or night, Tully had never courted a woman before. The longing to turn around and rush back to Brianna was one of the reasons why he'd avoided getting involved with a female.

At that moment, he cared more about lingering in her embrace, blending his mouth with hers in fervent kisses, than he did about the drunks having a high time in his town.

That kind of thinking could cloud his judgment and get someone killed.

Before he reached the saloon, Tully stopped and drew in a series of long, cleansing breaths. He had to cool his yearning for Brianna and clear thoughts of how much he was coming to care for her from his mind.

Later, after the troublemakers were gone or locked up for the night, he'd think about the flirty banter they'd exchanged, the flames that had flickered in her beautiful blue eyes, and how much he wanted to spend every day with her beside him.

For now, though, he had a job to do.

Swiftly pulling his gun from the holster at his hip, he pushed open the door to the saloon and focused on restoring order.

Chapter Thirteen

"If you don't hurry it up, it'll be hotter than the blacksmith's bellows out there. The berry bushes don't care if your bow is tied just so, or every hair is in place." Tully called up the stairs to Brianna.

He'd asked her join him on a picnic and promised to take her to pick both wild huckleberries and blackberries. Maggie would appreciate the berries and Brianna thought it sounded like fun.

Tully arrived right on time to pick her up, but she had yet to appear from her apartment.

Maggie grinned at him. "You realize hollering up the stairs isn't likely to make her hurry any faster, don't you?"

He forked his fingers through his hair and fiddled with his hat. "I know, but I'm not gonna wait on her all day. If she thinks I've got nothing better to do than…" Tully's words trailed off when he glanced up at Brianna. Like a lively schoolgirl, she bounded down the stairs with her hair woven into a long braid and a pail in one hand. She wore a dark navy split skirt with a blue-sprigged blouse that perfectly matched her eyes.

"I'm ready," she said with a bright smile, waving at Maggie before glancing at Tully. "From your yawping up the stairs, I thought you were anxious to go."

"I am. Time's wastin' and the temperature's climbin' higher than a creeping vine in granny's garden." Tully opened the door and looked back at Maggie. "Have a good day, Mags."

"You two have fun." Maggie winked at Tully as he escorted Brianna outside and shut the door.

Brianna offered Tully a curious look. "I didn't realize you have a grandmother."

"I don't," Tully said, lifting her to sit in the saddle on Hoss' back. "It's just a saying."

She settled herself in the seat and looped the handle of her pail over the saddle horn. Tully handed her the reins and she took them with a smile. "Your quaint colloquialisms are charming."

"Is that a fancy way of saying you like the way I talk?" Tully teased, swinging up on Cotton and leading the way down the street.

"Perhaps. Or maybe it's a polite way of saying you speak with an interesting rural point of view."

He tossed her a glare then clucked to Cotton. The horse sped up to a trot as they headed out of town toward the hills.

"How far are we riding today?" Brianna asked.

"As far as we need to until we find a good patch of berries." In his travels around the area, Tully had noticed several patches of ripe berries. If no one had beaten them to the ripe fruit, they wouldn't have to ride too far out to find them. Although he looked forward to the good jam and pies Maggie had promised to make, Tully mostly wanted an excuse to spend the day with Brianna.

Work had kept him busier than usual the last few days and he hadn't been able to spend any time with her.

The way his blood heated just looking at her, it probably was for the best anyway. He'd never felt like this about a woman before and the strange, unfamiliar feelings left him more than a little worried.

From Thane and Ian's recent experiences in the miserable bliss of falling in love, Tully worried he may have caught the same incurable illness.

While Brianna studied their surroundings, Tully watched her. Enchanted with everything about her, he couldn't get enough of seeing her, being with her. The golden-brown rope of her hair bounced against her back with every step of the horse, making him want to tug out the ribbon and let it flow freely around her.

A distraction from his improper thoughts arrived in the form of a little used lane.

"I know where we are," Brianna said, smiling as she rode beside him. "Are you sure that's where you want to go?"

"Where?" Tully asked.

"There." Brianna pointed to a ramshackle dwelling as they guided the horses down the trail toward Clive Fisher's place. They slowed the horses to an easy walk as they approached.

Tully motioned for Brianna to stop. "You wait here. Clive usually fires a warning shot or two before anyone gets this close."

"He illustrated that tendency upon my first visit." Brianna glanced around. "I hope Mr. Fisher is well."

"I'll check the cabin, but you wait here, just in case." Tully rode ahead and dismounted by Clive's abode. After knocking on the door and getting no response, he stuck his head inside. It was empty, so he tied Cotton's reins to a post and walked out to the mine.

At the entrance, he cupped his hands around his mouth and hollered into the mine. "Clive! It's Tully Barrett! Are you in there?"

He listened for a moment then called again. The sound of someone cussing made him grin as a figure emerged from the depths of the mine.

"Unless you're here to arrest me, you best get off my property, Sheriff," Clive warned. He wiped his sweaty face on a bandana that looked like it might have been used to scrub the hindquarters of a filthy swine.

Tully tried not to wrinkle his nose, concluding the bit of cloth certainly smelled like it had. He took a step back and turned his head to the side, drawing in a breath of untainted air.

"What do you want?" Clive tersely asked.

"Your partner and I were riding by and thought we'd stop." Tully grinned when Clive made a disgusted face and looked toward the clearing where Brianna waited.

"That little missy sure can't seem to stay out of trouble. Don't you have criminals to arrest? Or have you been demoted to escortin' troublesome women around?" Clive offered him a smug sneer.

"As a matter of fact, it's my day off and Miss Dumont is helping me with a project." Tully walked upwind of Clive as they headed back to the cabin. "I thought she might like to check on the progress at the mine, since she owns part of it."

Clive scowled. "Don't rub it in, son. It's bad enough I had to take a partner in the first place, but now I've got to put up with that pretty, prissy princess."

Tully held back a smile and motioned for Brianna to ride up to the cabin.

It took only a moment for her to reach them. She smiled at Clive as she swung out of the saddle. "Good morning, Mr. Fisher. How does this day find you?"

"It finds me interrupted for no reason when I'm this close…" He held his forefinger close to his thumb, "to makin' a big strike. That gold is just sittin' in there, waitin' for me to dig it out. Instead, I'm out here wastin' my time palaverin' with you."

Brianna ignored his gruff tone. "It's a pleasure to see you, too."

Clive winked at her and stuffed his filthy handkerchief into his pocket. "In truth, missy, ain't nothin' changed since the last time you was here. I got about two ounces of gold dust and that's it. But don't give up. I can feel it in my bones. There are riches in that hole and I ain't quittin' until I find it."

"I appreciate your tenacity, sir. Is there anything I can do to provide assistance?" Brianna took a shallow breath, wondering how a human could smell so bad and still be among the living.

"Not unless you're plannin' on getting' your nice clothes dirty and comin' into the mine to work." Clive looked at her and cackled. "That'd be like puttin' a rose in a bucket of coal. I don't need nothin' from you, honey, but I do thank you for askin'."

Clive motioned toward his cabin. "Would you like me to put on some coffee?"

"No, thank you," Brianna said, glancing at Tully as he subtly shook his head.

He moved forward and took her elbow in his hand. "We really should get going, Clive. We'll check on you another day."

"I suppose if you think you need to, that'd be fine." The miner shaded his eyes, watching as Tully lifted Brianna up to the saddle before he took Cotton's reins in his hands.

Tully tipped his head to Clive and swung onto his horse. He almost fell off when the old man stepped close to him so Brianna wouldn't hear him speak.

"When you gonna marry that lil' gal?" Clive asked in a raspy whisper.

"What?" Tully shot him a surprised frown. "What in tarnation made you ask that?"

"Because you're sweet on her, sure as I'm standin' here, and I'd say she feels the same about you." Clive cackled again, slapping his leg. "Never thought I'd see the day the mighty Tully Barrett fell in love."

"Oh, shut your pie hole, you loony ol' coot." Tully grinned at Clive then rode over to where Brianna waited on Hoss.

"What were you two talking about?" she asked, turning around in the saddle to wave one more time at Clive.

"Nothing of your concern," Tully said. He'd rather chew tacks than tell her what Clive said. Although he'd allowed the idea of marriage to flit through his head a few times in the past, the notion had lodged firmly in his brain the last few weeks.

Not that he wanted to, but he couldn't get Brianna out of his mind. Somehow, between him throwing her in jail and the night they'd stared up at the stars, she'd taken up a permanent place in his heart.

Uncertain what to do about his feelings, Tully wasn't ready to say anything to her, to make any promises. For all he knew, she'd head back to Rhode Island soon and he'd never see her again.

If only she'd be completely honest with him, tell him what really drove her from her home, he'd feel better prepared to contemplate a future with her.

Until he discovered her secret, though, he had to keep up his guard. Otherwise, he knew he was in for a world of heartache.

Deep in his musings, he glanced over at Brianna and noticed her fixated on something in the trees. He smiled as a deer and fawn hid at the base of a tree.

"They're beautiful, Tully," she said, whispering quietly as they continued on their way. The melodic lilt in her voice cascaded over him like a cool breeze on a scorching day. Refreshed, invigorated, and intrigued, he wanted to keep her talking.

Intently studying her, he held her gaze. "There are many beautiful things created by the Maker's hand. Have you ever seen ducks land on the water or watched a fiery sunrise fill the sky or noticed the way flower petals nestle together so perfectly?"

Brianna shook her head. "I haven't, but I do believe I'd like to experience those things with you. The way you speak about them so…" She searched for just the right word, "passionately and poetically makes me want to see them as you do."

Pleased, Tully smiled at her and pointed out a bird's nest, another deer, and a flock of wild turkeys before they reached the spot he had in mind for their picnic.

Close to a creek, plenty of trees provided shade. Twenty feet or so up the hill from the creek, a large patch of huckleberries ripened in the sunshine. Thirty feet down the creek, they could pick plenty of blackberries.

As he stopped and swung off Cotton, Brianna released a happy sigh. "It's so lovely here, Tully. It's more inviting than any park I've seen."

"I should hope so," he said, lifting her out of the saddle and setting her down before leading the horses to the creek for a drink.

Once Cotton and Hoss both grazed, Tully took an old quilt from behind his saddle and unrolled it, spreading it on the grass. He lifted his saddlebags from Cotton and carried them over to the quilt then held his hand out to Brianna.

"Will you join me for lunch, Miss Dumont?"

The boyish look on his face and the warm light shimmering in his eyes made her heart turn into a pool of syrup.

Courteously, she tipped her head to him. "It would be my pleasure." She took his hand and settled onto the quilt then watched as he bent his long legs and sat beside her.

From the saddlebags, he removed paper-wrapped sandwiches and pickles along with a tin of cookies.

"I've got water in my canteen, or we can drink from the creek if you're thirsty," he said, handing her a sandwich made of a thick piece of smoky ham and bread fresh from the oven that morning.

"This looks delicious, Sheriff. Did you make it yourself?" she asked.

He chuckled. "No, I did not, but the restaurant just down the street from my office often makes food I can take with me."

Brianna took a bite and fished a handkerchief from her pocket to use as a napkin. "It's very good. Thank you for bringing lunch."

"You're welcome. I can't expect to work you like a slave this afternoon if I don't make sure you're properly fed."

"I should say not." She took another bite and swallowed before staring at the sandwich in her hand. "I suppose we should have offered to share with Mr. Fisher. No doubt, he would appreciate a good meal."

Only marginally guilty, Tully shrugged. "I considered it when we were there, but I couldn't stomach the idea of sitting through a meal having to smell ol' Clive."

Brianna grinned. "He was rather pungent today, wasn't he?"

"That's a nice way to put it." The last thing Tully wanted to discuss was how bad the old miner smelled. He really didn't want to discuss anything at all.

Even if he didn't plan to act on it, kissing Brianna until they both lost the ability to reason seemed like a much better idea. Mindful of his wayward thoughts, he changed the subject. "Did you have a good time helping Mrs. Greenfield yesterday?"

"I did. I've never had to clean before and I learned so many helpful tips from her and Maggie and Jemma. It was fun to spend the day with them." Brianna recalled something from the previous day and laughed. "You should have seen Lily. Jemma tied a handkerchief over her curls to keep them clean. Instead, Lily decided she could use her head as a dust rag. She was down on her hands and knees, rubbing her head back and forth across the floor until Jemma put a stop to it."

Tully chuckled. "Lily is quite a girl. I'm afraid Thane's got his hands full and then some with that one. She and Jack couldn't be more different if they tried."

"How so?" Brianna asked.

"Jack's very responsible and often serious. He's a hard-worker and wants to please everyone, always eager to learn. Lily, on the other hand, is full of giggles and sunshine and tomfoolery. She's independent and sassy and isn't afraid to tell you what she thinks the minute the thought enters her head. When Ian was trying to win Maggie's affections, Lily sat him down and had a talk with him about how he should give Maggie slobbery kisses if he wanted her to like him."

Brianna almost choked on the bite she'd just swallowed and coughed into her handkerchief. "Slobbery kisses?"

"You know... kisses that aren't just a quick peck on the cheek. Apparently, Lily had witnessed Jemma and Thane kissing and decided that's what Ian and Maggie needed to do."

"I'm still not certain I understand what she meant by slobbery kisses." Imploringly, she gazed at him with soft and inviting blue eyes. "Perhaps you would be so kind as to demonstrate."

Tully set his half-eaten sandwich on the quilt and wiped his hands on the legs of his tan canvas trousers. He scooted closer to Brianna until his legs bracketed her on either side and his face was close to hers.

Slowly, he traced his thumb over her cheek, along her chin, then over her bottom lip. When a tremor passed over her, he looked into her eyes, gratified by the longing that flickered in their depths.

"A slobbery kiss," he whispered in a husky tone, "is something like this." His lips caressed hers, teasing and tempting until she leaned into him. Immediately, he deepened the kiss, skillfully pushing them both to the edge of something wild and wonderful. Finally, he lifted his head, smiling at the glazed look on her face.

He kissed her forehead and moved away. If he remained so close, he'd give in to his need to love her completely and thoroughly and that would never do. Not yet, anyway.

"That, Miss Dumont, is a slobbery kiss."

She swallowed hard as she gathered her composure. Nervously clearing her throat, she looked everywhere but at him. "I see, Sheriff. Although I'm generally a fast learner, I may require further demonstrations to firmly understand the concept." The teasing smile on her just-kissed lips and the twinkle of mirth in her eyes when she glanced at him grabbed hold of Tully's heart.

Desire blazed in his eyes as he nodded his head. "Name the time and place, Fred, and my lips and anything else you want are at your service."

"Mercy!" she gasped, hastily turning her attention back to her sandwich.

Tully finished his second sandwich and pickle then opened the tin of cookies. He helped himself to several of the chocolate macaroons, leaning back on one elbow and contentedly eating the sweets.

Brianna finished her sandwich and pickle. After selecting a cookie, she nibbled it as she watched him from beneath her lashes.

Aware of her gaze, Tully put the lid back on the cookie tin, wadded up the wrappings from their food and shoved the ball of paper into his saddlebag. He removed his Stetson and set it aside. In a smooth motion, he maneuvered around until his head rested on Brianna's lap.

"Ah, that's better," he said. Folding his hands so they rested on top of his chest, he stretched out his legs as his eyes drifted shut.

"What are you doing?" she asked, glaring down at him.

"I thought you liked to let mischievous boys sleep on your lap." He opened one eye and shot her a devilish smile.

"Little boys are far different than full-grown men," she said, pushing at his shoulders.

Determined to tease her, he refused to move, releasing a contented sigh. "This is just what I needed after our tasty lunch and those even tastier kisses."

"Oh! You are a wicked, crude man." She shoved at him again.

Tully didn't budge, settling more comfortably onto his back as he relaxed.

Only a minute or two passed before Brianna released her tension and stiff posture. Tully fought a grin as her cool hand brushed the hair away from his forehead. When she trailed her fingers along the sides of his face, tracing the line of his jaw and chin, heat surged through his veins, but he didn't move.

Tentatively, she explored his face, running a finger along his nose, over his eyebrows, and lingering at a scar right below his lip. A wisp of her hair brushed over his cheek as she bent and kissed his forehead.

While she assumed he'd fallen asleep, Tully only pretended. He enjoyed her light, tender touches too much not to remain awake.

"Tully Barrett, what am I going to do with you?" she asked quietly.

He had several suggestions, none of which he'd voice, given the fact she'd feel obliged to slap his face if he mentioned them. Most likely, Pastor Eagan wouldn't approve of them either. However, it was hard not to feel them with her enticing fragrance filling his nose while the very aura of her filled his heart.

Thoroughly at ease, Tully remained unmoving while each touch of Brianna's hand pushed him closer to the brink of losing his self-control.

"It's completely unfair of you to be so handsome and charming, Sheriff. Don't you know how hard it is for a woman to stay on guard around you?" She spoke in a whisper, unaware he listened to every word. "How is it you possess the ability to cast some sort of spell over me?"

Tully knew what she meant. He'd felt bewitched ever since she'd arrived in town.

"You are the most frustrating, maddening, vexatious, gorgeous, wonderful man I've ever encountered." The feathery touch of her lips brushing his almost made Tully give her another demonstration of slobbery kisses. By sheer determination, he managed to keep up his ruse. "Why must you be so undeniably attractive? It's not right that you have such a kissable mouth."

Unable to stop himself, Tully wrapped his arms around her and pulled her to his chest.

A startled squeak escaped her and she glared at him with wide eyes.

"How long have you been awake?" she asked, pushing against him.

"Who said I ever went to sleep?" He released her when she shoved against his chest again and sat up, irritated and embarrassed. "Now, don't go getting your bloomers in a bunch, Fred. I appreciated every single word you said. It's nice to know my good looks and charm aren't wasted on you."

"Oh! You are... you're a..." Too upset to think of a response, Brianna rose to her feet and stomped over to the creek bank. She knelt and splashed water on her hot cheeks then looked over her shoulder at Tully.

He rose up on his knees, wishing he'd let her think he slept a little longer. It sure was nice to rest with his head on her soft lap.

After he stuffed the cookie tin into his saddlebag, he settled his hat on his head, rolled the quilt and carried it back to his horse. He tied the quilt behind the saddle, tossed the saddlebags over Cotton's back then lifted the pails he and Brianna had both brought along.

As she stepped beside him, he handed one to her and carried the other two. "Let's pick the huckleberries first. They'll take longer than the blackberries," he said.

"Lead the way."

They needed to cross the creek to get to the berries, so he wrapped his arm around Brianna's waist and lifted her against his side.

"What are you doing?" she spluttered as her feet bumped his calves and the pail in her hand smacked against his chest.

"Carrying you across the creek, unless you'd rather get your feet wet. I can set you down right now if you prefer." He let her slide down a few inches when he reached the middle of the creek. The water wasn't deep or the current strong, but Brianna would be soaked from above her knees down.

"If that's the reason for this, then thank you." She lifted her feet, afraid they might drag in the water.

Tully chuckled as he made it to the other side of the creek and up the bank. He set her on her feet and resisted the yearning to kiss her again.

He pointed to the berry bushes a few feet away. "You start on this one and I'll go around to the other side. Only pick the purple berries and if they seem soft, don't put them in the pail. You want firm, ripe fruit."

In need of a little distance from the woman, Tully walked around to the far side of the bushes and went to work filling his pail.

"How'd you get to be an expert at berry picking?" Brianna asked.

"I did a lot of it as a boy. Once we moved here, Maggie liked to cook with berries and we didn't mind eating her pies and jams, so we always helped her pick them."

"When you say we, I assume you mean Thane."

Tully nodded, even though she couldn't see him. "That's right. I guess Thane will either help Jemma pick or not get any berry pie this year."

"Jemma mentioned something yesterday about picking berries later this week. She said Thane had an outing planned for her and the children."

Tully chuckled and shook his head.

"What is providing your current source of amusement?" Brianna asked.

Humor remained evident in his voice when he spoke. "I'm just picturing Lily helping with the berry picking."

Giggles floated over the bushes. She stopped picking, envisioning the mess Lily would make on a berry picking adventure. "That would be something to see. If she does it as enthusiastically as she does everything else, she'll be covered in berry juice."

"So will everyone else," he mused.

They worked in silence for a while until they'd picked all the ripe huckleberries. Tully poured the two pails together, filling one of them almost to the top.

He carried the pails across the creek then came back for Brianna.

Rather than tug her along next to his side, he swept her into his arms. Her hands locked around the back of his neck and her lips lingered tauntingly close to his.

"Are you ready?" he asked, taking a step into the creek.

"Yes," she whispered, although her gaze focused on his mouth.

He stumbled and took a hurried step to keep from dunking them both in the cold water. Frustrated that a single look from her could leave him so distracted he couldn't keep his wits about him, he set her down the moment his feet hit the other side of the bank.

"We need to get the rest of the berries picked so we can get back." Tully had no reason to rush into town, other than he didn't trust himself to be alone with Brianna. The emotions she stirred in him, the relentless force of his longing for her, left him so disturbed, he knew the best thing was to get her back to Baker City as soon as possible.

Since they still had two pails to fill with blackberries, he figured they could stay out of trouble for the next hour or two.

Tully led the way down the creek to where blackberries grew in wild profusion. He took a stick and shoved it into the bushes to make sure no critters or snakes lurked beneath the branches before he let Brianna start picking.

While the berries were bigger and easier to pick, the bushes had painfully sharp thorns. After she poked herself several times, Brianna glared at Tully. "I don't believe I care for blackberries."

"Why's that?" he asked, popping a ripe berry into his mouth before adding a handful to his pail.

"Because the thorns are quite painful."

Tully smirked. "Then stop picking them. It's the big, juicy berries you want."

Brianna's gaze narrowed as she glowered at him.

Several minutes passed in silence. Tully glanced over and noticed she had purple stains on her lips from snitching berries.

"Are you eatin' or pickin' berries, Fred. We'll be here all night if you don't get on the right track."

Indignant, she huffed. "I'll have you know my pail is nearly full. These are much faster to pick than the huckleberries."

"Yep. And juicier," he said, eating another handful of berries.

"How dare you accuse me of eating them when you've got berries smeared all over your face and hands? You are every bit as bad as a recalcitrant child."

Tully rocked back on one hip and stared at her. "Is that so, Miss Dumont?" He waved a berry-stained hand at her. "And I suppose you are a paragon of virtue, someone we all should emulate?"

Astonished by his choice of words, she blinked at him then noticed his teasing grin. "That is exactly what I have endeavored to convey to you, Sheriff Barrett."

"You know what I think, Fred?" Tully moved around the berry bush, approaching her with ornery determination.

"I have no idea what goes through that thick skull of yours." Troubled by the twinkle in his eye and the boyish grin on his face that brought out his dimples, she backed away from him.

"I think you need taken down a peg or two, Miss Sassy Britches."

Tully lunged for her, but she dodged away from him, running around the other side of the blackberries. She scooped up a handful of discarded berries and lobbed them at him.

One hit him on the chin, and another on the cheek.

"You are in for it now, missy!" Tully tossed several squishy berries at her, hitting her face and chest.

"Stop, Tully! You..." One caught her right in the mouth. She spluttered, spitting it out.

He wrapped her in his arms and swung her around. She squirmed and wiggled with such vigor, she knocked him off balance and they both fell to the ground.

Tully cushioned the fall by turning so he hit the ground with her held to his chest.

"Now look what you've done," she said, brushing hair from her eyes with a berry-coated hand. Purple juice smeared across her forehead.

Tully inhaled a deep breath and before he let his common sense take over, he crushed his mouth to hers, savoring the flavor of the berries as it mingled with Brianna's own sweet honey taste.

With slow strokes, he rubbed his hands up and down her back, concluding he'd never think of berry picking the same way again.

At first, Brianna held herself away from him, but he recognized the moment she surrendered to whatever it was that sparked between them. Her body relaxed and her hands crept up to bracket his face.

Still cradling her in his arms, he rolled over and continued lavishing her with his love. Kisses covered her eyelids, her cheeks, her chin, before he returned to her delicious, delectable mouth.

It didn't matter if they kissed for one minute or a million, he'd never tire of it.

Not ever.

Brianna Dumont was the one woman Tully would never get out of his mind or system. Truthfully, he didn't want to try.

What he really wanted was to do more than share a few stolen kisses in the summer sunshine with blackberries all around them.

Finally grasping the last few threads of common sense he possessed, Tully kissed her one last time, conveying his longing through the connection of their lips.

Abruptly, he raised his head and leaned over her on one elbow. The fire burning in her eyes matched the flames still glowing hot in his, but he forced himself to ignore it. To block out the temptation of loving her.

His long fingers pushed a wispy strand of hair behind her ear before he cupped her chin in his hand. "Come on, Fred. At this rate, it'll be next July before we finish picking Maggie's berries."

He stood and held a hand out to her. She took it and allowed him to pull her to her feet.

Dismayed, she glanced down at her berry-covered clothes. "I suppose we should finish."

Tully laughed. "Well, there's no hiding what we did today."

The frantic look she cast him made him laugh again. "I didn't mean the kissing, although that was the best part of the day. I meant berry picking."

Relieved, she released her breath and stepped next to the berry bush where she'd been picking. "That's good to know."

It didn't take long to finish filling their pails. Tully helped her mount Hoss then handed her one of the pails to carry.

"How are you going to carry two pails?" she asked as he handed her a second one to hold while he mounted.

"Like this," he said, carefully mounting Cotton while holding one pail. He pulled two lids from his saddlebags and fastened one on the pail in his hand then took the extra pail she held and placed a lid on it. With the handles of both in one hand, the pails rested on his thigh.

"Smarty," Brianna said, grinning at him as they turned the horses back in the direction they'd come.

On the way to town, she snitched a few more berries.

Entertained by how much she enjoyed the fresh fruit, Tully raised an eyebrow and gave her a cautionary look. "You best be careful, Fred, or you'll give yourself a bellyache."

"But they are so good, Tully. I've never had such fresh berries." She popped another in her mouth.

He stared at her. "Where did you get your produce in the city?"

"Our cook purchased what was needed. When I was very young, sometimes I'd go with her in the summer to the market. Farmers would bring in their produce and sell it from the backs of their wagons. The apples were always so good. Big and bright red, I'd bite into the crisp peel and an explosion of juicy flavor would burst forth in my mouth. It was like taking a bite of honey-laced autumn." She closed her eyes, lost in her memories.

Tully watched her face, mesmerized by her expressiveness. He could almost taste the apple she'd described. The way his mouth watered, though, had nothing to do with fruit and everything to do with how much he wanted to kiss her again.

"What else did you enjoy from your childhood?" If he kept them both distracted, they might make it to Baker City without him ravaging her luscious lips with more kisses.

"Father had a sailboat and we'd go out on it sometimes. That was grand." Brianna cast him a coy glance. "I was a good swimmer back then."

Surprised she'd get in the water, he grinned. "Do you still swim?"

"Goodness, no. One of the women from church took Father aside when I was ten and told him it was time for me to behave like a lady instead of a heathenish ruffian. After that, I wasn't allowed to do many things in which I'd previously found great pleasure."

"I bet you were a handful." Tully studied her a moment. "In fact, I'm sure you and Lily Jordan have a lot in common."

In a most unladylike response, Brianna stuck her tongue out at him.

He chuckled and pointed his index finger at her. "That is exactly what I'm talking about, Fred. I figure you'll eventually get over all this proper nonsense and have some fun."

A smile softened her features when she looked at him. "Today was wonderful, Tully. Thank you for thinking of it. Are we taking the berries straight to Maggie?"

"Yes, if you don't mind. I think she planned to have us stay for supper." Tully tipped his head to a few people as they rode into town.

"That sounds lovely, although I might need to change my clothes first. I'd feel sorely out of place eating in their immaculate home dressed like this." Brianna glanced down at her berry-stained blouse.

"Mags and Ian won't care. Even his mother wouldn't object, but Ian's folks left on this morning's train."

"Oh, I didn't know they were leaving or I would have bid them goodbye when I saw them yesterday." Brianna genuinely liked the elder MacGregor couple. Ian took after his father, although she could see bits of his mother in him, too.

"They promised to come back for a visit next spring, before it gets too hot. I think Ian said…"

"Brianna! Brianna Dumont!" A male voice called out her name.

Together, they watched a dapper gentleman hurry across the street, appearing excited to see her. The man wasn't someone Tully recognized and the way he gazed at Brianna set him on edge.

"Davis? What on earth are you doing here?" Brianna asked, as the man placed a possessive hand on her knee and gazed at her with adoration.

"I came to take you home, my darling, where you belong." The man rubbed his hand along her thigh. Brianna shifted slightly, trying to move away from him. Hoss sidestepped, but the man followed.

"Aren't you happy to see me, Brianna?" He offered her an exaggerated pout that most likely endeared him to the majority of females.

Tully wondered if he could punch the man in the nose without dropping the berries.

"It's not that, Davis. You caught me by surprise," she said, smiling brightly.

Tully had seen enough of her smiles to know it was fake and forced. Disturbed, he glared at the stranger. "Who are you and why are you bothering Miss Dumont?"

The man turned and studied him a moment, as though he spoke to someone far beneath him. "The better question would be why she's with you and in such a disheveled state. It's positively indecent to see her riding astride."

"Indecent?" Brianna's anger sparked and Tully waited for it to catch and burn Mr. Fancy Pants.

"Now, don't get upset, dearest. Let's get you down from there and cleaned up. I brought a few trunks of your things with me, in case you needed them." Fancy Pants took the pail of berries from her and handed it to Tully then reached up to help Brianna dismount. Before he could touch her, she swung down on her own.

"Come along, dear one, let's go to the hotel. I've taken a room there." The man tugged on her hand, but Brianna dug in her feet.

"I have my own place, Davis. Why don't we meet later?"

"No. I won't let you out of my sight, now that I found you." The man draped his arm around her shoulders.

Brianna sighed and shot a pleading look at Tully.

He tipped his head toward Mr. Fancy Pants. "Do you want me to haul him in for bothering you, Fred?"

"That won't be necessary," she said, glancing over at the man. "Sheriff Barrett, this is B. Davis Gordon, my fiancé."

Chapter Fourteen

"This is B. Davis Gordon, my fiancé," Tully mimicked under his breath as he rode out to Ian and Maggie's home.

What kind of woman failed to mention she was engaged to be married when she'd fully participated in the type of heated, passion-filled kisses he and Brianna had shared.

Furious and hurt, Tully reined in Cotton at the gate to the MacGregor home and left his two horses tied to the hitching rail.

Irate, he stalked down the walk and up the steps before pounding on the door. Footsteps tapped across the floor inside and Maggie swung the portal open with a welcoming smile.

"My goodness, Tully, did you take a bath in the berries? You've got them all over you." Maggie stepped aside so he could enter. The thunder riding Tully's brow didn't escape her notice and she place a hand on his arm. "What's wrong? What happened?"

"Brianna's fiancé just arrived in town."

Maggie's mouth fell open and she gaped at him for a long moment. Finally, she took one of the berry pails from him and motioned for him to follow her to the kitchen.

The sunny, open room provided a cheerful center to Ian and Maggie's home. However, Tully was too upset to notice.

He set the berries near the sink then slumped back against the counter.

Maggie filled a glass with tea and a few precious chunks of ice, and handed it to him then gave him a nudge toward the table situated in front of the window.

Reluctantly, Tully took a seat and drank half the tea. Maggie slid a plate of cookies his direction and he absently took one, biting into it without tasting anything.

"Tell me everything that happened." Maggie refilled his glass then returned to her seat across from him. "How do you know he's her fiancé?"

"Because that's how she introduced him." Tully affected a falsetto, imitating Brianna. "This is B. Davis Gordon, my fiancé." He fluttered his eyelashes and pulled such a comical face, Maggie had to work to hold back her laughter.

He glowered at her. "It isn't funny, Mags. It's dang serious and I'm so mad I could march into town and shoot Mr. Gordon then throttle Brianna for lying to me."

"Did she lie to you, Tully? Did you ask her if she was engaged?" Just as shocked as Tully by the news, Maggie assumed there had to be more to the story.

"Of course, I didn't ask her. I assumed when she let me kiss her like…" Tully snapped his mouth shut at Maggie's delighted grin. "She should have told me straight up that she was engaged. It's a lie by omission."

"Well, I suppose you could call it that, but maybe she has a good reason for not saying anything about him. Did she act excited to see him? Like she'd missed him?"

"No. Not really." Tully leaned back in his chair and removed his hat, hanging it off his knee. "In fact, she seemed rather upset at his arrival. From the way she acted, I assumed he was a person she didn't particularly care to be around until she introduced him."

"Maybe she doesn't like him. Perhaps he's someone her father wanted her to marry and she ran away to escape the confines of a loveless marriage."

Tully snorted and shook his head. "You've been reading those sappy books I told you to use for kindling, haven't you?"

Maggie glared at him. "What I choose to read is no concern of yours. Nonetheless, you should reserve judgment on Brianna until you know the whole story, Tully. There might be any number of trying circumstances behind all this of which you are unaware."

He took another long drink of tea. "You might be right, but it doesn't change the fact that he's here and Brianna is with him."

"I know, but…" The sound of the door opening interrupted their conversation.

"Maggie, my love, I hope you whipped up a berry pie for supper. I can hardly…" Ian strode into the kitchen and took in the long faces of his wife and friend.

"What on earth happened to you, Tully?" Ian kissed Maggie's cheek then sat beside her at the table.

"Brianna Dumont happened." Tully ran a hand through his hair and sighed. "The man she's supposed to marry arrived in town today."

"I didn't realize she was engaged." Ian glanced from Maggie to Tully.

"Neither did I."

Ian placed a hand on Tully's shoulder and gave it a squeeze. "I'm sorry, Tully. That is hard news to take." As though he suddenly recalled something, Ian sat up and pointed to Tully. "Is he a rather dandified-looking fellow? Pale and slight of build, wearing a linen suit?"

"He could have been dressed in burlap for all the attention I paid to his clothes, but yeah, he did seem rather citified and sissy-like."

Maggie rolled her eyes and stood. "If he's engaged to Brianna, I have to assume he's probably a handsome man, despite the description you two shared."

"Not nearly as handsome as the fine gents right here, lass." Ian popped her on the backside as she stepped away from the table.

She cast him a flirty smile and opened the oven to remove a roaster pan. "Are you still staying for supper, Tully?"

"I won't be very good company, Mags. Right now, I'd rather go home."

Maggie shook a spoon his direction. "Go home and pout, Tully, but you stay away from Brianna and that man. Your temper is simmering too close to the surface to think straight and I don't want you getting into trouble. As the sheriff, you need to set a good example for others, not waver on the line."

"I promise I'll go straight home, Mother." Tully stood and settled his hat on his head. "I'll talk to you both later."

"Are you sure you'll be fine, Tully? You know you're welcome to stay." Ian walked with him to the front door.

"Thanks, Ian. I do appreciate the offer, but I need to go."

Tully shuffled down the steps and over to his horses. Rather than mount Cotton, he led both horses past the lumberyard to the road that skirted around the edge of town.

By the time he arrived at his house and turned the horses loose in the pasture, he was even angrier with Brianna.

A cold bath did nothing to cool his temper. Long into the evening, he sat on his front porch, shirtless and barefooted, staring into the gathering darkness, wondering how he'd fallen for a woman who was nearly wed.

Mad at himself and Brianna, he decided the best thing to do was pretend he'd never met the infuriating, enthralling woman.

Chapter Fifteen

Brianna's father once mentioned something about the importance of keeping one's friends close and enemies closer.

At the time, what he said made no sense to her. Today, she understood the words with perfect clarity.

Forcing another smile as she sat at dinner with Davis in the Hotel Warshauer's dining room, she listened to the annoying man prattle on and on about how distraught he was when she disappeared.

"I left no stone unturned in my search for you, my dearest. I hired a detective to try to locate your whereabouts with no success." Davis took a sip from a glass of wine and gave her a look meant to be endearing.

It only made Brianna want to slap him. She gripped the fork in her hand tighter before she gave in to the urge.

Davis set his glass down and smiled. "It was entirely providential I happened to be in New York and picked up a copy of the paper the day they ran your article, Brianna. If it wasn't for that, I may never have found you again."

"How did you know I'd written the article?" she asked, assuming he'd gone to the editor and paid handsomely for the truth.

"I've read a few things you've written over the years. It held the same flair you tend to use when writing. Also, B.E. Dumont could have been none other than you. The moment I finished the article, I returned home and had your housekeeper pack your trunks. Stuck out here in the wilds of Oregon, I thought you might be in need of your things."

"Your thoughtfulness is beyond words, Davis. What did I do to deserve such a kind, generous man?" Brianna cut into the chicken on her plate, wishing it were the egotistical dolt sitting across from her.

No doubt, he was rifling through her father's papers the entire time the staff packed her things. She'd caught Davis snooping around her father's desk on more than one occasion, but the thought he'd been searching for her father's ledgers never entered her mind. Not until the day of her father's funeral.

The man reminded her of a doll she'd once seen as a child. If she held it one direction, it was lovely and inviting, but if she tipped it over, the face was hideous and frightening. The doll had scared her so badly, she'd run out of the store in tears.

Davis Gordon went to great lengths for people to see him as a successful, charming, kind man, but Brianna knew better.

The fact that he didn't know she was wise to his deception, though, was the only reason she maintained the ruse of being his fiancé.

When he'd asked her to wed, she told him she needed time to think about it. She never intended to marry him, but she feared he would call in her father's loan early or some such thing if she refused him outright.

Her father insisted she send Davis on his way and not worry about what might happen with the loan. In spite of her father's wishes, she'd continued to allow Davis to court her, counting the days until her father paid off the loan and she could tell the loathsome man farewell.

Before that day arrived, though, her father died and left Brianna to her own defenses.

The evening after his funeral service, people had gathered at her home to offer their condolences and partake of an elaborate meal Davis declared must be served in her father's honor.

Brianna had no appetite or interest in entertaining people. As soon as the guests began leaving, she retreated to her room. Intrigued by the papers she'd found in her father's safe in the library the day after he died, she'd taken them to her room to study. In the hours after the dinner guests departed, she read through every piece of correspondence he had from Clive Fisher. Curious where she might find Baker City, she'd been on her way to the library to study a map when she overheard Davis speaking to his assistant.

Every vile word the man spoke still echoed in her ears, as though he'd just uttered them.

"I've put up with that troublesome girl far longer than I thought this situation would require.

At the very least, I assumed I would have charmed her into my bed by now. I'll give her until the end of the week to come to her senses and marry me or I'll take what I've wanted all along. Either way, I'll have her. If I have to ruin her in the process, she'll make a lovely mistress. My preference is to have her as my wife, but I'll take whatever I can get. If she wasn't such a tempting little morsel, I'd have finished her a long time ago."

She recalled the ribald comments from his assistant that followed her up the stairs as she returned to her room and frantically packed her bag and trunk. Once Davis and his assistant left, she made plans to disappear and paid a driver to take her to the train station in the wee hours of the morning.

Fearful Davis would follow through with his threats if she remained at home even one more day, she wrote him a letter saying she needed time to grieve her father and would be in touch with him soon. Distance was the only thing that would keep her safe until she figured out the best way to pay the bank, clear her father's name, and break off her engagement.

Davis arrived at her house the following afternoon to find her gone and nothing but an envelope with her note waiting for him.

As she thought back to the day of her father's death, Davis had been the one to arrive at the house and tell her the tragic news. He'd also been the one to assure her the bank would take everything she and her father owned if she didn't come up with the money by August. He did emphasize marriage to him would cancel the debt, but she remained firm in her refusal to exchange vows immediately.

Now, she was grateful she hadn't given in to his incessant demands they wed as soon as possible.

After meeting Tully, she couldn't imagine spending her life with anyone but the teasing, trying, tempting Sheriff.

However, with Davis' unexpected arrival, she doubted Tully would have a thing to do with her. The pain in his eyes and hard clench of his jaw as he rode away left her aching to run to him and confess the truth.

Until she figured out a way to get rid of Davis and come up with the money to pay the bank, she had to push Tully away.

"Are you wool gathering, my precious, or weary from whatever ordeal you endured today?" In spite of the pleasant smile on his face, Brianna detected a hint of venom in his voice as he spoke.

She released a careworn sigh. "I suppose I'm rather weary. Wonderful surprises, like your arrival, are taxing to a body."

"You poor little dear. After we finish our meal, I'll escort you back to your apartment and you can get some rest."

"Thank you, Davis. You are so understanding and such a considerate gentleman." The words almost choked her as she spoke them. She wondered if lightning might bolt out of the sky and strike her dead for speaking such lies, but she didn't know what else to do.

Treading light and careful around Davis was the best way to keep her virtue intact until she could figure out why he'd tracked her down and what he wanted.

He might pretend to be a doting fiancé, but she had an idea their supposed relationship was the last reason he traveled all the way across the country. If he merely wanted her return to Rhode Island, he would have sent one of his assistants to bring her home.

No, there was some other motive that drove Davis Gordon to track her down, and she'd figure it out soon enough.

In the meantime, she'd just hope and pray Tully would forgive her for her deception.

Once he finished eating, Davis took Brianna's elbow in his hand and escorted her out of the dining room and through the hotel lobby.

She waved at Mr. Isaac as he worked at the front desk. He returned her greeting, although he seemed rather confused by her appearance with Davis.

"Are you certain you wouldn't rather stay here at the hotel, dearest? I can get you a room next to mine." Davis placed his hand on her back as they stepped onto the boardwalk and began meandering down the street toward Maggie's shop.

Brianna would prefer Davis have no idea where she was staying, but in a small town, the information would be hard to keep a secret.

Terrified of what he would do when he found out the door she needed to enter was in a back alley, she scrambled to come up with some reason to get away from Davis before they reached the shop.

"It's such a pleasant evening, let's stroll to the park," she said, turning down a busy side street.

"Pleasant? Has this primitive atmosphere addled your sense?" Davis asked with what he probably assumed was a playful smile.

Brianna thought it looked more like he had a bad case of indigestion.

With a dismissive gesture, he waved a hand around, as though encompassing the entire town. "I've never experienced such unyielding heat, dust and misery. I insist on taking you to your apartment before this hideous sun scorches your delicate skin." As though he just noticed the lack of it, he stared at Brianna. "Where is your parasol? Don't tell me you've abandoned every trace of civility. Really, darling, you must not allow the lax behavior of these westerners to corrupt you entirely."

Barely suppressing the urge to roll her eyes, Brianna slowed her pace as Davis turned her around and directed her back the way they'd come.

A block away from the shop, Brianna spied Dugan Durfey walking on the other side of the street.

Relief filled her as she grasped a means to escape Davis, at least for the evening.

"Deputy Durfey!" she called, waving to him.

He jogged across the street and tipped his hat to her. "Howdy, Miss Dumont. How does this evening find you?"

"Perfectly well, Deputy. Are you on duty this evening?"

"I sure am." Dugan glanced over at Davis. His face remained impassive even though Brianna sensed his dislike of the man.

"I'm sorry, Deputy. This is B. Davis Gordon. He was my father's banker," she said, sidling away from Davis as he glared at the lawman.

"You forget to tell him I'm also your fiancé, my dearest." Davis held out his hand to Dugan. "Is the town always so…" Davis gestured to the street, "like this?"

Dugan took a step back and spoke with pride in his voice. "Yep. It's one of the largest cities in the state and attracting more businesses all the time."

"Did you hear Mr. and Mrs. Greenfield purchased the boarding house?" Brianna asked, looping her arm around Dugan's, much to Davis' displeasure.

"Sure did. I helped Edwin move in a table this afternoon. He was trying to unload it himself and having quite a time of it." Dugan noticed the stranger's cold stare as Brianna chatted about the wallpaper she'd helped Hattie select the previous day.

"Oh, Deputy, I just recalled the sheriff asked me to drop by the office to sign a statement regarding Mr. Darcey's arrest. May I take care of that now?" Brianna asked, offering Dugan a sweet smile.

"Sure, Miss Dumont. It will only take a moment then you and Mr. Gordon may get on with your evening." Dugan noticed Davis glowering at him.

Much to the bafflement of both men, Brianna turned to Davis. "Why don't you return to the hotel, Davis? I'm sure you're exhausted after such a long trip in this heat. Deputy Durfey will escort me home." She turned to Dugan with a pleading look. "Won't you?"

"It would be my pleasure," he said. After giving Davis a curt nod, he and Brianna strolled down the boardwalk.

She looked over her shoulder at her fuming fiancé and waved at him, rambling enough that it was even getting on her nerves.

When Davis turned and marched back to the hotel, she released a relieved sigh and snapped her mouth shut.

At the sheriff's office, Dugan located the paperwork, but Brianna had already signed it.

"Silly me, I must have forgotten," she said, batting her eyelashes at Dugan. "I apologize for being such a bother."

"You're no bother, Miss Dumont. Do you want to go back to the hotel to see Mr. Gordon?" Dugan asked as they stepped outside.

"No!" Brianna shouted, panicked. She lowered her voice and forced another smile. "It's been a long day and I'd prefer to go back to my apartment, if you don't mind escorting me."

"Not at all." Dugan matched his pace to hers as they walked back to Maggie's shop and down the alley. The deputy waited as she unlocked the door then tipped his hat to her and left after she closed the door and locked it.

Brianna hurried up the stairs and collapsed on the sofa, weary beyond anything she'd ever experienced in her life.

Living a lie might prove more taxing than she had the strength to endure.

Chapter Sixteen

"Confounded, dad-blamed, goldurn..." Tully fumed around his office, slamming a desk drawer. When that didn't bring the satisfaction he sought, he slammed it again for good measure.

"Somethin' eatin' at you, boss?" Dugan asked from his seat behind the desk across the room. Tully had been in a rank temper from the moment he arrived that morning. Generally, the sheriff was full of smiles and teasing. However, the past few days, he'd gone from surly to downright cranky. No one seemed to know the cause of his foul mood, but everyone hoped it would soon pass.

Tully shot a scathing glare his direction then returned to mumbling under his breath as he searched through papers on his desk, tossing around files.

From what Dugan observed, he wasn't actually trying to find anything, although he made a good show of it.

Suddenly, Tully stopped and stared out the window. Dugan followed his glance, observing Brianna Dumont stroll by on the arm of her fiancé.

The town seemed to have little else to talk about since B. Davis Gordon arrived and announced his plans to wed Brianna once they returned to Rhode Island.

As much as the man appeared to despise Baker City, Dugan didn't know why the couple remained in town. He got the idea, though, that Brianna wasn't in a hurry to leave.

In fact, Dugan didn't think she seemed sold on the idea of marrying Mr. Gordon. The citified dandy was handsome, in a pasty sort of way. He had charmed many of the women in town with his idle flattery and impeccable manners. As the son of a banker, Dugan assumed he probably had plenty of money.

Yet, something about the man didn't seem quite right to Dugan. Seth said the same thing after he met Gordon.

They'd both tried to discuss their thoughts with Tully, but as soon as they mentioned Mr. Gordon's name, the sheriff's jaw clenched and his eyes took on a cold, deadly glint.

Unaccustomed to seeing him in such a state, they quickly changed the subject.

Tully stood and his hand dropped to the gun strapped on his hip as he followed the couple's progress down the street.

"Boss?" Dugan asked, concerned by the sheriff's actions. "Everything okay?"

"No. No, it's not okay." Tully slumped into the chair and slammed another drawer. He took a deep breath and another. Visibly calming, he straightened the scattered papers on his desk then read each one.

An hour later, he looked at Dugan. "What do you know about all these robbery reports?"

"Robbery reports? I've filed a few the last month or so." Dugan took the file Tully held out to him and scanned through the paperwork. He sat in a chair in front of Tully's desk and read them again. Baffled, he looked at his boss. "What's going on here?"

"That's what I'd like to know." Tully had been so preoccupied with Brianna, apprehending Dale Darcey, and trying not to shoot Davis Gordon, he'd somehow overlooked the variety of thefts that had taken place in his town.

After seeing Brianna stroll by earlier with her sissified husband-to-be, Tully concluded it was time to forget about her and move on.

He'd forced himself to sit at his desk and read through a stack of reports he'd ignored the past few weeks.

The individual robberies didn't seem that unusual, but when he put them together, it made him question if the same person committed all the crimes.

Mr. Irwin claimed a basket of peaches vanished. The bakery turned in three reports of stolen bread. The butcher declared a roast and a chicken had disappeared. Frank Miller was missing an entire box of handkerchiefs, a tin of crackers, and two bottles of cough syrup. Four women in town reported stolen eggs. One woman claimed her son's clothes were taken right off the clothesline as they dried. The creamery turned in six reports of missing bottles of milk. Mr. Patterson reported the theft of a berry pie from the windowsill where his wife had set it to cool. A dozen other reports contained similar claims of missing food.

In addition, there were Brianna's two reports for her missing bag and shoes.

Of all the thefts, her bag seemed the most valuable, but her losses didn't fit with the other thefts.

"I think we've either got a thief living on the streets, stealing to stay alive, or someone too lazy to work." Tully tapped his finger on the file Dugan set on his desk. "What do you think?"

"I believe you're right, boss. We've all been taking the reports, knowing consumables aren't going to be recovered, but not putting them together as an ongoing problem with one thief." Dugan leaned back in the chair. "But Miss Dumont's missing bag and shoes don't fit with the other crimes and neither do the handkerchiefs. Everything else that was stolen was food, except for the Palmer boy's clothes."

"I'm inclined to think Miss Dumont's missing bag was pinched by someone who jumped on the train. Her shoes… I haven't figured that out yet, but I'd be willing to bet money all the other thefts are tied together. The handkerchiefs and cough syrup make me think someone is sick, either the thief or someone close to them. Maybe it's someone with a child and that's why they stole the clothes off Mrs. Palmer's line." Tully glanced out the window and noticed Sammy watching Brianna and Davis saunter down the street. "Or maybe it's a child trying to take care of someone."

Dugan looked outside. "You don't think Sammy is the thief, do you? He's no bigger than a minute, and he works part-time for Bowen. Does he know anything about him?"

"I keep forgetting to ask him, but I'll make a point of doing that soon."

"What if Sammy was stealing all that stuff because he's an orphan? We can't throw that kid in jail, boss."

Tully's voice was gruff when he spoke. "I know that. What kind of bully do you think I am?"

Dugan grinned and shrugged. "Normally, I wouldn't take you as one at all, but you've been as crotchety as a sore-footed mule in the Sahara since Mr. Gordon arrived."

The slightest hint of a smirk lifted the corners of Tully's mouth. "How would you know anything about the Sahara? Do you even know what continent it's on?"

"Africa," Dugan said with a self-satisfied smirk. "I'm not nearly as dumb as I look."

Tully laughed and pointed toward the door. "Why don't you get out of here and enjoy what's left of the day. I'll see if I can make a little progress with our thief."

Chapter Seventeen

"Do you recall the Vandergards?" Davis asked as Brianna lingered over a cup of tea at the hotel after he'd insisted she join him there for lunch.

Bored with Davis' jabbering conversation, she wanted to hold her hands over her ears and run out of the room.

The past few days had been the most trying she'd ever known. Not only did he talk nonstop, Davis also operated under the false assumption she actually cared what he had to say.

She wondered how a man with so little intelligence had done so well in his father's banking business. Then again, Bertram Gordon was the one who handled the big decisions and accounts. It was easy to see why he'd question his son's judgment and abilities.

When Davis looked at her, waiting for her response, she swallowed down a frustrated groan. "I do recall the Vandergards. They have that lovely home with the wisteria that grows over the front gate."

Davis took a breath and continued speaking in a voice that grated on every one of Brianna's nerves. "Well, their daughter Mildred ran off with one of the Carlyle boys. Quite a scandal erupted, since his father owns the cannery down at the pier. Can you imagine? Why, I heard…"

Ready to scream, Brianna took a final sip of her tea then stood. "Pardon my departure, Davis, but I really must go. I have work to attend to this afternoon."

A disapproving glare accompanied his haughty sigh as he rose to his feet. "It is unseemly for my wife-to-be to run around this town writing articles for the paper. It is of the topmost importance for you to begin practicing discretion, my dear."

"And I will, Davis, but I do have assignments I agreed to finish for Mr. Packwood and I intend to keep my word. Now, if you'll excuse me." Brianna took a step toward the door, but Davis' hand on her arm stopped her.

"I'll accompany you. The wild ruffians in this town can't be trusted and I'm not of a mind to let you out of my sight. By the way, you look ravishing in that gown, my precious darling." Davis left money on the table to pay for their meals then lifted his straw hat and settled it on his head. "If you refuse to heed my advice, I suppose I shall have to spend my afternoon escorting you around town."

Davis took her elbow in his hand and guided her out the door. Heat bore down on them as though they walked around the perimeter of a blazing fire.

Expertly snapping open her parasol, Brianna held it over her head, scrambling for some excuse to get rid of Davis. The headache that started as a faint thumping in her head had grown to a persistent pounding that made her want to shove her handkerchief into his mouth for a few moments of quiet. Thoughts of Dale Darcey with his stinky sock stuffed in his mouth made her smile until she recalled the wonderful moments she'd spent in Tully's arms.

Filled with an acute ache in the region of her heart, she wanted to curl into a ball and cry out her frustrations. Rather than give in to the desire, she stood a little taller and lifted her chin.

No matter what Davis said, she did have a deadline to meet on an article she'd started about Edwin and Hattie Greenfield taking over the boarding house. She could finish it back at her apartment, but she certainly wouldn't divulge that detail to her irritating fiancé.

Instead, she wracked her brain for something that would give her an hour or two of relief from the annoying man. Struck with sudden inspiration, she changed direction and headed toward the livery stable.

"I say, Brianna, where are you going in such a common manner? It's most unbecoming. Decorum, precious. Walk with decorum and let those around you know you are unhurried and have no need for haste," Davis scolded, lengthening his stride to keep up with her.

"A story I'm working on requires me to ride out to one of the mines." Brianna slowed and looked at Davis with big, pleading eyes. "Will you ride along with me? The trail there is dusty and hot, and there's nowhere to stop for a rest. Horseback is the only way to reach the location. The arduous journey wouldn't seem so challenging if you'd go along."

A look of horror crossed his face and the façade Davis maintained slipped. The only thing he feared more than committing a social blunder or poverty was horses.

Amused, Brianna watched the wheels in his head spin as he tried to concoct an excuse not to go. "My dear, I just remembered I need to send a telegram to Father. I should see to that right away, lest I forget. Why don't you run along and do your little story? I'll meet you back at the hotel at four. We can enjoy a spot of tea."

A becoming pout rode her lips as she looked at Davis, pretending she found his news distressing. "I shall miss you. Somehow, I'll manage to make the trip on my own, if you're certain you must stay here."

"I'm certain, but I'll walk you to the livery." Davis took her elbow in his hand again and walked her down the street to the livery.

When he lingered at the door, Brianna had to carry through with her ruse, asking Milt to place the sidesaddle on a horse for her. Taken aback by her request, he didn't say anything as he saddled the horse she often rode and led it outside for her.

Brianna looked to Davis and smiled. "Will you help me mount?"

"Of course," Davis said, taking the parasol from her hand then stepping back. "Now you have both hands free."

The urge to roll her eyes or lambast Davis for being such a cowardly milksop made her turn her back to him. Milt gave her a hand up to the saddle. She settled her skirts before taking her parasol from Davis and holding the reins in her other hand.

"Enjoy your ride, my dear," Davis called as she rode away from him toward the south end of town.

"At least I won't have to listen to your incessant blathering for a while," she muttered under her breath. Her dress wasn't meant for riding and rubbed in places it shouldn't, but she'd do most anything to escape Davis for an hour or two.

One thing she could be thankful for about his unexpected visit was the clothes he'd brought along. Three trunks of her belongings traveled with him on the train. She was happy to have every shoe, stocking, and gown the staff at home had packed.

Aware of how his mind worked, he'd most likely assumed she'd run off without a change of clothes, or some such nonsense.

Repeatedly, he'd questioned her about why she traveled to Baker City, of all places. The story she gave him was the same one she'd told everyone else in town: she came to check on her father's holdings in a mine and it turned out to be nothing more than a hole in a hill owned by a very filthy, testy old man.

Davis offered to pursue a lawsuit for false representation with Clive Fisher, but Brianna refused. No matter what else happened, she liked the crusty miner, even if he did stink to high heaven and back again.

Thrilled with an hour or two to relax without Davis looking over her shoulder, she rode past Ian's lumberyard then took the road that circled around the back of town. The horse moved at a plodding gait, but even so, she'd only been gone about fifteen minutes when she reached the north end of town.

Turning the horse around, she headed back to the lumberyard. As she rode past the office, Ian hurried out, waving to her.

"What are you about on such a bonny day, lass?" he asked as she reined in the horse.

Brianna smiled, knowing she could be truthful with him. "I'm hiding from Davis. I needed a little quiet time."

Ian laughed. "The man does like to talk and talk."

With a grin, she nodded in agreement.

"So why are you out here?" Ian rubbed a gentle hand along the horse's neck and glanced up at her.

"The only means of escape was to go for a ride. Davis is terrified of horses. He is under the assumption I'm riding out to a mine to work on an article, which is only partially untrue. I do have an article I need to write, but I didn't need to ride anywhere to do it."

"Ach, lass, pardon my bluntness, but why is it ye're engaged to Mr. Gordon? I know for a fact one of the finest men in town would be happy to court ye." Ian's brogue thickened as he spoke, which it often did when he was mad or excited. "Deep are the wounds ye've caused him."

Emotions that simmered close to the surface threatened to spill over as Brianna looked at her friend. "It's complicated, Ian. If I were free to choose, Davis would be on the first train heading east and I'd beg that fine man you mentioned to forgive me." A remorseful sigh rolled up from her soul. "Since I can't do as I please, I'm trying to do the best I can in a less than ideal situation."

Ian studied her then pointed to his house across the meadow. "Why don't you make yourself at home this afternoon? I guarantee Mr. Gordon won't bother you there. You can finish your article for the newspaper and no one will be any the wiser."

The thought of spending the afternoon at the beautiful MacGregor home sounded too good to be true. "Are you sure I won't bother you or Maggie?"

"Not a bit, lass. I'll be here and Maggie's at her shop. The back door is unlocked. Go right on in. You can leave the horse down by the barn. No one will see him there from the road. If you'd rather, I can take him back to the livery."

"Thank you so much, Ian. If I hope to maintain my ruse, it's best I ride the horse back into town later." Brianna smiled at the kind man. "You don't know how much I appreciate this."

"I think I might have an idea. Help yourself to anything you like at the house. Maggie made a delicious cake yesterday and there's a pitcher of lemonade in the refrigerator."

"That sounds delightful," Brianna said, waving at Ian as he walked back to the office.

She rode across the meadow to his home, left the horse tied to the hitching rail by the barn, then hurried to the house. As she walked across the yard, she admired the colorful flowers blooming in profusion.

Maggie mentioned something about Charles and Martha Byron working for them to take care of the yard and the spotless home. Brianna wondered if either of them would be at the house.

Rather than rush inside, she tapped on the back door and waited to see if someone opened it. When all remained quiet, she stepped inside. The house felt so much cooler than the heat outdoors.

Relieved to have somewhere quiet to work away from Davis, Brianna removed her hat and gloves, poured a glass of lemonade then took a notebook and pencil from her reticule.

The kitchen table provided the perfect spot for her to work the next hour, finishing the story. After she penned the final sentence, she relaxed in the calm luxury of Maggie and Ian's home, grateful to have such good friends.

In all her life, she'd never met, or even imagined meeting, such open, kind people as she'd encountered in Baker City. Thoughts of her friends, of people she'd come to care a great deal for, led her mind straight to Tully.

He'd stayed far away from her since Davis arrived in town and she missed him so much, she ached to see him.

She missed the scruff on his face, the dimples in his cheeks and his teasing smile. She longed to hear the deep baritone rumble of his voice, see the mischievous sparks dance in his hazel eyes, and watch his shirt stretch across those broad shoulders as he moved.

In love with the man, she had no idea what to do about it.

The arrival of Davis had made it clear to Brianna that no matter how much she cared for

Tully, she'd rather break both their hearts than allow anything to happen to him.

Although Davis assured her that her father's death was a robbery, she wasn't convinced someone hadn't wanted him dead. The question was why. Why would anyone want her big-hearted, jovial, wonderful father dead?

Dwelling on questions to which she had no answers wouldn't help anything, so Brianna finished her lemonade then washed and dried her glass. Hastily writing Maggie and Ian a note, she thanked them for allowing her to hide in their house for a while, and gathered her things.

It took a little work to mount the horse without any help, but she finally settled her skirts and headed past the lumberyard. After waving at Ian, she once again took the road that skirted around the back of town then rode in from the north.

In case Davis watched for her, she wanted to make her afternoon trip appear real. She returned the horse to the livery and paid Milt then walked to the newspaper office and left the article.

Mr. Packwood gave her another assignment to work on then she exited through the newspaper office's back door and wandered to the park.

Barely had she taken a seat on a bench in the shade when Sammy plopped down beside her.

"How are you, Sammy? I haven't seen you much the last few days." Brianna gave the boy a one-armed hug, pulling him against her side.

The child gazed around, as though he expected Davis to materialize. Finally, he pointed to Brianna with a questioning look.

"You want to know who the man is that's been with me. Is that it?" she asked.

Sammy nodded.

Brianna settled against the back of the bench and Sammy leaned against her. "Well, that man is from the town where I used to live. I'm supposed to marry him and he wants me to go back with him."

Sammy sat up and shook his head.

"I don't want to leave." Brianna bent down close to Sammy's face and dropped her voice. "I'll even tell you a secret. I don't like Mr. Gordon and I have no interest in marrying him. In fact, nothing would make me happier if he'd just disappear."

The boy wrapped his thin arms around Brianna and gave her a tight hug. Rather than let go and run off, the child held on, offering his own bit of comfort.

Brianna blinked back the tears that burned her eyes at the child's affection and pasted on a bright smile. "It's much too lovely a day to be sad, Sammy. Do you think a dish of ice cream might make us both feel better?"

The boy hopped to his feet and tugged on Brianna's hand. She laughed as she stood and together they made their way to the drugstore where they each ordered a scoop of caramel ice cream.

Tully had been making his rounds through town after lunch when he noticed Brianna and her fiancé exit the hotel and stroll down the street.

The woman appeared so lovely, it made his heart hurt. A satin-striped gown the same shade as her blue eyes looked like she'd pulled down a piece of the summer sky and wrapped around herself. The gossamer sleeves and ruffle around her neck might have been accents made from bits of the fluffy clouds overhead.

A white hat decorated with blue plumes and ribbons sloped at a saucy angle on her head, and she carried a white parasol in one gloved hand.

He followed the couple as they meandered down the street, admiring the swish of Brianna's skirts as she walked.

Davis kept close to her side, talking nonstop. Something he said irritated Brianna. Although she turned and smiled, Tully knew her well enough to discern the smile as fake and catch the flash of anger in her eyes. That alone gave him hope that she wouldn't leave town with the simpering fool.

As he skulked along behind them, he wasn't the only one keeping an eye on the couple. Tully caught a glimpse of Sammy trailing along, almost out of sight. Humored that he and the boy both lurked in the shadows behind Brianna, Tully remained silent.

Without luck, he'd been trying to find Sammy to see if he could get the boy to respond to some questions. Now that he'd located the child, he wasn't of a mind to speak to him. He was much more interested in seeing what Davis was up to with Brianna.

From the alley across the street, he watched as she mounted a horse at the livery and Davis walked toward the hotel. Sammy scampered off in the direction of the park.

Tully wondered at Brianna's choice of riding attire. The gown belonged in some fancy parlor, drinking tea. It certainly wasn't made for riding, even if she had asked Milt to use the sidesaddle.

Concerned she might fall off in her getup, he hurried down the street after her. Someone stopped to ask him a question then he noticed old Mrs. Jepson trying to butcher a chicken and having a time of it. Tully helped her before rushing toward the edge of town. He'd nearly reached the lumberyard when Brianna rode up.

Tully ducked behind a tree and observed as she spoke with Ian then rode off toward his house.

"Why don't you talk to her?" a voice asked as a hand thumped him on the back.

Tully spun around with his gun drawn, scowling at his best friend.

Thane held his hands up in front of him, smirking.

Flustered and frustrated, Tully holstered the gun and pointed an accusing finger at Thane. "Are you trying to get your dang head blasted right off your idiotic body? Do you know what kind of trouble that would stir up with your wife if you made me kill you?"

Thane chuckled and slapped him on the back again. "What's got you so peevish today, other than Brianna's fancy pants fiancé?"

Tully sighed and leaned against the tree. "Isn't that enough reason?" He removed his hat and ran a hand over his head before settling it back in place.

"I don't know what to do, Thane. What if she leaves with him?"

"Give her a reason to stay," Thane said, looking at Tully like he'd missed the simplest solution. "If you marry her first, Mr. Gordon sure couldn't drag her back to Rhode Island as his bride."

"Marry her?" Tully shouted, then dropped his voice and looked around the tree to make sure no one heard him over at the lumberyard. "What put a crazy notion like that in your head?"

"You." Thane shook his index finger at his friend. "Deny it all you want, but you are smitten, besotted, in love with, and otherwise taken by Miss Brianna Dumont."

The truth in Thane's words left Tully without the ability to protest.

"The way I see it, the chance for a happy future is right in front of you, my friend. All you need to do is reach out and grab it before someone else takes it from you." Thane grinned, mindful his next words would spur his friend to action if nothing else would. "I never knew you to be such a coward. All this time, I thought you were a man, but it looks like I may have been mistaken. Only a boy would lurk around corners, whining about missing out on something he could just as well have, if he was brave enough to lay claim to it."

"You better watch your mouth, or I might just have to punch it." Tully's scowl darkened and he straightened to his full height.

"Just telling it like it is. You've been worse than a rabid badger in a cage ever since Brianna came to town. If you don't at least tell her how you feel, you'll regret it the rest of your life." Thane gave Tully a serious, solemn look. "I mean it, Tully. If your heart's telling you she's the one, listen to it."

Tully slumped against the tree again. "I can't just walk up to her and say, 'Pardon me, but I'm in love with you, let's get married.' That isn't how things are done."

Thane pulled Tully away from the tree and settled his hand on his shoulder, walking with him back into town. "No, that isn't how things are done. You need flowers, maybe a box of those chocolates Frank carries in his store." Thane wrinkled his nose in feigned disgust. "Take a bath. Have the barber give you a trim and splash on some shaving lotion. Definitely put on some clean clothes. Then here's what you should do…"

As they sauntered back through town to the jail, Thane gave him step-by-step directions, all of which he planned to ignore.

"Why are you here, Thane?" Tully asked as he opened the door to his office and they moved inside.

"I came in to place a lumber order with Ian. We're making improvements out at the Double D Mine. I'd finished my business with him and thought I'd swing by the store and pick up a little something for Jemma and the kids when I happened to notice you slinking around town like a lovesick peeping Tom."

Tully growled. "I wasn't slinking, I'm not lovesick, and I'm absolutely not a peeping Tom."

Thane laughed and stepped back outside. "Whatever you say. If you get tired of mooning for your ladylove, come out to the ranch for supper some evening. We'd enjoy having you."

"I might just take you up on that." Tully held out a hand to Thane.

Thane took it and gave him a hearty handshake then turned back toward the mercantile where he'd left his horse before he started following Tully. "Just think about what I said, Tully. The worst she can do is say no or slap your face. If memory serves me correctly, she's already done that, so what have you got to lose?"

With a dismissive wave, Tully returned inside the office and sat at his desk. He managed to do a little paperwork before he started wondering if Thane's words might hold some merit. In need of some fresh air to clear his head, he went to make a round through town and happened to see Brianna and Sammy enter the drugstore. The two of them sat in front of a window, enjoying a dish of ice cream.

The child seemed at ease with the woman. Tully wondered again about the boy's home life. As soon as things settled down with Brianna, he'd get to the bottom of the strange thefts and the boy's possible involvement.

In the meantime, he needed to come up with a way to send Davis packing and convince Brianna she belonged with him.

Chapter Eighteen

Unable to force herself to meet Davis for tea at the hotel, Brianna returned to her apartment and found Maggie had left early.

She unlocked the back door and slipped inside, turning the lock behind her.

Up in the apartment, she changed out of the gown that smelled of horses and took a refreshing sponge bath before dressing in a lightweight summer gown and pinning her hair up for the second time that day.

As she poked in the last hairpin, the back door rattled, as though someone tried to open it. No one knocked and she found it strange, but didn't give it another thought as she pinned on a hat that matched her cream-colored frock and tugged on a pair of gloves.

Mindful that Davis would be in a tizzy if she didn't appear soon, she hurried down the stairs. Voices outside stilled her feet.

Quietly pressing her ear to the crack at the door, she listened as Davis spoke to someone.

"I'm tired of playing these games. You do what I told you to take care of days ago while I keep her occupied. Before we leave, I still intend to make Brianna mine, whether it's willingly or by force. Perhaps I need to buy my way into her affections since nothing else seems to work. That troublesome woman better be worth it."

The other voice was muted as the two men walked down the alley.

Brianna held a hand over her mouth to keep from screaming out her anger and frustration. It seemed Davis still held despicable plans where she was concerned and had enlisted someone else to help carry them out.

In the few days he'd been in town, she couldn't recall seeing him with anyone in particular. Certainly not someone he'd speak to with such open frankness.

Davis might think she was incapable of taking care of herself, but she'd prove him wrong.

Several minutes passed before she opened the door and peered outside. With no one in sight, she slipped down the alley, cut across another and hurried to a store she'd walked past several times but never entered.

A man with a bright red, shaggy walrus mustache gave her a surprised glance as she strode inside the shop that specialized in weaponry and mining supplies.

"May I help you, ma'am?" he asked with a wary look as she hurried to the counter.

"Yes, sir, I certainly hope you'll be able to help me." Brianna motioned to a display of revolvers. "I need to purchase a weapon."

His bushy eyebrows nearly touched his flaming red hairline, but he opened the display case. "My name's McIntosh and this is my store. Who might you be?"

"Miss Dumont. It's a pleasure to meet you."

The dubious look on his face let her know he'd decide if it was a pleasure or not later. "What are you interested in purchasing?"

"I need something light enough to carry with me, but with enough power to hit the intended target and inflict damage." She pointed to a forty-four revolver. "How about that one?"

Mr. McIntosh handed her the gun but shook his head when it pulled her hand down. "That one will be too heavy, I think. You need something smaller and easier to handle."

He glanced at her and the reticule she'd placed on the counter. "Where are you planning to carry the gun? Your pocket or your reticule?"

"In my reticule." She held the Colt in her hand and sighted down the barrel. "No, that one won't do."

Surprised by the way she handled the weapon, as though she was familiar with guns, the man studied her a moment. "Have you previously owned a gun?"

"No, I haven't owned *a* gun. I owned three, but I left them behind when I moved here. My father taught me to shoot and we used to shoot targets all the time." Brianna handed the weapon back to him.

She tried a few other pistols, but none of them felt right in her hand.

"I just remembered I have one in the back. Wait here," Mr. McIntosh said, disappearing through a doorway. He returned carrying a revolver that made Brianna smile.

"It's so pretty, Mr. McIntosh." Admiration filled her face as she studied the gun in his hand. "I'd buy it just for that fact, but I really do need to be able to shoot it."

"Give it a try," he said, holding it out to her. She took it in her hand, pleased with the way it felt — well balanced, not too heavy, yet sturdy enough to get the job done.

"Tell me why I should purchase this one," she said, sighting down the barrel then examining the cylinder.

Mr. McIntosh leaned an elbow on the top of the display case. "It's a thirty-two-caliber center-fire double-action revolver with exhibition-grade engraving. See the beautiful floral scrollwork on the two-stage barrel? It goes across the frame and cylinder. And it's got that pretty pearl grip on it, like it was made for a beautiful lady like you."

Brianna frowned. "Flattery will get you nowhere, but I do like this one. What's the price?"

"That one is used, so I'll let you have it for ten dollars."

She shook her head and set the revolver down. "I may be a female but that doesn't mean I'm stupid. I'll give you eight dollars and you'll throw in a box of cartridges."

Mr. McIntosh grinned. "You drive a hard bargain, but it's a deal."

While he wrote out a receipt for her, she dropped five cartridges into the chambers and snapped the cylinder closed.

"You sure you don't need a lesson in how to shoot that thing?" Mr. McIntosh asked as she stuffed the gun in her reticule then tried to find somewhere to hide the cartridges.

"I'm quite certain, sir. Might I prevail upon you to deliver these cartridges to me tomorrow? I'm late for a meeting and would prefer to not carry them with me."

"I reckon I can do that for you. Where do you live?"

She gave him the address of Maggie's dress shop then hurried to the door. "Thank you, Mr. McIntosh. You've been extremely helpful."

"You're welcome, Miss Dumont." He shot her a teasing smile and waggled a finger at her in warning. "Just don't kill anyone with that."

"I only shoot to maim," she said, suppressing a laugh as his eyes goggled in astonishment.

No matter what Davis had planned, at least Brianna wouldn't be completely at his mercy. The man was nothing but a bully and a sissy. She doubted he'd ever handled a weapon of any type. If the situation became dire and she pulled the revolver on him, odds were high that he might faint.

The thought of him doing such made her giggle as she hurried down the street and up the steps of the hotel.

Davis sat in the lobby reading the newspaper. He set it aside and glared at her. As he rose to his feet, he pointed to the clock on the wall behind the front desk.

"You are eighty-six minutes late, my precious. Where have you been?" Davis roughly grasped her elbow and guided her into the dining room.

The waitress seated them at a table in front of one of the tall windows on a shady side of the building. A welcome breeze blew in, cooling Brianna's hot face.

"After returning from town, I was utterly exhausted and needed a rest. I just wanted to look my best for you." Brianna pretended to dab at tears. "My sincere apologies, Davis. I didn't mean to upset you."

"No. I suppose not." He gave her a long glance as the waitress set glasses of water on their table.

After they ate, Davis insisted Brianna join him for a stroll. Normally, he was the one who preferred to stay indoors, so the fact he wanted to go out caught her off guard.

Together, they made their way down one side of the main thoroughfare, crossed the street and meandered down the other.

"You've yet to invite me to see your apartment, dearest. I'd very much like to see what your rooms above the dress shop are like."

Brianna shook her head and slowed her step, since they were nearly to Maggie's store. "Now, Davis, you know it's not proper at all for a gentleman to enter a lady's living quarters when she lives alone and has no chaperone."

"That's exactly why you're going to open that door and we're going to have a little fun." Davis grabbed her upper arm and propelled her around the corner and into the shadows of the alley.

"No, Davis. You don't want to do this," she said, struggling to get away from him.

"Believe me, when I say I do. I've waited a very long time for this," he said, pulling her against him and pressing a vile kiss to her lips.

Struggling against him, she attempted to suck in a gulp of air. Suddenly, he released her. Something sweet smelling covered her face and filled her nose, leaving her groggy and lightheaded right before her world went black.

Chapter Nineteen

A sharp pain behind Brianna's left eye made her wonder if her head might split in two. Slowly opening her eyes, she stared up at the evening sky.

Disoriented, dizzy and nauseous, she sat up and swallowed. A glance to her side brought her to her knees as she scrambled over to Davis, pressing her hands to his chest. Blood turned the flaxen-colored linen of his suit crimson as it flowed from two wounds.

Glazed eyes stared at her, full of pain and shock.

"It's okay, Davis. Help will come and you'll be fine," she said, certain he wouldn't be fine. No one could sustain wounds such as his or lose that much blood and survive. As her mind regained the ability to function, she wondered how she'd blacked out and who had shot Davis.

"Book," he croaked then drew a shuddering final breath.

"No, Davis! Don't you dare die!" she screamed. "I don't want you to die."

Tully ran into the alley and slid to a stop at the sight of her hovering over the dead man. As he broke up a fight a block away, he'd heard two gunshots rock through the evening air. Racing toward the sound as fast as he could, he rounded the corner of the alley.

Brianna's blood-coated hands and horror-stricken gaze made his heart fall into his boots. Any number of thoughts entered his head, but not one of them proclaimed she was guilty of killing a man. She might not have liked Davis, but she wouldn't shoot him.

He hunkered down and placed a hand on her shoulder as tears dripped down her cheeks. "What happened?"

"I don't know, Tully. He kissed me and I struggled. The next thing I recall is waking up to find him shot. None of it makes sense," she said, sitting back and staring at her bloodstained gloves.

Tully picked up a revolver on the ground near Davis. "Have you seen this before?" he asked, showing her the weapon.

Her eyes widened. "Yes. I bought it this afternoon, before I met Davis for dinner."

"Did you plan to shoot him?"

On the verge of going into shock, she shook her head so forcefully, hairpins fell out and her hair tumbled around her shoulders and down her back. "No, Tully. I didn't. I wouldn't shoot to kill even if I had pulled the gun on him. How could you even ask that?"

Before he could say anything further, the alley filled with people who'd heard the ruckus. Hastily placing himself between the crowd and Brianna, Tully motioned for them all to get back.

"Someone run fetch Doc, please. And if you see my deputies, send them over," he asked, hoping to calm everyone. "Please folks, don't panic. Everything will be fine. If any of you saw anything suspicious, though, come see me at my office tonight or in the morning."

The crowd dispersed, although a few lingered, waiting for the doctor to arrive. A few moments later the man did. With his shirt untucked and his collar only half-fastened, Tully assumed Doc had been getting ready for bed when he was summoned.

It took only a moment for Doc to pronounce Davis dead. Tully knew he was, but wanted an official declaration.

"Mr. Palmer, would you mind letting the undertaker know about this?" Tully asked the saddle shop owner who often offered his help when it was needed.

"I'll go right now," he said, hurrying down the alley and around the corner.

Tully sighed in relief when Dugan and Seth both raced into the alley.

"Holy smokes, boss! What happened?" Dugan asked, taking in Davis' body as well as Brianna's bloody hands and dress.

"Someone shot and killed Mr. Gordon," Tully said, stating the facts. "Miss Dumont was here with him when I arrived on the scene of the crime."

Dugan leaned toward Tully and dropped his voice to a whisper. "You don't think she did it, do you?"

"Of course not," Tully snarled. "But the evidence points to her. It's her gun that killed him and she was the only one in the alley. Until we find who did it, I have to take her in."

Dugan and Seth both stared at him. The two deputies glanced at each other then Seth stepped forward. "We'll take care of things here until the undertaker arrives. You do what you need to do."

"Would one of you send for Maggie and Ian?" Tully shoved the gun that had killed Davis into his pocket then bent down and placed his hands beneath Brianna's elbows, lifting her to her feet. "Miss Dumont, I need you to come with me."

In a daze, she nodded and allowed him to guide her through the alley and behind Maggie's shop. She tried to stop at the back door, but Tully took a firmer grip on her arm. He knew she needed to clean up, but she couldn't do it at her apartment. It was far too close to the scene of the crime. "Brianna, darlin', you have to come with me to the jail. As much as I hate to, I need to hold you as a suspect in Davis' murder."

"What?" Brianna seemed to snap out of her stupor and glared at Tully. "I didn't kill him. I didn't even shoot him. Didn't you listen? I told you what happened. How can you do this to me?"

"I don't want to, but I have to uphold the law. If it was anyone else, I'd do the same thing."

"Even Maggie, or Jemma?" she asked, feeling sick to her stomach.

"Even them." Tully placed a hand to her back and nudged her forward. "Don't hate me for doing my job. I have to do this."

"No, you don't. You don't," she said, leaning against the building and losing the contents of her stomach.

Tully held her hair out of her face then handed her a handkerchief. As she wiped her face with it, blood smeared across her cheek.

"You can do this, Fred. You must," Tully whispered in her ear. He wrapped an arm around her waist and let her lean on his strength as he walked her along back alleys to the jail.

Instead of locking her into a cell, he sat her down in a chair by his desk and carefully removed her bloody gloves, placing them in a bag he pulled from a box in a storage cabinet.

He filled a pitcher full of water from the pump outside and rushed back into his office. After she washed her hands and wiped her face, he poured her a glass of cool water.

As she sipped it, he studied her ashen skin and the despondent look on her face.

For the time being, he had to distance himself from his feelings and need to protect her. Whether he liked it or not, he had a job to do.

If it were anyone else, he would have already shoved them in a cell and locked the door.

However, he couldn't do that to Brianna. Not yet.

The door banged open and Maggie and Ian rushed inside. "What in the world happened?" Maggie asked as she took in Brianna's shocked state and Tully's sullen look.

He motioned for them to step away from Brianna and moved to a corner across the room, dropping his voice to a whisper. "Two shots were fired. I ran into the alley and found her with Davis Gordon's body. He'd been shot with a gun she purchased this afternoon. She claims she blacked out and when she came to, he was dead. I believe her, but all the evidence points to her being the one to shoot him. It's going to take time to unravel the truth and I need to keep her safe. The best place to do that is right here."

Tully glanced back at Brianna as she sat in morose silence at his desk. "I hate to ask, but can she come to your house long enough to get a bath and change her clothes? She has his blood all over her and…"

Maggie placed a hand on his arm in understanding. "Of course, Tully. We'll take care of her then bring her back."

"I'll escort her there, get a change of clothes, and bring her back. I just wanted to make sure you wouldn't mind having her there since many in town are going to say you harbored a murderer under your roof."

Ian scoffed. "Ach, man, I dinna think the lass capable of such madness and neither do ye. She'll come home with us, for certain."

"Perhaps we should go now, while everyone is still somewhat occupied." Maggie moved toward Brianna and placed a hand on her shoulder. "Brianna, Ian and I are going to take you home so you can clean up. Okay?"

She nodded her head and rose to her feet, clinging to Maggie's hand as they walked together to the door where Tully and Ian waited.

"I can get her there safely, Tully," Ian said, looking around outside to make sure no one lurked in the shadows. Although Tully hadn't said anything, he knew the sheriff feared for Brianna's safety, and rightly so.

"I trust you, Ian. I'll get her clothes and be there soon." Tully motioned for Maggie and Brianna to step outside with Ian.

He followed them as far as the edge of town then jogged back to Maggie's shop. Although he had his own key to the place, he hadn't told Brianna. It would have unsettled her to know he could come and go anytime he pleased.

Quickly unlocking the door, he rushed upstairs and went to her bedroom. He rifled through her dresses, finally choosing one of her riding skirts and shirtwaists, assuming it would be more comfortable than the fancy clothes she'd brought with her from back east.

The second dresser drawer he opened contained the items he sought. He wrapped her unmentionables up in the skirt along with the blouse then clomped down the steps and out the door. Before he left, he pulled the spare key from the beam above the door, determined to keep anyone from sneaking in.

He glanced in the alley and observed as the undertaker oversaw moving the body while Dugan watched and Seth kept the crowd back.

Tully hurried down the alley and cut across a few yards to the lumberyard. With darkness falling, it was easy to reach Ian and Maggie's home unseen. Not that he felt he was doing anything wrong, but he didn't want to set a precedent for future arrests. He certainly wouldn't have allowed any of his male suspects to go home and take a bath before he locked them up.

Nonetheless, it would be hard enough to keep Brianna in jail, so he wanted to make things as easy for her as possible.

He tapped on the back door and opened it then stepped inside. Ian poured tea into a cup on the counter and held up the pot in his hand. "Want a cup?" he asked.

"Sure," Tully said, setting the clothes he'd brought on the counter.

Ian poured a cup of tea for Tully and set it in front of him then motioned to the sugar bowl and pitcher of cream on the kitchen table. "Help yourself," he said, before he dashed out of the room with Brianna's clothes.

Gone only a moment, he returned and added sugar to a cup of tea, taking a seat beside Tully at the table. "Maggie said they'll be down soon. Brianna hasn't said a word. What do you think happened?"

"I think someone wanted Davis dead and decided to make it look like Brianna did it. It seems awfully strange he was shot in the chest the same day she purchased that gun."

"Who would do such a thing?" Ian asked, sitting forward in his chair. "What kind of person would pin the blame on an innocent woman?"

"A spineless coward or a deranged monster." Tully had seen far too many of both during his years as a lawman. He drank his tea and glanced up when Maggie walked in with Brianna.

Tully stood and waited for the two women to take a seat at the table. Ian poured tea for them both and carried the cups over to the table.

Maggie gave hers a liberal spoon of sugar, but Brianna picked hers up and mindlessly sipped the hot brew. She returned the cup to the saucer and looked at Tully. "I didn't kill Davis."

Tully reached across the table and patted her hand. "I know that, Brianna, but it was your gun that killed him and you were the one in the alley with his blood all over your hands. The evidence looks bad and no matter what I want to do, I have to take you in."

"But I didn't kill him. Even if I wished he'd disappear, I wouldn't kill him." Brianna lifted her chin, a hint of defiance returning as she sat a little straighter.

"We'll figure out who did, but I have to get you back to the jail." Tully took another swig of his tea and stood.

Brianna sighed and rose to her feet, holding out her wrists. "Just cuff me and get it over with."

Tully took her hand in his and gave it a gentle squeeze. "That won't be necessary, but I do need to get you to the jail." He looked to Maggie and Ian. "Thank you for your help."

"It's the least we could do," Maggie said, giving both Brianna and Tully hugs. "If there is anything at all we can do to help, please ask."

"Do you think Brianna could borrow a blanket and a pillow? She won't want to use what we've got in the jail."

"We'll gather some things and be there soon," Ian said, giving Brianna a kind smile.

"Thank you," she said, following Tully out the door and across the meadow.

He kept to the shadows and guided her to the back of the jail. After waiting for a wagon to pass, he hurried her around the side of the building and inside his office.

He'd just locked her in a cell when Dugan returned.

"Where's Seth?" Tully asked as Dugan closed the office door behind him.

"There's still a crowd lingering near the alley, so he stayed to keep people out of it. I figured you'd want to take a look at the area in the morning, in the daylight," Dugan said, grabbing a box of cartridges from the desk drawer and shoving it in his pocket.

"Are you planning on a shoot-out?" Tully gave him a speculative glance.

"Nope, but I don't plan to find myself in need of more and not have them handy, especially with a bunch of men drinking at the saloon down the street. I told Seth I'd be right back, but I wanted to make sure you didn't need anything." Dugan looked around the doorway to the jail cells where Brianna stood in numbed silence in the first cell. The deputy dropped his voice and moved closer to Tully. "Is she gonna be okay, boss?"

"Eventually. We need to figure out who did this, and I want to keep it quiet that we're searching.

For now, you and Seth get the word out that it was her gun and she was found with the body."

Dugan gave him a knowing look. "So, whoever did it thinks we aren't looking for him. Is that the idea?"

Tully nodded. "I knew you were smarter than you look." He thumped the deputy on the back as the younger man opened the door. "You two be careful out there and if you need me, send someone to get me."

"Will do." Dugan disappeared down the street.

Tully had barely closed the door when Maggie and Ian arrived.

"Open her cell, Tully," Maggie ordered as she and Ian stood with full arms. "And for goodness sakes, take that filthy mattress out of there. Do you want something nasty to crawl on her?"

"I'll have you know I keep these cells spotless and vermin free."

Ian chuckled. "At least when they aren't occupied."

Tully unlocked the cell and opened the door. He pulled out the mattress and tossed it in one of the other cells.

Maggie examined the cot frame to make sure it was free of bugs before Ian plopped a feather mattress on it. She covered the mattress with a blanket, added a fluffy pillow, and left a second blanket at the foot of the bed. "That should at least get you through the night, Brianna. I'll bring more things in the morning. If there is anything you need, I'll get it for you."

"I don't know what I ever did to deserve such wonderful friends." Brianna sniffled and hugged Maggie. "Thank you."

"You're welcome. Try not to fret. Tully will make everything right." Maggie patted her shoulder then she and Ian left.

Every single part of Tully wanted to pull Brianna into his arms and offer her comfort. He wanted to shield her from whatever might come, protect her from what she'd already experienced.

Instead, he shut the cell door. If he gave in to his need to hold her, to touch her, he'd never be able to let her go.

Right now, what she needed was a sheriff who found the real murderer, not a shoulder to cry on. Their friends could provide that.

"Try to get some sleep, Brianna."

"I don't think I can." She grasped the bars of the cell door in her hands, as if she needed something sturdy to keep her upright. "If I close my eyes, I see Davis."

"Do you feel up to talking about what happened?" Tully asked.

At her nod, he opened the cell door again and took her hand, leading her to one of the chairs in front of his desk.

For her safety, he locked the exterior door then took a seat at his desk and picked up a pencil and a sheaf of paper.

"Let's start at the beginning. How do you know B. Davis Gordon?"

"My father and his father were friends. His father owns the bank where we do business. Davis is the vice president of the bank and extended Father the loan that I must pay back soon." Brianna clasped her hands in her lap, chilled even though the air was still warm from the heat of the day. "I've known Davis my whole life."

Tully scribbled a few notes. "When did you become romantically involved with him?"

Her head snapped up. "I've never been romantically involved with him. Not the way you mean. He began pursuing a courtship with me about three years ago. Not long after Father had to take out the loan, Davis asked me to marry him. Father told me not to accept his proposal, but I worried Davis might make things difficult with the loan. Reluctantly, I agreed to an engagement and kept putting him off whenever he wanted to set a date."

Tully studied her for a long moment. "You are not now nor have you ever been in love with Davis?"

Brianna shook her head. "No. Not ever. I despise the man. He's nothing like his father and I've never liked him. Father always said he was too pampered and spoiled to grow up to be anything but completely rotten."

"Can you recall the details of the day your father died?"

"Father was on his way to the bank to make the final payment on the loan. He was only a block from the bank when he was stabbed and the thief made off with the money." Brianna fell silent and brushed at the tears that trickled down her cheeks. Tully handed her a clean handkerchief he pulled from a desk drawer. She wiped her cheeks and took a deep breath. "Davis arrived at the house not long after it happened to tell me Father had been killed. His assistant was the one who found Father's body in the alley next to the bank."

"And you said he was stabbed?" Tully asked.

"Yes, once in the back and once in the chest." Consumed by her memories, an important detail came to mind. "A police officer did come by the house to ask a few questions that evening. It was after Davis and his father had left. He said the stabbing matched several other murders in the area, which I assumed meant they were also victims of robberies."

"What else do you remember?" Tully asked, taking thorough notes.

"The day of the funeral, a dinner was held at our home. I just wanted everyone to leave, but Davis insisted it was important to put on a brave face, as he called it, and mingle with the guests. Finally, I couldn't take anymore and went up to my room. I'd moved all of Father's papers and ledgers he kept in a safe in the library up to my room to read when I couldn't sleep. Anyway, I was studying several letters and came across the partnership and correspondence between Father and Clive Fisher. By then, the guests had all departed, or so I thought. I went downstairs to the library to find a map because I didn't even know where Baker City was located. I was outside the door when I heard Davis and his assistant talking. It sounded like they were looking through drawers, rifling papers. Davis said some rather disturbing things and that's when I decided to leave."

Tully looked at her. "What kind of disturbing things?"

When she didn't answer, he stared at her until she met his gaze. "What did he say, Brianna?"

Uncomfortable with the direction the conversation headed, she shifted on the chair. "He indicated that he, um… that he planned…"

"Come on, darlin'. We've talked about your corsets and bloomers, it can't be worse than that." Tully's teasing grin failed to make her smile.

Nervous, she kept her gaze on her lap, twisting her hands together. "He said that if I didn't marry him by the end of the week, he'd take what he'd always wanted from me. Davis said if he ruined me in the process, I'd make a wonderful mistress."

Tully's jaw clenched and angry sparks shot from his eyes. It was a good thing Davis was already dead because he wanted to throttle him. Forcibly tamping down his fury, he cleared his throat. "Go on."

"I snuck upstairs and packed one truck and my bag. Early the next morning, before any of the staff awakened, I called for a ride to the train depot and bought a ticket that brought me here. No one saw me leave, so I hoped to escape Davis. I needed to get as far from him as possible until I could figure out what to do. Baker City seemed like a place he'd never search for me and I really did hope to be able to acquire enough cash from the mine to pay the remainder of Father's loan. It's important to me to do so."

Remorse settled on her features and she released a long breath. "I made the mistake of submitting an article to a newspaper in New York and Davis happened upon it. That's how he located me." Brianna fiddled with the handkerchief in her hands. "I don't believe he came here because he wanted to marry me. I think there was something in my father's ledgers or paperwork that he wanted."

"You brought them with you?" Tully asked. Hope filled him that a motive for the whole mess would be easy to detect in a review of the accounts.

"I did, but they were in the bag that was stolen."

Deflated, Tully slumped back in the chair. "Okay. What about today? What drove you to purchase the gun?"

"Obviously, I was distressed to find Davis here and I worried that he might make good on his plans to… well, you know… I thought the safest thing to do was to go along with the ruse of being his devoted fiancée until I could either figure out why he came or a way to get him to return home." Brianna looked up at Tully with her heart in her eyes. "I never meant to hurt you, Tully, or lead you on. The time we spent together was unbelievably special to me. I need you to know that."

Unable to speak without confessing his love for her, he nodded his head.

Brianna looked wounded, but she continued her story. "Today, I'd had all I could stand of Davis' constant blathering and recalled his fear of horses. I told him I had to ride out to a mine to work on an article. I did have an article I wanted to finish for Mr. Packwood, but I merely needed a quiet hour to write it. At the livery, I rented a horse, knowing he wouldn't go with me. I ended up at Maggie and Ian's house where I spent the afternoon in blissful silence. After I finished the article, I returned the horse to the livery, delivered the article to Mr. Packwood, and adjourned to the park where I ran into Sammy. We went to get a dish of ice cream at the drugstore near the park."

Tully knew most of what she shared from spying on her a good part of the afternoon. In spite of that, he had no idea she truly despised Davis, and with good reason.

"When did you meet back up with Davis?" Around suppertime, he'd seen her head to the hotel, but lost track of her after that until he heard the gunshots.

"I returned to my apartment to change after I parted ways with Sammy. There would have been no end to Davis' complaints if I showed up for dinner smelling like a horse. While I was changing, I thought I heard the back door rattle, like someone tried to open it. I didn't think anything of it until I went downstairs and heard Davis speaking to someone in the alley by the door. He restated something very similar to the comments I heard the day of my father's funeral. I did hear him tell the man he was with to get what they came for while he distracted me. They walked off. I didn't hear the other man's reply or see what he looked like. As soon as I thought I could leave without either of them spotting me, I made my way to the mining supply store down the street from the livery and purchased the revolver."

"From McIntosh?" Tully asked.

"Yes, I believe that was the gentleman's name. He has bright red hair and a big mustache." She used her index fingers to draw the bushy lines of the man's facial hair on her own face.

"That's McIntosh. What did you plan to do with the gun?"

"I mostly planned to frighten Davis with it. Honestly, I thought if he threatened me, I'd pull the gun on him and he'd most likely faint. He wouldn't have attempted to wrest it away from me, of that I'm sure. If necessary, I was prepared to shoot him in the leg or arm to stop him from carrying out some detestable act against my person. However, I never, not even for a moment, entertained the notion of killing him."

"You purchased the gun then met him for dinner at the hotel. Is that right?" A big piece of the puzzle was missing, but Tully couldn't put his finger on it.

"Yes. I suffered through another meal with him. When we finished, he suggested going for a stroll, which I found unusual. He much prefers to sit indoors and talk than move around outside. He directed me toward Maggie's shop, saying he wanted to see the apartment. When I resisted, he pulled me into the alley and…"

Brianna blushed, hesitant to continue.

Tully's jaw clenched again. "What did he do to you, darlin'. You need to tell me everything."

"He forced a kiss upon me. I struggled against him and drew back. The next thing I remember is awakening with a headache and feeling nauseous."

"Chloroform." Tully eyed her. "When you struggled with Davis, did you smell something sweet?"

"Yes, but I thought it was his cologne."

"That's chloroform. Davis had an accomplice. My hunch says the man who was supposed to help subdue you turned on him. We just need to figure out who that man is." Tully leaned back in his chair. If he hadn't been so mad at Brianna for being engaged and flouncing around town with Davis, he might have noticed a stranger lurking in the shadows. "Did you see anyone with Davis? Someone you recognized from home?"

"No. I didn't see him with anyone except people who live here." She sniffled and fought down more tears. "I didn't want Davis to die, Tully, and I really don't want to go to prison for something I didn't do."

The quiver of her bottom lip was his undoing. Tully rose from his seat at the desk and pulled her into his arms. He kissed the top of her fragrant head, still slightly damp from the bath she'd taken at Maggie's. Her hair hung down her back in a long braid, but tendrils already escaped to wave temptingly around her face.

Comfortingly, he rubbed his hands up and down her back then along her arms. Before he could think about his actions, he lifted her up until their lips met in an urgent, needful exchange.

Unaware of anything except her glorious, fervent kisses, Tully failed to hear a series of knocks on the office door.

"Tully! What in glory's name are ye doing in there?" Ian's brogue carried into the office as he pounded the door with his fist.

Tully grinned at Brianna then set her on her feet and hurried to unlock the door.

Ian barged inside with a gun in one hand and a large basket in the other. He took in the fact Brianna was not in a cell and tried to hide her red-cheeked, just-kissed face. Pleased, he smiled. "Maggie thought you might need coffee and she sent along sandwiches and cookies." He set the basket on Tully's desk.

"And why is it you're toting a gun around?" Tully asked, knowing the Scotsman preferred not to carry one unless it was absolutely necessary.

"Maggie insisted I bring it. With a murderer running around town on the loose, she's more than a little worried." Ian holstered the gun and removed a pot of coffee along with several tin cups from the basket. "Coffee?" he asked, holding out a cup to Brianna.

Grateful, she accepted it, holding the warm cup in her chilled hands and taking a sip. Although she'd felt warm and safe in the circle of Tully's arms, the moment he stepped away, bone-chilling cold settled over her again.

Tully noticed her discomfort and hurried into her cell, grabbing the blanket Maggie had left on the end of the bed. With tender care, he wrapped it around her shoulders.

She sank onto a chair and pulled the blanket around her.

Ian set out the sandwiches and a tin of cookies as Dugan raced in the door and slammed it behind him.

"We got trouble coming, boss."

Tully stared at him. "What's going on?"

"A bunch of men have been drinking down at the Rusty Nugget and got it in their heads that a little vigilante justice is in order for a murdering, lying wench." Dugan glanced apologetically at Brianna. "Their words, not mine. Seth and I tried to talk them out of their plans, but a group of them are heading this way. They plan on busting in here, taking Miss Dumont and stringing her up as an example to keep the rest of the women in this town in line."

"Over my dead body," Tully muttered darkly. He lifted Brianna out of the chair and set her in the jail cell, locking the door and pocketing the keys. "The safest place for you is right there, darlin'. I won't let any harm come to you."

Fearful not so much for herself, but for Tully and his men, she nodded her head, unable to speak.

Tully shut the door between the cells and the office then unlocked a cabinet and took out two shotguns and a revolver, along with cartridges. "How long before they get here, Dugan?"

"Seth was going to try to slow them down while I came to warn you. Most of them are so drunk they can barely walk, but a few of them are just on the other side of sober. In the dark, I couldn't exactly tell who brandished the spoon that stirred up the pot of trouble, but a dozen or so men are headed this way."

Tully checked to make sure each gun was ready to fire, then walked to the office's lone window and looked out. He could see a group walking toward the jail in the gaslights lining the street.

"Ian, you stay in here with the door bolted. Do not, under any circumstance open it." Tully looked to his friend as he closed the heavy metal shutters the blacksmith had crafted to cover the window for just such an occasion. "If the worst happens, shoot to kill because that group is out for blood."

"Understood." Ian gave Tully a reassuring nod.

Dugan reached for the door but it opened as Thane Jordan and two of his men stepped inside.

Tully smiled. "You have no idea how glad I am to see you."

"You didn't think we'd miss out on all the fun, did you?" Thane grinned and slapped Tully on the back. "Ben, here, happened to be in town earlier and heard what happened. He thought you might need some reinforcements before the night was through. Looks like he's right."

Tully nodded to the young cowboy who'd come to the rescue. "I appreciate that. Let's greet them outside. Nobody shoot unless I give the signal, and then aim for legs or hands. It'll be hard to do anything if they can't walk or hold a gun. We don't need to drum up any more business for the undertaker tonight."

The men moved outside and spread out across the front of the sheriff's office, guns cocked and ready to fire.

Tully listened for the click of the lock on the door then turned his attention to the approaching group of men.

Seth appeared out of the darkness and took a position to Tully's left. In the lamplight, he swiped at blood trickling from his lip.

"You okay, Seth?" Tully asked, giving him a quick glimpse.

"Yeah. One of the men decided to tromp through our crime scene." Seth wiped more blood away. "You could say we had a slight difference of opinion on the matter. I left Palmer keeping guard down there."

"Good." Tully stepped forward as the drunken crowd descended.

Not expecting half a dozen heavily armed men to be waiting for them, confused looks passed among the inebriated faces.

"You men turn around and go on home, and we'll forget this happened," Tully said in a loud, authoritative voice.

A man who kept to the shadows with a hat pulled low over his face spoke. "Seems to me you're outnumbered, Sheriff. Give us the girl and you won't have to bother with bringing in a judge for a trial."

"Oh, I don't mind doing that at all. In fact, Judge Anders happens to be a good friend. I'm sure he'd be thrilled to see each one of you brought before him for the list of crimes I'm about to slap on you."

A few of the men looked uncertainly at each other, but the designated spokesperson appeared undeterred. "That woman shot a man in broad daylight. The only reason you're defending her is because you're sweet on her. Maybe you helped her, since the man she killed was her fiancé."

His words stirred up the drunks and they yelled, calling out for justice and vengeance.

"Settle down, the lot of you," Tully roared, taking another step forward and pointing his revolver at the lead troublemaker.

"John, you know for a fact I was keeping you and Rutland, there, from pounding each other into the dirt when the shots went off, so don't go casting blame on me. That woman in there deserves a fair trial, same as anyone else. If it was your wife, would you be standing here, ready to hang her from a tree?"

Three of the men lowered their guns and backed away from the group. Two others appeared hesitant. One of the drunken men laughed and swayed on his feet. "If it was my old woman, I'd bring the rope."

The leader of the gang boldly raised his gun at Tully. "String her up, boys. String her up!"

Two men lunged forward. Tully shot one in the knee while Thane hit the other in his thigh.

Their howls of pain scattered the remaining drunks who took off running before they ended up at the doctor's office or at the undertaker's. The ringleader finally lowered his weapon and stalked away.

Tully turned to Dugan and gave him a subtle nod to follow the one who'd apparently prodded the men into trouble.

Dugan slipped into the shadows while Thane and his men helped Seth drag the two injured drunks to Doc's place.

Tully pounded on the door to the office. "You can open up, Ian."

"How do I know ye're not being held at gunpoint, insisting I open this door?"

"Because I'll bust the door in and shoot you myself if you don't open it right now," Tully threatened.

The door opened and Ian grinned. "Just had to be sure." He glanced behind Tully and caught a glimpse of Thane and Ben helping a limping man down the street. "Is everyone okay?"

"Two of them took bullets in their legs. Once they sober up, they'll probably rethink joining a vigilante committee the next time someone stirs up trouble."

"Who was the instigator of all this?" Ian asked as Tully closed the door.

"A man I didn't recognize. He made sure to stay in the shadows and had a hat pulled low over his face. My guess is he's probably involved in this somehow. I sent Dugan to follow him."

"With any luck, the deputy will turn up something that clears Brianna of any wrong doing."

"I hope so." Tully opened the door to the jail cells and checked on Brianna. She remained on her knees by the cot, her head bowed in prayer. "Brianna, it's over. Everything is okay." He spoke quietly.

She rose to her feet and reached through the bars, taking Tully's hand in hers. "I'm so glad to hear that. This is all my fault, Tully. If I'd never come to town, if I'd never tried to run away from Davis in the first place. If I'd…"

"He didn't give you much choice. You had to leave and I'm powerful glad you came here." His fingers brushed across her cheek and he gave her a tender smile. "I'm gonna leave you locked in here for the rest of the night, just because it's the safest place for you to be right now. Try to get some sleep, darlin'. Don't you worry about a thing. We'll find who did this."

"Thank you, Tully." She pressed a kiss to the palm of his hand then stepped back and sank onto the cot. "Thank you for keeping me safe."

"It's what I do, Brianna, especially for you." He backed toward the doorway. "Go to sleep and we'll talk more in the morning."

Tully partially closed the door to the cells then held out a hand to Ian. "Thank you for your help, Ian. I appreciate being able to count on you."

"Anytime, Tully. I'm going home to my wife before she decides to come looking for me. You know how Maggie is."

A grin lit Tully's face. "I'm surprised Mags wasn't right in the thick of things. It would have been like old times if she'd showed up wearing your britches with a gun strapped to her hip."

"Ach, Sheriff, me bonny lass is a married woman, now. She can't be joining yer posse and chasing down criminals." Ian smiled as he opened a door. "Be safe, Tully."

"You, too. And thank Maggie for the food. It's appreciated."

Ian left with a wave and Tully sank onto his desk chair, exhausted. He poured a cup of coffee and drank it in a few swallows then poured another.

Thane returned with Ben and Walt. The three of them stood inside the door, looking expectantly at Tully. "What can we do to help?" Thane asked.

"I'm hoping nothing more happens tonight." Tully glanced behind them. "Where's Seth?"

"He went back to the alley by Maggie's shop. He said someone needed to keep an eye on it until you can look it over tomorrow."

Tully nodded. "Good. If one of you wouldn't mind going to help him, I'd sure be grateful. With the alley open on both ends, it might be hard for him to keep any interested parties from wandering where they shouldn't."

"I'll go," Ben volunteered. He snagged one of the sandwiches off Tully's desk then hustled out the door.

"Do you need help anywhere else, Tully?" Thane asked. When the sheriff shook his head, Thane turned to his other employee. "Walt, you go on home and let my wife know that we're all fine. Tell her I'll be home tomorrow and not to worry."

Walt grinned. "I'll tell her, but Mrs. Jordan is likely wearing a groove in the floor of your new parlor."

"Probably, but she'll be fine." Thane thumped the man on the back. "Thanks for your help."

"Anytime, boss." Walt ambled out the door, closing it behind him.

Tully motioned for Thane to have a seat in a chair at his desk. "You might as well go home, too,

Thane. There's nothing else that can be done tonight."

"I can keep you company while we figure out what's really going on." Thane poured himself a cup of coffee and took a drink. "It wouldn't be the first time we've sat up all night guarding a prisoner and I bet it won't be the last."

Tully grinned. "In case I've never mentioned it before, I'm really glad to have you for a friend."

"Don't go getting all sappy on me now, Tully." Thane smirked at him. "I'm glad you've got me, too. Now, tell me what you know."

Chapter Twenty

The first fingers of dawn barely stretched across the sky when Ian and Maggie arrived at the sheriff's office with another pot of coffee and a basket of freshly baked muffins.

Tully opened Brianna's cell and she joined them for breakfast. When they finished eating, Tully turned to Ian. "Will you two stay here and keep an eye on her? There are a few things I need to check on."

"We'd be happy to," Ian said, smiling at his wife as she nodded her head in agreement. "Go on and do whatever you need to do."

Brianna looked at him from her seat at his desk. "I remembered two things, Tully. Right before Davis died, he said the word 'book.' I don't know if it's relevant or not, but his personal assistant's name is Booker Smith. He was the one Davis was speaking with at my home the night before I left."

"What's the other thing you remembered?"

"It seemed silly at the time, but I thought I saw Mr. Smith in the park the day of the Fourth of July celebration."

"Can you describe him?"

Brianna nodded. "He stands about six feet. He's stocky and bald. I believe he's in his thirties, dresses well, but looks like he could be a boxer. Oh, and he has a strange-looking mole on his neck, shaped like a star."

Tully gave Brianna a long, studying glance then left without a word. Thane tipped his hat to the women and followed his friend out the door.

Their first stop was the alley where Tully had found Brianna leaning over Davis' body. Ben and Seth guarded both ends of the location. Although bleary-eyed, they joined Thane and Tully as they studied the footprints and impressions in the dust.

The two men were kneeling to study the print of a shoe made in a spot where someone had dumped out a bucket of water when the undertaker raced down the alley.

"Sheriff! There's something I need you to see." Godfrey Williams motioned for them to join him.

Tully glanced at the excited undertaker then at Seth. "Have you seen Dugan?"

"Not since you sent him off last night." Seth rubbed a hand over his face.

A frown crossed Tully's features. "If you two can somehow secure this alley, put up a temporary fence of sorts, go get some much-needed rest."

"We'll take care of it," Seth said, looking to Ben.

Tully and Thane left with the undertaker and hurried to his place. Davis Gordon's body rested on a tall, narrow table with a sheet draped over him.

"I thought something seemed strange last night, but I wanted to take a look in the daylight," Godfrey said, pulling the sheet down to Davis' waist. "Mr. Gordon was shot twice, but that isn't all." He pointed to the two bullet holes. "This shot came from the front, but the other is an exit wound from the back."

"The back?" Tully asked. He rolled the body onto its side and studied the holes in the back that were opposite to the two on the front. "What's this, here?" He pointed to a jagged cut just above one of the bullet holes.

"That's the thing I really wanted you to see," Godfrey said, holding up a magnifying glass. "I believe Mr. Gordon was stabbed twice then shot. The knife entered right here." Godfrey handed the magnifying glass to Tully who carefully studied the wound.

When he finished, they rolled the body onto its back. "There is a similar wound, barely visible at the edge of the bullet holes."

Tully straightened and stared at the undertaker. "What you're saying is that Davis was stabbed in the back and chest then shot in the same locations to hide the knife wounds?"

"Yes. My best guess would be someone stabbed him in the back with a hunting knife, then in the chest. He was shot the same way, once in the back and once in the chest."

"Why would someone go to the bother of shooting him if they'd already inflicted a fatal stab wound?" Thane asked, trying to understand the reasoning.

Tully continued to study the fatal wounds. "They might do that if they didn't want anyone to know this was a stabbing and not a shooting, especially if they wanted it to look like Brianna was the one who fired the shots." Tully stared at Godfrey. "In your expert opinion, could Miss Dumont have inflicted the stab wounds to this man's chest?"

"I don't believe so. From what I can tell, the one in his back was made with brutal force." Godfrey rolled the body over again, pointing to bruising around the wound. "The ability of a woman the size of Miss Dumont to inflict that sort of damage isn't likely. I also believe the attacker stood taller than Mr. Gordon from the angle of the cut. You can see that, right there at the edge. Despite the bullet holes, the edge where the knife entered the skin remains visible."

Tully smiled at the man and clapped him on the shoulder. "Good work, Godfrey. For now, could you please keep what you found just between us? We've still got a murderer to catch and I'd like for him to think we aren't on to him quite yet."

Thane and Tully left the undertaker, heading back to the jail to ask Brianna a few more questions about people who might have wanted Davis dead. They were almost to Milt Owen's livery when the man ran outside and wildly waved to Tully.

The two men rushed inside to find Dugan Durfey sitting on a bench by the door, holding his head with both hands.

Tully hunkered down and placed a hand on his back. "Dugan? What happened to you?"

"I followed the man you asked me to last night. He ducked into an alley and I chased after him. The next thing I knew, I woke up in a stall here with my hands and feet tied together and a whale of a headache."

"You ought to see Doc and have him check you over." Tully stood and studied a raised bump on the back of Dugan's head. "Looks like somebody hit you hard on the back of that thick noggin' of yours."

"Feels like they used a club." Dugan rose to his feet, with Tully and Thane's help. He squinted at Tully. "I'm sorry, boss, but I never got a good look at his face."

"Don't worry about it, Dug. You just take care of yourself, we'll handle the rest." Tully patted his shoulder and gave Thane a questioning look.

"I'll help Dugan to Doc's office," Thane said. "Go on with your duties, Sheriff."

"Thank you." Tully hurried out the door, eager to return to his office. He'd just turned the corner to walk around to the front of the jail when Sammy raced toward him, little legs pumping for all he was worth.

Tully bent down as the child ran right into his arms, sobbing and frantic. Quickly picking up the child, Tully carried him inside the office. Ian, Maggie, Brianna, Seth, and Ben all turned startled eyes to him as he entered.

Brianna stood from where she and Maggie sat together in front of Tully's desk and took the little boy from him.

"Oh, sweetheart. Whatever is the matter?" she asked, kissing Sammy's tear-streaked cheek. She nearly dropped the child when he spoke.

"The bad man that shot Mr. Gordon was in your apartment. I followed him there and he almost caught me. I ran straight here, but he was right behind me."

So stunned by the fact the child could talk, it took them all a moment to gather their wits.

Tully was the first to come to his senses and took Sammy, sitting him down on the corner of his desk. Kneeling in front of the child, he stared at him. "I thought you couldn't talk?"

"I can talk and you better listen right smart to what I'm saying. The man who killed Mr. Gordon turned Brianna's apartment upside down looking for something. I snuck up the stairs and watched him. One of the boards squeaked and he saw me, but I ran lickety-split down the stairs. He almost had me until I lit a shuck through Mrs. Jepson's yard."

"What did the man look like, Sammy?" Tully's voice sounded low and pleasant, as though life and death didn't depend on the child giving them a helpful answer.

"He was big and mean-looking and he had a bald head. His hat flew off when he was chasing me."

"How do you know it was the same man who killed Mr. Gordon?"

Sammy rubbed a finger along his freckled nose. "Well, I was on my way home last night when I saw Mr. Gordon grab Brianna's arm and pull her into the alley, so I decided I best keep an eye on her. A man stepped out from the other end of the alley, like he'd been waitin' there all along. Mr. Gordon went to slobbering all over Brianna like she was a piece of candy." Sammy glanced at Brianna then back at Tully. "She wasn't enjoying it, Sheriff. Not like when you kiss her."

Maggie stifled a giggle while Ian, Seth, and Ben did their best to hide their chuckles.

Absently, Tully wondered how many times the child had seen him kiss Brianna. "Then what happened?" he asked, hoping to direct the conversation back to the matter at hand.

"Brianna was struggling against Mr. Gordon when another man put a cloth over her face and she went as limp as an overcooked carrot." Sammy demonstrated by suddenly going lax and flopping back on the desk before sitting upright again. "While she was down for the count, the bad man stabbed Mr. Gordon in the back. Mr. Gordon stumbled forward and the other man grabbed him and turned him. The bad man stabbed him in the chest. I closed my eyes and heard gunshots." Sammy held out his thumb and index finger, pretending they were a gun. "Pow! Pow! When I opened my eyes, the two men were gone. I was gonna follow them, but they'd already disappeared. I hid across the street to make sure someone came to help Brianna then you done hauled her here."

"What did the other man look like, Sammy? The one who held the cloth over Miss Brianna's face?"

"He was short and he smelled bad, like he forgot how to use soap." Sammy's little nose wrinkled on the end. "And he had a scar on his cheek."

"Thank you for telling us what you saw, Sammy." Tully patted the child on the back and glanced at Seth and Ben. "I know you two are tired, but do you think you could help me?"

"Sure, boss," Seth said, rising from where he'd leaned against the desk he shared with Dugan. "Whatever you need."

"Let's go find our killer and his friend." Tully glanced at Ian. "If you can stay a little longer and keep an eye on these two hardened criminals, I'll be back as soon as I can."

"Am I gonna go to jail?" Sammy asked, his lip rolling out in a pout and tears filling his eyes.

"No, Sammy, but we do need to have a talk about some things when I get back." Tully took the stubborn little chin in his hand and winked at the child. "You stay out of trouble and help keep Miss Brianna safe."

"I can do that," Sammy said, sliding off the desk and taking Brianna's hand in his.

Tully, along with Seth and Ben, hurried outside.

"What's the plan?" Ben asked, tugging his hat down as he walked beside Tully.

"I think a well-dressed bald man in his thirties would stick out, now that we know who it is we're looking for. He has to be staying somewhere in town. Ask at the hotels. If we don't find anything, we'll start checking the saloons and brothels. I'll take everything on the east side of Front Street. The two of you divide up the west side."

On a hunch, Tully made a quick detour that took him into Chinatown. Often times, if there was trouble he'd find whoever was behind it hiding there.

Tully had just walked past the Joss house when he noticed several people gathering at the banks of the nearby river. Breaking into a run, he pushed through the crowd and sucked in a breath at the sight of a body floating in the water. Most likely, it would have floated down the river undetected, but the jacket the man wore had snagged on the root of a tree.

Quickly removing his gun belt, Tully slid down the bank to the edge of the water. He waded in waist deep and untangled the body. When he reached the bank, several people helped lift the body from the river. A strong hand reached down and clasped his, pulling him upward.

He smiled at Thane. "You following me?"

"Yep. I was on my way back from Doc's office when I saw you head this direction. Glad I tagged along?"

"Always." Tully turned the man's body over and noticed the scar on his cheek. He hated to make Sammy identify the body, but he had a strong notion this man helped the bald man get away with murder.

Experience taught him that most criminals didn't like loose ends and generally tied them all up before they finished their dirty work.

"Someone fetch Godfrey Williams, please," Tully shouted as he strapped on his gun belt. He noticed two children take off running and assumed they'd bring back the undertaker.

Once Williams appeared with his wagon, Tully and Thane walked downtown. Tully informed his friend of the details Sammy shared.

"I can't believe that little scamp can talk," Thane said, incredulous the child had fooled them all. "Did he say why he pretended to be mute?"

"Nope, and I didn't take time to ask. There are a few more pressing matters to handle today."

"How are we going to find this mysterious bald man?" Thane asked as they walked into the Hotel Warshauer.

"He has to be staying somewhere in town. Seth and Ben are checking everywhere he could possibly have a room. Since Davis was staying here, I thought we might luck out," Tully said as they approached the front desk.

"Good morning, Sheriff. Mr. Jordan." Mr. Isaac greeted them with a friendly smile. "How may I be of assistance to you gentlemen?"

"I'd like to take a look in Davis Gordon's room. Can you give us a key?" Tully asked.

"I'd be happy to, but his friend took the key and went up a few minutes ago."

"His friend?" Thane asked.

"Yes. Mr. Smith has also been staying with us. I assumed he and Mr. Gordon were business associates."

"What are their room numbers?"

"Mr. Gordon was in room 212 and Mr. Smith is staying in room 203. Would you…"

Tully and Thane raced up the stairs and around the mezzanine to the second-floor rooms. Guns drawn, they hurried down the hall on silent feet, approaching Davis Gordon's room. The noise of drawers slamming alerted them to someone inside.

With a glance at each other, Tully kicked open the door and ducked as a knife flew so close to his head, it drew blood from the rim of his ear before embedding itself in the hallway wall.

The shot he fired hit his intended target. Booker Smith grunted in pain before snatching a ledger from the desk and diving out the open window.

Thane had the sense of mind to grab the knife and race back down the stairs while Tully followed Booker out the window.

Like a ghost, the man had seemingly disappeared in the seconds it took Tully to jump down to the ground.

Thane raced out the door of the hotel and met Tully on the boardwalk. "Where'd he go?"

"It's like he vanished," Tully said, studying the ground and noticing a few drops of blood. "Or maybe not." Although the drops were light, they left a trail down the alley and around a corner leading into an area full of fine homes.

The drops were closer together and easier to follow. They'd gone another block when they caught sight of a limping figure duck behind the bushes in someone's yard.

Silently, Tully motioned for Thane to go around to the back of the house while he came in from the front.

Swiftly opening the gate, Tully stepped around the shrubs with his gun pointed at the fugitive. "It's over, Booker. Put your hands in the air and surrender."

"Not while I'm still breathing," the man said, slowly sliding his hand downward.

Tully pulled the trigger and shot him in the hand.

Booker howled in pain and dropped to his knees as Thane rushed into the front yard. A sigh of relief rolled out of him as he helped Tully get the criminal to his feet then held him while the sheriff fastened handcuffs on his wrists.

"I won't talk and nothing you do can make me," Booker sneered as they made their way to the jail.

"I have an eye witness who not only saw you rifling through Miss Dumont's apartment this morning, but also watched you stab Davis Gordon. We already found your dead accomplice in the river, so it seems to me there isn't much more for you to share."

"There is the matter of this," Thane said, holding up the ledger he'd grabbed from Booker. "What were you trying to find in Brianna's apartment?"

"I told you I'm not talking."

"Well, that's too bad," Tully said, coming to a stop and staring at Booker. "I was planning to have Doc give you medical attention, but if you really plan to make things difficult for me, I'll make them hard for you."

Thane smirked. "The wounds will get septic and the pain will drive you right out of your mind. Gangrene sure is a nasty way to die."

"You wouldn't do that," Booker said uncertainly.

"You sure you want to try me? I've done it before and I'd be happy to do it to you," Tully said. The cold, ruthless gleam in his eyes left Booker completely unsettled.

"Fine, I'll talk, but you have to let the doctor see to my wounds."

"Talk first then I'll have someone fetch Doc."

Thane opened the door to the jail and Tully marched Booker inside. The conversation died as they entered. Brianna rose to her feet while Sammy yelped in fear and moved to stand beside Ian.

"Sammy, is this the man you saw kill Mr. Gordon?" Tully asked.

The child nodded and pointed a finger at Booker. "He's the one. He chased me this morning and called me names my mama would make him suck soap for saying."

"I'll be sure to wash his mouth out later," Tully said, winking at the boy before turning to Brianna. "Miss Dumont, do you recognize this man?"

"Yes. His name is Booker Smith. He worked at the bank with Davis as his personal assistant." She took a step closer to the criminal. "Why did you kill Davis?"

"Same reason I killed your father — they got in my way." Booker looked surprised when Brianna slapped him across his face.

The man would have lunged at her, but Tully strong-armed him into a cell and locked the door.

Tully shut the door to the cell area and turned in time to watch Brianna's legs give out on her. Wrapping her in his arms, he held her close and kissed her cheeks, murmuring words of comfort.

Chapter Twenty-One

"I still don't understand why you killed Brianna's father," Tully said to Booker as the doctor treated the bullet wound in the man's hand. Tully questioned the criminal while Brianna silently listened from the doorway of the examination room at Doc's office.

"George Dumont, like his daughter, wouldn't mind his own business." Booker sneered at Brianna then sucked in a gulp of air when the doctor poured disinfectant over the wound. He ground his teeth, took a breath then continued speaking. "I don't know how he found out Davis had a few less than scrupulous enterprises on the side, but he did. He'd kept detailed notes of it in a journal. Davis found out about it the day George came in to make the final payment on his loan."

"He made it to the bank?" Brianna asked, taking a step into the room. "Davis said he was robbed on his way there."

"Of course, he did," Booker said, looking at Brianna like she was the dumbest female he'd ever encountered. "Your father came in, made the payment in full, and was on his way out the door when Davis made some off-handed remark about you. Your father told Davis he wanted him to leave you alone. That's when he said he had written proof of Davis' illegal schemes and would take them to the old man if Davis didn't stay away from you."

"And who is the old man?" Tully asked.

"Bertrand Gordon, Davis' father. The old geezer thought Davis could do no wrong and turned a blind eye to most of his dealings."

Brianna clenched her hands at her sides, wishing she could pummel the man who murdered her father instead of calmly questioning him. "Father said as much, more than once. You stabbed my father after he left the bank?"

"Yeah. Davis told me to take care of him, so I did. I pulled the receipt for the payment and his wallet, to make it look like a robbery." Booker appeared quite pleased with himself as he recalled the details.

"The factory, the house, and all of Father's holdings are mine, free and clear?" Brianna asked in a quavering voice.

Booker nodded. "Davis was counting on you agreeing to marry him so he could rightfully claim ownership to everything."

Brianna took another step forward but Tully gave her a subtle glance that kept her at the door. He turned to Booker with an impassive look. "It's quite fortunate you prefer to stab your victims once in the back then in the chest because your local police have a long list of unsolved crimes that tie you to more than a dozen deaths."

Booker's countenance fell at this bit of news.

Tully tapped his pencil against the tablet. "Why did you come to Baker City? What did Davis hope to find?"

"The ledger George kept that implicated him in numerous crimes. The evening of the funeral, we searched all over the library at the house for it, but we couldn't find anything." Booker narrowed his gaze toward Brianna. "Apparently, Miss Dumont found it before we did and packed it, along with the jewels, before Davis could find them."

"Jewels?" Tully asked, looking to Brianna.

Ignoring Tully's question, she focused the conversation back on Booker. "How did Davis find me?"

"Your father had mentioned his partnership in the mine to old man Gordon. Davis kept prying information out of him about George's various investments and finally concluded Baker City would have been a perfect place for Brianna to hide from him. He sent me ahead to make sure she was here. The article she wrote for the paper in New York provided the perfect excuse for him to arrive."

"What article?" Tully glanced at Brianna again.

"Later," she said, refusing to meet his gaze. "Why did Davis bring my trunks with him?"

"That gave us an excuse to be at the house and search for the ledger. At that point, Davis only speculated that you had it. While your idiotic staff packed the trunks, Davis and I went through every inch of your father's library and found his empty safe." Booker winced as the doctor started digging out the bullet in his leg. "That's when Davis knew for sure you had the ledger. I was supposed to figure out where you kept it while he distracted you. With the dressmaker always at the shop, the first opportunity I had to search the apartment was this morning and then that bratty kid snuck up on me."

"And what about the ledger you stole from Davis' room when Thane and I caught up to you?" Tully asked, writing meticulous notes.

"It's a record of all the dealings he'd rather no one know about. My name is mentioned in there, as well as our associates."

Tully's mouth thinned to a hard line. "And the associate I pulled out of the river? Where did you meet him?"

"I needed some help when I decided to off Davis. With him out of the picture, I could have taken care of old man Gordon and everything they had would have been mine, after I doctored a few documents and their attorney mysteriously disappeared. The other night, I ran into a miner down on his luck. He seemed willing to do anything to make a few bucks, so I enlisted his help last night. He handled Miss Dumont while I took care of Davis. I sent him to that saloon to stir up the men then joined him once the group was drunk and thirsty for blood. My hope was that they'd either turn on him and take care of that loose end for me, or they really would hang her from a tree. I've hated her and her father since the first time I met them."

"You cowardly…" Brianna stepped toward Booker, but Tully moved to block her.

"Would you please go to Maggie's and check on Sammy while I escort the prisoner back to his cell. A U.S. Marshal will be here in the morning to transport him to Rhode Island." Tully gave Brianna a gentle nudge out the door.

"You can't put me on a train in my condition. What if I get an infection?" Booker gave the doctor a worried glance. "He can't do that, can he?"

"He's the sheriff." Doc shrugged as he wrapped a bandage around Booker's leg. "He can do whatever he likes."

"Go on, Brianna. I'll catch up with you soon," Tully said, giving her another push toward the door.

She scowled at him, but stomped down the hallway and out the door.

When Doc finished wrapping the bandage, Tully thanked him for his help then hauled Booker back to the jail where Seth kept watch over him.

"You look dead on your feet, boss. Why don't you go home and get some rest?" Seth asked as Tully dropped the tablet he'd taken notes on into a desk drawer.

"I've got one more criminal to interrogate and another matter to attend then I might sleep for a whole day." Tully thumped Seth on the shoulder as he walked past him. "Thank you for all your help. I appreciate being able to depend on you and Dugan."

"It's why you hired us, Tully." Seth grinned and leaned back in his desk chair, propping his boots on top of the desk. "I imagine your next interrogation might go better if you took along a piece of candy or two. I heard Sammy's partial to sassafras drops."

"I'm not gonna reward the kid for lying to me," Tully said, stepping out the door. He stuck his head back in, "but he might need one for turning in Booker."

"Yep. You're the toughest, meanest sheriff in the west." Seth laughed as Tully scowled at him then left.

He hurried to Maggie and Ian's home. Maggie had agreed to keep an eye on Sammy while Ian went to her shop to see what kind of damage Booker had done when he broke in that morning. Before he went home, Tully planned to help clean up whatever messes were there. He hoped to convince Brianna to stay with Maggie and Ian for the night. She'd feel safer there than the apartment even if a threat no longer loomed over her.

At the back door, he tapped once then opened it and stepped inside the sunny kitchen.

Brianna and Maggie sat at the table with Sammy. The boy finished the last few sips from a glass of milk then wiped crumbs from his mouth on his sleeve. He slid out of his chair and walked over to Tully, looking up at him with sad eyes. "Are you gonna arrest me and make me stay in jail?"

Tully removed his hat and hunkered down so he didn't tower over the boy. "No, I'm not gonna arrest you or throw you in jail, but we need to have a talk about some things I think you may have taken."

Sammy stared at his bare toes instead of meeting Tully's direct gaze.

Brianna sank down on the floor next to him and put a hand on the boy's back. "Did you steal something, Sammy?"

The little boy nodded.

Brianna gave Tully a questioning look and he sighed. "I recently reviewed an astounding number of reports for theft and it made me wonder if one person was responsible for the crime spree." Tully reached out with his index finger and tipped Sammy's chin up until the boy looked at him. "You know all about what was stolen, don't you, Sammy."

Another nod.

"Why did you steal, Sammy?" Brianna studied the boy, wondering what the child had done and what had driven him to do it. "What did you steal?"

"Mostly food, and a few things for my mama. She's sick and I wanted to make her feel better."

Maggie sniffled from behind them and Brianna worked hard to hold back her own tears. She wrapped her arms around the little boy and pulled him onto her lap, giving him a tight hug. "What's wrong with your mama? Does the doctor know she's sick?"

"Yeah. He comes to see her. I didn't want to steal, but I get so hungry sometimes and the money I make from Mr. Packwood doesn't pay much more than Mama's doctor bill. She doesn't know that, though. She thinks my papa sends us money to buy things."

"Can you take us to see your mother, Sammy? I'd like to meet her." Tully lifted Sammy into his arms and stood then held out a hand to Brianna, helping her to her feet.

"You aren't gonna do anything to my mama." Sammy didn't ask it as a question but offered it as a statement as he glared at Tully.

"I promise I won't do anything to upset your mama, but I do want to meet her and see where you live. Would you please take us to your house?" Tully looked over Sammy's head and mouthed "thank you" to Maggie before he and Brianna went out the back door.

"Are you sure you have to meet Mama?" Sammy squirmed against Tully as if he wanted down. Too tired to chase the little imp if he decided to bolt, he continued carrying him as they walked into town.

"Absolutely sure. Where do you live?" Tully glanced down at Sammy with a look that let the child know he wouldn't tolerate any nonsense.

Sammy gave him the name of a street and they started that direction. The house was in a neighborhood where many families of miners lived. The small homes weren't fancy, by any means, but they were snug and sturdy.

They were almost there when Sammy reached out and touched Brianna on the shoulder. "Promise you won't hate me?"

Brianna took his hand in hers and kissed the little fingers. "I promise, Sammy. No matter what, I could never, ever hate you."

"Put me down, Sheriff."

Tully set the boy on his feet and he scampered up the steps of a house with no yard, although a few flowers grew in an old rusty bucket near the door.

Sammy pointed to the two adults. "You both wait out here for a minute then I'll let you in."

"Don't you dare go running off out the back, Sammy," Tully warned. "I don't have another chase through town in me today."

The child grinned. "I won't. Just wait out here." He disappeared inside the house as Tully and Brianna slowly made their way up the steps to the door.

They heard Sammy call out to someone and the sound of his footsteps racing through the house. The door opened and they looked down at a little girl in a pale blue dress. She smiled and motioned them inside.

"Welcome to my home, Sheriff, and Miss Dumont."

Too dazed to speak let alone move, Brianna numbly let Sammy pull her into the house while Tully followed.

Aware of their shocked expressions, Sammy tugged on Tully and Brianna's hands until they bent down close to her. "My mama doesn't know about me dressing like a boy, neither. If you wouldn't mind keeping that a secret, too, I'd sure be grateful," she said in a confidential whisper.

Both adults nodded and followed Sammy into a bedroom where a thin, frail woman rested on a frilly pink pillow with a quilt tugged up to her chin.

"What kind of trouble have you been in now, Samantha Margaret Howe?" Mrs. Howe asked her daughter before she raised a handkerchief to her mouth and coughed from deep in her chest.

When she pulled the handkerchief away, blood stained the white fabric. Tully and Brianna looked at each other then at the child who had fooled them all with her appearance.

"She's not in a bit of trouble, Mrs. Howe. We wanted to let you know how helpful she was in bringing in a criminal wanted in three states. She witnessed him in the midst of a crime and reported it to me this morning." Tully smiled at Sammy. "You have an incredibly brave little girl anyone would be proud to call their own."

"Your daughter is a bright, wonderful child, Mrs. Howe," Brianna said, smiling at the dying woman. "I met her through my work at the newspaper."

Sammy's mother beamed at her daughter before she began coughing again. When she finished and could get her breath, she weakly nodded her head. "Samantha has been such a help to me since we moved here. I do so appreciate you both coming by today."

"You're most welcome, Mrs. Howe. If there is ever anything we can do for you, please let us know. We both think the world of your girl." Tully swallowed hard to clear the emotion clogging his throat. "If you have no objection, Mrs. Howe, perhaps I could return to visit you another day."

The woman smiled. "I'd like that." Unable to keep her eyes open, Mrs. Howe let them drift shut.

Sammy led them out of the room and closed the bedroom door. She walked into the small parlor and turned to stare at them with wariness in her eyes.

Brianna dropped to her knees and hugged the child to her chest, kissing her cheeks. "Sammy, why on earth didn't you tell us you were a girl, that you could talk, that your mama is so sick?"

"No one in town would give a job to a little girl, but I knew Mr. Packwood hired boys. He thought I was too young for the job, but I convinced him I could work hard. I'm actually eight, but most folks assume since I'm kind of small, that I'm younger." Sammy sniffled and pulled a little handkerchief out of her dress pocket then dabbed at her nose. "I didn't talk because it made it easier to pretend I was a boy and no one asked me questions about anything that way."

"Does the doctor know how sick your mother is?" Tully asked, kneeling beside them and rubbing a hand over Sammy's short blond hair.

"Sure. He comes by every week to check on her. He doesn't know about me pretending to be a boy, though. I always make sure I have on a dress when he comes." Sammy shrugged, as if it should be simple to understand.

"What about your father? Where is he?" Tully asked, noticing the house had a few pieces of quality furnishings.

"My papa moved us here back in May. We had a nice house in Olympia, but he got the gold fever, or that's what Mama calls it. He sold off most of our stuff and we rode the train here. Papa rented this house. He paid for six months rent when we moved here. If he hadn't, I don't know what I would have done with Mama. Anyway, he went off to work in a mine somewhere to the north. He came home about a week later without any money in his pockets. He took most of what we had here and said he was going to try another mine near Sumpter. That's the last we heard from him. I think he either got himself killed or he run off. Ain't like he's been a good papa or husband since my mama got sick. She's convinced he'll come back home any day, but I don't think he ever planned on coming back."

Sammy stared down at her toes. "With the doctor bills, I didn't have money left to buy food and the things Mama needs, so I started stealing. I'm sorry. I tried not to do it too often." Sammy hugged Brianna again. "And Brianna has been so nice to me, buying me treats and a beautiful book, and being my friend."

Tears rolled out of the child's pretty blue eyes and soaked the front of her dress.

Brianna rocked her back and forth, whispering softly that everything would be fine. "We'll help you take care of your mama, sweetheart. I promise."

Convicted, Sammy pulled back and looked at Brianna. "That ain't why I'm crying like a big baby." Sammy sniffled and wiped her cheeks. "I done something terrible to you, Brianna. Something that will make you hate me forever and then some."

"What did you do, honey?" Tully asked, picking her up and setting her on his bent knee. "What did you do to Miss Brianna?"

"I stole something of hers that I know she needed back, and I kept it anyway." Sammy's lip puckered out and she drew in a few choppy breaths. "I stole it before I knew who you were. When I did, I just thought you were the prettiest, best-smelling lady I'd ever seen, and I wanted to bring home something nice for my mama. Then, after I knew you, I was afraid to give it back. Afraid you'd be so mad at me, you wouldn't be my friend anymore."

"I'll always be your friend, Sammy." Brianna kissed her cheek. "What on earth did you take?"

Sammy hopped off Tully's leg and disappeared through a doorway. A few seconds passed before she reappeared, carrying Brianna's bag.

"Oh! My bag!" Brianna took it from Sammy and looked inside. She pulled out the ledgers that had belonged to her father. "You'll need those," she said, handing them to Tully, then dug deeper into the bag. A smile lit her face as her hand connected with the treasure she'd been seeking. "It's all here."

"I didn't take nothing. Once I saw what was in it, I decided there wasn't anything my mama could use, but I couldn't throw it away."

Brianna hugged Sammy and kissed her forehead before looking at Tully. "If Sammy hadn't stolen this, Booker would have found it and that would have been beyond disastrous."

"I reckon so." Tully handed the ledgers and papers back to Brianna then picked up Sammy and sat on the sofa with her on his lap.

"Samantha Margaret Howe, I don't want you to ever, ever steal anything again as long as you live. Do you promise?" Tully asked in a solemn tone.

The little head nodded in agreement so rapidly, Brianna thought the child might injure herself.

Tully held the girl's gaze. "From now on, if there is something you need, you will ask me or Miss Brianna. Is that understood?"

"Yes, sir. I promise," Sammy said, throwing her arms around Tully's neck and squeezing. Before she let go, she whispered in his ear. "I wish my papa was a nice man like you, Sheriff. You'd never run off and leave your little girl and wife all alone."

Tears burned the backs of Tully's eyes and he had to stare at the ceiling a moment before he could speak. "I wouldn't ever leave you, Sammy. You're one of the finest little girls I've ever met."

"Does that mean I'm not in trouble?" she asked with a charming little pout.

Tully set her back on her feet. "You are not in trouble, young lady, but I expect you to go to Mr. Packwood tomorrow and tell him the truth. I'm sure you can keep your job, but you tell him the truth just the same."

Sammy appeared to consider his request then finally agreed. "I'll do it. I won't like it, but I'll do it."

Tully stood then pulled Brianna up. She handed him her bag then hugged Sammy again. "Will you stay here with your mother the rest of the day, Sammy? Or do you prefer Samantha?"

"I like Sammy just fine and I was planning on staying here with Mama the rest of the day. Mrs. MacGregor stuffed me so full of food that I may not be hungry for a week."

Tully chuckled then placed a hand to Brianna's back as they moved toward the door. "I'll check on you tomorrow, Sammy. Thank you for all your help today. I meant what I told your mother. You are a very brave, smart girl and I'm proud to know you."

Sammy's lip started to quiver again and she pointed to the door. "You better leave now before you set me to blubbering again."

"Good night, Sammy," Brianna said, following Tully outside.

He took her hand in his as they walked away from the house. "Well, I sure didn't see that coming. How could we all be fooled by that little girl?"

"Because we saw what she wanted us to," Brianna said. Drained from the events of the last twenty-four hours, she felt numb. Her heart ached with such pain for Sammy and her mother, it took all her energy to put one foot in front of the other as they neared her apartment.

Tully lent her strength as she leaned against him. He glanced down at her with a tender look. "Don't you think you should stay with Maggie and Ian tonight? You could get a room at the hotel, if you'd rather."

"I'm so tired, I don't care where I sleep as long as I have a bed and a pillow. However, if I'm going to Maggie's, I'd like to take a few things with me." Brianna smiled at the man who worked to install a new back door at Maggie's shop after Booker had busted through it earlier.

"Looks like you're doing a fine job, Bill," Tully commented as they walked by him and up the stairs.

Booker had gone through everything in the apartment, upending cushions, dumping out every drawer and cupboard.

Emotionally sapped, Brianna righted the cushions on the sofa and plopped down, utterly out of strength.

Tully took a seat beside her then set her bag on the floor between them. He studied her as she leaned back against the sofa cushions and closed her eyes. "Brianna?"

"Yes?"

"You promised to tell me two things later. One is about jewels, and the other is about an article in a paper back east. I'd like to hear about both subjects before you fall asleep."

Brianna opened her eyes and sighed. She sat up and turned toward Tully. "You recall the day we apprehended Dale Darcey?"

"Of course. We had quite an adventure." Tully took Brianna's hand in his. Recollections of how much he enjoyed holding her in his arms, kissing her beneath the stars, made him grin.

"Yes, we did. I thought people in a big city might like to know that the things we dream about the West, the things we imagine to be true, really exist. I wrote about a horse rustler and the determined, handsome sheriff who tracked him down. In the article, I described all the things you taught me." When Tully suggestively waggled his eyebrow at her, she playfully smacked his leg, pretending to be affronted. "About the native plants and animals as we rode back to town. And sleeping under the stars by a campfire. Of course, I painted a picture with you as a Wild West hero. The newspaper printed the article by B.E. Dumont, making it sound as though the author is a man."

"May I read the article?" Tully asked, brushing his thumb along the inside of her wrist, savoring the smooth feel of her skin against his work-roughened fingers.

His touch made it nearly impossible to concentrate on anything beyond how much she craved his kisses. Reluctantly, she pulled her gaze away from his enticing mouth. "As soon as the copies the newspaper mailed arrive, you may."

Tully slid a little closer to her. "And the jewels? What's that about?"

"Do you remember the day I arrived in town and you forced me to say what I really wanted from my bag? That I needed my corsets?" Brianna managed to say the word without blushing.

"I sure do. You were so cute, angry and fuming, demanding that I do my job," he said, offering her a teasing grin.

"Well, I really did want my corsets back." She reached into the bag and pulled out three expensive, lace-trimmed corsets.

Tully's mouth went dry as he imagined her wearing them.

When he continued to stare at the fancy corsets on her lap, she held out her hand to him. "Do you have a pocket knife?"

He rolled up on one hip and shoved his hand in his pocket, pulling out a knife. After folding it open, he handed it to her.

Before he could protest, she cut along the seam of one of the corsets and removed a beautiful sapphire necklace. She held it up as light from the setting sun shined in the window and refracted through it.

Carefully taking it in his hand, Tully studied the necklace. Curious, he looked to Brianna. "Where did this come from?"

"I have four necklaces, three bracelets, and five rings that belonged to my family. My father gave my mother that necklace when I was born." Brianna cut open another seam and lifted out a ring set with a large diamond. "This was my mother's wedding ring. It belonged to my great-grandmother."

Confused, Tully held the priceless pieces in his big hand. "How did the jewels end up in your corsets?"

"Right after Christmas, my father came home with them. We kept the jewelry at the bank in a vault. Father didn't say why he brought the pieces home, although now I suspect it had something to do with Davis. Father told me to put them somewhere no one would ever think to look for them and to make sure it was something I could easily take with me." Brianna sat back against the cushions as she slit open another seam and removed a gold bracelet set with rubies. "I wonder if Father somehow knew I might need to escape from Davis. If so, I'm thankful for his foresight."

"You could have sold the jewels to pay the loan." Tully studied the diamond in the ring he held up to catch the light.

Brianna shook her head. "I'd never sell them, no matter how much I needed the money. They aren't just precious jewels. The jewels are precious because they remind me of my family."

Tully set the jewelry on a side table and took the corsets from Brianna, placing them back in her bag. After he returned the knife to his pocket, he picked her up and settled her across his lap.

"You realize this is highly improper, especially with Mr. Thomason right downstairs working on the door," Brianna whispered, leaning her head against Tully's solid chest. She listened to the steady beat of his heart, grateful he knew the truth, the whole truth about everything, and still cared about her.

"As you've probably heard Maggie mention, I've never been overly concerned about what's proper."

Brianna grinned, although Tully couldn't see it. Content and comfortable with his arms around her, she closed her eyes, ready to give in to her exhaustion. "I don't think I can handle any more excitement today," she mumbled, snuggling closer to him.

"Are you absolutely sure about that?" Tully asked in a teasing tone that made her open her eyes and turn her head to look up at him.

"What are you planning, Sheriff Barrett?"

Tully set her on the sofa then knelt in front of her, taking both of her hands in his. "This sure isn't how I planned to do this, darlin', with my socks sloggin' in my wet boots from wadin' in the river and both of us so tired we can barely think, but I don't want to wait another minute to tell you how I feel." He kissed the backs of both of her hands before his gaze fused to hers. Flames flickered in his hazel eyes as he smiled at her, causing dimples to pop out in his cheeks. "I love you with every single bit of my heart and then some. I've never felt so miserable and alone as I did the day Davis arrived and said you belonged to him. I want you to be mine, Brianna, forever and always. Will you please marry me? Be my wife and spend a lifetime telling me what a detestable, conceited, arrogant man I am?"

"Yes! Oh, yes, Tully!" she squealed with excitement. "Absolutely, yes!" She wrapped her arms around his neck and hugged him. He lifted her in his arms and stood, swinging her around and around.

"Is everything okay up there?" Mr. Thomason called up the stairs.

"Couldn't be better, Bill," Tully replied. He captured Brianna's lips with his, pouring all the passion she stirred in him into the loving exchange.

Breathless and euphoric, she smiled at him when he finally lifted his head. "Do you think we might wed soon?"

"Would tomorrow work for you?" Tully asked, kissing her again then giving her a teasing wink. "I think I might be able to wait that long to see you model those corsets we've talked about so much.

A blush made pink blossoms bloom in her cheeks, but she smiled. "Tomorrow would be just fine. I love you so much, Tully Barrett. More than you can possibly know. You're the finest, gentlest man I've ever known and I can't wait to be your bride."

Chapter Twenty-Two

Much to Tully's dismay, the wedding did not take place the next day. In fact, it was almost two weeks before he stood in the church with Thane and Ian beside him, waiting for his bride to walk down the aisle.

The evening he proposed and Brianna accepted, she packed a few things in her bag and Tully escorted her to Maggie and Ian's home where they shared the happy news of their plans to wed.

Somehow, between the time Tully kissed Brianna good night and he stopped the next morning to kiss her hello, Maggie had talked her into having a real wedding with a reception and fancy gown.

If that wasn't bad enough, Jemma arrived in town mid-morning and joined in the plans with the help of Hattie Greenfield.

The only thing the women asked him to do was stop by the tailor's shop to try on the new suit Brianna had ordered for him. From the many hushed conversations he'd interrupted the last few days, he assumed Brianna had a surprise or two in mind for him.

He had a few surprises of his own planned, though, and smiled as he thought of them.

At the look on his face, Thane leaned toward him with a smirk. "Do you know Jemma and Maggie bet on when you would marry Brianna?"

Tully turned to him with a disbelieving look. "You're joshin' me."

"Honest truth," Thane said, tipping his head toward Ian. "We both heard them discussing it. They wagered between August and September. Here it is the eighth day of August."

"What can I say?" Tully grinned at his friends. "I know when it's time to surrender to the inevitable."

Thane and Ian laughed as Pastor Eagan moved into place beside them. The men watched Jemma then Maggie stroll down the aisle, carrying bouquets of carnations with daisies.

Dressed in a pale blue dress fit for a princess, Sammy flounced behind them tossing flower petals from a basket. Although the child argued she was much too old for the job of flower girl, she happily accepted when Brianna mentioned there would be a new dress for her to wear.

After all that transpired with Davis' murder and the arrest of Booker Smith, Brianna wrote an article about the tiny hero who helped save the day. Not only did Bowen Packwood print it, but the story also ran in newspapers across the country.

Sammy had been so proud when Brianna shared the article with her. The little girl had cried at the last paragraph:

The actions of Miss Howe prove that it is not the size or age of a person, but the grand depths of one's heart and the expansive breadth of one's bravery that make a true hero. Our world would be a much better place if more souls that are selfless, like this valiant child, existed. The West has a new champion — a little girl with a heart full of love.

True to her promise, Sammy had gone to Bowen and apologized for tricking him into hiring her. He allowed her to keep the job, but told her he wouldn't tolerate any further subterfuge. She'd gone around town and humbly asked forgiveness from anyone she'd fooled into thinking she was a boy who couldn't speak.

Brianna and Tully made sure every person she'd stolen from received monetary compensation for their lost goods. However, since Sammy wasn't the one who stole Brianna's shoes, their loss remained a mystery.

Now, as the little girl stood next to Maggie, she looked up at Tully with a happy smile. He winked at her then turned his gaze to Brianna as she floated down the aisle on the arm of Edwin Greenfield.

Overwhelmed by the vision she made in the dress Maggie created for her, he drew in a sharp breath. Her small waist appeared impossibly tiny above the peplum of her gown. Rich lace dripped from the sleeves and skirt while a veil and train trailed several feet behind her down the aisle.

The bouquet of assorted roses, gathered from yards all around town, offered a subtle hint of fragrance as Brianna took her place beside him.

Heedless to what was proper, he bent down until his lips nearly touched her ear. "You are the loveliest bride I've ever laid eyes on, Fred. Thank you for agreeing to marry me."

When Edwin had escorted her inside the church and they started walking down the aisle, her breath had caught in her throat. In her eyes, Tully Barrett was the most handsome man she'd ever seen as he stood near the pastor in his dark suit.

From the shoulders that looked as though they could carry the weight of the world to the long, solid legs made for standing strong, Tully was her hero, her defender, her champion, and soon to be her husband.

All her girlish dreams of falling in love fell far short of the splendid bliss of being loved by the good-looking, lighthearted sheriff.

When he took her hand in his, flashing those dimples, Brianna questioned whether her knees would continue to hold her upright for the duration of the ceremony. The husky tone of his voice as he called her Fred nearly left her undone. Weeks ago, she'd decided the teasing endearment was the sweetest word she could possibly hear.

She nodded her head and the ceremony proceeded smoothly. A tear rolled down Brianna's cheek when Tully placed her mother's wedding ring on her finger. Although she dearly wished both her parents could be with her, she felt incredibly blessed to marry Tully, a man she loved with her whole heart.

A quiver of anticipation rolled through her when Tully lifted her veil and stared into her eyes for a moment before he claimed her lips in a tender, sweet kiss.

His deep voice rumbled near her ear as he whispered, "I love you," then raised his head with a warm smile full of promises.

Filled with happiness, Brianna squeezed his hand and smiled in return as they faced the congregation. Together, they strolled down the street to the boarding house where the Greenfields insisted on hosting the reception in their large back yard.

As they sat at a table eating cake and drinking fruity punch with their friends, Brianna and Tully shared a smile as Jack Jordan trailed after Sammy. Aware of the boy's interest in her, the little girl coyly glanced over her shoulder at him and tossed her hair.

"She took the news of her father's death well," Brianna said, leaning closer to Tully.

"Yeah, she did. She expected it, though. If I'd known he was missing, I would have asked around sooner. At least it didn't take long to track down the information. It is unfortunate he died in a mine blast and no one knew he left a family behind. Sammy said she figured he either ran off or got himself killed." Tully watched Sammy take Lily Jordan's hand in hers as the two little girls giggled at something Jack said. "It's what will happen when she loses her mother that's got me worried."

Brianna's voice softened. "We'll take her, of course."

Tully whipped his head around and stared at his bride. "You mean you'd really take her in? I'd love to keep her, but I thought maybe you were teasing about that when you mentioned it in passing."

"I don't tease about such serious matters." Brianna kissed Tully's cheek. "When the time comes, she'll have a home with us."

"Have I mentioned how much I love you?" Tully slid his arm around Brianna's shoulders and placed a moist kiss just below her ear.

She smiled and closed her eyes, savoring the touch of his lips to her skin. "Mmm. You have not made any mention of your affections for me in the last five minutes. Please feel free to continue."

"I adore your smile, Mrs. Barrett." Tully nibbled on her ear. "I cherish your laughter." He kissed her neck again. "I treasure the love shining in your beautiful blue eyes." A peck to her cheek. "I..."

"Mrs. Barrett!" A raspy voice carried across the yard as Clive Fisher hurried their direction as fast as bowed legs could carry him. "Brianna! I done brung you a weddin' gift."

Tully and Brianna both stood, smiling at Clive as he stopped next to their table and held out a surprisingly clean hand. In fact, it appeared as though he'd broken his rule of only one bath a year and had taken one. A hair trim and shave, along with a set of clean clothes, gave him a respectable appearance.

Sunlight glinted off the large gold nugget resting on his callused palm.

"Mr. Fisher, what's this?" Brianna asked, taking the nugget in her hand and giving the old miner a curious glance.

"I done told you I was getting close and I was right. I hit a vein a few days ago and have been digging like a mad man every living minute of the day." Clive grinned and pointed to the nugget in her hand. "There's loads more where that came from. Maybe you and the sheriff will come out and see it soon."

"We'd be happy to do that, Clive," Tully said, taking the nugget from Brianna and examining it. "As soon as we return from our honeymoon trip, we'll ride out to see you."

Unaware of any plans for a trip, Brianna glanced at Tully then Clive. "I'm so glad you decided to come today, Mr. Fisher. After you told me you'd rather be dragged through the streets in your birthday suit than join us, I didn't think we'd see you here."

"Don't get any ideas. I come into town to bring you that and wish you both well. Just because some of us didn't have a happy marriage, don't mean I can't wish the best for the two of you." Clive's eyes filled with moisture and he took out a stiff new handkerchief, swiping at his nose and dabbing his eyes before stuffing it back into his pocket.

Brianna gave him an impulsive hug then stepped back. "Please stay a while, Mr. Fisher. There's plenty of food, cake, and punch. It would make me so happy for you to stay and enjoy yourself."

"Well…" Clive glanced around, noticed the food table, and nodded his head. "I reckon a few minutes won't hurt."

He ambled off in the direction of the wedding cake and Tully handed the nugget back to Brianna. "It looks like your father's investment in Clive's mine paid off."

"Yes, it did. Father would be so excited if he could see this." Brianna gave the nugget one more look then slid it into Tully's suit coat pocket for safekeeping. She lifted her gaze to her husband's and tilted her head. "What's this about a honeymoon trip? You didn't mention a thing about it to me earlier."

"I wanted it to be a surprise. We'll leave on tomorrow's train for Warwick, Rhode Island. I thought you might like to go home."

Brianna took Tully's face in her hands and smiled with her heart in her eyes. "You silly man. Don't you know my home is here with you, in your arms, but I can't tell you how much it means to me to be able to show you where I grew up. I can pack the rest of my things there and you can help me decide what to do with the house and our holdings."

"I figure we'll be gone about two weeks. Maggie and Ian will keep an eye on Sammy and her mama while we're gone. Our absence will also give the workers plenty of time to finish." Tully kissed her forehead and slid his arm around her shoulders again, drawing her close.

"Workers? What workers?" Brianna asked, staring at him.

"The men I hired to add a bathroom onto our house and install running water in the kitchen."

A squeal of excitement burst out of her and she threw her arms around his neck. "I love you, you fabulous man. Thank you for such a wonderful wedding gift."

Tully chuckled and stood, pulling her to her feet then taking her hand in his. "That's not your wedding gift, darlin'."

"It's not?" Puzzled, she followed as Tully led her out of the yard and down the street. When they reached Hotel Warshauer, he swept her into his arms and carried her inside.

Mr. Isaac greeted them as they passed through the lobby. "Congratulations on your nuptials, Mrs. Barrett."

"Thank you, Mr. Isaac," she said, glancing over Tully's shoulder as he carried her up the steps to the second floor. Brianna pointed to the elevator as he maneuvered across the mezzanine. "You could have saved yourself some work."

He grinned and turned down a hallway. "The elevator takes longer than I'm willing to wait. If you can dig your dainty little hand into my coat pocket..." His head tilted to the right, indicating which side, "you'll find the key to our room."

"Our room?" Brianna asked, retrieving the key.

Tully bent down and she inserted it in the lock. When it clicked, she turned the knob and he toed the door open to the hotel's finest suite.

"I thought you might enjoy a fancy room tonight, one with a bathroom and a big tub." Tully grinned at her. "A tub big enough for two."

Heat burned her cheeks at his implication and she turned to glance around the well-appointed room. A basket with fruit, cheese, and bread sat on a table in front of a settee, along with a bouquet of fragrant flowers.

Tully let her slide down until her feet touched the floor. His gaze held hers as he closed the door and locked it. With unhurried movements, he removed his suit coat, vest, and tie then took off her veil.

"It's much too warm for so many layers, Mrs. Barrett," he said in a deep husky tone that made her tremble.

Filled with nervous anticipation, Brianna remained silent, uncertain what to say or do.

Tully moved behind her and placed a light kiss to the back of her neck before he reached down to undo her buttons, only to realize there weren't any.

"How am I supposed to get you out of that thing, pretty as it is?"

Brianna lifted her left arm, revealing a row of hooks.

Tully bent his knees and planted his tongue in his cheek as his big fingers worked to undo the tiny fasteners.

At the look of pure concentration on his face, she giggled. "How are you going to put me at ease if you look so serious?"

"This is serious business, Fred." He glanced at her and smiled, revealing those glorious dimples. Fingers fumbling, he continued to make slow progress. "Did Maggie intentionally make this hard for me?"

Another blush filled her cheeks. "No. She thought it would be easier than buttons."

"Well, she might be wrong." Tully considered yanking on the hooks and ruining them, but he didn't want to upset his bride at that particular moment. "I've been greatly anticipating the moment when you'll model one of those fancy corsets for me, but I might have to postpone the show."

Embarrassed but intrigued, she gave him a questioning look, inhaling the minty aroma of his breath. "Why is that?"

"Because I'm not stopping until every speck of your clothes are on the floor."

Her mouth rounded in an "O" as her eyes widened, shocked by his words.

Once the hooks were unfastened and he removed Brianna's gown, he took the pins from her hair and watched the golden-brown waves fall around her face.

"You are so enchantingly beautiful, Brianna." His thumb traced across her. "I can't quite believe you're finally mine."

Brianna reached up and unfastened the buttons of Tully's shirt. "You said you had another gift for me. Is it here?" she asked, pushing the shirt off his shoulders and tentatively running her hands over his chest.

Her fingers seared his skin everywhere she touched and set his temperature on a fast boil. Flames burned bright in his eyes as he buried his hands in her hair and breathed in the soft rose fragrance of her. "The gift I want to give you is me."

"I can't think of one I'd like better," she whispered, pulling his head down until his lips connected with hers.

Tully swept her into his arms again and carried her into the bedroom.

Much later, as they both fought to keep their eyes open, Tully held her close and kissed her temple.

"There's one thing I promised you, wife of mine."

She tipped her head back to look at him. "And what might that be?"

He trailed a hand down her side and along the length of her leg until he touched her foot. "Finding out where you're ticklish."

She squirmed, trying to get away, but Tully held fast to her foot, tickling it until she giggled so much she had to work to catch her breath.

He chuckled and drew her back into his arms. "You know what I think?"

She feigned a perturbed look then smiled. "I have no idea."

"Being married to you is gonna be the most fun I've ever had. Even if I wouldn't admit it, I knew the first time I saw you there was this amazing, special thing about you. Something more magical than snow flurries in June and more wonderful than a symphony of summer stars." He kissed her tenderly and brushed the hair away from her face with a gentle hand. "I truly do love you, Brianna. With all my heart."

"And I love you, Tully." She raised up on one elbow, trailing her finger across his tempting mouth. "You have to promise me one more thing."

"Anything, darlin'."

"Never stop calling me Fred."

He wrapped his arms around her and lowered his head. "That's a promise I'm happy to keep."

Keep reading for a preview of another Baker City Brides story!

Chocolate Macaroons

Although Brianna doesn't cook, Tully does enjoy his sweets. This cookie is easy to make and so yummy. The recipe comes right out of my grandma's 1903 cookbook!

Chocolate Macaroons
3 egg whites
½ cup sugar
4 ounces grated semi-sweet chocolate
1 teaspoon vanilla

Preheat oven to 375 degrees. Line a baking sheet with parchment and set aside.

Beat egg whites until very stiff. Add in sugar then gently fold in chocolate and vanilla. Place walnut-sized drops on the baking sheet and bake about eight minutes, until cookies are just firm to the touch but still soft in the middle. (It's okay if they seem a little sticky when you remove them from the oven, they will harden as they cool).

Remove from the oven and cool.

Author's Note

The first time I wrote Tully Barrett's name in *Crumpets and Cowpies*, I knew he needed his own story.

After all, Tully, Thane and Maggie have been friends for years, so it only made sense the three of them would each need their own romance.

Many of you thought Tully would marry Maggie in *Thimbles and Thistles*, but she was already in love with Ian MacGregor (even if she didn't realize it yet!).

Tully needed to fall for a girl far different from any he'd ever met, and that's when the idea for Brianna Dumont came to mind.

Brianna's missing shoes came from an old advertisement I read about "leaving your shoes in the hall for a polish." I thought it would be funny if someone like Brianna set out her shoes and ended up having them stolen.

I used the historic Slater Mill in Rhode Island for the inspiration for her father's business. It was the first successful cotton-spinning factory in the United States and was dedicated exclusively to the production of cotton thread until 1829. From then, until 1921, a variety of owners and renters used the facility to produce such things as tools for the jewelry industry, coffin trimmings, cardboard manufacture, and bicycle sales.

As I wrote *Corsets and Cuffs*, I dove deeper into the history of Baker City and found some very interesting details.

In July 1886, the weather bureau established a reporting meteorological station in Baker City. Reports of weather conditions were telegraphed to the chief office every day at 5 a.m. and again at 5 p.m. The office was equipped with barometers, thermometers, anemometers, rain and snow gauges to report all conditions of the weather.

Speaking of the weather, I've been reading *The Diaries of Harriet "Hattie" Dillabaugh*. Hattie lived in the Baker City area during the 1890s and I've found so much helpful information in her brief daily entries in her journal. One I had to include in the story was a notation about a summer snowstorm.

As for other details about the town, some of the history books I found stated that a creamery opened at the edge of town in 1889. A soap factory opened facilities in 1890 for the manufacture of fifty boxes of laundry soap per day.

Hotel Warshauer is mentioned in the first two *Baker City Brides* books. It provided an important part of the setting in this story. The hotel was eventually purchased by the Geiser family. Today, visitors to town can stay at the Geiser Grand Hotel in one of the renovated rooms.

One of the photos I happened across from Baker City's 1891 history was of a Fourth of July rock drilling contest. As mentioned in the story, rock drilling was used to drill holes into rock and provide a place to set explosives. While the work was originally completed by hand, eventually machines took over the process. In the photo of the contest, a large crowd gathered to watch it, dressed in suits (can you imagine how hot it would be?). A few brave women stood around with parasols, observing the competitors. Several children (mostly boys) watched from the sidelines, too.

Baker City was home to many Chinese people. They arrived in the 1860s during the area's first gold rush. In 1879, the Chinese residents made up 13.9% of Baker City's population. The number dropped in the next decade, then gained steam in the 1890s with the second gold rush period. Their population peaked in 1900 with 264 citizens.

A "China Town" was located a few blocks away from the town's main thoroughfare, near the river. There were a few Chinese stores, a gambling establishment, and a temple, also known as a Joss house. The area also boasted a garden. Most of the Chinese residents were men. Today, a Chinese cemetery is located near the freeway and visitors may stop there to learn more about the Chinese community in Baker County.

Baker City was dubbed, "Queen City of the Mines," and was also referred to as the "Denver of Oregon." At one point, it was the fastest growing community in the old west as people flocked to the area, intent on making their fortune mining.

It was the third largest city in the state and the Hotel Warshauer could proudly boast it installed the third elevator west of the Mississippi.

Education was also important to the residents of the area. Baker City was home to Oregon's second high school.

I do my best to make my stories as historically accurate as possible, right down to the phrases my characters use. When I had Sammy say Brianna was "down for the count," I decided I'd better make sure the phrase would have been used then. For those unfamiliar with the term, it refers to the time when a boxer is knocked down to the mat and the referee begins counting. The earliest recorded use of the phrase is supposedly from the *Newark Daily Advocate* newspaper from 1900. In reporting a boxing match between Jack Root and Dick O'Brien, the reporter wrote:

"O'Brien was in poor condition or probably the result would have been different, as he had Root down for the count three times in the second round."

Since it was close to the time of this book, I decided to keep it.

Special thanks to Camilla U. for providing the name of the villain in this book and Kathy C. for choosing Rhode Island as his home. And huge thanks to Ann, Charity, Cindy, Danielle, Marcia, and Shauna — without you ladies, I wouldn't be able to do what I do!

I hope you enjoyed Tully and Brianna's story. Read more adventures with the Baker City characters in ***Bobbins and Boots***!

Thank You!

Thank you for reading ***Corsets and Cuffs***. Now that you've finished Tully and Brianna's story, won't you please consider writing a review?

I would truly appreciate it. Reviews are such a wonderful way for readers to discover great new books.

Also, if you haven't yet signed up for my newsletter, please consider subscribing?

You'll receive a free book or two, and what I call The Welcome Letters with exclusive content and some fun stuff!

My newsletters are sent when I have new releases, sales, or news of freebies to share. Each month, you can enter a contest, get a new recipe to try, and discover details about upcoming events. Don't wait. Sign up today!

Shanna's Newsletter

And if newsletters aren't your thing, please follow me on *BookBub*. You'll receive notifications on pre-orders, new releases, and sale books!

Bobbins and Boots Preview

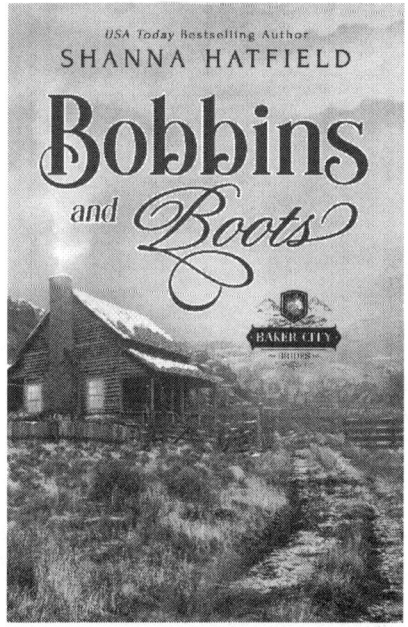

Baker City, Oregon
September 1891

Fear churned in Allie Tillman's nervous stomach like a butter paddle in a jar of thick cream. Since it was far too late to change the plans already set in motion, she stepped across the platform at the train depot and glanced around.

Questions about her future husband's appearance pecked at her thoughts from the moment she received Joe Lambery's letter. The missive confirmed his acceptance of her as his mail-order bride and included a train ticket to Baker City, but didn't contain a photograph. Would he be tall and handsome or short and balding? Was he still in possession of all his teeth? Although he sounded nice enough in the one letter they'd exchanged, what if he was cruel and spiteful.

A flicker of adventure nudged away a little of her anxiety as she glanced around the Eastern Oregon town she'd never heard of until she happened upon Joe Lambery's advertisement for a bride. The sagebrush covered hills to the south and east, and the thick forest to the west and north was unlike anything she'd ever seen growing up on the flat prairie of Nebraska.

A deep breath filled her nose with fresh, clean air. Redolent with a hint of pine and a sprinkling of sage, she also detected the delicious smell of roasting meat. If she hadn't teetered on the edge of full-fledged panic at what she was about to do, she might have paid more attention to her gnawing hunger.

In all her life, she'd never traveled more than ten miles from the sod house where she'd been born. Now, she was more than a thousand miles away from everyone and everything she'd ever known.

A quick scan of the faces of those still waiting to board the train revealed none of them seemed to be the rancher she'd come to wed. Not one of them wore a hat like the cowboys she'd seen on the train. Like she imagined Mr. Lambery would wear.

She pictured him as tall and broad-shouldered, with a friendly smile and a warm light in his eyes. Another glimpse around the depot confirmed no one appeared to be the right age for her intended. Two crusty old miners and a gentleman in a fine suit were the only people left outside, and they all busily gathered supplies into wagons parked next to the platform.

Concerned, Allie hurried into the ticket office and stepped up to the counter.

"May I help you miss?" The man barely glanced up at her as he shuffled papers from a stack on his left to one on his right.

"Yes, sir, I'm looking for a man named Joe Lambery. Have you by chance seen him today?" she asked.

The papers stilled in the ticket agent's hands and he slowly raised his gaze. One eyebrow traveled upward and he gave her a long, studying glance. "What in the world do you want with Joe Lambery?"

Startled by the disapproving tone of his voice and the disparaging look on his face, Allie took a step back from the counter. "He sent for me. We're to marry and live on his ranch."

"On his ranch?" The man's second eyebrow joined the first, stretching close to his hairline.

Much to Allie's dismay, the man guffawed loudly and slapped the counter with one hand. Tears leaked from his eyes and he bent over, holding his stomach as laughter rolled out of him in great, uncontrollable waves.

Suddenly realizing she was quite serious, he curtailed his humor and straightened, giving her an apologetic glance.

"I'm sorry, miss, but I haven't seen Joe Lambery for weeks." His eyes held a hint of sympathy. "To my knowledge, there is no way to get a message to him, so you'll have to find somewhere to wait until he wanders back into town. If I see him, I'll mention your arrival."

"Oh, I…" Stunned by Mr. Lambery's failure to meet the train and the ticket agent's odd behavior, Allie nodded her head. "Thank you, sir."

She shifted the worn carpetbag in her hand and returned to the platform. The few coins in her bag wouldn't secure a decent place to stay for the night let alone purchase enough food to fill all the empty spaces in her belly.

Tears pricked the back of her eyes but she held them in check as she stared down the train tracks, watching the train chug on its way to the next stop along the line. So much for her dreams of her future husband being a gallant, romantic sort. In fact, from the way the ticket agent acted, she couldn't help but think Joe Lambery might be rather disreputable.

A pleasant, masculine voice spoke from beside her. "Pardon me, miss. I couldn't help but notice you seem to be waiting for someone. May I be of assistance?"

Allie turned and smiled at the man in a suit she'd seen loading his wagon with supplies. He appeared to be in his fifties, with gray touching his temples. It gave him a distinguished appearance while his British accent made him seem like royalty. If she'd known how to curtsey properly, she would have.

"I came to town as a mail-order bride, but the gentleman who sent for me isn't here. The ticket agent said he had no idea how to get word to him I've arrived. It seems I'll have to wait for him to come to town." Allie looked into the man's friendly face and kind eyes, hoping he would be more helpful than the chortling ticket agent had been.

The man doffed his hat and grinned. "Edwin Greenfield at your service. You must come home with me. My wife and I run a boardinghouse and we'd love to have you stay until your intended arrives in town."

"Oh, Mr. Greenfield, that's a lovely offer, but I'll tell it to you straight. I don't have any money for a room. I don't think I have enough to even buy a decent meal." Allie hated to admit it, but her mother had taught her to tell the truth, no matter how painful it might be.

Greenfield settled his hat on his head and rocked back on his heels. "Would you be interested in a job while you wait for your fiancé?"

"Would I?" Allie's blue eyes lit with hope. "You bet your britches I would. I'm a hard worker. If I don't know how to do something, Ma says I learn real fast."

"Splendid. Come along then, and we'll get you settled." Edwin took her elbow in his hand. She started to jerk away, but realized he was only being kind and helpful. He guided her down the steps and offered his hand as she climbed up to the seat of his wagon. "Do you have any trunks?"

"Nope. This is it." Allie set her carpetbag at her feet.

As he drove through town, Edwin pointed out Mr. Miller's Mercantile, Maggie MacGregor's dress shop, and Mr. Palmer's saddle shop. He waved at the sheriff as he strolled down the boardwalk with his arm around the waist of a beautiful woman while a little girl skipped along beside them.

Edwin stopped the wagon outside a large two-story residence with a lush yard and wrap-around porch. The fancy trim dripping from the house caused Allie to wonder if her shoes were clean enough to step foot inside such a grand house.

"Welcome to our home," Edwin said. He wrapped the reins around the brake and climbed down. When he offered her a hand, Allie's fingers barely grazed his as she jumped down then followed him up the steps and inside the front door.

"Hattie, my love, we have a special guest." Edwin smiled at Allie and motioned her to precede him into a parlor. A woman his age sat on a tufted velvet sofa cuddling a curly-haired child. Across from the duo, on a matching sofa, a lovely auburn-haired woman smiled as she held a cup of tea in her elegant hands.

"Hello!" The older woman set the child on the cushion beside her and rose to her feet. "Welcome, welcome. I'm Hattie Greenfield. This is Lady Jemma Jordan and her daughter, Lily."

"It's right nice to meet you, Mrs. Greenfield, Mrs. Jordan. I'm Allie Tillman." Allie tipped her head toward Edwin. "Mr. Greenfield said you'd hire me for a few days until the man I came to marry makes it into town."

"Did you just arrive on the train?" Hattie asked, gently pushing Allie down into a side chair and pouring her a cup of tea.

Without any past opportunity to drink tea out of a china cup, Allie tentatively took it, puzzled by what she should do with the saucer. Covertly, she watched Mrs. Jordan as she held the saucer in one hand and daintily took a sip from the delicate cup.

Emulating the woman's posture, Allie took a drink of the sweet, rich brew then returned the cup to the saucer. "Thank you. I did just arrive. The man who sent for me wasn't around to meet the train. The ticket agent didn't seem to know when he'd show up in town, although he seemed to find the notion of my husband-to-be getting married quite funny."

Eager to participate in the conversation, Lily skipped over to Allie and leaned against her chair. She tilted her head one way then the other before grinning at her. "You're tall," she said.

Strawberry-blond curls sprung up around the girl's head like a downy halo while copper-colored eyes snapped with mischief and excitement. Allie thought Lily looked like a little autumn fairy in her coral and cream striped frock.

"I suppose I am tall for a girl," Allie said, grinning at the charming child. "Do you think I'll grow into a giant?"

"No!" Lily giggled and shook her head, making her curls dance. "You'll be a princess and live with a handsome prince and eat cake twice a day."

"Twice a day? My, goodness! Wouldn't that be something?" Allie asked, accepting the plate of food

Hattie handed to her. Tiny sandwiches, fruit-filled tarts, and buttery cookies made her mouth water. She took a bite and forced herself not to eat like a mannerless heathen. Already feeling out of place in the Greenfield's immaculate home in her simple calico dress, she didn't want to draw any more attention to herself.

"Yep! I'd eat cake twice a day if Mama would let me," Lily said. She scampered over to her mother and plopped down beside her then took a bite of a cookie Jemma gave her.

Jemma turned to Allie with a pleasant smile. "Miss Tillman, if you don't mind my asking, whom did you come to wed?"

"Joe Lambery. Do you know him?" Allie asked. Surely, someone would be able to locate her missing fiancé.

Jemma shook her head. "I don't, although his name seems familiar for some reason. When my husband arrives, we'll ask him. He knows most people in the area."

Allie nodded and focused on eating the food on her plate and sipping her tea. "Are you all related?"

Hattie Greenfield shot Jemma a motherly look then turned her attention back to her guest. "No, dear. Mr. Greenfield and I used to work for Jemma's family, when we all lived in England. Jemma's sister wed a man named Henry Jordan and they blessed us with two delightful children. Sadly, Jane passed away, and then Henry. Jemma took over raising both children. Henry's brother, Thane, came to settle his estate, only to discover the existence of Jemma and the children. They wed and moved to America, but we missed Jemma and the children so terribly, we decided to come to Baker City to be near them."

"Oh, that's wonderful." Abruptly realizing what she'd said, she darted a glance at Jemma. "I don't mean about your sister and her husband dying. I just meant it's wonderful you all are so close and can be together."

She wondered what it would be like to be loved so much someone would follow you across an ocean and the country. She'd traveled across half of America to wed a stranger but he hadn't even possessed the courtesy to show up to meet her. Her experience with men was limited to her pa and brothers. What she knew from dealing with them left her rather wary of the male species.

The door opened and the jangle of spurs rang into the parlor before a brawny, handsome man stepped into the parlor, holding a cowboy hat in one hand. He looked so much like the vision Allie held of her rancher, she stared at him in fascination, taking him in from the top of his head to the tips of his dusty boots.

Lily ran to him with her arms outstretched. "Daddy!"

"Hi, honey. Are you being a good girl?" he asked, moving farther into the room.

Allie watched as his eyes softened when they landed on Jemma and he shot her a tender smile. There was nothing she wanted more in the world than to be loved like that, but her lot in life was to make do with what she could get. Apparently, she couldn't even get the groom who'd sent for her.

Jemma stood and tipped up her cheek as Thane pressed a kiss to it. He offered a greeting to Hattie and Edwin Greenfield then noticed Allie.

"Thane, this is Miss Allie Tillman. She just arrived on this afternoon's train," Jemma said, making introductions. "Miss Tillman, this is my husband, Thane Jordan."

Thane politely tipped his head and offered her an amiable grin. "Nice to meet you, Miss Tillman. Welcome to Baker City. What brings you to town?"

Allie rose to her feet, noting Thane's surprised look when she stood only a few inches shorter than his tall height. "Please, call me Allie. To answer your question, Mr. Jordan, I came as a mail-order bride, but the man I'm to wed didn't meet the train. The ticket agent wasn't sure when he'd be in town."

Thane shifted Lily in his arms to free a hand and accepted a cookie from the platter of sweets Hattie held out to him. He gave her an appreciative nod, but turned back to Allie. "What's the name of the fellow who sent for you?"

"Joe Lambery." Allie's eyes widened in shock when Thane choked on the cookie he'd popped into his mouth. He handed Lily to Jemma while Edwin whacked him on the back and Hattie poured him a cup of tea.

Thane swallowed the contents of the teacup in a gulp. He coughed one more time before pinning Allie with a penetrating glare. "Joe Lambery? Are you sure that's the name?"

"Yes. That's what the letter said." Allie opened the carpetbag she'd left by the chair and pulled out the newspaper advertisement and the letter Joe had sent to her.

Thane read the newspaper advertisement aloud:

Handsome, wealthy rancher, 27 years of age, seeks a bride to share home in Eastern Oregon. Lady between 18 and 30, of gentle disposition with love of outdoors preferred. To correspond...

He scanned the letter then handed it and the advertisement back to her with his jaw clenched in irritation.

"Thane? What is it?" Jemma asked, placing a hand on his arm. "What's wrong?"

"Not what. Who." Thane motioned for Allie to take a seat. Once she did, he and Jemma sat on the sofa. "Look, Miss Tillman, you seem like a sensible girl, a nice girl. That's why you can't marry Joe. I don't know what inspired him to send for a bride, but the only thing in that advertisement that might be remotely close to the truth is that he's twenty-seven. He's not wealthy, doesn't own anything beyond his horse and saddle, and the handsome part is farfetched considering he's missing a few teeth and has never had more than a passing acquaintance with soap and water. Joe is a lazy, mean, worthless cuss. I have to assume the only reason he wants a bride is because your train ticket was cheaper than continuing to spend what little money he has at the Rusty Nugget on har..." Thane grunted as Jemma's elbow connected with his ribs. The disapproving glower from his wife caused him to alter his statement. "Female companionship of a disreputable nature."

Allie's face lost all color and she leaned back in the chair. Lightheaded, she struggled to make sense of what Mr. Jordan said. According to the man sitting across from her, Joe Lambery was a liar and sent for her because he couldn't afford to continue seeking out soiled doves.

Precariously balanced on the edge of shock, Allie worked to swallow the bitter bile rising in her throat. What had she done? What had she gotten herself into by agreeing to marry a man who misrepresented himself and his ability to provide for a wife?

Jemma set Lily down and snatched up a fan. She flicked it open and waved it in front of Allie's face. "All will be well, Allie. We won't allow him to marry you."

Thane offered her a look of encouragement. "We certainly won't. Believe me when I say the last thing you want to do is marry Joe Lambery. You'd be signing up for a lifetime of regret and misery. No one deserves that."

Allie glanced at the two couples as they hovered around her. "But I don't know what I'll do. He paid for my train ticket and I don't have money to pay him back."

"Don't you worry about a thing," Hattie said, patting Allie's hand. "You'll stay here with us until you decide what you'd like to do."

"That's why I offered her a position with us, love," Edwin said, smiling at his wife. "You know, that special position we need to fill."

Hattie patted Allie's hand again, fully aware they didn't need any help and there wasn't any special position. Obviously, the girl needed a job and they'd give her one. "It's settled then, Allie. You'll work for us and that's that."

Overwhelmed by the kindness of these people she'd just met, Allie didn't know whether to laugh or cry at her strange, completely unexpected situation.

"Have a tart, Miss Tillman. It'll make you feel all better," Lily said, placing a tart on a plate and handing it to Allie.

Allie accepted the sweet. "Thank you, Lily. I believe it will."

Later, after the Jordan family left with a promise to check in on her in a few days, Hattie showed Allie upstairs to a bedroom near the back stairs.

The woman opened the door to the sunny room and stood back, allowing Allie to enter. "I hope you don't mind this room. It's a tad small, but it's comfortable and quiet."

Allie took in the pale yellow curtains fluttering in the afternoon breeze. A yellow and white quilt covered the bed, a beautiful braided rug rested on the gleaming floor, and matching maple furniture shone from a recent polish.

Sunshine spilled through the sparkling windows, making Allie long to stand in the beams to soak up the warmth and light.

She turned to her hostess. "Oh, Mrs. Greenfield, I couldn't stay here. It's too lovely, too…"

Hattie squeezed her hand and smiled. "It's your room for as long as you like. The bathroom is directly across the hall. You'll share it with two other boarders. Some of the rooms have private baths, but not all."

Impulsively, Allie gave her a hug.

The woman hugged her back then pulled away with a smile. "I serve dinner at six, breakfast at seven, and lunch at noon."

"I reckon we better get to fixing something for supper." Allie set her carpetbag on the floor by the bed then turned back to Hattie, ready to work.

Hattie laughed and shook her head. "For today, you are a guest, Allie Tillman. Do anything you like this afternoon. Take a nap. Sit on the swing out back. Go for a walk. Read a book."

"I can't read a lick, although my Ma tried more times than you can count to teach me," Allie admitted. "But sitting in a swing sounds nice. I don't have a hankering to wander around town and I'm too wound up to settle down for a nap. Besides, I haven't had one of those since I was in diapers."

Hattie grinned and held out a hand to Allie. "In that case, come with me and I'll show you the swing."

The two women walked down the back stairs and along a short hallway to the kitchen. Hattie opened the back door and they stepped outside onto a shaded porch. A large fenced yard held a variety of flowers and plants. Birds darted among the feeders and flowers, happily chirping. A large swing hung from thick ropes tied around a sturdy branch of a tree at the back corner of the yard.

"It's perfect, Mrs. Greenfield!" Allie meandered down the steps, admiring the profusion of flowers blooming around the yard. Foxglove, hollyhocks, bellflowers, sweet peas, and pinks scented the air while providing a burst of color. "Everything is so pretty."

"Thank you, Allie. Please, call me Hattie and my husband Edwin. There is no need to be so formal among friends." Hattie smiled at her again. "Come in when you're ready. You have nearly two hours before we eat, so enjoy yourself."

"Thank you, Hattie." Allie sat down on the swing big enough for two and grabbed the rope in her hands. By some unexplainable miracle, she'd gone from a jilted, homeless bride to having a job in a home that seemed more like a castle than a house. It was by far the nicest place she'd ever been. And to think, she'd get to stay there for as long as she liked.

Her long legs pumped as she set the swing into motion and let her thoughts wander. Worry niggled at her about Joe Lambery, about what he would do when she refused to marry him. Determined not to let it steal the joy of the moment, she jumped off the swing and hurried inside, intent on earning her keep.

Available now on Amazon!

More Sweet Romances

Hardman Holidays Series
Heartwarming holiday stories set in the 1890s in Hardman, Oregon.

__The Christmas Bargain__ (Book 1) — As owner and manager of the Hardman bank, Luke Granger is a man of responsibility and integrity in the small 1890s Eastern Oregon town. When he calls in a long overdue loan, Luke finds himself reluctantly accepting a bargain in lieu of payment from the shiftless farmer who barters his daughter to settle his debt.

__The Christmas Token__ (Book 2) — Determined to escape an unwelcome suitor, Ginny Granger flees to her brother's home in Eastern Oregon for the holiday season. Returning to the community where she spent her childhood years, she plans to relax and enjoy a peaceful visit. Not expecting to encounter the boy she once loved, her exile proves to be anything but restful.

The Christmas Calamity (Book 3) — Arlan Guthry's uncluttered world tilts off kilter when the beautiful and enigmatic prestidigitator Alexandra Janowski arrives in town, spinning magic and trouble in her wake as the holiday season approaches.

The Christmas Vow (Book 4) — Sailor Adam Guthry returns home to bury his best friend and his past, only to fall once more for the girl who broke his heart.

The Christmas Quandary (Book 5) — Tom Grove just needs to survive a month at home while he recovers from a work injury. He arrives to discover his middle-aged parents acting like newlyweds, the school in need of a teacher, and the girl of his dreams already engaged.

The Christmas Confection (Book 6) — Will Hardman's sweet baker be able to soften Fred Decker's hardened heart?

The Christmas Melody (Book 7) — Can a determined woman bring holiday cheer to a man in exile?

The Christmas Ring (Book 8) — Will Christmas ring with romance for two hearts longing for a home.

The Christmas Wish (Book 9) — Will a holiday at home heal his shattered heart?

The *Regional Romance Series* features books with three connected sweet romances.
Discover how one matchmaker ends up traveling to Oregon to set one reluctant groom on his ear in
<u>Grass Valley Brides</u>.
And read about a romantic rancher who will do anything to avoid falling in love in
<u>Romance at Rinehart's Crossing</u>.

About the Author

PHOTO BY SHANA BAILEY PHOTOGRAPHY

USA Today bestselling author Shanna Hatfield is a farm girl who loves to write. Her sweet historical and contemporary romances are filled with sarcasm, humor, hope, and hunky heroes.

When Shanna isn't dreaming up unforgettable characters, twisting plots, or covertly seeking dark, decadent chocolate, she hangs out with her beloved husband, Captain Cavedweller, at their home in the Pacific Northwest.

Shanna loves to hear from readers.
Connect with her online:
Website: shannahatfield.com
Email: shanna@shannahatfield.com

Made in the USA
Monee, IL
28 August 2024